# THE LOST CONCERTO

## A Novel

## HELAINE MARIO

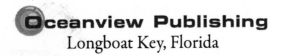
Oceanview Publishing
Longboat Key, Florida

ISBN: 978-1-60809-221-5

Published in the United States of America by Oceanview Publishing Longboat Key, Florida

www.oceanviewpub.com

10 9 8 7 6 5 4 3 2

PRINTED IN THE UNITED STATES OF AMERICA

# ACKNOWLEDGMENTS

I especially want to acknowledge—and express my heartfelt appreciation for—our service men and women, and their families, for their remarkable patriotism, bravery, strength and sacrifice. Colonel Beckett and Zachary Law could not have "come to life" without their stories and inspiration.

A special thank you, also, to my Ace Assistant Stella "Fantastico" Shea, a very beautiful three-legged rescue dog in Georgia who was the inspiration for Shiloh.

I am very grateful for my two early manuscript editors, Ron Mario and Gail MacLean, whose careful reading, talents and excellent, thoughtful comments and suggestions made *The Lost Concerto* so much better. The very complex Victor Orsini was originally a very minor, "one-note" character and only came to life with Ron's encouragement.

A very personal acknowledgment to Pat and Bob Gussin and the staff at Oceanview Publishing for their remarkable publishing and writing skills, and their love of books. Thank you for believing in Maggie's story.

*This book is dedicated to*

*my children,*
*Jessica, a beautiful mother, friend & woman*
*& Sean, my Piano Man, who inspired the*
*classical music in this novel,*

*to my grandchildren,*
*Ellie, Tyler, Clair Violet, & Declan,*
*who fill my world with magic.*
*Always love music.*

*and to*

*Ron—always, only you*

*Please do not shoot the pianist.*
—Oscar Wilde

# THE LOST CONCERTO

# OVERTURE
(In music: an opening, preceding a larger work)

*The bright day is done, and we are for the dark.*
—Shakespeare, *Antony and Cleopatra*

BRITTANY, FRANCE. LATE SUMMER

They fled from Rome on a rain-swept August night.

First in the black Citroën, speeding north into the darkness. Then two trains, the small fishing boat, the final climb up a steep path through thick, swirling mist. Moving from shadow to shadow for two days, until they stood before the high, locked iron gates of the sixth-century Benedictine convent. *Couvent de la Brume*...the Convent of the Fog. The nuns welcomed them in silence.

She had chosen their hiding place well. The tiny Breton isle lay seven kilometers off the French coast, lost in the immense blackness of the ocean. Isolated by dangerous reefs and haunted by rolling, dense gray fogs, the island was a world apart—a final sentinel before the vastness of the misted sea.

The woman thought they would be safe, finally, here at the very edge of the world.

For five days, they hid in the convent, sheltered by thick stone walls and the island's fog.

Each morning the woman stood at the arched window, keeping watch. Outside, beyond the small cloister, the island appeared and then was gone as mist swirled like veils across the hills. She watched the nuns plant vegetables in the garden, scrub whitewashed walls, kneel by the stone cross in the cloister to pray.

Each night, the woman sat vigilant in the watery darkness, listening to the soaring Gregorian chants, the muffled thunder of waves against jagged rocks, and the small breaths from the cot under the eaves.

Generations of seafarers had called the place *l'Île de la Brume*. Fog Island.

She thought it was the last place on earth a man would look for his missing wife.

\* \* \*

On the first day of September, the soft cocoon of fog began to shimmer with light. The woman watched with growing dread as, one by one, the cottages and pines and bright boats beyond the convent walls emerged from the haze. Too soon the sky turned clear as glass, and she hurried to gather their belongings while the sun spun like a golden coin toward the sea.

When all was ready she waited at the window, willing the sun to set. The light shimmered on the black pearls around her neck and caught her marble-pale face, once beautiful but now etched by fear and despair. *Hurry*, she pleaded with the glowing sky. *We need the protection of the night.*

But still the bright day lingered, fighting the dark.

Bells called the nuns to evening prayer, and she watched them cross the ancient cloister, their white wimples shining like birds' wings in the changing light.

A trawler's horn sounded a warning. Startled, she looked toward the harbor, saw the man leap easily from the deck of a fishing boat just as the setting sun flashed on the mirrors of his glasses.

Terror, sudden and sharp, exploded in her chest.

She slammed the shutters closed, reached for her cloak and backpack. Then she woke her companion, settling a small knapsack over his thin shoulders. They clattered down the narrow stairs as the sky became a great sea of light, awash with the fiery crimson and burnished brass of one last summer's sunset.

Against this glimmering curtain, the two figures running

across the deserted beach showed black and distinct. They were perfect silhouettes. Perfect targets.

The island cliffs rose like dark ships before them. Just below the rocks, on a small crescent of sand, a tangle of wind-battered sea pines promised shelter.

On they ran. One hundred meters. Fifty. Twenty.

They disappeared into the shadows.

Only then, deep within the pines, did the woman slow their pace. She raised her eyes to search the cliffs. There. On the rock face some twenty meters above them, a lamp flashed orange in the splintered half-light.

The stone chapel clung to the cliff like a wild bird's nest wedged into the rock. The blinking light shone from the medieval belfry, casting its warning to unwary sailors far out over the hunched and shining reefs. She could hear the crash of waves, fierce against the rocks. Soon the rising tides would completely cut off the tiny chapel of Notre-Dame du Sauf Retour from the shore. Our Lady of the Safe Return.

It was the perfect refuge.

Very gently, the woman set a Red Sox baseball cap on the dark head by her side and pointed to the distant light. "That's where we're going," she whispered. "To the very top."

She clasped the hand of her child tightly and they followed the ancient track through the sea pines as the last brightness fell from the day.

* * *

The hunter moved away from the window under the eaves. In his hand he held a heavy cardboard tube, some fifty centimeters in length, that had been left behind. *Empty*. He hurled it to the floor, watched it roll across the stones.

He had only missed them by a few minutes. The door had been left open, the sheets on the rumpled bed still warm.

No matter. He had seen their flight across the beach. Now he knew where they were headed.

He lifted the mirrored glasses and bent to study his map of the island, following the shoreline as it left the village, curved towards the forest, then climbed the headland toward the cliffs. His finger stopped on the symbol of a small black cross.

"There," he murmured.

* * *

The mother and child stood silently on the black cliffs. Worn steps disappeared over the edge into a deep void of thundering surf. Their faces glowed briefly as the lamp in the tower blinked on and off in the darkness.

"Are we there yet?"

The woman smiled at the ageless question. "Our Lady's chapel," she whispered, gesturing toward the church.

The small boy was young, not more than five years old. The dark terrors of the night were forgotten as he watched the blinking light. "Like fireflies, Mama!"

"Just like fireflies," agreed the woman, reaching to caress his cheek. A large sapphire ring flashed blue in the moonlight, jarring with the simplicity of her Breton clothing.

"Mama!" cried the boy. "I want to—"

"Hush, Little Firefly," she said quickly, touching his lips. He nodded, understanding beyond his years, his small fingers reaching trustingly for her hand. Sudden fear for her son engulfed her in waves.

*I won't let him hurt you ever again, my darling.*

In need of reassurance, the woman slipped her hand into the deep pocket of her cloak. Money and passports. A flashlight and cell phone. And the small journal. Her fingers lingered on the smooth leather.

"Come, Tommy," she urged. She tipped the baseball cap back from his head and, very gently, brushed a dark curl from the child's eyes. Then she drew the thin journal from her pocket. "We should go into the chapel. I have a very special hiding game for you."

The boy's eyes widened. "Can Paddy play, too?" he asked in a stage whisper as he tugged a worn stuffed bear out of his knapsack.

"An excellent idea. But you and Paddy must make me a promise, too. You must promise to never, *ever* tell our secret..."

Sofia Orsini drew her son toward the chapel as she described their game.

Behind them, the mist crept like smoke over the edge of the cliffs.

* * *

Enclosed in a blinding white shroud, the hunter stood motionless and listened. Was that a child's voice, trapped and echoing in the mist?

Below him, the incoming surf pounded on the old steps that hugged the cliff, reaching for his boots. He pressed his hands against the wall of rock.

She was close by. He sensed it.

He always knew when she was near. So many times, when she was unaware of his presence, he'd watched her at the villa in Rome. Her scent, the low voice, the graceful movement of her skirt. Once, late at night when he passed through the villa's gardens, he'd seen her through a lighted window as she brushed her hair with long, smooth strokes in front of a mirror. Her bare arm moving up and down. The way the silky hair sparked with black fire in the lamplight.

The hunter touched the needle-sharp Laguiole knife in his belt and felt the excitement stirring in his body as he climbed higher. Toward Sofia and the little boy.

Far below him, the sea crashed against the rocks. "Like as the waves make toward the pebbled shore," he quoted, "So do our minutes hasten to their end."

* * *

The chapel smelled of lingering incense and the sea.

Sofia Orsini sat with her son in one of the shoulder-high pews. She had lit the tapers set in heavy candlesticks, and now they flickered next to the red sanctuary flame on the stone altar. The statue of Our Lady of the Safe Return glimmered in the dusky light.

*Sanctuary...*

Her eyes swept the carved pulpit, the cracked baptismal font, the faded frescoes of ships that decorated the walls. Hollow plaster statues stood in narrow niches, their suffering eyes raised heavenward. An arched door led to the medieval belfry. In a dark corner a musty curtain of once-scarlet velvet hid a small confessional. Someone, she noticed, had placed fresh chrysanthemums on the white altar cloth. High above the altar, a round rose window waited to filter the morning's sunlight down onto the gentle-faced virgin.

So many places to hide a small journal. She nodded with satisfaction.

With a long sigh she looked down at her son. The boy slept deeply, his head nestled in her lap, the stuffed bear still clutched in his arms.

She had found such infinite joy with this child, conceived so unexpectedly and late in her life. He was the very center of her world—her son, her heart. Perhaps one day he would forgive her for hiding him from his father.

Her fingers traced the purple bruise that marred the pale skin of her son's cheek. Someday, she told him silently, when you're older, you will learn about your father. Then you will understand why I did not have a choice.

Beyond the chapel walls, the opalescent fog swirled, muffling the cries of the seabirds as they were frightened from their nests in the cliffs.

* * *

The Madonna stood in a halo of light, holding out her hand. Sofia Orsini raised pleading eyes to the statue as she held her son close. Protect us, she prayed. Keep my child safe in your—

*The sound came from the right.*

A dark figure stepped into the light and grasped her son, swinging him away from her arms.

"Mama!" cried the boy, struggling to free himself.

She lunged toward the man, but froze at the sight of the silver dagger, held so close to the boy's ear.

"God in Heaven, what are you doing? Let him go!"

Familiar, frightening mirrored glasses glittered at her. "I'm taking him back to Rome where he belongs."

"He belongs with me."

"So you thought you could just disappear with him? A beautiful woman and a boy in a too-big baseball cap." He shook his head, taunting her. "People remembered you."

"His cap..."

"You have a fatal flaw, Sofia. You are far too trusting. And once again you trusted the wrong person to help you escape."

Her eyes were locked on the knife. "Please, if you'll just let him go, I will—"

"I want the journal you stole. And the manuscript..." The dagger flickered with candlelight and the boy whimpered. "You see? You have made him afraid of me."

The mother looked down at her son. His eyes were wide with uncomprehending terror.

*Get the knife away from her child.*

"Please," she pleaded. "He is just a child, he cannot hurt you!"

"But *you* can, Sofia." The words were chilling. "You've read the journal, haven't you? You've discovered the truth."

She closed her eyes. "Yes. I know." She reached into the depths of her cloak. "Just let Thomas go, and I'll give you what you want." Her fingers closed around an object in the deep pocket.

"Give them to me, Sofia." The hunter smiled as the tip of the dagger touched the boy's skin.

The child cried out.

She hurled her flashlight at the mirrored lenses.

The man flung his hand up. She lunged, grabbed her son's

sleeve, spun him away from the knife. Twisting, she raked sharp nails across the hunter's face.

Bright blood ran down his cheek. "A mistake," he said. His fingers reached out to caress her neck as he smiled down at her.

The child had buried his face in the folds of her cloak. One last time, Sofia Orsini held her son fiercely against her body and bent to press her lips to his hair. "Hide," she whispered. "I'll find you."

The hunter moved. Desperately she pushed her child away, toward the shadows. "Run, Thomas!" Her voice was an anguished command.

Clutching his stuffed bear to his chest, her son ran.

As the man lunged for the child, the woman wrapped her thin arms around his neck. Pouring all of her strength into the struggle, her teeth sank into his ear. She heard his curse of pain and felt his fingers brutally gripping her hair, pulling back her head. "Hide, Thomas!" she screamed.

Breath coming in sobs, she hit out wildly. Her fingers touched the candlestick and in an instant the heavy brass club was in her hand. She struck out at the back of his head and an animal sound erupted from his throat as he fell to the floor.

She whirled to search the high pews. "Tommy!"

The hunter surged up from the floor and grabbed the hem of her dress.

* * *

"*No!*"

The boy ran out from behind a choir stall. He saw his mother and the man he feared locked together, their giant shadows wavering like monsters from his nightmares against the stone wall. They fell against the statue of Mary and it toppled to the floor.

The crash was loud, terrifying.

A sharp cry. A man's hand, held high.

A terrible flash of silver in the candlelight.

A gasp. A heavy thud.

His mother's voice, murmuring his name in a strange, choked sound.

The child stared at the cloaked figure, motionless on the stone floor.

"Mama! Mama!" His cries echoed throughout the chapel.

He ran down the aisle, out through the heavy doors into the black night. He could hear the sounds of footsteps running after him. Coming closer!

*Hide! Hide from the man with the knife.*

The roar of the surf grew louder and then the earth fell away. He felt himself tumbling over and over into a vast and silent darkness.

* * *

The young nun found the woman at dawn, crumpled and still on the cold stones amid the scattered shards of the Madonna statue. Black pearls rolled and crunched loudly beneath her shoes as she moved toward her.

Morning flowed through the stained-glass window. Sofia Orsini lay in a brilliant halo of light, splashes of emerald and amethyst and blood-red ruby lighting her ivory face and shining like fallen stars in the dark stain on her breast.

Her ringless hand was stretched toward the scattering of toys that spilled from a small torn knapsack.

There was no sign of the child.

# CONCERTO

A musical composition in which a solo
instrument is contrasted and blended with
the orchestra, usually in three movements
of symphonic proportions.

# PART I

*Lost*

*Why, woman, what are you waiting for?*
—Sophocles, *Electra*

# CHAPTER ONE

"Luze? Are you here? Hello?"

Maggie O'Shea closed the blue door of The Piano Cat music shop and stood motionless, listening.

Too quiet.

The large, book-lined room was cool and empty of customers. Late-day sun spilled through the huge bow window onto scattered sheet music and the Steinway grand piano that stood in the curve of the window.

Deliberately turning her back on the piano, she pulled her sweat-soaked t-shirt away from her skin and kicked off her running shoes with a sigh. The afternoon had been too hot to run, after all. You need a shower, she told herself, lifting the heavy mass of her hair away from her neck just as her grandmother's wall clock began to chime.

Seven o'clock. Finally. Turning to lock the front door, she caught her reflection in the glass. The face staring back at her was a pale oval, all cheekbones and eyes too large for her face, surrounded by a cloud of black hair.

*You have hair the color of a summer's night, Maggie-mine.*

She froze.

You never know, she thought, when you will be ambushed by grief.

Almost nine months after her husband's death, there were good days and bad days. Still, unexpected moments triggered the flood of memories. A voice, a word, a gesture from a stranger on the street. The sight of an empty chair at the end of the day. A reflection in a glass...

And earlier, as she'd run through the Boston Public Garden, it was the scent of the roses.

Johnny had always given her roses. "Red for passion," he'd say in his great rumbling voice, his arms full of huge crimson blooms, "and roses because their scent is like your skin." Once, in a crowded restaurant, he had leaned across the table and slowly, maddeningly, tucked a rose between her breasts. Then he'd teased her when she blushed like a schoolgirl.

She turned her head, her gaze once more seeking the piano. This time, the Steinway drew her across the room. She sank to the piano bench and clenched her fingers in her lap. In the cluster of silver-framed photographs on the Steinway, Johnny smiled at her from a Martha's Vineyard dock. One arm was flung affectionately around her son Brian, the other held an enormous bass high in the air. Her husband's bright blue eyes stared into hers.

*We lost you too soon, Johnny.*

For almost twenty years, it had been just mother and son. Single mom Maggie Stewart and her son, Brian. A good life, but a quiet one—filled with baseball and school, scouting and piano lessons, and later with girls and jazz concerts and late-night talks over huge bowls of popcorn. She could never understand why her son stayed so thin.

And then, the summer before Brian's last year at Penn, the journalist John Patrick O'Shea had stormed into their lives at a Red Sox game and swept both of them into his magical orbit. A great bear of an Irishman with his wild red beard and rumbling voice, he had filled their small apartment, and their hearts, with joy and laughter.

Now the apartment was quiet again. Brian and his seven months pregnant wife were living on Cape Cod. And the voice of her husband no longer filled the silence.

The soft click of computer keys drifted from the music

shop's rear office. So that was where her friend Luze was hiding. Working late, as usual.

Even the clicking reminded Maggie of her husband. An award-winning investigative journalist, Johnny O'Shea was always banging on his antique Corona late into the night. "Come to bed, Johnny," she would say. "Finish the story in the morning." Then the clicking keys would fall silent, and she would feel his weight all warm next to her and breathe in the woodsy scent of his skin...

She closed her eyes, trying to see his face. But all she could see were broken silver sails spinning in ink-black water. On the bad days, the images repeated in her head, again and again, like the notes in a Bach fugue.

Bach...Maggie's breath came out in a long sigh as she raised her hands to the Steinway keyboard. Very slowly, her fingertips brushed the ivory and ebony keys, once as warm and alive as her husband's touch. Now the keys were cold as river stones beneath her rigid fingers.

The Steinway was deafeningly silent. She looked down at the words printed in bold letters on her damp t-shirt. *You are the music while the music lasts. T. S. Eliot.* "Magdalena O'Shea, concert pianist," she said aloud. But the music hadn't lasted...

Her throat tightened. *Ex*-concert pianist, she reminded herself.

God, she missed her music. Some days the longing was almost unbearable. The piano was one of her first memories. And music—it was as essential as air in her life. It was in her blood, her bones, her very soul.

So many times, since her husband's death, she had forced herself to sit in front of the keyboard and begin the simple scales and chords that would stretch muscles grown stiff with disuse. But each time she tried to play, all she could see was the small shattered sailboat. And her fingers would freeze on the silent keys.

*If only I hadn't asked him to go. If only I'd gone with him. If only he hadn't gone sailing that day. If only, if only.* Sometimes Maggie thought she would go mad with the compulsion to reshape the past.

She sat staring down at her narrow fingers. Johnny had loved to listen to her play the Steinway. "Make your music for me, Lass," he would say, coming to her and swinging her around in his arms. "Tonight I need to hear Scarlatti." And she would play for him.

"I need the music to come back, Johnny," whispered Maggie. Once again tears threatened behind her lids. *I will not cry,* she thought furiously. She knew that if she ever really let the tears come she wouldn't be able to stop the storm until she was completely hollow inside. Until her bones rattled.

"I've really made a mess of things, haven't I, Johnny?"

Sometimes, when she talked to him like this, she could see him so clearly. Her phantom lover, looking at her across the piano, his eyes so blue and electric, his beard red and soft and curling around his smiling mouth. She ached for him, ached for the sound of his voice describing the simple moments of his day.

She closed her eyes. In the stillness of the room, she could feel him now, standing behind her.

*Johnny?* she tried.

His voice answered, low and close.

*Yes, Lass. I'm here.*

*Johnny! Oh Johnny, I'm missing you so today.*

*Always near, Mo Graidh.*

*Sometimes I see your shadow in the mirror. Am I going crazy? Why can I see you?*

*Because you need to see me, Maggie-mine. But you're too thin.*

*You were always the better cook...*

*No more pills, though, Maggie? No more scotch?*

*No. I poured everything down the sink.*

*Holy Mother! Not our Cabernet collection too?*

*I'm lonely, Johnny, not crazy. But the wine can't keep the nightmares away.*

*I know, Lass.*

*It's not over, is it, Johnny?*

*No. It's not over.*

*Don't go. I need to know...*

*You need to live your life, Maggie-mine. I love you...*

He was gone.

Maggie opened her eyes, surprised to find herself alone at the piano. She touched her cheek, certain that she could still feel the gentle caress of her husband's fingers.

*It's not over...*

Fear brushed her, like a shadow in a dark theatre. Behind her the clock chimed the half hour. Seven thirty. Soon it would be dark.

She stood and moved to place the *Bach Tomorrow, Offenbach Sooner* sign on the blue shop door. Clicking on the radio, she stood very still as the bright opening notes of a Mozart concerto flooded the room. It was the No. 19 in F major. She had played it two summers ago at Tanglewood with the Boston Symphony Orchestra. Johnny had been watching her from the sixth row.

Damn, damn. Where was a melancholy nocturne when she needed one? Catching up her damp hair with a tortoise clip, her eyes fell on the crystal decanter that sat on a small table by the sofa.

Shower or drink?

"Drink," she said out loud.

\* \* \*

The dark-skinned man sat at one of the small tables outside the Charles Street Café. In the last moments of sunset, the deep-hued red brick across the street glowed with fire. He tapped a pencil thoughtfully on the rim of his coffee cup as he watched the woman's shadow through the music shop window.

The waiter appeared at his elbow. "A nice glass of Napa Char?"

"Just one more java, pal," said the man. "Black." His pencil hovered over the folded newspaper in his hand. "And gimme a fourteen-letter word that means 'sense of the body in space.'"

The waiter just shook his head as he turned away.

The man dropped the newspaper, with its half-finished crossword puzzle, to the white tablecloth as his iPhone buzzed for the fifth time in as many minutes.

*The clock is ticking on this one...*

Once more he looked toward the window in the music shop across the street.

He'd seen her return, watched her disappear through the blue door. A small, slender woman. Some looker, with all that wild black hair. Funny, how life worked sometimes. Because just last week, in Cairo, his friend Ahmed had predicted that there was a woman with hair the color of night in his future.

*Just let her be the one.*

# CHAPTER TWO

Guilt.

*Your problem, Mrs. O'Shea, is that you blame yourself for your husband's death.*

Oh, you think so, Doctor? She didn't need a damned therapist to tell her that.

Curled like a cat into the soft sofa pillows, Maggie closed her eyes until the voice was gone and only the notes of the Mozart concerto filled the air. She drank deeply from the glass of topaz-colored wine and waited for the cool liquid to ease the tightness in her chest.

She'd bought the two-story brownstone from a Turkish carpet dealer decades earlier, after she had fallen in love with the Dickensian Beacon Hill neighborhood of gas-lit lamps, steep cobbled streets, and tiny secret gardens. She and her son had lived in the small two-bedroom apartment above the shop until he'd graduated high school.

Her eyes dropped to the Persian carpet of faded gold and blue, a parting gift from the shop's previous owner that filled the air with a faint, lingering spicy scent when the tall windows were closed. In spite of its questionable ancestry, the Persian provided an island for the old sofa where Maggie sat, and for the two red leather wing-chairs that faced each other across Johnny's antique chess set.

She pictured her husband, sitting in his favorite chair, his too-blue eyes smiling at her over the chess pieces. *Checkmate, Lass. It's time for bed.*

Maggie took a deep swallow of wine and gazed around her. Full of color and light, the room was more like a private study than a shop. Oak bookcases and glassed cabinets held a wide collection of musical scores and books. Glimmering watercolors of Martha's Vineyard lit the walls. An antique glass lamp cast an amber pool over a long refectory table. By the huge bow window, her mother's Steinway glowed with purple light.

She smiled, caught by a memory of her son sitting at that piano, pounding out Dave Brubeck. Her son loved that piano as much as she did.

*Brian.* Her tall, talented, tenderhearted son, with that charming devil-may-care smile and, now, all the cockiness of a soon-to-be dad. So bright, so funny and fine. He'd married his Laura two years ago, and settled on Cape Cod to teach and play jazz. Their baby would be born in two months, close to Johnny's birthday. And would, no doubt, have the same charming smile as her son.

Johnny would have been crazy about his grandchild. *If only—*

An enormous creature the color of ripe melon appeared at Maggie's shoulder.

"Gracie to the rescue," murmured Maggie. She settled the huge old cat on her lap and poured another glass of wine. Fifteen years earlier, on a bright winter morning, Brian had found the one-eyed kitten, hungry and squalling, in the rear garden. For boy and cat, it was love at first sight.

"I'm calling him Rocky," announced Brian.

"Rach-y, like Rachmaninoff?"

"Rocky, like the boxer!" groaned Brian, rolling his eyes.

But the cat had turned out to be a female. And since Brian had just discovered the James Bond movies, he had named her Grace Jones.

By evening, Gracie had been curled on the Steinway, enraptured by Brian's pulsing, if erratic, jazz rendition of Ruby Tuesday. So enraptured that she'd begun to sing along with bellowing meows. After that night, Stewart's Music Shop became, simply, The Piano Cat.

Smiling at the memory, Maggie scratched Gracie behind her

golden ears. The Piano Cat would never make her rich, but it had allowed her precious time to practice her music. It was her concert fees that financed nights at the symphony, Vineyard summers at the cottage in Chilmark, and Brian's years at Penn.

Maggie drained the last of the wine and loosened her hair. Very deliberately, she turned her back on the silent Steinway across the room.

*How do I find my way back, Johnny?*

Sensing her mood, Gracie leaped from Maggie's lap and disappeared. Maggie set the wine glass down on the table and gazed around the empty room. In her mind, she began to play the opening notes of Scarlatti's Sonata in E major.

* * *

Across Charles Street, Special Agent Simon Sugarman of the United States Department of Justice leaned back in his chair and signaled the waiter.

"Found that word yet, bro?"

Sugarman grinned and held up the completed crossword puzzle. "Fifteen across. You're lookin' at the master, pal. *Proprioception.* Sense of the body in space."

"No kiddin'? Proprio...ception?"

"I've changed my mind. I need to celebrate. Bring me a Tanqueray Martini. And, pal, just whisper the word vermouth over the gin."

Sugarman returned his gaze to The Piano Cat's bow window.

In spite of the heat, he did not mind the vigil. In a sense he had been waiting for a very long time. Now the wait was almost over. Soon, he knew, the woman would open the envelope he'd left for her. The final act in this little drama would begin.

And Magdalena O'Shea's life would change forever.

Sorry, babe, but I need you. You do what you gotta do.

*Open the envelope, Magdalena. Look at the faces in that photograph.*

# CHAPTER THREE

Night fell early in this part of the world. Already, black shadows edged the cold waters of Penobscot Bay. The only light came intermittently, blinking from the lighthouse on the far cliff. Light, darkness. Light, darkness.

On a low bluff above a protected cove, a man stood waiting. Stamping his feet nervously, he checked his watch, then scanned the restless water. Light lit his face for an instant. Then darkness.

Stepping deeper into the shadows, he lifted his lamp. One brief flash, two, scattering on fingers of fog. Soon the mist would make the cove impossible to find. The man felt an odd sense of relief.

Then he turned and saw the boat spear silently out of the mist.

A tall man dressed in a blue windbreaker vaulted over the gunwale and strode onto the rocks. His hair was very blond, almost white, and much longer now. He'd grown a long drooping mustache since the spring—but the hawk nose was unmistakable. He still wore those damned mirrored glasses. Even in the dark.

The boat disappeared back into the mist. Dousing his lamp, the contact stepped from the shadow of the boulders and held out his hand. "Welcome to the US, Dane."

The man called Dane eased a backpack off his shoulders. Light touched the hard planes of his face for an instant, and he turned away. "Don't use my name again."

The man dropped his hand and turned toward the sea. "Navigating in the dark isn't—"

"You have what I need?" The low voice was silky and unnerving in the shadows.

"Yes. But we have a problem."

The blond man unzipped the leather sack. "I'm waiting."

"The traitor did her work too well. She did more than lure Victor to Paris. She got his photograph. Now, one of the stars at the Justice Department has a photograph of Victor, taken just weeks ago at the Café de la Paix."

Dane turned and looked directly at his contact for the first time. The man saw himself reflected in the mirrored glasses and felt his stomach tighten.

Light touched them briefly. Then darkness.

"Someone in the Attorney General's office has a recent photograph of Victor?"

"That's what my source at Justice said."

"No doubt Victor will be amused. Who has the photograph?"

"An agent named Simon Sugarman."

Powerful fingers tightened on the backpack. "Sugarman. The agent who investigated Sofia Orsini's death—"

"Yes."

"I see." Dane's body was very still. Then he asked, too casually, "Was anyone else in that photograph?"

"No idea. Justice has the lid clamped tight."

"I need to know what's in that photograph. Anything else?"

"My source said that Sugarman went to Boston to see an M. O'Shea. That's all I know."

"M. O'Shea," repeated Dane.

The contact held out a set of keys. "Okay, then. Car's parked just up the road, black Corolla, full tank. You've got a nine, maybe ten-hour drive to DC. Curtain's at eight tomorrow night. Good luck."

He turned his back on Dane and walked into the fog.

\* \* \*

*Luck? I will control my own destiny*, Dane thought, staring at the departing figure. *And you have seen my face.*

He shook his head and moved quickly, slipping his knife from its sheath. A glint of steel, arcing through the air. The sharp, upward thrust. A shocked grunt. Then silence.

"Just death, kind umpire of man's miseries."

Cursing under his breath, Dane wiped the knife on the agent's jacket, re-sheathed the blade and hefted his backpack as he glanced at the inert body. The man had been useful to Victor. But Dane could no longer take any chances. The news of the photograph had jarred him—badly. *Control,* he told himself, trying to still the loud clanging of the warning bell inside his brain.

For he, too, had been with Victor at the Café de la Paix two weeks earlier, on the day that photograph was taken. He had joined Victor and the others for a glass of Absolut. Dane remembered glancing up just as a dark-helmeted stranger on a motorbike had roared up to the curb, snapped a photograph of all of them, and disappeared into the swirling traffic of Place de L'Opera.

This was no longer about Victor. Now, he had to protect himself.

There had been no trace of the biker when he raced out to the boulevard. But he knew where the photo had been sent. Irony of ironies. Someone at Justice has a photograph of Sofia Orsini's killer—and they don't even know it.

The laughter, when it came, was startling and hollow. It was simply a matter of execution.

He shifted the heavy backpack and disappeared into the shadows.

Light. Darkness.

# CHAPTER FOUR

"There you are!"

Luze Jacobs stopped and caught her breath. Deep purple light filled the front room of The Piano Cat, silhouetting a sleeping Maggie against the luminous bow window. Maggie's hair, fanned in disarray across the sofa cushion, flamed with black fire. Starred lashes fluttered against ivory skin, dark hollows sculpted the high cheeks. The fitted t-shirt and nylon running shorts emphasized a body as slender as a sapling. Not for the first time, Luze was struck by the intense, fragile beauty of her friend.

The two women had met years before in a seminar on medieval music. Maggie was supporting herself and her preschooler by teaching and pursuing her doctorate in music at night. Luze, a transplanted New Yorker, simply "had to have music in her life." Their professor had called them "the bow and the cello." Smoothing a hand over her soft, pear-shaped hip, Luze smiled at the memory.

Yes, we're exact opposites, physically, thought Luze. Maggie slight, darkly beautiful, and understated, while she was, well—Rubenesque. Luze smiled to herself, comfortable with her eccentric, gypsy look of bright swinging dresses, bangle bracelets, and the heavy gold hoops in her ears.

"Hey, Bow," said Luze, giving Maggie's shoulder a gentle shake. "Sleeping on the job again?"

Maggie stirred and opened eyes that seemed enormous in her pale, drawn face. It hurt Luze to see the new wariness in them.

Maggie O'Shea was like two different women since Johnny's death. She'd always been strong, Luze thought, but now there was a new vulnerability about her. The public Maggie worked tirelessly in the music shop, visited her family, exercised, attended board meetings. But when she was alone, she withdrew to endure her pain in some silent inner world.

"Hi, Cello. How was your day?"

Ever protective, Luze shaped her mouth into a bright smile. "I sold the Ravel collection this afternoon. And the symphony office called. They want us to order the sheet music for Chopin's Double Thirds Etude in G-Sharp."

"That piece is impossible!"

"*You* managed it." Luze looked down at Maggie's Reeboks, forgotten on the floor. "So how was your run? Not that you need the exercise." Her smile faded when she saw the empty wine glass on the coffee table. *One of the bad days.* She raised one black eyebrow and waited.

"You've got that look," said Maggie into the silence.

Luze's face softened as she sat down next to her friend. "It's almost the Fourth. You'll be watching fireworks with that beautiful family of yours in two days."

"I might stay here," Maggie ventured.

The bracelets jangled on Luze's wrists as she reached for her friend's arm. "You can't disappoint Brian, Maggie. Look at you, so pale and bony. You need sun, girlfriend! Calories. A good night's sleep. Better yet, a cute young lifeguard?"

"I'm going to be a *grandmother*!"

"You're barely forty-eight, Maggs."

"Luze, I miss Bones like crazy," said Maggie, using her son's special nickname. "But I saw them last month. And Brian has his own life now, his own family to look after. You know how giving he is. It would be too easy for me to...let him fill my emptiness."

"Okay, it's Jewish mother time," said Luze firmly. "You won't see friends, you've lost weight, you've canceled your concerts. You won't even cry, dammit!" Luze's eyes moved to the Steinway.

"You haven't touched that piano once since the night of the accident. And you were born to play, Maggie. You have an amazing gift."

"Responsibility goes with that gift," said Maggie. "I'm numb. I can't make beautiful music for people anymore."

"Music is life affirming!" cried Luze. "You *need* it. It's just not fair to—"

"It's Johnny's dying that's not fair! I get slammed by memories everywhere I look. I open a closet and see bare hangers... Who knew there were so many ways to miss someone?"

"Grieving is never what we imagine or expect it to be."

"I didn't just lose my husband too soon. He *drowned*! Alone, far away, in a godforsaken place I never heard of. Because of *me*! Oh God, I close my eyes and see the black water pulling him away from me. *Two* people drowned that night," she whispered. "I'm as lost as he is..."

"It won't always be this way, Maggie."

"At least the pain means Johnny was alive. Luze, you're going to think I'm crazy, but sometimes I see Johnny. I *talk* to him. And he answers. Going on means losing Johnny."

Luze put her arms around her friend. "You're going to get through this," she murmured. "You're going to be okay."

"I don't feel strong enough," said Maggie against her friend's shoulder.

"Are you kidding?" said Luze. "It takes a woman with great strength to raise a child all alone. You started this music shop, you've soloed with the Vienna Philharmonic. In *Austria*!"

Luze moved closer, looked directly into her friend's eyes. "You're going to be someone stronger, Maggie. The secret is to start caring about something again. Some *one* again."

"Sometimes," said Maggie quietly, "I pretend he's just upstairs asleep, or reading..."

"It's okay, honey," comforted Luze. "You're still in love with your husband."

"Very much." Maggie shook her head. "I don't know *how* to be a damned widow."

"What would Johnny want you to do?"

"Find my way back to life." She made a face. "I hate it when you're right."

"Okay, then, so how about some pizza tonight?"

Maggie turned to her friend with a faint smile. "Right now I'd settle for just being able to sleep at night with the lights off."

Luze waited a heartbeat. "So...other than that, Mrs. Lincoln, how was your day?"

"You're good," Maggie murmured.

The two women sat together quietly, arms linked, watching twilight cloak Beacon Hill beyond the bow window.

\* \* \*

"...the nightclub bombed in Amsterdam last night was popular with Americans," said the voice on the radio, "and is just the latest in a series of anti-US attacks in Europe. Back in Washington, the Senate Intelligence Chair has accused the Director of the CIA of spying on Senate investigations into CIA abuses..."

"Washington." Luze bolted upright. "The envelope! A man from Washington came by just before closing, asking for you. Tall guy, easy smile. Gorgeous."

Maggie shook her head in confusion. "What *envelope*, Luze?"

Luze gestured toward a thin 8 x 10 manila envelope on the desk. "*That* one. Said he needs to talk with you about the contents tomorrow morning." She was searching her pockets. "He gave me his card. Damn—it's here somewhere."

"I don't need any more drama in my life." But Maggie felt the small spark of interest leap in her chest.

Luze held up a business card in triumph, then squinted at the small print. "Where are my glasses when I need them?"

"On your forehead."

"Oh." Luze dropped the glasses to her nose. "His name is Simon Sugarman. Who is he?"

"He's the agent from Justice who investigated Sofia's death. I haven't seen him in months, not since he returned from France.

I badgered him for information for weeks. Nothing. And then Johnny died and, well—everything just stopped." She grasped her friend's hand. "Maybe he finally has news about Tommy?"

Her husband's voice whispered in her head. *It's not over.*

Luze put a hand on her arm. "What is it, honey? What's wrong?"

"It's just one tragedy after another. Sofia, Tommy, Johnny. Hearing from Simon Sugarman brings it all back. My best friend murdered less than a year ago. My godson vanishing into thin air. God only knows if he's even alive! Then Johnny, gone just a month later..."

"You've got a bad case of survivor's guilt tonight, Maggs. But trust me, Jewish women *own* guilt. It's like carrying around a huge bag of bricks." She stood, moved to the desk, and held out the envelope. "So, one brick at a time. Maybe it's *good* news."

Maggie reached for Sugarman's envelope.

*Let it be good news.*

The cat leaped from the piano and followed them from the room. It was just beginning to rain.

# CHAPTER FIVE

*My name is Sofia. But everyone calls me Fee.*

Maggie stood at the tall window in her upstairs front room, listening to the rush of wind in the trees, surrounded by memories of her friend. *I miss you, Fee.*

Simon Sugarman's still-unopened envelope was gripped in her hand. Despite Luze's protests, she'd kissed her friend goodnight, nudged her firmly out the door, set the locks, and climbed the back stairs to her small apartment.

She needed time alone to think, to remember. And, to be honest, to prepare for whatever was in that envelope. Sofia's death last September had been such a shock, such a terrible loss. Had Sugarman found Fee's murderer? Her son?

Needing courage against the ghosts of the night, she switched on a lamp to dispel the shadows and clicked on the radio. Yo Yo Ma's Bach Cello Suite No. 1. Perfect.

She gazed down through night-blue glass at shining cobblestones and gas lamps blurred by rain. She'd met Sofia Orsini on just such a wild night, more than thirty years earlier. She closed her eyes and listened to the rain drum against the panes as the memories washed over her.

* * *

Rain hurled and beat against the hood of her coat as she ran across the shining cobblestones of Harvard Square. The rain was cold, stinging her face, blinding her. Where was that coffeehouse?

Just as Maggie rounded the corner onto Brattle Street, she'd heard a woman's sharp scream. In a pool of blurred light from a streetlamp, like a film noir, a woman fought off two dark figures.

"Hey!" shouted Maggie, running toward the trio without thought.

The two young men suddenly rushed at her, shoving her against a parked car as they dashed past and disappeared around the corner. Maggie swung around, searching for the woman. There, on her knees in the shadows. She was hiding something in a dark backpack as Maggie ran toward her. The woman stood and shouted, "Follow me!" Then, head down, she dashed through the driving rain toward the lights of the coffeehouse.

Headlamps stabbed the black fog, too close.

"Watch out!" Maggie lunged into the street, colliding hard with the cloaked figure. They crashed together to the cobble-stones as the car rushed past with a long echoing blare of its horn.

"Bloody hell!"

"Whoa, damn!"

Both women struggled to sit up, looked at each other through the curtain of rain—and burst into laughter.

"Are you okay?"

"Yes, yes, and you?" The stranger quickly checked the contents of her backpack, breathed a sigh of relief. "Thank God you saw the car."

Maggie was the first to stand, and held out her hand. "C'mon, I'm soaked and I'm freezing."

Strong wet fingers grasped hard. "I owe you. Twice." They entered the smoky warmth together. Only one table free, in the far corner. A lone student was winding his way toward it. They locked eyes once more.

"Last one there buys the coffee."

Whipping past the surprised student, they claimed the wooden chairs. Maggie blinked rain from her lashes and looked across the table into dark eyes framed by black hair as wild and untamed as her own. "I hate storms."

The striking young woman across from her waved a hand to the waiter behind the coffee bar, held up two fingers, and called in a low voice, "Davio! *Due caffè, grazie!* And a bowl of *acqua, per favore.*" Shifting her backpack, she searched for her purse, lit a slender cigarette, and raised it to ruby lips. A silver bracelet flashed in the light. Gazing at Maggie through a stream of gauzy smoke, she said, "I love the rain."

Maggie pulled her jacket closer to her body, shivering. "Boston in November? You can have it. Pitch black at three o'clock... God, I'm cold! What on earth was going on out there?"

"Those two kids, they were hurting her, I couldn't let it happen."

"Her?" Maggie looked around. "Hurting whom?"

The bulge in the leather backpack moved, shifted. The young woman smiled and lifted the flap. A soft brown muzzle appeared and sniffed the smoky air.

"A puppy!" gasped Maggie, reaching out to touch the smooth silky head of the chocolate Lab. "Oh, she's a lucky one, aren't you, girl? What will you do with her now?"

"Aren't we responsible for the lives we rescue?"

For a heartbeat the woman's words hung in the air, electric with prophecy. Then she said, "I'll keep her, of course. And name her after you."

Two steaming mugs of coffee appeared on the table. "Hi, Fee, didn't know you had a sister."

"*Grazie*, Davio." The woman arched an eyebrow at Maggie as she handed a ten-dollar bill to the smitten waiter. "Sisters?" She studied Maggie's face. "Yes...except for your green eyes and appalling lack of makeup, I almost feel that I'm looking in the mirror. I think we were fated to meet tonight." She set the puppy down by the water dish and raised her cup to Maggie. "To the woman who rescued *me*."

"You're just lucky you weren't drowning. I'm scared to death of deep water. I'd have run the other way!"

"Somehow I doubt that." The woman smiled, cocked her

head. "So you don't like storms or being cold or deep water. What *do* you like?"

Maggie shrugged, cupped the warm mug gratefully and drank. "Ah, hot caffeine, for one thing. Salvation! You are a goddess. Now *I* promise to name my first daughter after you. Fee, is it?"

Fee held out her hand. "Sofia Chambers. Everyone calls me Fee."

"Sofia is a beautiful name. I'm Maggie Stewart."

Sofia Chambers held the soft squirming puppy up to the light. "Ah, little one, you're not to be a Maggie after all, it seems. So you will be...Magnus! Yes, Magnus suits you."

"Hello, Magnus," said Maggie. "And if I have a son instead of daughter," she added, "then he will have to be...a Phinneas? No, a Sophocles!"

"You're sounding dangerously like a Harvard girl, Maggie Stewart."

"Hardly. I'm studying music at the conservatory across town."

"You play—"

"Not well enough." Maggie moved her fingers in the air. "The piano is my life. And most certainly will be my death as well," she muttered darkly. "You?"

"Don't know a sharp from a flat. I'm studying Public Policy."

"Government." Maggie shook her head.

"I'm crazy, I know. But I'm a diplomat's brat. I *love* politics. Can't wait to get to DC."

Maggie raised her own cup in salute. "Then here's to the future—what?—Senator from Massachusetts? Ambassador to the Court of King James?"

"Why think small, darling?"

"Ah, then someday when you're Madame President, I'll come and play for you and Magnus at the White House."

"Now I'm interested. And you'll bring little Sofia or Sophocles with you."

And they'd sat and talked for two hours, while Magnus slept

contentedly at their feet, and outside in Harvard Square the night rain beat against the window panes.

\* \* \*

Maggie blinked at the rain. A friendship born in a storm, so many years ago. She'd never played at the White House, nor had a daughter named Sofia. But her son's name was Brian Zachary *Sophocles* Stewart. And Fee...well, Sofia Chambers had made it to Washington, eventually won her promotion to the US Embassy in Rome, and then surprised everyone by running off with an expat art collector. Her young son, Thomas, was Maggie's godson.

And now Fee was dead.

*We are responsible for the lives we rescue...*

The call had come on an early September night. She remembered that moment so clearly. She'd been standing on the porch of the Vineyard cottage, wrapped in a heavy shawl, watching stars shimmer on Menemsha Pond while Johnny worked on a story in the back room. The air was cold against her face and smelled of fall grasses and wood smoke. In the distance she could hear the call of the wild geese. And then the ringing of the phone.

"Madame O'Shea? Magdalena O'Shea?" A woman's voice, soft, accented. Unfamiliar.

"Yes."

"I have—" Static. Then the deep chime of bells.

"Sorry, I can't hear you. The chimes—"

"I have called to warn you, Madame." Louder. "I am sorry, but your friend Sofia Orsini is dead. Her son is missing, you must find him—"

"What? Oh, God. No, no, you're mistaken. It can't be true! Who is this?"

"I cannot say more." Just those words, and the connection was lost.

*She never found out who had placed the call.*

Maggie had been on the first morning plane to Washington. Fee had told her about a good friend at the Justice Department, and Maggie was waiting for Agent Simon Sugarman outside his office door by nine a.m., demanding answers.

But he'd had no answers. And now, ten months later, Agent Sugarman was in Boston. And an envelope left for her by Sugarman was in her hand.

What if—? Just *do* it, damn it.

Maggie turned away from the rain, tore the seal, and tipped out the contents. An 8 x 10 black and white photograph spilled into the light. Stunned, she dropped the photograph to the carpet as if it burned her fingers.

"My God. It can't be—"

# CHAPTER SIX

*This is impossible.*

Maggie shook her head in disbelief. The gold cat, asleep on an easy chair, stirred, looked squarely at her, and turned away to contemplate the rain-washed window.

"Thanks for the support, Gracie."

She bent to retrieve the photograph and ran down the hall to her son's old bedroom. Turning on the lamp, she brushed past the new cradle, nestled so close to Brian's boyhood bed, and stopped before his bureau. The cat had followed her, curious. She could hear the small creak of rocking wood behind her as Gracie settled into the cradle Maggie had bought for her first grandchild.

Her fingers shook as she searched the cluttered surface of Brian's bureau, where framed snapshots were scattered among Red Sox mementos and sports trophies. She lifted one picture, then another. Brian at the piano, and with his Little League team. His favorite photo of her, bowing on the stage of Carnegie Hall. And there—Johnny and Brian, brown and windblown, on Johnny's sailboat, the *Green Eyed Lass*.

*I will not cry.*

The small silver frame she sought was hidden behind a forgotten baseball mitt. Maggie lifted the photograph of Brian's biological father, Zachary Law. Zachary Law, MIA, disappearing somewhere in the deserts of Lebanon in the fall of 1983—just weeks before his son Brian was born.

Maggie stared at the youth trapped forever behind the dusty

glass. This photo was one of the few keepsakes Brian kept of the father he had never known. It was a small black and white snapshot of Zach—sensitive dark eyes shadowed by tortoise-framed sunglasses worn, as always, slightly askew and low on his nose, face still unlined by experience—taken the day he left for the Middle East.

*Zach.* Turning to the window, she leaned her forehead against the cool windowpane. A pale, hollow face was reflected in the glass. Then the wind blew raindrops hard against the dark glass and blurred her image with silver tears.

*The rain is full of ghosts tonight,* she thought. My husband. Sofia and her little boy. And now, Zach. My life would have been so different if Zach had come home. *If we had married...*

The pregnancy had been totally unexpected, undiscovered until her third month. A shocked and frightened Maggie, barely eighteen and with no family to support her, had written to Zach in panic. But his reply never came. Months later she'd received a brief message suggesting she contact the State Department. Instead she'd called Zach's estranged father in New York. And Cameron Law had told her, in a curiously flat voice, that Zach had been working with a multinational force for a USAID program in Lebanon and volunteered for a special mission. It was a dangerous time, with the Lebanese involved in a terrible civil war.

Her breath caught in her chest, remembering.

October 23, 1983. Two truck bombs had struck the barracks housing US and French forces. The numbers of dead were engraved in her memory. Two hundred ninety-nine dead.

"Two hundred twenty Marines," she whispered, remembering every terrible word of Cameron Law's unemotional recitation. "Eighteen navy, three army. Sixty Americans injured..."

Zachary Law had been listed MIA following the explosion. His body was never found.

*Not to have known!* The black, awful shock of it. She had vomited right there, in her tiny kitchen. Even now, after all these years, the memory still sickened her.

By then seven months pregnant, she'd gone to the Vineyard to grieve. Sofia had joined her, insisting that she shouldn't be alone.

That night, she'd gone into labor. Sofia had held her hand and kissed her forehead and cajoled and threatened her through the worst of it. Fifteen hours later, on the last day of November, Brian Zachary Sophocles Stewart was born. When she'd called Zach's father from the neonatal unit to tell him he had a grandson, he had asked her, coldly, how many men could lay claim to the child.

And so Maggie and Brian were on their own.

It was many years before she spoke to Zach's father again, and only because Johnny worked so hard to set things right between Brian and his grandfather. "The boy should know his blood," Johnny had insisted. "His father is gone. But he should know his grandfather." And because it was impossible to say no to Johnny O'Shea, grandfather and grandson, both so tall and hawk-nosed and stubborn, finally had come to know each other.

Over the years, so often when she'd looked into her son's dark eyes, she'd seen Zach. Thought of all the things Zach had missed, not knowing his son. Brian's first words, the home runs, the cigarettes behind the garage, prom night. Brian's music.

A grandchild coming...

Maggie looked down at the stiff, smiling figure of young Zachary Law in the silver frame. Her son's father.

Her husband's words echoed in her ears. *Brian should know his blood.*

I need to know the truth, she thought. For Brian.

Under the strong light of Brian's lamp, Maggie held the two pictures side by side, her eyes moving back and forth, comparing the youthful Zach to Sugarman's photograph.

Sugarman's print showed four people grouped beneath an umbrella at a crowded European café. A beautiful young woman, her fashionably cut short hair fringed around a gamine face. A tall male, fair-haired with a hint of mustache, caught in mid-motion as he rose from his chair. His lean wolf-like face, partly hidden by mirrored aviator sunglasses, wore an expression of anger as he stared directly into the camera.

Towering above the people at the table stood an older, barrel-chested man dressed in the loose clothing of a laborer. His face, too, was shadowed by dark glasses and a cap pulled low over his brow. But the strong, square-shouldered body was familiar. She'd met him only once, six years ago, after Fee's son was born. Victor Orsini, Sofia's husband.

"You rotten bastard," whispered Maggie.

Orsini's thick, ringed hand rested with familiarity on a third man's shoulder. Sitting to the woman's right, he was slender, his graying bearded face upturned, profile sharply defined against the light. Maggie's eyes locked on the handsome, bearded face.

The thrusting chin beneath the close beard. Glasses askew, slipping low on a nose that jutted out like the prow of a ship. The boney ridge of forehead. A strong silhouette, angular and unforgettable. It was a profile exactly like Cameron Law's. Exactly like Brian's.

*Exactly like the face of her son's father, staring out from the silver-framed photograph.*

Maggie turned off the lamp and sat alone in the dark on the bed of her son.

"Zach?" whispered Maggie into the blackness.

*Are you alive?*

# CHAPTER SEVEN

*The black Steinway concert grand piano stood at the edge of the rocky beach, stark against a sky that pulsed with dark-blue light and flickered with wild rain.*

*As Maggie sat down on the bench, the wind caught the long gossamer scarf on her shoulders, lifting it behind her like a ghostly banner. With a crash of chords she began to play the Grieg Piano Concerto in A minor.*

*A tiny sailboat, just a glimmer of white in the ink-blue darkness, speared through the curtain of fog. It slid across the wild water toward rocks thrusting black and sharp as dragon's teeth.*

*At the moment of impact there was no sound. Just the small bright boat, slamming silently into cold stone. Spinning, end over end, in slow motion, high into the air. Then down, down through the darkness. Suddenly a ball of water blossomed, like some monstrous black flower, against the rain swept night sky.*

*Johnny!*

*She ran toward the swirling black water and flung herself into the sea.*

*PleaseGodPlease. Then she saw his hand, just beyond her reach. Take my hand, hold on to me!*

*Black water engulfed him.*

*Then fingers, pale and wavering, gripped her ankle and began to pull her down. Her lungs filled with water as she spun down, down into a swirling vortex of terrifying black.*

*Somewhere beyond the blackness, as if from the bottom of a well, the shrill ringing of a telephone and the deep, sorrowful chime of bells.*

*Then only silence.*

Maggie's eyes flew open. She flung out her arms blindly, gasping for breath. Drowning.

*Johnny…*

Her heart was beating frantically against her chest like a trapped bird. She struggled to sit up, clutching the tangled sheets to her trembling body. The white nightshirt she wore, an old Oxford shirt of Johnny's, was soaked with sweat.

The same nightmare as always. The stark terror of the hand. Sinking into the cold blackness. And—something more. Something she desperately needed to remember.

She turned on the radio for company and sat very still, holding her knees tightly.

\* \* \*

Maggie stood in the hot, stinging shower trying to scrub away the lingering coldness of the nightmare. Just concentrate on today, she told herself. Simon Sugarman will be here in thirty minutes. You need to know about that photograph.

*You need to know if Zach could be alive.*

She arched her neck under the hot water and closed her eyes.

For so long, she'd believed that Zach was dead, lost to her somewhere in the deserts of the Middle East. She tried to imagine him—a man now, thirty years older—living somewhere overseas. Deliberately choosing not to come home. Had her letters ever reached him?

*Would he even know that he had a son? A grandchild coming?*

Maggie turned off the taps and reached for a towel.

There had to be another explanation for the photograph. A stranger who resembled Zach. But why else would Sugarman have left the photograph for her to see?

*Why else*, her brain hammered at her.

The shower had not washed away her fears after all. But her thoughts had triggered another long-forgotten memory. Quickly she drew a terry robe around her body and moved into the bedroom to search the drawers of her desk. The yellowed newspaper clipping lay forgotten in the bottom drawer.

It was a Boston Globe music review from late 1982, just after she had met Zach. Her eyes skimmed the small print. "Last night, Bostonians were treated to a rare performance in the Jordan Concert Hall," it began. "Pianist Zachary Law, native New Yorker and graduate fellow at the New England Conservatory, performed Tchaikovsky's Piano Concerto No. 1 in B-flat minor with uncompromising, dazzling virtuosity, more than a century after the first performance took place in this very city in 1875. From the moment the imperious horn opens the concerto, Mr. Law's consummate skill..."

Maggie sat back on her heels and closed her eyes, remembering. She was a girl again, shivering with excitement in the balcony, as Zach's fingers flew across the keys with the inspired touch of a sorcerer conjuring forth a new world. She still could see the way his eyes, dark and shining, had sought hers at the moment when the audience surged to its feet and shouts of Bravo! rang like cymbals in the air.

It was all so long ago, thought Maggie. A relationship between two innocent young lovers, both strangers to her now. Let the past stay buried.

And yet... She dropped her eyes to the last lines of the clipping. "Zachary Law is indeed a new force to be reckoned with in the musical world. Expect to hear his name again and again. In Moscow's competitions. In Europe's concert halls. In New York City. This young pianist could well be the Horowitz of the future."

*If you really are alive, Zach, then whatever happened to your music?*

Her face was ashen in the vanity mirror. Small wonder, she

thought. My husband and dearest friend die, just one month apart. And now, my son's father might be alive.

Maggie dressed, swept a brush through her hair, and closed the bedroom door behind her. For just a moment, she paused on the landing at the top of the stairs. Then she went down the steps to face her past.

# CHAPTER EIGHT

The powerful, brilliant first four notes of Beethoven's Fifth Symphony filled the front room of The Piano Cat, surrounding Maggie with deep vibrating sound. Fate knocking on the door, the composer had explained. A perfect choice, thought Maggie. Come ahead and knock on my door, Agent Simon Sugarman, I'm ready for you now. *I hope.*

Outside on Charles Street, as if on cue, a red cab slid to a stop in front of the music shop. A tall, broad-shouldered African American in a fitted suit stepped out of the cab. He turned his head slowly toward the window, as if he sensed her presence behind the purple panes. Maggie took a step back and moved to the door.

Simon Sugarman entered the shop. Suddenly the doorway seemed too small, as if a dark granite spire blocked out the light.

In his mid-fifties, Sugarman was built like an athlete, his close-cropped hair the color of coal and skin black as asphalt. A thin sheen of whiskers surrounded his jaw. Luze was right. Gorgeous.

He wore the standard bureaucratic uniform—dark suit, white shirt with striped tie—but night-blue Nikes took the place of polished wingtips. The deep brown eyes conveyed a sharp intelligence and some impatience. And the well-cut suit barely seemed able to contain his strength and energy.

She took a breath and moved toward him.

"What the hell is going on, Agent Sugarman?"

* * *

Sugarman tried to hide his shock. Good God, he thought. She'd lost weight in the ten months since he'd seen her, but...*hair the color of night*, just as Ahmed had predicted. And as beautiful as the Nile at sunrise. He'd forgotten—or suppressed?—how much she resembled Sofia Orsini.

She stood in front of him, the angry question in her eyes. He'd have to be careful...

Giving Maggie a rogue's grin and holding out his hand, he broke the silence between them. "So this is Chez O'Shea. Nice."

"Thank you. And you're here because...?"

"Because we need to talk." He bent toward her. "Last time I saw you, you were demanding justice outside my office door, with your duffel packed for France. I had one helluva time convincing you to let the professionals do their job." His hand closed around hers like a boxing glove. "How are you holding up, Mrs. O'Shea?"

"I'm fine."

Her voice, deep and resonant as a cello, was surprising in one so small. "Liar," he said gently.

"Okay, so I'm a mess. But I'm not your problem. Have you found Tommy Orsini, Agent Sugarman?"

"No, Mrs. O'Shea, I'm sorry."

"Have you found Sofia's murderer?"

"No. Not yet."

"Then why have you shown up *now*, ten months after Tommy disappeared? Are you here to tell me you're giving up the search? Because Tommy is *alive*, Agent Sugarman. My godson is out there somewhere. You can't stop looking for him."

"You take no prisoners, do you, Mrs. O'Shea? No, that's not why I'm here either. Exactly."

"Then why are you here, Agent Sugarman? Exactly."

"Ouch," he said. "We're on the same side here, Mrs. O'Shea."

She went still. Her eyes locked on the Steinway for a long moment, then moved back to him. "God," she breathed. "I'm sorry. I'm not ever this rude. But it's been one hell of a year, and I haven't heard from you, and my godson is still missing. And all you have for me is a damned photograph."

"Let's sit down, Mrs. O'Shea, and I'll explain everything." Sugarman moved toward the wing chairs, but stopped in front of the Doctorates of Music diplomas framed on the wall. "*Two* Doctorates?" he murmured, turning to her. "Do people call you Doc?"

"No."

He smiled, then tapped a score left open on the music cabinet. "Vivaldi's Four Seasons. Love it."

"You're a fan of classical music, Agent Sugarman?"

"Call me Simon. My mama insists I'm rhythmically challenged for a black man, but I know my way around a concert hall." His eyes dropped to the words on her t-shirt—*Bend It Like Beethoven*. "Can't beat Beethoven's Fifth," he murmured as he finally settled into one of the red wing chairs.

The look on her face told him he'd chosen her husband's chair.

Maggie took a deep breath and sat down across from him. "I need to know why you're really here. You haven't found Sofia's murderer or my godson. What else do you do at Justice that could possibly involve a classical pianist?"

"My job is finding lost 'Cultural Property.' I specialize in illicit importation and distribution, illegal trafficking of stolen art, antiquities, sculptures. There's a hell of a black market for private collectors."

She was staring at him.

"Even music," he went on. "Helped track down a stolen Stradivarius last year, found it in a decaying palazzo. Who knew there was a vast global business empire in stolen violins? "And a long-lost Mozart manuscript discovered in a Philadelphia seminary was just auctioned off for $1.7 million! That's big money."

She held up a hand to stop him. "I read about that. I only thought...maybe you were here because of my husband."

"Your husband?" His voice was suddenly careful. "Why would you think such a thing?"

"I need to know. My husband was Johnny O'Shea, the journalist. He had a great many contacts in Washington. He died not long after you and I met."

"I heard about his death. I'm sorry."

"You knew Johnny?"

"Only by reputation. Foreign Affairs expert, internationally syndicated columnist. My pals in the government swore they read Johnny O'Shea every morning so they'd know what was *really* goin' on in the world."

She looked down at her fingers, clasped tightly in her lap. "That was my husband. Always in search of the big story."

Sugarman watched her. "Didn't I read that he died somewhere in Europe?"

"Off the Marseilles coast. A boating accident, in a storm, last October." Her voice was barely audible. "He always loved to sail..."

Sugarman let out his breath. She'd told him what he wanted to know. "An accident," he repeated, shaking his head. "I'm sorry. One hell of a loss."

She looked down at the gold wedding band on her finger. "They found his boat...broken against the rocks. I thought, when you asked to see me..." her eyes searched his. "You might know something more?"

Sugarman shook his head and told his first lie. "No, Mrs. O'Shea. This visit has nothing to do with Johnny O'Shea."

"I just had to be sure. Of course you've really come to discuss this." She lifted the photograph of the French café from her coffee table and held it out.

Sugarman nodded, relieved to be on safer ground. "This photograph could lead us to your godson," he said. "Let me bring you up to speed."

He leaned forward in the chair. "The first thirty-six hours are always the most critical in missing cases," he admitted. "Took me twenty-four hours just to get to that damned island—and that convent on the edge of nowhere, where Sofia Orsini died." He closed his eyes. "The nuns showed me where she was buried. On a hillside wreathed in fog, looking out toward the sea. She gave her life to protect her son..."

Slowly he took her through the investigation. The images were stark, powerful. Partial footprints made by a child—and by a pair of size eleven boots. A small Red Sox cap, a trace of Tommy Orsini's blood on the rocks. The abandoned villa in Rome. Sugarman watched her face as his quiet, terrible words washed over her.

"You have the look of Sofia," Sugarman murmured as he reached into his jacket pocket. "I found this with her things. Maybe you'd like to have it." He held out a small photograph of a boy about five years old, with black curls and a pensive, shy smile.

"Tommy. Pictures are all I have," she said quietly. "I haven't seen him since his christening, almost six years ago. When Fee stopped our visits. Victor didn't want me in her life."

He waited, his eyes on her. Just let her talk, he told himself.

"After that, all I had were her letters," said Maggie.

*He hadn't known about the letters. Where were they?*

"Fee wrote that he was a resourceful kid," Maggie was saying. "Dear God, he must have fought. He must have tried to protect her..." She stopped, paled, as if horrified by the images in her mind.

"Maybe there's something in those letters Fee sent you that could help us?"

"She told me to burn them."

He didn't believe her. "Okay, whatever. But if you—"

"It's been almost a year, Agent Sugarman," she interrupted. "Do you really believe that my godson is still alive?"

"All our leads to Tommy ran cold," he admitted. "*Until now.*"

She raised shining eyes to his. "Tell me!"

"I'm bettin' my Arlington condo that your godson's been hidden somewhere in Europe by his father."

"If Tommy is with Victor, then he's in real danger." She held up the photograph of the four people in the café. "You think this will lead us to my godson."

Suddenly the leather chair could not contain his energy. Sugarman stood and pointed a finger at her. "I do. This photograph was taken in Paris very recently." He bent over her shoulder and tapped the older, barrel-chested man standing behind the café table. "You recognized Victor Orsini, of course."

Clearly surprised, Maggie stood to face him. What had she expected him to say? He watched her stare down at Orsini's half-hidden face.

"He's gained weight since the one time I met him, and the clothing is far less elegant, but yes. That's Fee's murderer."

"Maybe, maybe not. But I'm absolutely certain that you're looking at the face of her killer."

Once more she looked down at the faces in the photograph. "One of these three men?" Confusion—and fear—flickered across her face.

"Yeah. Or the woman. Ever seen her before?"

She took a step back, as if she knew where his questions were irrevocably headed. "No."

"Or the blond guy staring into the camera?"

She suppressed a shudder. "I'd remember him. So let's get to the point, shall we? What do you really want from me? "

"Okay, Doc, cards on the table." Sugarman steepled his fingers against his lips. "Ten months ago, in my office, you said you would do anything to find your godson. Now I'm asking, Doc."

Her hand moved to her chest, as if to calm a rapid heartbeat. "Asking what?" she whispered.

"You know the one person who can lead me to that missing kid. You've recognized the third man in that photograph, haven't you, Mrs. O'Shea?"

"The bearded one," she said, almost inaudibly, "the man speaking to Orsini." Her voice sounded hollow. "He looks like someone I loved a long time ago. His name was Zachary Law. But it can't be Zach..."

"Are you sure?" asked Sugarman.

"And so it all falls into place," she murmured, "like a well-ordered Bach Invention." She looked Sugarman in the eye. "I'm sure. Zachary Law died thirty years ago."

Sugarman gazed down at her, aware that his next words were going to hit her like a punch in the stomach.

*Just tell as much of the truth as you can.*

"Then that means," said Sugarman, "that not too long ago Law's daddy got a letter from a dead man."

# CHAPTER NINE

"Zachary Law is alive." Sugarman looked directly into Maggie's eyes as he spoke. "Late last summer he sent a letter to his father, Cameron Law, from Vienna. Now here he is again, just one year later, in this photograph. He's as alive as I am, Doc."

Maggie shook her head in denial. "Not possible. I don't know who sent Cameron Law a letter, Agent Sugarman, but it wasn't his son. They were estranged. And Zachary Law is dead." Her voice was low and stony. "He was listed MIA in Lebanon. The Beirut bombings, in 1983. His father received confirmation from the Pentagon."

"Means nada. Was Law wearing a dog tag?"

"A relief agency ID. It was delivered to his father." She swallowed. "His body was never found, but—"

Sugarman shook his head. "Those tags made too much noise, you know? A few men hid them in boots or hats. But most left them behind."

Maggie felt lightheaded and sick. "But...Cameron Law is my son's grandfather. Surely he would have called us." She shook her head back and forth in confusion. "And even if Zach *is* alive, how is he connected to finding my godson?"

"Just hear me out, Doc." Sugarman tapped the photograph again. "Zachary Law is a means to an end. Just look at the expressions on their faces, Orsini's hand on Law's shoulder. These men are friends, they know each other well. Law is the link I've been searching for. If Law is close to Victor, he could get us to Victor's kid."

"Maybe," she conceded finally, "but only *if* he's alive." She felt as if she were trying to learn a piece of new music when half the notes were missing. "This man you think is Zach—you don't know where he is now?"

"I've been working with Interpol. They've found no trace of a Zachary Law in France or Italy. Or Europe, for that matter. I was hoping *you* could tell me how to find him."

She raised shocked eyes to his. "*Me*! I'm a pianist, Agent Sugarman, I don't rub lamps for a living. Until last night, I thought Zach died in a far-away desert. And frankly, you still have not convinced me otherwise. A letter and photograph prove nothing."

Maggie watched Sugarman's muscles shift with impatience under the fine fabric of his suit. But when he spoke his voice was neutral. "Just let me tell you what I know. I found a guy who survived the Beirut explosion that day. A medic. Turns out he knew Law. He said—" Sugarman stopped. "You sure you want to hear this?"

"No. But I need to."

Sugarman shrugged. "It was a surprise attack. Just after dawn. Six twenty-two a.m., to be exact. A 12,000-pound truck bomb does a lot of damage. The medic said that his unit carried a whole lotta injured out that day, including Zach Law. The guy saw him under a tarp, waiting for evac."

She closed her eyes as if they were shields. *Could it be true?* Taking a jagged breath, she asked, "What were his injuries?"

"Bad. Real bad, was all he could say. Then another medic took over, and my guy never saw Zach again."

"Bad injuries..." she swallowed. "So he didn't survive."

"Maybe. I went to the Pentagon, found a record of a Zachary Law treated at a field hospital near Beirut. Then—nothing. The trail went cold. Until the official death confirmation." Sugarman gestured toward the photograph. "But that's his face we're looking at, isn't it?"

"So you're saying Zach survived but chose not to come

home." The words sounded in her ears like cold stones dropping into the room.

"Violence changes people. Maybe he lost his memory. Or maybe Law just needed to stay lost, Doc."

She stared at him. "But why? How..."

"If people want to disappear, they can grow beards, gain or lose weight, get tinted contact lenses, shave or dye their hair, change their names. And people don't look for a dead man."

There was something in his voice. Her head came up quickly, but he was turned away from her.

What was she missing? *The letter*. "You said that someone you think is Zach sent a letter to Cameron Law from Vienna. What was in it? And exactly how did you find out about a letter sent to Zach's father? What are you not telling me?"

"What are you, a mind reader? Yeah, there's something more you don't know, something you're not gonna like."

"Just say it, Agent Sugarman. This all happened a long time ago. It can't possibly hurt me now."

"You sure about that?" Sugarman began to pace back and forth across the Persian rug. "I may not have been entirely honest with you."

She took a deep breath. "About?"

"About your husband." He held up a hand when he saw the expression on her face. "When Cameron Law got the letter from Zach, last summer, he called your husband."

Maggie took a step back, shaking her head as if someone had hit her. "Last summer? That's not possible."

"Yeah. It is."

"Johnny *knew*? But...he would have told me!"

"Not if it concerned your son, Mrs. O'Shea. Those men bonded because of Brian. Your husband loved his stepson; Cameron Law loves his grandson. Neither man wanted to raise false hopes for you—and especially for your son. So—"

"So Cameron asked Johnny to help him find out the truth."

"Bada-bing."

She closed her eyes, trying to fit the pieces together. The thoughts skipped through her mind like arpeggios across a keyboard. All of Johnny's overseas travels—of course he would have used every contact, done everything he could to help. "But *you* didn't know Zach's father—*or* my husband."

The dark eyes gleamed at her. "You're good," he murmured with admiration. "I never met your husband, that's true. But he knew about *me*. You told him yourself—that I was the agent in charge of investigating Sofia's death."

"Of course," she said, remembering. "I told Johnny about meeting you in DC after Tommy disappeared."

"Your husband told Cameron Law about me. That he should contact me if ever...well. Old Man Law got in touch with me after your husband's death."

She gazed blindly out the bow window. "But that was last October."

"I went to see Cameron Law in New York when he called," said Sugarman. "He told me that your husband had been searching for his son Zach, thought he was getting close. Law showed me old photographs of his son."

*The photograph.* Suddenly the dots were connecting. "And when you saw this photo of Victor Orsini, you recognized Zach as well."

"Yeah, so I flew to New York and showed my café photo to old man Law. He recognized his son, all right. Said it was time you knew."

She stared at him. *Was he telling her the truth?*

"And all your threads suddenly came together." Maggie ran her fingers lightly over the photograph. "The search for Sofia Orsini's missing child. Cameron Law's search for his missing son, Zach. And a photograph connecting Zachary Law to Victor Orsini, the child's father."

"The threads are still tangled as hell, but—yeah."

Her eyes locked on his. "You think Victor has his son hidden somewhere. You think Zach can lead you to him. All you need is someone to find Zach."

"You're playin' sweet music, Doc!"

"More like broken chords, Agent Sugarman. How did you get this photograph?"

"A source. Contacted me last month. We had a meeting late at night, outdoors, in a cold hard rain." He shook his head. "The informer says I might find Victor Orsini in Paris. I just pulled on the string to see where it went. Our agent caught up with Vic at the Café de la Paix. That photograph in your hand was sent directly to my iPhone from Paris. But he disappeared like smoke."

She sensed there was a great deal he wasn't saying. She could hear the false note in his voice, as clearly as she could detect the off-key notes on a concert grand piano. "There's more."

Sugarman spoke behind her. "There was something else with that letter to Cameron Law. A CD."

She swung around to face him. "What's on that disc, Agent Sugarman?"

"Music. Cameron Law said it was a piano concerto."

Maggie's stomach constricted. "Which one?"

"Got me."

"I want to hear it. And see the letter you say is from Zach."

"You'll have all of it, Doc. Because I'm lookin' for a guy I've never met. His father is in a wheelchair. You're the only other person left who still might give a damn about him." His eyes flashed at her. "It's all connected, Zach Law and the kid and the music. You feel it, too, I know you do."

She looked away.

"Do you speak French, Doc?"

Maggie spun around as if he'd hit her. "You want me to go to France?"

He smiled. "*Cherchez l'homme*, as they say. Find the man, and he'll lead us to Tommy Orsini."

"Just how do you expect me to find a man who's been missing for three decades?"

"I've done my homework, Doc. You're a concert pianist. And Law was a piano player, too."

"A 'piano player'..." she repeated wryly. "Zach was on the edge of a brilliant musical career when he went overseas."

"Okay, whatever. Music is a key connection here. Listen to that CD, Doc. Zach may have changed his name, his appearance, but I'll bet he's still into music. And there are some major music festivals in France this month." He gestured at a poster on the shop wall. "Avignon, Nice, Aix, Orange—"

"You expect me to run into Zach at a French music festival? Someone whose appearance would be totally different. And say what? 'Hello, I'm the mother of the child you never knew.'"

Intense eyes, wavering. "Okay. Not exactly. We would arrange for you to give a few concerts. The publicity alone would draw him out of hiding."

"*No*! No concerts."

The raw, unexpected pain in her voice surprised both of them.

"Hey, Doc, you're it! People who'd recognize Zachary Law after thirty years are not exactly beating down my door. And I'll do anything to find that kid."

She moved closer, looked up into his eyes. "So will I. But my best friend and my husband both died in France. Isn't there any other way I can—" She stopped, hearing the hollowness of her words.

"Sorry, Doc, but you're my only shot." Sugarman hesitated. "What's really going on here, Mrs. O'Shea?"

The anger welled up, tore from her throat. "If Zachary Law is alive, then the man I loved with all my heart wanted me to think he was *dead*. He lied to me, he abandoned me! Why would I ever want to see Zachary Law again? I don't want Brian to know that his father didn't want to come home to us!"

"Lies just cover truth." Sugarman's eyes darkened. "This isn't about Law, or even your son. It's about finding Fee's son. We're alive, Doc, she's not. Are you gonna sit at that silent piano and mourn forever? Or are you going to get up and help me find your godson?"

She could hear her husband's words in her head. *You need to live your life.*

"This isn't about Tommy," Maggie said suddenly. "You want Orsini. Why?"

"I want your *godson*. Victor is our best shot at finding him." He handed her a manila envelope. "Here's the CD, and the letter from Zachary Law." He snapped the case closed and moved toward the blue door. "You know you're going to France, Doc. Hell, we both know you'll do anything for Fee and her son. But take a few hours to think about it. Listen to that music."

"Think about it?" she whispered, staring at the envelope in her hand. "Really?"

"One more thing," said Sugarman. There was a determined light in the dark-brown eyes. "Our lives begin to end the day we become silent about the things that matter. Doesn't your son deserve to know if his father is alive? Do right by him, Doc."

As he closed the blue door, his words hung in the air around her like the final coda of a symphony.

# CHAPTER TEN

Dane moved toward a tall mirror in the formal wear shop on Capitol Hill. There he saw the reflection of a stranger—a tall, dashing figure in a well-cut designer tuxedo. Blue-tinted glasses, long, newly-brown hair secured at the nape of his neck, the trimmed, darker mustache, the beard skimming his jaw. The diamond flashing in his left ear.

It was almost time to play his latest role. The years of acting had taught him to change his appearance—and his voice, his character—at will. It had allowed him to remain faceless all these years.

*Until now.*

Now, suddenly, it was all at risk. An agent with the US Fucking Justice Department had his photograph with Victor Orsini. If they caught him, he could lose everything.

On the long drive from Maine he had researched every "M. O'Shea" in Boston. One child. One eighty-six year old in a nursing home. And one Magdalena O'Shea, classical pianist.

Sugarman had visited one of them. His money was on the musician.

Dane said the name over once more, slowly, in his head. *Magdalena O'Shea.* Why would Sugarman show her the photograph? What connection could she possibly have with Victor?

*With him?*

"Nice fit," said the tailor approvingly, entering the room. "Armani suits you."

Dane stared at him.

"Never go to these galas myself," said the tailor, to fill the silence. "But they say Washington has more black-tie affairs and limousines than any other city in the United States, including LA. You from the West Coast?"

Dane shook his head. He had only spoken once since he entered the shop, to give his suit size.

"Right out of GQ magazine," said the clerk in a satisfied voice. He made one more adjustment, smoothed the broad shoulders one final time. "Big Fourth of July bash?"

Dane remained silent as he removed several one hundred dollar bills from his wallet. The tailor eyed the cash and the tall stranger warily. Dane watched the tailor's hand touch the drawer beneath the cash register—where he kept his gun? Dane flexed his fingers, waited.

But the man just took the money and nodded.

Smart decision, Dane told him silently. And a lucky one. The only reason you are going home tonight is because I altered my appearance.

Dane lifted the garment bag and turned to the door. Behind him he heard the tailor let out his breath, unable to resist one last parting shot. "Knock 'em dead tonight, Prince Charming!"

Dane closed the door behind him and stepped out into the rain. "Now that's funny," he said to the empty street.

# CHAPTER ELEVEN

BOSTON. SUNSET, JULY 3

*Inhale. Exhale. Inhale. Exhale.*

Laughter followed Maggie as she ran past the Swan Boats that floated in the bright lake in Boston's Public Garden. The sun was setting in a shower of golden sparks and kids were smiling and it was just another day in the park.

My husband is gone, thought Maggie starkly, but life has to go on.

She dodged the traffic on Beacon Street, heedless of the angry horns, and turned right toward the Hill. Before her husband's death, she had taken great pleasure in the row of narrow, gracious brownstones that lined the revolutionary street like fading dowagers adorned in their velvet and fluttering lace. But tonight she ran past the lovely old buildings without a glance.

In the darkest days, just after her husband's death, Maggie had discovered that she could crowd out the memories with sheer, unrelenting physical activity. She'd started running, pushing muscles beyond endurance until she was too tired to think, too exhausted to do anything but pass out on her empty bed.

Running had become her one escape. Now Maggie ran every day, often at sunset when the evening air was cool and purple with twilight. After the first few miles, she would find herself deep in a trance-like oxygen high, lost in her own private, painless world.

Ironically, she'd found herself to be in the best physical condition of her life, hard and lean and strong. "I'll be running in the marathon by spring," she'd said to Luze with a trace of her old wry humor.

"There's a huge difference between running and running away," Luze had answered. "Why must you go on punishing yourself?"

*Inhale. Exhale. Inhale. Exhale.*

Because I'm angry, damn it. So angry I'm blind with it! Angry with Johnny for keeping secrets. For leaving me. Angry with Zach's father for asking Johnny to find Zach. Angry with myself for asking Johnny to look for my godson. I run because a hurting body is infinitely preferable to a hurting heart.

If only you hadn't gone to Europe, Johnny. Damn you! I hate you! Oh, God.

*I love you.*

Don't think about Johnny. Don't think about the letter and CD waiting unopened on her desk. Don't think about a best friend who died trying to protect her little son. Don't think about a sweet innocent child who vanished into the fog.

Just keep running.

*Inhale. Exhale. Inhale. Exhale.*

Sugarman's words pounded into her head as steadily as the worn Reeboks that pounded the cobblestones.

*Will you go to Paris for your son?*

She ran on, not slowing until she reached Revere Street.

There, finally, she stopped on the corner, bending at the waist and breathing deeply.

The two-story Bulfinch building across the narrow, crooked street sat on the corner in genteel glory. Caught by the setting sun, The Piano Cat's deep-hued brick glowed golden with fire and the lavender window panes shined like antique mirrors. Tonight, even the beauty of light on ancient stone failed to calm her.

Tonight, waiting for her in the music shop, was the package from Simon Sugarman. Once more, she was struck by the sinking feeling that her life was about to change. Once more, not ready, she'd run. Run *away*. But it was time to stop running.

It was time to open Sugarman's package.

# CHAPTER TWELVE

Simon Sugarman shifted down as he eased into Washington's rush-hour traffic on the George Washington Parkway. Rain hurled toward him out of the black sky. Hell of a night to be on the road.

He'd been uncharacteristically moody and unsettled since his encounter with Maggie O'Shea in Boston. Why did she have to be a dead ringer for Sofia Orsini?

All these years, and he still couldn't get Sofia out of his mind. They'd been friends, and then lovers. And now she was dead. It had all gone to hell when Victor Orsini surfaced in Italy. And it was Sugarman's fault.

Sugarman listened to the metronome of the windshield wipers and let the memories spin into the darkness. He had first crossed paths with Victor many years earlier at Yale. They'd been house mates in the Gothic, residential Trumbull College, older than most of the other students, and eventually cautious friends. Orsini was a wealthy, brilliant scholar who double-majored in religious art and music, a man who preferred museums, libraries, and concert halls to the down and dirty bars of New Haven where Sugarman could usually be found. Yet they'd forged an unlikely bond during the long nights of that first year, sitting in front of the fire with full tumblers of good scotch, arguing politics, philosophy, and religion until the sky turned pink and the bells tolled in the clock tower.

And then Orsini was inducted into one of Yale's powerful secret societies—Skull and Bones, a clandestine club for Yale's brightest and wealthiest—whose veiled activities and powerful "cloak and gown" connections continued until death. Over the years, Orsini grew even more secretive and driven.

Sugarman went on to Georgetown Law, while Orsini surprised the hell out of everyone by moving immediately to Washington and, inexplicably, joining the intelligence community. Sugarman had watched as Orsini was drawn deeper and deeper into the darkness.

Orsini's fall from grace had come, finally, in Washington, in the secret corridors of the CIA. Five agents lost their lives under his watch. And in 1985, Victor Orsini left the CIA and disappeared from the public eye.

Sugarman had been friends with two of the agents who died. Because of Victor?

Eventually Orsini had surfaced in Rome, an elusive, expatriate multimillionaire with a rumored museum-quality art collection. What had he been doing during those years he'd dropped off the radar? And where had all his damned money come from? Blood money, Sugarman was convinced. Oh, yeah, he had his suspicions, all right. But no proof. He'd needed someone on the inside.

But one of Sugarman's agents was found floating in the Tiber River. The other found in a dirty alley near the Vatican, the apparent victim of a mugging.

And then, seven years ago, Sofia had called to tell him she'd been offered an extended tour at the US Embassy in Italy. Within a month, she'd met the fascinating expat named Victor Orsini in a Roman art gallery.

She never knew that Sugarman had orchestrated that introduction, hoping one last time to infiltrate Orsini's organization.

*Way to go*, thought Sugarman. *I decided to use the love of my life to infiltrate a terrorist organization.*

The one thing he had never expected was the pregnancy. Or the hastily arranged marriage to Orsini. His very moral, very Catholic Sofia.

Sofia's letters had described her husband as a Svengali-like mentor. "There is a Lippi oil of the Archangel Gabriel in Victor's collection," she'd written. "Victor sees himself in that painting—a powerful archangel in people's lives."

Sugarman shook his head as he eased the car onto the rain-slick exit for Arlington. When, how—*why*—had the darkness replaced Victor's light? The questions throbbed in his brain, insistent as the rhythm of the windshield wipers.

The letters had stopped when Sofia gave birth to her son. He remembered the icy foreboding and helplessness he'd felt. He'd broken his own rules then. Called and told her his suspicions about Orsini.

But she'd stayed in Rome. Because of the child.

Sugarman slowed for the right turn into his condo parking entrance. End of the line. And the end of Sofia's story. Because last September one final letter had come. The words still haunted him.

"I've discovered the truth about my husband," she'd written from a remote French island. "It's all in a journal I found hidden in his safe. Victor is a criminal. Worse, a traitor. I've taken my son away from him. Soon, God willing, I will place the proof in your hands."

Her last sentence had chilled him. "Victor fell from the sky like a proud and faithless Lucifer with his wings on fire—the brightest Dark Angel of all."

And every bit as tormented and dangerous. *But what had caused his fall from grace?*

Eventually the letter had found its way to his desk in Washington. But Sofia Orsini never came home. She was never able to give him Victor's journal.

*Traitor.* For years, Sugarman's team of hand-picked agents from the CIA, FBI, NSA, DIA, and Justice had been searching for the dangerous cadre of men who financed acts of terror. Terrorists needed money, big money, to succeed. Somehow, he was sure, Sofia had stumbled on the information he needed.

The financial structure of Orsini's organization—the secret clients, bank accounts, network of contacts, targets. Follow the money.

"Where did you hide Orsini's journal, Sofia?" he said into the silence of the car.

And the journal wasn't all she'd taken from Orsini.

He closed his eyes, saw again the empty cardboard tube he'd been given at the small police station in Brittany—left behind by Sofia when she'd run from the convent. An eighteen-inch long tube that could have held a small, rolled up canvas. Something from Orsini's private collection? A painting, a manuscript? Music? What had been in that tube?

He pulled into an empty parking space, turned off the engine and lights, and sat alone in the rain-filled darkness.

Did you confide any of your secrets in all those letters to your best friend, Fee? Does Maggie O'Shea know more than she's let on? Because then she could be the next to die.

"You do what you gotta do," he murmured. *Just don't get caught...*

But on the bad nights, like this one, Simon Sugarman still wondered how much he was to blame for Sofia Orsini's death.

# CHAPTER THIRTEEN

"So the good news is," said Luze, "Brian's father could be alive."

"And maybe the bad news as well..." Maggie murmured into the phone.

"What can I do, Maggs? Shall I come over?"

"I'm a soloist, remember? We'll talk in the morning. Love you."

*I'm a soloist.*

Maggie clicked off her phone, pulled the quilt around her shoulders, and hugged her knees to her chest. Now, alone in her bedroom, she had to face the questions—and the doubts—raised by Sugarman. And the anger.

Closing her eyes, she allowed the anger to wash over her in waves. How could Zach have just stopped loving me? Why would he let me think he was dead? Where did he go? What has he been doing for thirty years? What happened to his music?

The answers could well be waiting for her in the package sent to Zach's father. She eyed the small envelope, tossed unopened on her quilt. Sugarman had said it contained a CD of music and a letter mailed to Zach's father from Vienna last summer.

Vienna. *I want to take you to Vienna someday, Slim. It's a city of music. More composers have lived there than any other place. Music is literally in the air...*

She'd gone to Vienna years later. Alone. And now—whatever this package held, it had been enough to convince Cameron Law that his son might still be alive.

She reached for the manila envelope, shook it slightly, examined the address. She did not recognize the handwriting.

Don't open it.

Maggie took a deep breath and tore open the package.

* * *

*Father,* the letter began.

Had Zach written the words? The dark script with the big uneven letters did not look at all familiar.

*It seems that Fate decided to play a huge joke on both of us and spare me. I am well. As I trust you are, despite the years, since you always said that only the good die young.*

*At the risk of disappointing you one final time, Father, I never did become that man you always hoped for. I tried, but it all went very wrong.*

*Until a few months back, when someone came into my life. Someone who reawakened long-buried feelings. Helped me to stop blaming the past, take responsibility for my own actions. To know what it is to feel love again. I'm sending you one of the results—perhaps, after all these years, you will understand your only son when you listen to the CD. Perhaps not. Either way, for me it is a validation.*

The note was signed, simply, *Zach.*

That was all. She re-read the words slowly.

*To love again? What happened to you, Zach?*

She touched the small silvery disc in her lap. After all this time, would she hear his voice? Somehow, she knew, whatever was on this disc was going to change her life.

She slipped the CD into the slot, held her breath, and pressed the "Play" button. She heard the whir of the CD. Then a piano began to play.

Maggie felt her body quiver like a cello string as the first minor chords—D minor, that haunting, saddest of keys—beckoned and promised. The orchestra answered with its beautiful, nostalgic opening theme, rising like a moon in a black night sky. Then the piano once more, mesmerizing as a first love, casting its spell around her. The throaty sonority evoked images of starry darkness and soft winds around the hot white moon. The music was haunting, elusive and yet...familiar, like a half-forgotten dream.

*I've heard this music before.*

Maggie felt suspended in the calm before the storm as elements of classical jazz, pure and turbulent, began to weave in and out of the theme, gathering power.

She closed her eyes, felt the notes touch her, reach inside.

The music sent her spiraling back into the past. Hot summer nights, the piano, the feel of demanding hands on her skin. *God, we were so young.* But her body still remembered.

\* \* \*

She's seventeen, in her first year at the New England Conservatory of Music.

On a late autumn morning, she walks into the rehearsal room—and finds a young man sitting at the battered Steinway. Tall, dark-haired, and very thin, he has intense brown eyes and the spare, bony face of an artist. His glasses, slipping low on the jutting nose, are alarmingly askew. She can see his long fingers on the keys, hears the Rachmaninov Piano Concerto No. 2 played the way she's never heard it played before.

Suddenly aware of her presence, he stops playing, lifts his glasses impatiently to his high forehead, and turns to stare at the flustered girl with the waist-length hair who stands frozen in his doorway.

"You look like someone who plays the harp," he says in low, quick, New York syllables.

She shakes her head with indignance. "No. Piano."

"Then God help you. What are you working on?"

"Chopin's Concerto in E minor."

"Impossible." He rises abruptly from the piano bench, reaching for her. Long fingers easily encircle her slender wrist. "You're thin as piano wire, Slim. Way too slight to play this piece. You need to be much stronger, fierce—"

Wrenching her hand away, she shoots him a look and sits down, still and straight, at the piano. She can feel his eyes on her.

She plays the Chopin—his crazy difficult Concerto in E minor. When she is done, the stranger raises his black eyebrows. "Are you busy tonight, Slim?" he asks her.

And she is lost.

Three months later she celebrates her eighteenth birthday by moving in with him. Zachary Law is her first lover—and her first real love. One spring night, after a rehearsal, she returns very late to their tiny Cambridge apartment. A single candle burns low on the window ledge, waiting for her. In the flickering light, Zach's black shape is framed against the blue night that fills the open window.

She stops on the sidewalk to watch him.

Then music fills the night and she stays in the shadows, listening, as Zach plays. He is playing music she's never heard before. She climbs the steps, drawn inexorably by the haunting melody, and lets herself into the room.

He sees her, and stops with an angry crash of chords.

"Zach," she whispers. "That was so beautiful. What is it?"

"A work in progress, Slim. A piano concerto."

"But, you never told me—"

"Because I can't finish it! I don't know how."

She blows out the candle and moves into his arms. "You'll finish your concerto one day, Zach. You'll know how."

"Aren't you wearing too many clothes?"

Two days later he tells her that he's had another terrible argument with his father. He needs to go away, he has something to prove—to his father, and himself. He has taken a six-month assignment in the Middle East as an aid worker.

*Don't leave me*, she'd pleaded.

*I've got to. But I'll come home to you, my beautiful Slim. I promise.*

But he hadn't come home to her. She'd never heard that glorious music again.

*Until tonight.* Maggie opened her eyes and listened, rapt, to the final firestorm of complex harmonies. Now the music was much darker—haunting, threatening, ultimately heartbreaking. A treacherous run of blistering notes. Too soon, the last chords of the concerto trembled in the shadowed bedroom.

For a long time she sat in the dark, the enormity of what she'd heard still ringing in her ears. All these years, she'd thought the concerto was lost forever, along with her first love, somewhere in a hot dry desert.

*But Zach was alive! Brian's father was alive.*

He had to be.

Maggie let out her breath slowly. Oh God, the soaring power of the music! The brilliant timbre, the dark resonance, those shimmering left-hand tremolos.

He had found a way to finish his concerto after all. And now the music held much more than a boy's innocent passion. It held a man's depth of feeling and experience. It held pain. And loss.

*What has happened to you, Zach?*

Maggie felt suddenly cold and rose to close the bedroom window against the night. Something in the music frightened her. The answer skittered on the edge of her memory for a moment, and then was gone. But she couldn't shake the feeling that it was important.

She reached again for the "Play" button.

Once more the haunting music ran like water through her head. The concerto was composed by Zach, she was certain, but... She closed her eyes, focusing on the chords. She could still see his sculpted hands, so strong and sensitive, moving across black and ivory keys. His touch. That was it!

She knew his hands. Intimately. Zach's touch was his personal signature on the keyboard.

Alone in the shadowed bedroom, Maggie was absolutely certain that the piano concerto on this CD was *not* played by the hands of Zachary Law.

# CHAPTER FOURTEEN

Dane enjoyed killing women.

He liked the way their skin felt, cold and slick with panic, as they struggled. He liked it when he saw that final moment of pure fear in their eyes, that terrible moment when they understood they were going to die. It was sexual. Thrilling.

Sofia Orsini had not been his first female victim. She would not be his last. His eyes sought the traitor. There, standing on the curving staircase.

Dane stood alone beneath the bronze sculpture of John F. Kennedy in the Grand Foyer of the Kennedy Center for the Performing Arts. The icy glass of Evian water in his hand was almost empty.

Act II of Puccini's *Madama Butterfly* had just ended. The heavy scarlet curtains in the Opera House had lowered as the lovely, childlike Cio-Cio San knelt in her Japanese garden waiting for the return of her American lieutenant.

Now Dane, too, waited. In just a few minutes, the last act would begin.

But first he would enjoy the intermission in the great red-carpeted lobby. It was a spectacle all of its own, whirling before Dane's eyes and enveloping him with a sensuous, smoky warmth. In the shimmering wall of mirrors, jeweled women and crystal chandeliers reflected endlessly. A far cry from the small, dirty theatres of his youth.

He reached up and touched the diamond in his ear. What would Shakespeare have made of all this? he wondered.

There was a heightened murmuring and purposeful shifting as people watched the senator from New York and his lovely auburn-haired wife walk slowly down the long foyer. Then they disappeared into the swirling vortex of fawning glitterati.

This town is all about power, thought Dane. Proximity to power, gaining power, losing power. And, ironically, those perceived to have power. But the real power, he brooded, is the power over life and death.

*I have that power.*

He looked down at the heavy gold Rolex circling his wrist. Expensive watches, villas, women. He'd come a long way from that scared, filthy, little water rat who had found a place to hide on the Hamburg docks.

The voices around him suddenly faded, like applause muted by a heavy curtain sliding closed across a stage.

*The docks.* That was when his double life had begun. Barely fifteen, but tall and strong with hard, burning eyes, it had been easy to lie about his age. The rackets of the docks by day, the sleazy little backwater theatres at night. He took small jobs at first, then the heady graduation to narcotics, smuggled so easily through his theatre and dock connections.

The first murders were almost too easy. And just a natural progression. Suddenly the money was bigger, the jobs more frequent.

The curtain of his thoughts slid open, and once more Dane looked around the glittering foyer. This is my life now, he thought. Thanks to Victor.

Victor Orsini, the man he'd met over the baccarat table in one of the very private upstairs salons at Monte Carlo. Dane had had the money to gamble. But still he hadn't belonged. And then—there was Victor. Brilliant Victor, with his power and wealth and influence. His art. His music. Buying him a drink, asking questions, listening with those deep, obsidian eyes.

Victor, who taught him how to dress, what to say and when to say it, which wine to order. It was simple, really, for a man whose passion was Shakespeare. Just another role to play.

Then, when he was finally ready, Victor had given him the job in Athens. Another in Central America, testing him and paying more than he'd ever dreamed. Victor, who made it an easy leap to the exclusive society of successful executioners. An easy leap to the two Swiss bank accounts, the women, the Armani suits, the villa in Provence. The secret hilltop refuge in Greece.

Yes, Victor Orsini had changed his life. They'd had a good relationship over the years. But then—everything changed when Sofia Orsini died in Brittany. He had told Victor that her death was accidental, as she fought for the boy. But the trust was gone.

It was time to disappear. Only one more assignment, after this one. Next week, the final job in the US. And then—Greece. *Freedom.*

He just had to stay safe until then. He would never survive in prison.

Dane swallowed the last inch of ice water, wanting his usual Absolut vodka. But he never drank on a job. Victor had taught him that, too. Always be in control.

Once more his eyes scanned the faces in the crowd, searching for the traitor.

Suddenly, in the shimmering mirrors that lined the foyer walls, he glimpsed a woman whose hair sparked with black fire.

He swung around. The night fell away as pale faces floated beneath the glowing lamps. Like petals on dark water.

The last time he'd seen his mother, it had been in a setting just like this. He had been barely twenty, the guest of a wealthy French racketeer at a glittering party in Paris—and shocked to see his mother for the first time in thirteen years. Since that day he'd come home from school and she was just—*gone.* Leaving a frightened little seven-year-old boy alone and defenseless with an angry, violent father...

*Why didn't you want me?*

That night in Paris, his mother had come swirling like a half-remembered dream into the nightclub, her dark beauty still undimmed. He had stared at her from across the room the way a child might stare at a glorious exotic bird. She'd laughed, swinging the thick black hair he remembered, and he had been drawn inexorably toward her fire.

Standing close, he'd heard the low murmuring voice of his childhood. Her light spicy scent was achingly familiar. He was assaulted with fragmented images—the soft words of a lullaby, a hand caressing his cheek. The shine of her hair in the lamplight.

Her shawl slipped and he caught the silk, re-settling it on her shoulders. She turned to thank him and, for a moment, her hand had cupped his, jolting him with the memory of her touch. Golden eyes met his with no spark of recognition, and she turned away.

The fine stem of his own glass snapped beneath the pressure of Dane's fingers as flashing theatre lights drew him back to the Grand Foyer of the Opera House. Dropping the shards into the earth of a heavy planter, he pulled a linen handkerchief from his breast pocket and, as he had done countless times on the stage in the past, wiped bright blood from his fingers.

Dane stared at his reflection in the glittering glass doors that led to the terrace. In the mirror of the rain-streaked window, his eyes met the eyes of the dark-haired woman who had reminded him of his mother.

But she was a stranger.

*What was the matter with him tonight?* Losing control was inexcusable. He had to focus. Concentrate totally on the target.

Again his eyes scanned the crowd, lingered briefly on the striking brunette, then moved on. There, halfway up the right stairway. The traitor, champagne glass in hand, surrounded by sycophants, returning to the box seats in the first balcony.

Dane smiled as he moved toward the woman who had betrayed Victor Orsini. The traitor who had lured Victor out of hiding, to Paris. The one responsible for the photograph now in Simon Sugarman's possession.

At the foot of the curving stairs, he stopped for a moment close to the slender brunette who had kindled the memory of his mother.

The lights dimmed, went out. He heard the orchestra's opening chords. It was time. He turned away from the woman on the stairs.

Inside the theatre, he could hear the distant clanging of anchors, the far-off voices of sailors rising from a painted harbor toward the garden where Cio-Cio San knelt. Butterfly's night of waiting had passed. For Dane, too, the long night was almost over.

Very slowly, Dane climbed the red-carpeted stairway to the first balcony.

# CHAPTER FIFTEEN

Sugarman opened his eyes and looked around. Jesus! He'd fallen asleep at the kitchen table again. As usual, his tenth-floor Arlington condo was littered with empty take-out cartons, chipped mugs filled with cold coffee, and the Sunday *Times* crossword puzzle—completed in ink, thank you very much. Except for 33 Down. How was a kid from the Harlem tenements supposed to know that damned Cymbeline quote?

Restless, he wandered to the bank of windows that looked across the dark Potomac. Sugarman gazed at the lights of Washington and closed his eyes wearily as he thought about the city he called home.

No more deaths, he vowed. But how do I protect them all?

Sometimes, he thought, you just gotta get a break. Two weeks earlier, he'd been approached at the Café Milano bar by an old agency pal, just as he'd told Maggie O'Shea. *Always tell as much of the truth as you can.*

Pounding music, sexy lights, six deep at the bar. The perfect cover for a very private conversation. "There's someone you should talk to, someone who might have a lead to Victor Orsini. Be at the fountains outside the National Gallery of Art, nine p.m. tomorrow night."

He closed his eyes, let himself fall into the memory.

*The fountains, lit by floodlights against the black night, are blurred in the rain.*

*The informer approaches, body swathed in long raincoat, face hidden by a black umbrella. Rain drums steadily on the canvas.*

*"You're Sugarman. I can give you information on Victor Orsini."*

*"Why'd you come to me?"*

*"Because I'm scared out of my mind."* The whispered words are hoarse, edged with panic. *"I've fallen into something big. Now my family has been threatened..."*

*The fountain waters rise and fall, loud as rain and dazzling behind the shining black umbrella.*

*"Talk to me. And I'll take care of your family."*

*"Orsini is a collector. His Achilles heel is religious art. And rare music..."*

*Behind them, the spray from the fountain drifts like mist into the night.*

Sugarman shook his head. Funny how things worked. The information had led to a late-night meeting with a Left Bank art gallery owner in Paris named Vanessa Durand. A quietly arranged, very private sale of a rare Fra Angelico Madonna offered to interested collectors. Then the photograph, emailed to his iPhone, with four faces that sent him packing to see an old guy in a penthouse in New York. And finally to a music shop in Boston.

Sugarman loosened his tie. As he drank the last dregs of cold coffee, he stared at his cell phone, willing it to ring. *C'mon, Doc.*

Across the Potomac, the lights of Washington glimmered in the rain. The informer who'd betrayed Victor Orsini by the light of the fountains was over there at the Kennedy Center tonight, no doubt dressed to the nines, drinking French champagne in the VIP box, surrounded by glorious music.

*And here I am, dog-tired, in bad need of a shower and shave, and having another dinner-for-one from a cheap take-out carton. Waiting for a phone call from a beautiful woman who wants nothing to do with me.*

*What's wrong with this picture?* Sugarman asked himself moodily, turning his back on the bright city lights.

The phone buzzed. He whipped it to his ear, expecting

Maggie O'Shea's voice. But it was a state trooper, calling from Maine. He listened, felt his gut tighten.

"Dead guy, isolated coastline, no ID," he repeated. "So why are you calling *me*?" He went still. "What? He was dating one of *our* agents at Justice? How did he die?"

The answer chilled him. *A knife.*

He turned to stare out the window at the Kennedy Center, ablaze in lights across the river.

# CHAPTER SIXTEEN

BOSTON. LATE NIGHT, JULY 3

"I don't want to tell him."

It was just after ten o'clock. The old orange cat had jumped up onto the bed and now she looked squarely at Maggie, waiting.

Maggie scratched the torn ears. "What should I do, Gracie? How do I tell Brian that his father might be alive after all these years?"

Gracie turned away, her attention caught by a train whistle somewhere in the night.

"Okay," muttered Maggie. She reached for the phone.

One ring. Two.

She held her breath, listening to the distant ring of a phone in a weathered Cape Cod colonial perched on the edge of the Atlantic Ocean.

Three rings. Four.

She pictured a tall young man, opening the door, dropping some sheet music on a cluttered coffee table, lunging for the receiver.

Five.

"Stewart here."

Maggie's heart caught at the sound of her son's deep, familiar voice. *Okay. Just tell him the truth.*

"Hello, you!" she said, her voice relieved and full of love.

"Mom? Hey, Almost-Grandma! You caught me on my way to the club."

She smiled. "Don't rush the Grandma thing. How is Laura feeling?"

"Big. And ready. We can't wait to see you. And I can't wait for you to hear the guys, Mom. We're doing a lot of Charley Parker and Monk. Ella, of course. Hank Jones, Randy Weston, some kick-butt Basie. I'll do a Gershwin Prelude, just for you."

The warmth in her son's voice enveloped her. Closing her eyes, Maggie could picture Brian sprawled easily on the second-hand sofa, six feet two inches of bones and angles and dark curly hair that was much too long. The jutting nose, that wide crooked grin. The deepest brown eyes. *Zach's eyes.*

"One of my favorites," she whispered.

"I know." Her son's voice changed. "But it's Brahms I play for Laura and the baby every night. I keep thinking about you giving our kid the very first piano lesson. I'll have to warn him—or her—about your *March of the Middle C Twins.*"

She laughed. "Don't you think my grandchild needs to be able to sit up first?" *Keep it light.* "But, speaking of music—"

"Mom? What's wrong? You're not calling to cancel, right?"

She took a deep breath. "Just postpone, Bones. Only for a week or so—"

"Mom, no! You—"

"Please, just listen to me, sweetheart. I wouldn't change our plans without a really good reason."

Silence. Then, "Okay. I'm listening."

"I just spoke to your Grandfather Cam, and he and I agreed that it's time you know something."

She could hear him take a deep breath. "Should I be sitting down?"

"Wouldn't hurt." She waited a beat, then said, "Not long ago Cameron received a letter and a CD of music, mailed from Vienna. We think the letter was from your father, Zachary Law."

Her son made a sharp, shocked sound.

"Yes. The CD holds a piano concerto, a piece that I know Zach composed three decades ago. Oh, Bones, it's possible that your father is still alive."

And then, while her son listened, she told him everything she knew.

* * *

Finally, she was silent, her hand damp on the phone. What would he say?

Then her son's voice, low and loving against her ear. "So the agent who investigated Sofia's death seems to think you might be able to help find Tommy by tracking down my father. In France."

She smiled in spite of herself. "That's the gist of it, yes."

"It will be hard for you, going to France again so soon after losing Aunt Fee and Johnny."

Her narrow shoulders shrugged in the darkness. "Maybe just the opposite, a pilgrimage in a way. And I'll finally be doing something for Fee."

"Fee was murdered, Mom. I don't want you in any danger."

She thought about the shadows in Sugarman's eyes. "I'll be attending a music festival, Brian. I'll be careful. Agent Sugarman has promised that I won't be alone. And if I can help find my godson, it's the right thing to do."

"If you're sure—"

"Very sure. But—" She closed her eyes. "For me, this is not just about Fee and Tommy. It's about *you*, Bones, about finding Zach. It hurts your grandfather and me that you never had a chance to know your father. What if I don't find him? But, God, what if I *do*?" What if he wants nothing to do with us? "I don't want you hurt by this."

"Hey, Mrs. Guilty, whatever happens, I already got to know my father through you."

She could feel her son searching for the right words. Finally he said, "Okay, sure, it hurts sometimes, can't pretend it doesn't. I would have liked my father to know me, my thoughts, my music, my dreams." His voice changed. "Some nights, when I'm really playing well, I imagine that he is out there somewhere, in the audience."

He stopped, embarrassed. "I know about my father. But he never knew about *me*. I never existed for him. I wish he'd known he had a son, Mom. And a grandchild, to carry on his legacy. That hurts. But I keep it inside because I have an amazing mom and I don't ever want her to think she hasn't been enough."

"Bones. I would never think that. You've been a joy since the moment you were born. Before that."

"Geez, Mom..." She heard Brian's I-don't-want-to-deal-with-this-emotional-stuff-now tone as he said, "One day at a time. Just go to France and look for my dad, okay? We'll figure the rest of it out. Together. You just have to promise that you'll call me every day. Twice."

"I promise. I love you so much, Bones."

"Me too, Mom." His breath whistled out. "Hey, I'm late for the club. Ask Luze to send some of her cookies, will you? Chocolate chip. I'll call Granddad. Just be safe!"

The phone clicked and Maggie sat on the wide bed listening to the humming dial tone. She didn't know whether to laugh or to cry.

*Oh, Zach, you have such a fine, fine son. He's a good man, he'll be such a good father.*

The thought echoed in her head. Present tense. Was she really beginning to believe that Brian's father could be alive?

# CHAPTER SEVENTEEN

LANGLEY, VIRGINIA. LATE NIGHT, JULY 3

Sugarman stood in the driving rain beneath the life size statue of Nathan Hale, his hands and feet bound, blank bronze eyes on the horizon. He squinted up at the spot-lit concrete wings that soared over the entrance to the original headquarters of the Central Intelligence Agency. The futuristic complex of glass and steel, known as "The Company," was tucked into the Virginia countryside just eight miles northwest of the White House.

Home sweet home to all the spies and analysts and all that budget-busting-state-of-the-art electronic equipment. Tonight, the rain blurred the words chiseled into the white stone, but Sugarman knew them by heart.

*"...and the truth shall make you free."*

Not true, thought Sugarman. We all manipulate the truth when it suits us.

The son of a nightclub waitress and a railroad station redcap, Simon Sugarman had kissed his mama goodbye on his eighteenth birthday and left Harlem for Marine boot camp. Sent immediately to Southeast Asia, he was already a veteran of US intelligence by age twenty-two, and, in his own mind, came home de-humanized. The GI bill, Yale, and law school, saved his life.

Sugarman blinked in the rain, remembering.

It was during Sugarman's final weeks at Yale—on a scholarship and his very large GI loan—when the CIA first approached him. "Interested in foreign travel? Access to senior US officials?" they had asked. "Meet the challenges of a rapidly changing world?"

He, and two of his house mates, had been actively courted. He was one of the two who declined. The third, Victor Orsini, had said yes without hesitation. Sugarman had never learned why his brilliant, artistic friend had made a choice so shockingly out of character.

*The roads not taken*, Sugarman thought.

But his road, too, eventually had led to Washington, and three weeks after earning his law degree he found himself climbing the white marble stairs of the Justice Department. Two days after that he was seated at an old metal desk in a smoky fifth floor cubicle in a nondescript building on lower Pennsylvania Avenue, just blocks from the White House.

Eventually he and his team took on Cultural Property Crimes. They knew that there was huge money in the theft of antiquities and art. Money that could finance acts of terror. They had been "following that money" ever since. And now Orsini was in his sights.

Sugarman looked up at the lights burning steadily in the seventh-floor corner office where the Admiral waited for him. Rain was seeping down inside his collar. He pulled the plastic ID from his trench coat and moved toward the locked doors.

Walking past the large granite CIA seal on the lobby floor, with its compass spokes representing intelligence data from all over the world, Sugarman stopped, as he always did, in front of the agency's Memorial Wall. Flanked by the American flag and the blue-and-gold banner of the CIA, more than one hundred stars were carved into the smooth white marble, each representing an intelligence agent who died in the service of his country. At least a dozen had been his friends. Beneath the stars, the fallen agents whose names could be revealed were listed in the glass-enclosed Book of Honor. The other spaces on the page showed only stars.

The secret spies. Anonymous even in death.

He turned toward the security gate. "Hey, pal, how'ya doin'?" He flashed his laminated ID badge at the uniformed guard.

"Long time no see. Yeah, same old, same old. I'm here to see the admiral."

He passed through the security scanner and hurried down the hallway toward the small private elevator that would take him to the seventh floor.

He could feel the eyes of Wild Bill Donovan and all the past CIA directors watching him from the oil portraits that lined the long corridor. Sugarman saluted as he entered the elevator.

* * *

"Sugar! Come in and sit down. How are things at the DOJ these days?"

"Still too many bad guys out there, Admiral."

"Any more news on the Orsini boy?"

"There's a woman..."

Intense blue eyes flashed beneath a shock of pure white hair tied back in a thin ponytail. The eyebrows and mustache were jarring slashes of charcoal on the pale patrician face. "There's *always* a woman, isn't there?"

Sugarman shrugged. "Oh, yeah." His thoughts touched on Maggie O'Shea, then away. Focus. "Two weeks ago, a woman came to me. A big deal in the DC art world. She'd met Victor Orsini at an art auction in Europe a few years ago, had an affair with him. When she wanted out, he said no. Seems he had his eye on a Fra Angelico Madonna, wanted her help. She was successful, married, with a kid, the perfect blackmail victim. But she understood she'd never be free of him, so she turned to *me* instead. We were able to arrange for the Madonna to be privately auctioned in Paris."

"You lured him to Paris... Ah, so *that's* what led to the now infamous photograph taken in the Café de la Paix. Orsini was celebrating, no doubt. But he slipped through your fingers."

"Not for long." Sugarman's eyes shined. "I let it be known around town that *I have* that photograph."

"*You* are the leak? How Machiavellian of you, Sugar."

"Let's just say that the lure's been cast," said Sugarman.

"We need Orsini's damned journal, Sugar." The breath rasped. "The bank accounts, networks of names. Correspondence, logs of recent activities, movements, liasons... *Investors*!"

"Yeah. Protect our own, take down theirs."

"Just watch yourself, Sugar. Two weeks from now, I intend to be drinking the best French champagne at my granddaughter's wedding. Not appearing before some Special Prosecutor because we overstepped our boundaries."

For the first time that night, Sugarman grinned. "A wedding's a better alibi than most."

"Just make sure I don't need an alibi. Have you heard from Magdalena O'Shea?"

"Not yet. But she'll call. She's the kind of woman who does the right thing."

"Did she mention her husband?"

"Briefly. She doesn't know. Doesn't need to know."

"Precisely." The admiral looked down at his iPhone. "What are your plans for Paris?"

"There's a guy I know. Career military, a good man in case of trouble. I'm sending him in with her. If only..."

"Don't confuse weakness with morality, Sugar."

"It's been a long day, sir."

"And not over yet. Welcome to Operation Bright Angel, Sugar. The code name for Magdalena O'Shea will be..." The Admiral smiled. "Concerto."

# CHAPTER EIGHTEEN

Dane walked across the first balcony of the Opera House, past the life-size sculpture of Poseidon and the two red-jacketed ushers. On his right was the central President's Box, with its round presidential seal on the door. His contact had verified that the President and his staff were entertaining at Camp David this weekend. That meant no extra security.

He glanced back once more at the ushers. Both slight, in their fifties. Tonight, no one was expecting any trouble.

Satisfied, he moved quickly to his left. Around the curve, out of sight, he stopped in front of Box 11. He was alone.

Dane opened the door and entered a small, darkened anteroom—a coatroom, really—covered entirely in red velvet. A heavy crimson curtain hid the entrance to the box seats. Tonight, courtesy of Victor, he was the only patron in his box.

Dane parted the curtain and peered out into the shadowed theatre. Down on the stage, Cio-Cio San began to sing a lullaby to her son as she waited for the lieutenant to climb the hill. *Dormi amor mio*. Two boxes to his right, Victor's traitor and her guests sat transfixed by the doomed soprano.

The surgical gloves were in his back pocket. The silver dagger slipped easily from the back of his cumberbund into his fingers. The French Laguiole knife, with its signature bee at the tip of the fold, had originated with the shepherds in the rugged hills of the Massif Central. Now, it was his weapon of choice as well.

He glanced once more toward Box 7. The woman raised her eyes to look at him. Had she felt his eyes on her? He smiled, and she looked away.

Dane ran a finger along the razor edge of the blade and eased open the door onto the darkened balcony.

He edged around the curved velvet wall, saw the two ushers talking quietly near the far stairs, and waited until they turned away. Screened by the sculpture of Poseidon, he moved quickly to the door of Box 7 and disappeared inside.

Dane stood motionless in the dark anteroom. Beyond the heavy curtain, the traitor who had betrayed Victor and his organization sat listening to the tearful farewell.

*Just a few moments more.*

Cio-Cio San's voice rose, the music welled up.

It was the moment he always waited for, the moment when he stood alone on the very edge of the chasm. He felt no fear, just an incredible sexual rush. He moved to the edge of the curtain.

Out in the darkness, Butterfly's voice soared higher.

Dane parted the curtain, stepped silently into the shadowed box.

The traitor sat forward, spellbound, in her chair.

The soprano's voice shimmered to its highest note. Held.

Dane leaned down until his mouth was against the woman's ear. "Here is a message from Victor Orsini," he whispered to the beautiful Director of the National Gallery of Art.

The woman twisted around.

Dane smiled at the fear in her eyes and slid the dagger into her heart.

The woman slumped forward into the darkness with a soft sigh of surprise. He was already through the velvet curtains when her goblet of champagne fell to the carpeted floor.

As he descended the curving staircase, he heard the muffled

shout. Walk, don't hurry, he reminded himself. Don't call attention to yourself.

Out into the dark wet night, the sound of sirens in the distance. Now, he could enjoy that glass of Absolut.

# CHAPTER NINETEEN

*It's not over, Maggie.*

In the shadowed bedroom, Maggie swung around. Her husband's face looked out at her from the antique mirror above the desk.

*Oh, Johnny, I need you. I heard Zach's music tonight. A concerto. I thought it was lost forever, but...Zachary Law may be alive, in France.*

*Talk to me.*

*That's not Zach on the CD! Another pianist is playing his concerto. So Zach may well be dead, after all.*

*The answers are in France, Lass. Find your godson.*

*But that means I might have to face Zach. All the lies...*

*Then find the truth, Lass. Your son should know his own blood.*

The phantom image of her husband reached out. Stopped in mid-air. Began to fade.

*Begin with me.*

Maggie opened her eyes, gazed around the quiet bedroom. She was alone.

*I don't want to find Zach if it means Brian will be hurt.*

*But I won't abandon my godson.*

The orange cat leaped onto the bed and stared at her. "You knew I'd go all along didn't you, Gracie?" said Maggie, stroking the soft fur.

She pulled his robe more tightly around her, closed her eyes, and tried to imagine her husband breathing next to her.

*Begin with me...*What had Johnny meant?

An image from her nightmares swam into her head. The small white sailboat spinning through black water. Her eyes flew open.

*I know where I have to go.*

"You found something in France, Johnny. I'll begin with you."

# CHAPTER TWENTY

MARTHA'S VINEYARD. LATE AFTERNOON, JULY 4

She'd gotten the last seat, in the last row, on Cape Air's midday commuter flight to Martha's Vineyard. Good thing Fourth of July was a family holiday, thought Maggie. Not much call for a single seat.

Now, relieved to be off the tiny six-seat Cessna, Maggie stood on the weathered cottage porch and gazed out over Menemsha Pond. In the late afternoon light the water was the color of seaweed and smooth enough to reflect the high white clouds.

She loved the cottage, left to her so long ago by her mother. Leaning over the wooden railing, she breathed deeply. She could smell clam shells and the sea in the salted air. And maybe a hint of offshore rain.

Here in Chilmark, in the tiny fishing village of Menemsha on the southwest corner of the island, Maggie was in a secluded world far away from the tourists and pleasure boats—a world of winding dirt roads and ancient stone walls following the curve of hills. Wildflowers blooming across moors, sea pines tumbling down to lonely, windswept beaches.

She had come to this old gray cottage when she was happy and run to it when her life was shattered. As a child she'd practiced her scales on the old upright piano under the skylight in the living room. As a young woman, she had shared quiet walks with Sofia down to the pond and sat alone gazing into the fire on cold snowy nights. Brian had been born upstairs in the old brass bed, and when he was older, she'd taken him fishing off that pier. And years later, from this very spot on the porch, she had waved to Johnny on the deck of the *Green Eyed Lass*.

Now she searched the waters, willing her husband's distinctive white sails to appear on the horizon. But the *Green Eyed Lass* was in dry dock at the Menemsha boatyard, and her husband would never sail these waters again.

She turned her head, caught her breath as she saw Johnny's boots by the cottage door.

Oh, God.

Last October, when word had come of his death, she'd flown immediately to the South of France and stood alone on the Mediterranean beach of Hyères, stoic and dry eyed, looking out to sea, searching, waiting for her husband. In the distance she could see the Îles d'Or, the three Golden Islands, where Johnny's sailboat had disappeared. For almost two weeks she had waited while the French police searched the islands and deep water. Shattered remnants of the sailboat were recovered. But there was no sign of her husband. On the fifteenth day, she shook the hand of the sad-eyed gendarme, accepted the small package he placed in her numb fingers, and returned to Boston.

But home would never be the same. When she'd sat down at her beloved Steinway, her hands were still too cold and numb to play. And that night, the nightmares struck. At dawn she'd fled to the Vineyard, to run like a woman possessed across the wild autumn beach, shouting her husband's name into the roaring dark.

Late last night, she'd remembered the package given to her by the kindly French policeman. It was one of the reasons she'd come to the Vineyard.

The other reason was Sofia Orsini's letters.

Maggie straightened her shoulders, searching for her key as she reached for her suitcase. Then she stepped through the tall French doors into the cottage.

Tall spruce and pines were framed like paintings in the huge windows, their silhouettes strong and dark against the sky, and beams of sunlight shafted through the many glass panes, burnishing the high-beamed great room with a soft glow. She took a deep breath, comforted as always by the clutter of books and family photographs and the shabby chairs gathered around a fireplace fashioned of local stone.

*No one to share it with anymore...*

The cushions on one chair were out of place, and, after setting them right, she walked over to the old upright piano against the wall, laid a finger on a cold ivory key. Maybe if she—

*Footsteps on the deck.*

She froze as the silhouette of a man in a dark hooded sweatshirt passed by the window. Then he rattled the doorknob, walked slowly into the cottage, and came toward her.

"Stop right there!" cried Maggie. The man came closer, pushing the hood from his face, and she let out her breath. "Tully!"

The old lobsterman, her neighbor and caretaker of the cottage for decades, stepped from the shadows. "Missus."

"Sorry, Tully, you frightened me for a moment. I wasn't expecting to see you this afternoon." And then, seeing his expression, "What's wrong?"

"You've had a break-in, Missus. I discovered it this morning, when I came over to turn on your lights and heat for you." He flung out a gnarled hand. "That there back window was jimmied."

She swallowed, looking at the window with its shiny new latch. "When?"

"Not rightly sure, Missus. And I don't know if anyone got inside, everything looked in order, but..." The old man shrugged bony shoulders. "I've been watching for ya. Didn't want you in the cottage alone until I checked it out again."

"I appreciate that, Tully, thanks." She gazed around the quiet great room. Everything seemed to be in order. *Except for the chair cushions.*

Fifteen minutes later, when they were both satisfied that no one else was in the cottage, the caretaker left with a wave and a tip of his silvered head, and she was alone.

With a final glance toward the new window latch, Maggie

climbed the stairs once more. Had someone broken in to search the cottage? Who? And what were they looking for?

*There's been a break-in.*

She stopped on the landing, remembering, suddenly, the two strangers in their dark business suits. Showing up at The Piano Cat, standing before her, asking for Johnny's files. And then, two days later, the shop and her apartment had been searched. Robbers, the police assured her. But her jewelry and cash had not been taken. Only the contents of her husband's briefcase, found open on the floor. *Empty.*

No need for rocket science there. And now, a broken lock. *Was this about you, too, Johnny?* She glanced out the landing window, toward the boathouse.

But first—

The guest room was at the rear of the cottage. A small leather trunk stood at the base of the white-quilted bed, and Maggie dropped to her knees in front of it. The lock appeared to be unbroken.

Raising the heavy lid, she was enveloped by the evocative scents of sandalwood and Guerlain. Very gently she shifted the satin-wrapped albums and treasures that had belonged to her mother. And there, beneath a small cloth doll, was the false wooden floor. Hidden underneath it, the letters she'd come for. Letters from Sofia Orsini.

She touched the hidden latch, lifted the secret floor. Reaching inside for the letters, she froze. *What if someone had been searching for Sofia's letters?*

Maggie carried the small stack of airmail envelopes down to the porch and settled onto the old swing.

Thunderous rain clouds were gathering to the west. The night Brian had been born—two months early—she and Fee had been here at the cottage.

*The skylight above her had danced with lightning.*

*She'd been sitting at the old upright, playing Chopin, her huge abdomen pressed against the keyboard. Without warning, the pain had ripped into her and the music ended with a crash of chords.* "Oh Jesus God Fee! The baby—It's too soon!"

*The skylight swooped down toward her.*

*"I'm here, Maggie darling, hold on to me, Maggie, hold on tight!"*

Maggie gazed down at the letters in her hand. We lived through so much together, Fee. I missed you so when you moved to Rome.

But Fee had been so happy there, intoxicated by life. Her early letters had been full of her work at the embassy, new friends and explorations, a red motor scooter, and her favorite café in the Piazza Navona. And always the latest adventures of Magnus3— the third generation offspring of Magnus.

But then she had met Victor Orsini, and it all turned dark.

Maggie found the letter she wanted and slipped it from its ribbon.

# CHAPTER TWENTY-ONE

*I've met a man, Maggie. He's like no man I've ever known. We met in an art gallery at the foot of the Spanish Steps. He's an American expat, quite wealthy, I think. Collects religious art. Rubens, Botticelli, Tintoretto, da Vinci. And he's a music lover, like you. Has a small collection of rare sheet music, illuminated manuscripts, autographed scores. He's brilliant, Maggie, charismatic. Older than I, but strong and exciting.*

The breeze from the sea was picking up. Maggie unfolded the next letter from Fee just as the rain clouds surrounded the setting sun.

*I've news, Maggie darling, earthshaking news. I'm pregnant! Me, the ultimate "I've-no-time-for-children-because-I-have-a-career" woman. Now this, so late in my life. I still can't believe it! Victor has asked me to marry him. Last night he gave me a sapphire ring that belonged to his mother. The doctors say I'm strong and healthy, but Victor says I should move into the villa. Please come, the gardens are so beautiful. And you can finally meet Victor.*

But the visit was postponed, and then, within a month, the small wedding had taken place. *Just two witnesses, Maggie, friends of Victor's, he thought it best...*

Thomas James Orsini was born soon after. His christening was the only time she'd been able to see Fee. Six long years since she'd seen them. After that, in the months and years that followed, only letters that had grown darker and darker.

*Victor thinks it best if I take a leave from the embassy to be with Tommy...*

*I miss Magnus3 so much, but Victor says he won't have dogs in the villa...*

*No, this wouldn't be a good time for a visit, I took a fall yesterday...*

Victor says. Victor wants. Victor needs. Victor forgives... Over the years, with each letter, her strong, independent friend had grown weaker and more vulnerable.

*Why didn't I trust my instincts that you weren't safe? Why didn't I insist that you leave?*

Lightning lit the dark sky over the sea as Maggie slipped Fee's final letter, hastily written on a fog-bound French island, from the ribbon. A brief note clipped to it said, in an unfamiliar, flowing script, "Your friend Sofia asked me to send this to you. I fear she is in danger. You will find her at Couvent de la Brume in Brittany." The Convent of the Fog. It was signed, simply, Soeur Marie Clair.

So much more trouble than you knew, Sister. But by the time Fee's letter had arrived, Fee was dead. Maggie felt the guilt and pain wash over her in waves as, once more, she opened Fee's last letter.

*How did this happen to me, Maggie? Just five days ago, I was sitting in a sunlit garden in Rome.*

*Then Victor's body blocked out the light as he handed me the custody papers. I looked into his cold eyes, I heard the cruelty in the voice. "I must leave Rome. I am taking my son with me," he said. "Pack his clothes. He leaves with me tomorrow."*

*"My son," he said. I did not understand until that moment the dangerous extent of my husband's possessiveness. And I knew without a doubt that I would never see my son again.*

*Of course we argued. I tried to stop him and he hit me, right there in the garden. Tommy ran over to protect me. He's so brave, my darling boy. Then Victor turned and hit his son, Maggie! I will never forgive him. Or myself.*

*That was the moment our marriage ended.*

*I knew about Victor's secret safe, behind the Rubens. That night, taking our passports, I found he'd hidden thousands of euros, a journal, and the key to a case that held a very old manuscript of music. Of course I thought of you, although it's a violin concerto, I think. I took it all, Maggie. As insurance—and hopefully a rare musical score will be worth something if I need more cash. Then I ran with Tommy before sunrise. I had help, I have a friend I trust...*

Maggie gazed up at the flickering sky. Who was your trusted friend, Fee? Who betrayed you? And where are the journal and manuscript you took that night?

A sharp crack of thunder. Lightning flashed on the white-capped, gunmetal sea.

Hurry, thought Maggie. Her eyes found Fee's last words.

*There is a huge difference between love and possession, and I know now that Tommy and I were Victor's possessions, just like his priceless art. I've read his journal, Maggie. My husband is brilliant, vengeful, and a monster. He thinks he is all-powerful but he has one weakness. Me. And I will take him down.*

*When the fog lifts, I will try to make my way home to you. Whatever happens to me now, I deserve. But Tommy is innocent, he is your godson. I need you to remember the promise you made in the church that morning of Tommy's baptism. To always protect my son.*

*Please, just burn these letters. Fee.*

But she hadn't burned them. *We are responsible for the lives we save.* Something, some inner voice, compelled her to hide them. Fee had left her some clues in the letters, she was sure of it. She'd take them with her, study every word.

What had Johnny said to her in the dream? *Begin with me.*

Dropping the letters to the table, she stood and walked with determination out onto the windy terrace.

It was time to go to the boatyard.

# CHAPTER TWENTY-TWO

The log cabin was glowing like a lantern in the purpling light. Tall pines crowded against the redwood porch and whispered against a deck cantilevered out over the precipitous hillside like the prow of a ship.

Steep wooden steps wound down through the firs to a crescent of rocky beach, where a small lake glinted like a mirror. Not far from the shore, an arched fishing pole flashed silver in the light. The man sat hunched in a gently rocking rowboat, a stark silhouette against the darkening sky, gazing up at the cabin. The words on the old cap pulled low over his head said, *Fish Fear Me.*

The last sunlight of the day slanted in rays over the mountain peak, lighting the tips of the high firs like candles. A "V" of snow geese flew overhead, their call as haunting and mysterious as the whistle of a freight train disappearing into the hills of Virginia. Their wings caught the final flames of the sun as the man watched them vanish beyond the blue mountain.

How did they know where to go? If only he could be so sure of where he was going.

"Safe flight, darlins'," he murmured, raising his thermos in salute. Then he took a long drink of the bourbon.

He pulled back on the fishing pole, and a shaft of pain exploded through his side. He doubled over with an oath. Just seven months earlier, he'd been so hard and strong and healthy. And then his life changed in a split second. The fractured skull, the punctured lung, the hole in the side of his chest. The broken leg.

His peppered brows spiked as he looked down at his forearms, the bones so much more prominent now since his agonizing struggle back to life.

The empty line dangled in front of him. "Damned trout," he muttered.

Colonel Michael Jefferson Beckett scowled, his fist hitting against the old boat in frustration. Then he clamped his teeth together and pulled on the oars, ignoring the fire that shot across his chest. The air was deep blue with twilight as he turned the boat toward the shore.

Again his eyes found the cabin windows through the pines. Home. But empty. No one waiting for him there. He took another long swallow of the bourbon.

He missed his old hound dog, Red. He missed his old life. He missed—

The sudden scream of automatic gunfire split the air.

A flash of brilliant light.

"Incoming!" shouted Beckett, throwing himself down in the rowboat, hands over his head, heart pounding like ricocheting rocks in his chest.

More explosions, blooming in the sky. *He was on the ground, in the dusty square.* Bright flashes, screams. The whining spit of bullets, the smell of burning flesh. The roar of thunder, a searing blast of heat. A shout, *Allahu Akbar*! Dust exploding around him, shattered glass, blood everywhere. *Christ, the kid. No, Farzad! Don't...*

The rowboat rocked, spun gently. Beckett opened his eyes, sat up, shook his head. Looked up to see fireworks lighting the sky. Not gunfire. "Christ," he murmured. Today was the Fourth of July. Bloody fool. He drank again.

The rowboat scraped against the stony beach. Now it was the only sound disturbing the quiet, the fireworks and haunting call of the geese only a memory. Beckett gripped a heavy carved cane and grunted with pain as he climbed slowly over the bow.

In the blue dusk, he searched for the wooden steps that climbed the steep hillside through the pines up to the cabin. He'd built those stairs. Used to run to the top in under a minute. And now...one step at a time, the doc said. It would take him ten, maybe fifteen minutes to negotiate.

He froze as he heard the sound.

The dull roar of a motorboat, growing louder, coming fast across the lake.

Toward the cabin.

He squinted into the distance.

There. One small light. Aimed directly at him.

His rifle was locked in the cabin. One hundred steps up.

He looked up at the steep stairs, disappearing into indigo shadows, and grasped the railing.

The sound of the motorboat grew louder in the darkness.

\* \* \*

The motor cut off suddenly.

One-third of the way up the stairs, Beckett stopped and searched the dense forest and black beach below. He stood very still, tense and listening.

The only sounds were the sigh of the wind in the firs and the soft slap of lake water against the rocky beach.

Then he heard the footsteps, stealthy and quick on the wooden stairs, and the uneven, halting click of large animal paws. A low growl.

*Christ.*

Beckett pulled back into the shadows and waited. His left hand gripped the flashlight. In his right hand he hefted the cane, stiff and ready.

Two dark figures emerged from the shadows.

"Stop right there." Beckett clicked on the flashlight and stepped forward.

"Mike, is that you? Geez, you scared the shit outta me."

"Sugar. I should have known."

Standing next to Simon Sugarman was a large, too-thin golden retriever. Clearly nervous. Pulling back on the leash. Hard.

Beckett leaned closer, squinting in the darkness. *The dog had only three legs.* "Jesus. Don't tell me that's…

Sugarman was staring at him. "Helluva way to greet an old partner, Mike. Buy me a beer and I'll tell you everything."

Beckett scowled at the agent. "What the devil are you doing here, Sugar? Since when do you work on holidays?"

Sugarman looked down at the dog, still straining against the leash. "Maybe I just wanted to see how my old pal was doing." Beckett could hear the concern in Sugarman's voice. "You've seen better days, pal, if you don't mind me sayin'."

"Automatic fire at close range packs one hell of a wallop." Beckett scowled down at the shivering Golden. "Who's the dog?"

"All in good time. Aren't you gonna invite an old pal up?"

Beckett glared at him. Sugar had more secrets than a Mafia lawyer at a Mob funeral. He pointed upward with his cane. "You comin' or not?"

The agent placed a large hand on the colonel's shoulder. "It's been seven months, Mike. At least you could *act* happy to see me."

"When we work together, Sugar, people die."

The two men stared at each other, then began the slow climb toward the cabin.

* * *

The high-beamed room wavered with firelight. It was a beautiful space of glowing red woods, huge windows, and hand-made bookcases—dark and rough-hewn, like the colonel himself. Soft leather chairs were drawn close to the fireplace, and in the far corner, a circular staircase disappeared into the bedroom loft.

Beckett added more wood to the fire, his eyes on the dog. The Golden limped slowly to the far corner of the room, crawled beneath a table, whimpered. A head case. The dog's brown eyes locked on his. Darkened with—what? Recognition?

Beckett turned to Sugarman. "Beer's in the fridge. Is this Farzad's dog?"

Sugarman found two beers, handed one to Beckett, then sank into the leather couch and sighed with approval. "Just gimme a crossword puzzle and a cold Sam Adams, pal, and I'm your permanent house guest." He looked around the beamed room. "Nice. But the end of nowhere."

Beckett set a bowl of water under the table near the dog's nose. The Golden shrank back from him with a soft, wary growl. He could see the scars, white zigzags across the chest and hind quarters. Yeah. The dog recognized him, all right. "The dog, Sugar?"

Sugarman sighed. "Yeah, he's Farzad's dog. Just arrived at Andrews on a military flight yesterday. Couldn't leave him over there, Mike. We couldn't bring any animals home after 'Nam, remember? But now, from Afghanistan, we can. He's had a rough time, Mike."

Beckett stiffened. "I thought the dog died that day."

*No, Farzad! Don't...*

He closed his eyes against the sudden flashes of fire in the dark. The screams. The smoke. The first enormous punch of pain.

He shook his head, turned to walk haltingly toward Sugarman across the room.

Sugarman shook his head. "Dog survived. Chest and leg wounds, like you. Docs couldn't save his front leg. You both got stones, Mike, I'll give you that."

"I'm just too mean to die, Sugar. Only thing I know is to keep fighting."

Beckett eyed his friend. "You still searching for your terrorists? Following their money trails no matter who gets caught in your net?"

"Bada-bing!" A bright light sparked deep in the brown eyes. "Operation Green Quest is alive and well. Money is the lifeblood of terrorists, you know that. You can't tear down the terrorists without taking down their suppliers. But you've got to go through

Seven Veils these days to get to the source of the money—bank vaults, charities, secret Cayman accounts, private donors. Couriers smuggling cash across borders, or anything that can be turned into cash—jewels, drugs, weapons, whatever. I'm working the stolen art angle now, with Interpol. Museum pieces, oils and watercolors, sculptures and antiquities, even rare instruments and musical scores. 'Cultural Property,' they call it."

"And the real reason you're here."

"Okay, yeah. Something's coming down, Mike. There's been a huge uptick in chatter, all the intelligence points to an upcoming strike. New York, we think."

"And this has to do with missing art how?"

"Interpol thinks one guy is behind this. A major player, with a major network. Someone who controls international trade in illicit art, antiquities. Uses the money against us. Name's Victor Orsini."

"And you need to find him."

"Bingo. The clock is ticking."

Beckett glanced toward the Golden hiding under the table. "And the dog?"

Sugarman popped another beer, settled deeper into the sofa. "Oh. Yeah. About the dog. Did he ever have a name?"

"No idea. You're not leaving him here, Sugar. He's the last thing I need in my life. Or want."

"Yeah, yeah. Tick tock, tick tock. Now take a look at these photographs, Mike."

\* \* \*

"Paris Fucking France."

Beckett scowled at the Golden, still hunched far under his kitchen table, as the last sounds of the motorboat faded away across the black lake. "And why the devil did I let him leave here without *you*?"

A low growl.

He looked down at his cane, frowned. "And why in hell would Sugar want *me*?"

He stood, searched the fridge until he found the leftover brisket, began to cut it into chunks. "You like beef, Dog?" He set the dish down, locking eyes with the snarling Golden, and backed away. "I don't want you here anymore than you want me," he muttered. "Eat when you're hungry, or don't. Up to you."

He poured a full glass of Jack Daniel's, lifted the file of photographs Sugarman had left behind, and limped out to the deck. No sign of Sugar's boat. The night was dark, starless. Cold.

One photograph was of a woman, and he scowled down at the formal, magazine-like image. Dressed in a long, strapless black dress, she sat on a spot-lit piano bench, her back against the keyboard of the concert grand piano behind her, as if she had just finished playing and turned to face the audience. One graceful bare arm rested lightly on the glowing wood as she gazed into the distance. Wild cloud of dark hair, pensive. Eyes like bright water. Some looker, all right. Photo must have been taken just before her husband was killed. Sugar had said that was her last concert.

What the devil was Sugar thinking?

This was no operation for a goddamned amateur. Sofia Orsini's murderer had been brutal.

*No more deaths on my watch.*

He tucked the photograph back into the file with an angry oath. Pulling off the new gold-rimmed glasses, he rubbed his eyes wearily. A sound behind him, and he turned. The dog was sitting in the open doorway, staring past him into the dark sky.

"Guess you need a walk," he said. "At least you're not a damned cat!"

A sudden boom, and Beckett winced as the sky lit once more with fireworks.

The dog yelped, hunched down, then jerked back into the safety of the cabin.

Beckett watched the dog cower once more beneath the table. "Maybe we're two of a kind, you and I."

He turned once more to gaze out over the black water. *Paris, here I come. Ready or not. I just have to figure out what to do with a nutcase dog. And find a way to ditch the O'Shea woman.*

*Count on it.*

He shook his head, trying to concentrate on Sugarman's plan.

But when he closed his eyes, all he could see was the face of a beautiful woman with hair the color of night, sitting alone at a grand piano.

# CHAPTER TWENTY-THREE

*You can do this.*

Maggie stood in the gathering darkness staring up at the deck of the *Green Eyed Lass*. This section of the boatyard was quiet at the end of the day. The storm had blown off toward the east, and she was alone with the gentle sound of lapping water and the groans and creaks of swaying masts. The boats in this corner of the shed, including Johnny's, were in dry dock, suspended well above the dark water. *Above* the water. It was the only reason she was able to board. *That's why they call it dry dock, you idiot.*

Maggie very deliberately grasped the ladder and pulled herself up and over the railing onto the *Lass'* deck. The moment her feet touched the deck, terror uncoiled like a snake in her stomach. She froze, suddenly dizzy, and closed her eyes. *Just don't look down at the water.*

She was deathly afraid of the water. It was the reason she'd never been able to sail with Johnny. "And I was right to be terrified," she whispered into the shadows. "The sea took you from me."

Anger filled her, fueled her, gave her the strength to fight off the vertigo. After a moment she took a cautious breath. *Okay, then.* Gradually she became aware of the sounds around her—the gentle lap of water against pilings, the soft creak of wood beneath her, the distant cries of the gulls. She forced herself toward the hatch and clambered awkwardly down the metal stairs into the cabin.

Her fingers found the light switch and the cabin sprang to life. She'd forgotten how beautiful the small galley area was, graced by shining brass and teak and Johnny's old maps of New England's waters. It smelled of her husband and the sea. It felt intimate, shadowed with secrets.

The only other time she'd boarded the *Lass* was a month after Johnny's death. The sale contract had been drawn up, but Johnny had called the *Green Eyed Lass* his "other" great love so often that, at the last minute, she couldn't bear to part with it. So on that day she'd come to the sailboat simply to feel close to her husband. She'd touched his papers, wrapped herself in his clothes, stored his treasures and belongings in an old leather suitcase. Then she'd curled on the narrow bed to grieve.

Her chin came up. Tonight was not about grieving, it was about finding answers. Where had she put it? She searched the small space, finally found the old suitcase stowed under the bed. Still here, she thought, half surprised.

Again she thought of The Piano Cat and her apartment—broken into just days after her husband's death. And now the cottage? But no one could have known about Johnny's boat.

Maggie lifted the lid of the old suitcase. Beneath his soft flannel shirts, just as she remembered, was the small brown package from the French policeman that she'd hidden away. It contained the few personal items that had been found in Johnny's hotel room safe in southern France after the accident. That day she barely had been able to glance at the contents.

Now, very gently, she pulled the stiff paper apart. His passport, currency in euros, a pen, house keys, and a toothbrush spilled into her lap. The gold watch she'd given him on their fifth anniversary—she slipped it over her wrist gently. Tears threatened and her teeth clamped down hard on her lower lip as she lifted his leather calendar book, engraved with his initials, thick with his handwritten notes. She laid her fingers on the pages, his handwriting as familiar as a touch.

There had to be something here, in the items he had left behind. Something that would send her in the right direction.

She opened her husband's passport. His bright eyes, so electric and blue, caught at her. Trust you, Johnny O'Shea, to be handsome even in a passport photo.

She forced her gaze to the stamped pages. *Italy*. Of course. In October, concerned that there was still no word of her godson, Maggie had asked her husband to follow his journalist's instincts and conduct his own investigation into Sofia's death and Tommy Orsini's disappearance. Early on a Sunday morning, he had touched her cheek, kissed her lips. *I love you. I'll call you.*

And then he was gone.

The passport pages told the story. He'd started in Rome, where he had gone to the abandoned Orsini villa and questioned the shopkeepers and neighbors on the Via Borghese. From there, he had flown to the Breton coast of France, calling her in the middle of the night from the tiny fog-bound convent where Fee and her son had taken refuge.

And after that?

She lifted her husband's thick, 8 x 10 calendar book, scanned the pages for October. He'd always used his own peculiar shorthand code. Letters, numbers, abbreviations meant only for him, to protect his sources and investigations.

In Paris, he'd written "VD" followed by a local telephone number. And then, for some inexplicable reason, he had flown south and taken a room near the old port of Hyères on the Mediterranean Sea east of Marseilles.

On his first day in Hyères, Johnny had rented a small sailboat in the port. The next day, October 19th, he had drowned in a sudden storm, in the deep aquamarine waters some ten miles off the coast.

*Why? Why had he gone to Hyères? Why had he gone sailing that October day? You found out something that day, didn't you, Johnny? Something—or someone—that made you rent that damned sailboat...*

She lifted the hotel bill from Hyères and scanned the numbers. Charges for the room, whiskey, computer link, breakfast room service, telephone. There, her own phone number in Boston, the last time he'd called her.

*"Pick up, Maggie. Pick up the bloody phone. It's me! I've got something. Where the devil are you, Lass? I need to tell you—"* The message had ended abruptly.

Maggie's finger ran down the charges, stopped. Johnny had called a local number from his hotel in Hyères. It was close to midnight now in France. She would call both the Paris and Hyères numbers in the morning.

As she lifted his calendar once more, a folded paper fell from the book. On it Johnny had scribbled, *Morgan Library. National Library of Israel. Las Palmas Cathedral. G. Black. Vienna.*

*Vienna.* The word jumped out at her. City of music, the city where Zachary Law may have mailed a CD of a concerto to his father. She checked the passport quickly. Johnny had gone to Austria twice last summer, in July and again in late August. And then to Naples in September. Next to Naples, the letters BF were circled.

Maggie stared at her husband's notes, overwhelmed by too much information with too little meaning.

Two libraries, in New York and Israel. A cathedral in—where? Spain? Two cities, Vienna and Naples. G. Black—a person's name? And the letters BF. What did they have in common? What did they mean? And how were they connected to his search for Zach Law and her godson?

Her fingers touched the letters of his very last entry, on October 19th.

**_CFSMC, what am I missing?_**

And then, his final five words, in capital letters.

***GO BACK TO THE BEGINNING.***

Maggie sat back on her heels, profoundly unsettled. What beginning, what had he missed?

*I never fully knew you, Johnny, did I?*

With a sigh, she tucked the list of libraries, cities, phone numbers, and codes back into the calendar book, then slipped the leather calendar into her purse. She would look at everything again, very carefully, later tonight.

She looked down at Johnny's watch, now dangling like a huge gold bracelet from her wrist, and rubbed it thoughtfully. She knew the answer to why her husband had gone to Hyères. He'd found a lead to her godson.

A lead that had led to his death.

# CHAPTER TWENTY-FOUR

When Maggie returned to the cottage it was after eight o'clock. The lights were off.

She hesitated on the porch, peering in the window. *What's the matter with you?* It was just the storm, knocking out the electricity as it always did.

But the storm had already passed when she'd left for the boat.

She fumbled with the key, entered the kitchen. Stood still and listened. Wind in the firs, and the familiar settling sounds of an old house. She moved cautiously toward the great room. The last embers in the fireplace still glowed, casting wavering shadows across the skylight.

In the splintered light, she saw Sofia's letters scattered on the table, blue ribbon undone. Had she left them that way?

She found candles and matches on the mantel. Standing in the streaming shadows, she lit the candle.

And the memory struck.

*She stood in the streaming shadows and lit the candle...*

A sudden flare, and gold flickered across the water in the ancient stone baptismal font. Fee, tense and pale, holding her infant son in her arms.

"You will become a child of light, a child of God," intoned the old priest with his palm on the infant's head. He made the sign of the cross and poured holy oil into the water. The scent of incense was strong in the musty air.

They stood in a circle in a small chapel in the centuries-old church of Santa Cecilia in Trastevere—Maggie, the Roman priest in his simple vestments, Sofia radiant as a Madonna with her tiny son in her arms. And behind her, Victor Orsini, his deep-set black eyes locked on his child's face.

Off to the left, two white-habited Benedictine nuns peered through an iron grate. The only guests, thought Maggie, are those who are uninvited...

Maggie's gaze returned to the man Sofia had married. The day before, wandering in the villa's rose garden, she had overheard a frightening argument between Victor and his wife. He had not known that Sofia had invited Maggie to the christening and demanded that Maggie leave at once. His rage was brutal, cruel.

"...from the Greek word for immerse," said the priest, pulling Maggie back to the church.

Maggie held out her hands and Fee stepped forward, easing her son into Maggie's arms. The antique white lace baptismal garment draped the child like an angel's wings. Maggie looked down into her godson's eyes. Dark, so like his mother's.

"Hello, you," she whispered. "We're going to be great friends, you and I." The baby stared solemnly back at her.

She felt Orsini's black eyes on her and looked up. Very deliberately, he smiled. And she knew without doubt that he had known she'd been in the garden that morning—known she'd heard his vicious threats.

The priest lifted a small silver cup, dipped it into the water, and sprinkled it over the baby's dark curls. "I baptize you in the name of the Father, and of the Son, and of the Holy Spirit," he said in Italian. "I christen you Thomas James."

Thomas blinked in surprise as the cool water ran down his face, but he did not cry. As Maggie brushed his cheek with her fingertips, his tiny hand closed tightly around her fingers, and a chord struck deep within her.

"Are you ready, Magdalena O'Shea, to assist in raising this

child?" asked the old priest. "Are you ready to take responsibility for guarding his life?"

Orsini's eyes burned into hers, with something so dark behind the fire, and for a brief instant she hesitated, inexplicably afraid. Then her chin came up.

"I am," she had promised.

Maggie opened her eyes, blinking in the half-light of the cottage.

The memory had been so real. She gazed down at her outstretched arms, almost expecting to find an infant draped in white lace, nestled close to her heart.

*Leave him, Fee. Victor is dangerous. You've got to leave him. Now!*

"Oh, Fee," she whispered. "I begged you to leave him that night. I should never have left you and Tommy alone with him."

*We are responsible for the lives we save...*

She was still for a moment, then reached for her cell phone.

Deep down, she'd known the answer all along. In a small stone chapel in Rome, holding her tiny godson close, she'd promised to guard his life. It was time to bring him home.

*She'd given her word.*

* * *

Sugarman's phone buzzed to life. "Speak to me, pal."

He listened. And then, "Okay, so airport security found an abandoned car, good for them. Why are you bothering me with a local—*where'd* they find it? D fucking C? What did you just say? Goddamn it to hell! Get there. Now!"

He closed his eyes. The GPS in the stolen Corolla held Magdalena O'Shea's address in Boston.

# CHAPTER TWENTY-FIVE

Luze Jacobs switched on the Victorian lamp in The Piano Cat and looked around the large front room. Tonight the shop smelled spicy and sweet.

The silk of her dress rustled as she moved toward the music cabinets, competing with the jangle of her silver bracelets. She'd better hurry. Her husband would be back with the champagne in a minute. But it was a good idea to pick up the Berlioz scores tonight. Now she could stay up late with her husband to celebrate their anniversary. She grinned at her thoughts and smoothed the purple silk over her hip.

A sound.

She stopped, lifted her head. No, all quiet. Just the settling sounds of the old brownstone.

*Wait.*

Standing still in the darkness, Luze tilted her head, listening once more. Not quiet, after all. A faint sound in the back room. That old sink again? Dammit, she'd thought that was fixed. The last thing Maggie needed when she returned was a flooded office. Luze walked quickly down the shadowed, familiar hallway.

A shaft of moonlight fell through a high window, lighting a path along the carpet.

She was smiling at the pattern of light when the stranger stepped from the small rear office.

"Ill met by moonlight, proud Titania," he said softly.

She froze, saw him raise his hand.
A flash of silver. She felt the scream catch in her throat.
A crushing blow to her chest.
Darkness.

* * *

One hour later, at Boston's Logan Airport, a tall, fair-haired man with narrow, wolf-like features sat in the first-class lounge, staring down at the flickering screen of his cell phone. The digital image he'd requested just moments earlier began to take shape. He watched, fascinated, as the woman appeared before him. Arched brows framing huge shining eyes, high cheekbones in a heart-shaped face. The mass of dark hair.

"She comes more near the earth than she was wont," he said, "And makes men mad."

Othello's words. After all this time, he still found himself slipping back into Shakespeare's characters. But why not? For almost one year he had been Othello. Six nights and one matinee, every week. Such an intimate relationship forms when one plays a character for so long, he reminded himself. No wonder the lines between the role and reality blur.

The loudspeaker called his flight. He had to get home. To prepare.

The pianist was coming to Paris. It was time to warn Victor. He punched a number into his cell phone, listened to the distant ring as he gazed down once more at the photograph.

He flexed his hands. He'd gone to The Piano Cat music shop for information, nothing more. But it had been very late, and dark, and the woman working inside had taken him by surprise. No matter. He'd found out what he needed to know. The brochures, travel documents, and hotel reservations had been on her desk.

Magdalena O'Shea was coming to Paris.
*Why?*

# CHAPTER TWENTY-SIX

*She was standing there, tall and slender, on the moonlit stage. As beautiful as a goddess in the long ebony gown. She lifted the Stradivarius to her shoulder, set her chin on the glowing wood, closed her eyes. Waited for a heartbeat.*

*Then the storm of notes, soaring out over the valley.*

*He froze. Not Paganini. She was playing Tartini.*

*The Devil's Trill.*

*Why? Why was she playing another piece?*

*The first frisson of fear touched his skin.*

*He stood very still, caught up in the wild, virtuosic music.*

*Then he saw the face of the man on the far side of the stage.*

*Something was wrong.*

*He ran toward her, shouting, as the furious frenzied notes filled his head.*

*No!*

*The stage exploded in a fireball of flame.*

Victor Orsini woke with a start.

The phone on the table was ringing, sharp and loud as an alarm.

Sweat drenching his skin, heart thundering in his chest.

He opened his eyes. Dark.

The phone stopped ringing.

Orsini took a ragged breath.

The nightmare told him that final act had begun. Soon, he

would have his revenge. And at the center of it all was Magdalena O'Shea...

The agonized notes of the *Devil's Trill* still echoed in his head.

It had been a long time since he'd dreamed of Ravello.

# PART II

## Searching

*Fled is that music...*
—John Keats

# CHAPTER TWENTY-SEVEN

Colonel Michael Beckett shook his head with disbelief as he closed the report on the Bright Angel operation with an irritated snap and stared down at the thick file in his hand.

*Bright Angel.* Where the devil do you get these names, Sugar?

He gazed out the window of the Airbus A380 military transport. Stars off to his right, red wing lights blinking, pink dawning in the east. Already morning in Paris.

They'd left Andrews Air Force Base hours ago. Taking a long swallow of Jack Daniel's, he gazed down at the dog curled under the seat across the aisle. Courtesy of Sugar. The man could charm the fleas off a hound dog.

He drank again, wishing for a smoke. He pictured the last five Marlboros in their wrinkled cellophane pack and the heavy gold lighter, all stowed safely in his bag, then leaned his head back against the seat and exhaled wearily. Only five left.

*Okay, back to work. This is what we have...*

One: Ten months ago, US diplomat Sofia Orsini is brutally murdered in Brittany. Her son vanishes into thin air. And her husband, expat multimillionaire Victor Orsini, disappears. Simon Sugarman spends a week asking questions on a tiny French island in the middle of nowhere—and gets nowhere fast.

Two: Ten months of investigation, with every lead turning as cold as a January snow in the Blue Ridge. The search grinds to a halt. Then a photograph surfaces in Washington, proving Victor Orsini was alive and well just weeks ago in a café in Paris.

Three: Orsini, code-named "Bright Angel" by Sugar, is considered by Interpol to be a big-money player in the terror game. Orsini left the CIA in 1985 and resurfaced a decade later in Rome. So what had he been doing for those years he went missing? Where did the big money come from?

*And what happened to him in 1985 that made him want to disappear?* Every old case had a trigger. What was the trigger for Orsini? And why was everything happening now?

"More loose threads than my Sunday suit," muttered Beckett.

Four: Sugarman needs to track down Orsini fast, as he is suspected of bankrolling a major terrorist strike against the US. *Soon.* The clock is ticking.

Five: The only lead to Orsini is the younger, bearded man in the café photograph, a man who may—or may not—be an American MIA named Zachary Law. A man who may—or may not—be in up to his eyeballs with Orsini. A man who may—or may not—be Sofia Orsini's murderer. A man who may—or may not—be dead. So it all comes down to finding Zachary Law. Dead or alive.

And if he is alive, what the devil has he been doing for the last thirty years? And how did he end up in a photograph with Victor Orsini?

Six: Magdalena O'Shea, code name "Concerto." Beckett shook his head. A Boston musician. But according to Sugarman, the best person to find—and connect with—Zachary Law.

Right. He looked over at the Golden. "You don't go to a whorehouse to play the piano," he muttered. The dog did not respond.

Beckett flipped open the file and once more scanned the interview printed in the Boston Globe after a local concert last September. Magdalena O'Shea—acclaimed classical pianist, owner of The Piano Cat music shop, Conservatory board member, founder of Boston's *MusicKids* program, one married son.

His eyes focused on the quotes from the critics. "O'Shea's technical control, always pushed to the edge, is masterful," said one, "but beyond that, one is swept up by her passion as she becomes one with the piano."

One critic said, simply, "Maggie O'Shea looks like a nymph and plays like an angel."

*Glissando trills, pizzicatos, cadenzas...*and the sum total of his knowledge of classical music came from late-night Hitchcock movies.

Beckett scowled down at the picture accompanying the article. Pretty woman, with all that long dark hair and eyes as deep as the lake back home.

Okay, he told himself, so maybe she's damned good at what she does. But probably a prima donna, intense, temperamental as hell. And a total amateur when it comes to going head to head with Sofia Orsini's murderer.

He jammed the file into his briefcase and secured the steel locks with a small key attached to his belt. Pulling off his glasses, he rubbed his weary eyes. He felt so damned tired. What did he see when he looked in the mirror? A guy on the wrong side of sixty, with a hard, crooked face and hair curling gray around his temples.

His knee was aching again, and Beckett leaned back in the seat. He'd never expected to take a hit in a crowded Afghani square, never imagined that a hole in his chest and a bullet in the thigh would decide his retirement date. But at least life in the Blue Ridge was far better than being found one morning at the office, red-taped to death.

Wasn't it?

He gripped his aching knee, shook his head. He looked over at the dog, who was now staring at him with sad, liquid brown eyes. "Okay, okay, I know what you're thinking. So maybe I miss the action."

This operation, he knew, would be his last hurrah. Then back home to Virginia, where he could fish, read, carve, play his guitar, and try to bring back his tennis game. And try not to die of boredom.

But first, he would find Victor Orsini. On his own. After he ditched Magdalena O'Shea, the biggest unknown of all.

"I needed someone above suspicion, Mike," Sugarman had said in his briefing. "She's not an agent, she's not military, she has no rules or laws to follow. She's a musician, for Pete's sake! Who'd think a woman like her would be involved in this thing?"

"Orsini would. He knows her, Sugar."

"He knows she's a pianist. She's in France for music, what could be more innocent?"

"Damn it, Sugar, you're putting her life in danger. People connected to Victor Orsini die. Sofia Orsini was murdered—and she was his *wife!*"

"Get off your white horse long enough to see the big picture, pal. The only way to take this enemy is from inside the camp."

"Then do it with a trained team, not an amateur. I won't be her babysitter."

"If you want out, Mike, just say the word. Maggie O'Shea is all I've got. Zach Law was once in love with her. Now he's concealed somewhere deep in Orsini's empire. We need someone to get close. Real close. She can get into places we can't!"

That was Sugarman for you. A True Believer in the end justifying the means.

Outside the window, the black night rushed past and lights winked red on the Airbus' giant wings. The innocence of the O'Shea woman had struck home, stirring memories Beckett had tried to keep buried. Against his will, the memories of another woman pulled at him insistently, just as Europe now pulled him once again toward her shores.

*Kandahar.*

She'd been barely out of her teens. A sweet, inexperienced girl from a small town in Missouri, recruited by NATO and assigned against his objections to his team. Silky blond hair falling to her waist, and the bluest eyes he'd ever seen.

He'd thought the operation was going so well.

Until he found her in an old warehouse at the airport east of the city. Naked, tied to a chair, with her head falling to one side so that the blond hair, stained with dark blood, hung almost to the floor. The look of betrayal in the open blue eyes.

A damned waste of a young life. But she had wrecked an important operation that had taken months to plan. One wrong word to the wrong person. And she was dead.

The plane shuddered with turbulence, and Beckett opened his eyes with a start. The dog whimpered in his sleep. The innocents always die, Beckett thought savagely. And too often they drag you down with them.

He took a long pull of Jack Daniel's. He was damned if he would risk this operation—or his life—like that again.

He would establish contact with the O'Shea woman in Paris, find out the information he needed, then pack her off to the airport. Then—*alone*—he would begin the search for the kid and Orsini. On his own terms.

Forty-some years in the military had not kept him from making his own rules when it mattered, and his instincts had saved his skin more than once. But maybe it also explained why he had been passed over during the last round of promotions. That, and the double bourbons he seemed to need since his last tour in Afghanistan.

He gazed over at the Golden, now stirring with dreams. Nightmares? "We've all got them, Dog," he murmured. Okay, so maybe he'd lost his edge. But now he had another turn in the batter's box. He was going to get Orsini. Go out with a bang, not a whimper.

Once more he thought about the Bright Angel file locked in his briefcase and the woman code named Concerto. Magdalena O'Shea. Add in Zachary Law. Victor Orsini. What connected all of the players? What was the one thing they all had in common? Sofia Orsini? No. Education? No. Work? Friends? Passions?

"Music," he said suddenly.

*Music.*

What if the O'Shea woman had something Orsini needed? She was a musician, after all. If music was the common thread... then Magdalena O'Shea was at the center of the storm.

# CHAPTER TWENTY-EIGHT

Maggie O'Shea swallowed the too-sweet café au lait and gazed thoughtfully at the early editions of *Le Monde, Le Figaro,* and the *International Herald Tribune.* Each newspaper was folded to the style section, where her own face stared enigmatically back at her.

"American Pianist Magdalena O'Shea in Paris for Lecture Series at the Conservatoire de Musique."

Simon Sugarman had not wasted any time casting his lure. The articles were truthful—as far as they went. If Zach were still in Paris, he would know she was here.

But then what?

As she refolded the *Tribune* she glanced at two other headlines. "American Secretary of State in Paris to Meet with French Foreign Minister." She'd seen the black limos and extra security on the Left Bank. And below that headline, "U.S. Director of the National Gallery of Art Murdered in the Kennedy Center Opera House." Her eyes scanned the story. Another horrible knifing. She shuddered and dropped the newspaper to the floor.

Johnny's calendar book rested on the window seat beside her, along with several pages of her own research. She touched the smooth leather, and memory flared like a match. She saw her husband sitting in his red wing chair in Boston, writing furiously.

*I'm onto something, Maggie. Something big.*

How many times had he said those words to her, before he kissed her and disappeared to some far away place? He'd been on to something big this last time as well. It was all here, in his calendar. Very slowly, after days of research, she was beginning to put the pieces together. It was like learning a difficult passage of music.

And now, in a few hours, she would meet Colonel Michael Beckett and together they would begin the search for Zach. She couldn't just sit and wait. She had to *do* something.

She scooped up Johnny's calendar, locked it in the small safe in her closet, and reached for her running shoes.

* * *

"Damned French and their steps!" murmured Michael Beckett. Leaning heavily on a thick wooden cane, he looked down at the Golden Retriever. "Especially for guys like us, with three legs each." The Golden growled his agreement.

They stood on the terrace of the Sacred Heart Basilica, still out of breath, two feet apart, on a hilltop high above the rooftops of Paris.

Montmartre spread out over the hillside below them like the skirt of a Moulin Rouge dancer, full of color and mystery and promise. High pitched roofs angled over narrow alleys, blue shutters flung open to the sunlight, thin Parisian women drinking coffee behind curtains that stirred like long white skirts in the breeze.

It had taken them a long time to negotiate all the steps. The dog, on three legs, could barely manage a dozen steps at a time. And to be honest, thought Beckett, glaring down at his cane, he'd been grateful for the rest stops, too. Then they'd searched the huge domed Basilica for an hour, with no luck.

Now Beckett bent to give the dog the rest of the water just as the great bells of Sacré Coeur began to ring, and he looked up at the cupolas that towered like a fantastic wedding cake above all of Paris. Magdalena O'Shea hadn't been in the beautiful old church. So now he had to find his way to the cemetery.

Just for a moment, a shadow touched the stony eyes. Then his face hardened as he thought about his morning. Hung over and dog-tired, at seven a.m., he and the Golden had limped into the modern lobby of the Ambassador Hotel and been told that "*la belle Madame* had arrived early this morning, *mais oui, Monsieur*, but checked out immediately, who could understand Americans these days?"

He'd fumed in the café for thirty minutes, drinking an outrageously expensive cup of coffee, before thinking to ask for messages. There it was: "M. O'Shea can be reached at Relais Odette, off Rue Dauphine."

The sleepy concierge at the small Left Bank hotel had been very helpful. "I know the one you seek, *Monsieur*, but she is not in her room. She checked in two hours ago, then out running before breakfast was served. What is this fascination you Americans have with the exercise? *Ce matin, Monsieur*, she was off to Sacré Coeur. And she asked the way to Père Lachaise."

The concierge had gestured vaguely toward the east, and then squinted at the blank look on Beckett's face. "*Le Cimetière, Monsieur,*" he explained. "Père Lachaise is where the great ones are buried."

A cemetery. Just what he needed. "Haven't even met the woman yet and already she's making me crazy," he muttered to the dog. The Golden ignored him while keeping a wary eye on the loud, gesturing tourists climbing toward them.

He'd better hurry. The cemetery was just opening and the man who'd murdered Sofia Orsini was sure to take a very personal interest in this little operation. Sugarman had cast his lines well. Including the lure of a beautiful, brilliant pianist named Magdalena O'Shea. The man would be looking for her, all right.

And the man was a killer.

*But so am I*, the colonel told himself.

\* \* \*

At that moment, the man responsible for the violent death of Sofia Orsini was sitting in a café on Boulevard Haussmann drink-

ing a double espresso. His pale eyes were focused on the front entrance of the Paris Ambassador Hotel across the busy boulevard.

He'd seen the reservation confirmation on Magdalena
O'Shea's music shop desk in Boston.

She should be arriving at any moment. He smiled with anticipation.

# CHAPTER TWENTY-NINE

"I hope their love was worth it."

Beckett gazed down at the stone figures, stained green with lichen, who lay side by side for eternity under a canopy of shade-cooled rock. Abelard and Heloise, according to his map. The twelfth century abbot and his beautiful, pregnant lover.

The Golden hunched wearily at his side, clearly not interested in the age-old tragedy.

Père Lachaise was not at all what Beckett had expected. Built on a gentle slope of hillside in the northeast corner of Paris, the cemetery was like a very old, quiet town. The curving, narrow tree-lined lanes and alleys were crowded with mausoleums, statuary, altars, and obelisks, all standing shoulder to shoulder, guarding their dead like silent sentinels.

Beckett slipped on his glasses, fascinated by the ancient graves and sculptures. A mother gazing at her sleeping baby. A young poet frozen in white stone, pensive and dreamy. A man holding the detached head of a woman.

Beckett concentrated on the cemetery map. Where would an insomniac musician be? His finger moved down the list of names buried in the cemetery. Delacroix. Isadora Duncan. Sarah Bernhardt—a definite possibility. Balzac, Proust. Edith Piaf? Maybe. Jim Morrison. His silver eyebrows drew together. A classical pianist interested in The Doors singer? Not bloody likely.

He looked down at the Golden. "Any ideas?"

The dog shook his sleek head and turned away.

No help there. Gertrude Stein, Chopin. His finger stopped at Chopin. O'Shea would go for the composer. Frederic Chopin, section eleven. Up the hill to the left. *Up.* That figured. He ignored the knee, grasped his cane and the leash, and began to climb. The Golden resisted, then limped and hopped along behind him.

They found Chopin's tomb under a quiet arch of green. A delicate marble muse, head bowed, sat atop a high rectangle of stone. A yellow tomcat slept curled at her feet. Bouquets of flowers obscured the carved letters.

The Golden stared at the cat but remained surprisingly still. "Remind me to give you the 'Dogs Don't Like Cats' lecture," muttered Beckett.

The child-like muse was the only female in sight. *No, wait.* Over there. A woman, still as snow. So still he'd almost missed her. Beckett couldn't see her face. Only the chaos of black hair, long and loose, and one bare leg ending in a bright orange running shoe.

He pulled off his glasses as he moved toward her. Bloody fool, he mocked himself. "Mrs. O'Shea? Are you Doctor Magdalena O'Shea?"

She was lost in thought and turned quickly, as if startled to hear the male voice behind her. She stood with unconscious grace to face him.

"Yes, I'm Maggie O'Shea."

It was a voice made for reading poetry, low and sonorous as a church bell. He looked down into huge eyes of a deep, disturbing green. The kind of green you see in the heart of the forest. Eyes that had distance in them.

She was as slender as a boy and the simple running shorts and t-shirt, loose on her small frame, made her seem both innocent and tough at the same time. Winged brows above a straight nose, skin as pale as the alabaster statues surrounding her—except for the purple hollows that tinged the high cheekbones and shadowed the guarded eyes.

Pretty woman, he thought.

She took a step back. "And you are?"

He realized that he had frightened her. Suddenly conscious that he was staring, he stepped out of the shadows and tried to reshape his mouth into a smile.

"Good mornin', ma'am," he said. "I'm Mike Beckett. Colonel Michael Jefferson Beckett, United States Army, Retired."

Maggie O'Shea's eyes widened in surprise as she looked up into the face of the man towering above her. "I didn't expect to meet you here, Colonel. How did you find me?"

"Your concierge. You asked directions to the cemetery." He shook his head at her naiveté. "I've had to hit the ground running because you changed your hotel." The top of her head barely reached his shoulder. *What the devil was Sugar thinking?*

She stared at the tensing muscles in his jaw. "I *did* leave a message for you. The Ambassador Hotel was too huge and impersonal." Her chin tilted defensively.

"Does Sugar know?"

"He doesn't control my life, Colonel. No one does. I'm here now. Surely that's what counts." She bent to the Golden until she was eye to eye and offered the back of her hand for him to sniff. "Hello there, fella, good dog. What's your name?"

The Golden shrank back, and she raised an eyebrow at Beckett.

"He needs therapy, not a name," he said gruffly.

She stared at him. "Your dog deserves a name, no matter what."

"He's not *my* dog, ma'am."

She shook her head, raising one arm to lift the heavy hair off her neck. It was hard to look away from her. Damn, she surely wasn't what he'd expected. He thought about the small, romantic

Left Bank hotel she'd chosen, set in a misty cobblestone court-yard. *Yes, it suits you*, he thought.

* * *

His eyes had distance in them.

Eyes that had seen too much violence? But the sound of his voice—slow, deep and easy—was much more reassuring than the forbidding expression. She liked the way he moved, too—the easy grace, even with a bad leg, and the quick eyes. Except for the hint of wariness in his body.

And now those disturbing gray eyes were on her, assessing. Waiting, glinting at her with a deep and serious intelligence. This man would not suffer fools gladly.

Maggie stared at the crooked nose, the wide grim mouth, the silvery day-old beard. It was a battered face, she thought, a Tom-Selleck-without-the-mustache face, deeply scored by life. He was not a handsome man, and yet there was something compelling about his strong, angular features. Gazing at him, she thought of a forest—trees, earth, rock.

Beckett's eyes moved to the quote on her t-shirt—*Where words leave off, music begins.* "Sugar says you play with the Boston Symphony."

"I'm afraid I only sell sheet music these days. I don't play the piano anymore."

"I'm sorry to hear that, ma'am. My grandma always said that we need music in our lives so we'll know how heaven sounds when the angels sing."

Maggie liked the image and wondered why the words didn't match the expression on his face. That slight, self-mocking smile didn't quite reach his eyes—eyes as cold and dark as the winter sea off the Vineyard.

"We need to talk, Mrs. O'Shea."

The Golden bristled and Beckett's sudden tension silenced Maggie's response. She felt the instant reaction of his body and looked up to see a man in a black warm-up suit biking slowly toward them down the winding lane. She noticed, too, the subtle shift of the colonel's body, as if to shield her. What's going on here? Maggie wondered.

The biker passed, and Beckett turned to her. "Time to go," he said.

Maggie refused to move. "You're obviously used to giving orders, Colonel Beckett," she said, "but I'm not used to taking them."

Granite eyes glinted at her. Then he pushed his hand through the silvered fringe of hair in exasperation. "I can see that, ma'am. Let's walk." He waited a beat. "Please."

She relented and fell into step beside him and the Golden. "Why did you follow me here?" she demanded.

Clearly searching for time, he reached into his jacket pocket and withdrew a battered pack of cigarettes and a dull gold lighter. This colonel had carpenter's hands, ringless, scarred, and powerful. And just how did he get all those scars?

"Mrs. O'Shea?" Beckett was looking at her with an odd expression. He narrowed his eyes, smiled grimly, and slipped the cigarette back into his pocket.

"The Café de la Paix must be open by now. Shall we go ask about Zachary Law?"

"We? Well, ma'am, the dog and I are on our way to the Café de la Paix. You are going back to your hotel to pack your suitcase."

Her confusion sparked into anger. "Like hell I will!"

"Didn't see that coming," he muttered to the Golden.

"I'm not going anywhere until I find my godson," said Maggie, locking her arms across her chest. "I won't be told what to do."

His unyielding face was so close that she felt his breath on her cheek. This time she refused to step back. "This isn't Dodge City, Colonel. You can't just run me out of town."

"Sugarman must have been out of his mind to involve you in this. You're an amateur who will end up compromising the mission. You're—what? One hundred ten soaking wet?"

*Arrogant bastard.* She turned away to conceal the sudden temper that burned her skin.

"Don't fight me," he warned her. "I'll win."

The full force of his will hit her like a blow, but she stood her ground. "I. Won't. Leave," she told him with finality.

# CHAPTER THIRTY

The desk clerk at the Ambassador Hotel shook his head as he watched the tall, fair-haired man stride across the lobby. He'd spoken French, insisting he needed to see Madame O'Shea. Angry and rude. *Alors*. Perhaps he should not have revealed that Madame had moved to Relais Odette.

* * *

In the cemetery of Père Lachaise, Beckett stared at Maggie in disbelief. "I'm pitching but you're not catching, ma'am. I can't guarantee your safety."

"You're playing the wrong page of music, Colonel," she said. "I didn't ask to be here. And this isn't about my safety."

"Oh, but it is, Mrs. O'Shea. You've gotten involved in some very risky business and I—"

"I understand the risks only too well. My good friend was attacked in my music shop. I'm not so naïve as to think the intruder was after a Berlioz score. Especially since he had a knife."

He spiked an eyebrow. "A knife is vicious. Intimate. How is she doing?"

"Frightened. But she's going to be okay, thank God. She thinks her corset deflected the knife."

"A corset?"

She offered a faint smile. "Long story. But I hate that she was threatened because of me. Just one more reason why I'm here. It's the right thing to do."

He shook his head. "Right thing, maybe, but wrong reason when a knife is involved."

She glanced down at the Golden. "Is he always this difficult?"

The Golden gazed at her thoughtfully, as if considering her question.

"You may not know this, Colonel Beckett, but my home and music shop were vandalized after my husband died. His computer was stolen, as were several files. Someone wanted information from my husband. Not me."

The silver eyes locked on hers. "Not you..."

Something is wrong, thought Maggie. The colonel's words, like Tchaikovsky's huge introduction to his first symphony, were set in the wrong key.

"Musicians are not immune from danger, Colonel. Sousa fell through the stage floor while conducting. Vivaldi was born during an earthquake, Simon Barere died while performing at Carnegie Hall. The American composer Blitzstein was beaten to death by three French sailors."

"Maybe they didn't like his music." Beckett shook his head. "Where do you *get* this stuff?"

"I'm a trained pianist. I take care of myself, I don't need protecting. And I'm not afraid."

"Then you're naïve, ma'am." He eyed her slender arms, the narrow ankles just visible above the neon-orange Reeboks. "You shouldn't be here."

"I do many things I shouldn't do."

"I have no doubt. But things could get very rough." Beckett pushed his hands deep into his pockets, clearly frustrated.

"Things not going the way you planned, Colonel?"

He took a deep breath. "Just what the devil did Sugarman tell you?"

She looked down at the wedding band on her left hand. "Simon came to me because a very long time ago I was—involved— with Zachary Law. Simon is convinced that Zach is alive and the link to finding Fee's son. Because of the photo of Zach with Victor Orsini in the Café de la Paix."

"How much do you know about Orsini?"

She could sense the anger behind the controlled voice. "He was married to my good friend, Sofia Orsini. But you already know all this," she said, watching him. "What you don't know is that when my godson was born, I promised to protect him. I didn't. So here I am."

"How about this, Mrs. O'Shea? You go home, and I'll find your godson for you."

"How about this, Colonel? You're not concerned about my safety. You just don't trust me not to mess up your operation."

Beckett looked over at the Golden. "Welcome to Beckett-No-Win-Roulette," he muttered. "Your friend Sofia's involvement with Victor Orsini cost her her life. You know it, and so do I. Now you're looking for her son. And Orsini doesn't want his kid found."

"Do you believe Victor Orsini murdered his wife?"

"I believe he's a man with too many secrets. And a man with secrets to hide is a dangerous man."

"So the danger comes from Orsini. At least that explains why Simon insisted that I work with you. Although, like you, I would prefer to work on my own." She locked eyes with his. "Something wrong, Colonel?"

He nodded uncomfortably. "It's just...I've never met a lady piano player before."

"Then we're even." She watched his face as she put her suspicion into words. "Because I've never met an army intelligence officer."

# CHAPTER THIRTY-ONE

Chanel sunglasses and a swirl of silken scarf obscured the face of the elegant Frenchwoman who rode her bicycle down the Rue du Chat qui Peche. In the crowded square of Place Saint-Michel, she stopped by the Davioud fountain to gaze up at the huge stone sculpture of the Archangel Michael and the Devil. Sorbonne students in tight black t-shirts sprawled around the stone rim, smoking and deliberately ignoring the tourists who threw coins and photographed "*Le vrai Paris*" with their iPhone cameras.

She looked toward the small glass-fronted bistro on the north edge of the swirling square. Bistro de la Fontaine was charming with its art deco canopy above a red door and windows displaying artfully arranged wine bottles and baskets of bread and cheese.

Today three Gendarmes and several tall Americans with wires in their ears stood talking by the door. A line of official black SUVs were parked on the street in front of the bistro. Inside, the French Foreign Minister was having breakfast with the American Secretary of State.

The woman dismounted, leaning her bicycle against the fountain's rim. The small satchel in the rear basket was hidden by a bouquet of bright flowers.

Wandering away from the bike, she took photographs of the fountain, the square, a young Frenchwoman trailing her hand dreamily in the fountain's water. Then, with a last look at the glass-walled bistro, she turned and walked quickly toward St. Germaine, leaving her bicycle behind. In a moment the crowds swallowed her, and she was gone.

\* \* \*

In the dappled shade of Père Lachaise cemetery, Maggie repeated her question. "*Are* you an intelligence officer, Colonel Beckett?"

Beckett felt the muscle jump angrily in the hollow of his cheek. He glanced down at the Golden, searching for a distraction, but the dog looked away and he was on his own. "Why the devil would you think that?" he asked, too quietly.

"Because I think you are here because of Victor Orsini, not Fee's son. But frankly, I'm not interested in your political intrigue. This may be your job, but I made a promise to my husband and my godson, and I intend to keep that promise."

He bristled. "Political intrigue? I'm just a disillusioned old soldier who used to push papers through five miles of hallway at the Pentagon."

"Disillusion breeds a hard edge of cynicism."

"This is just another run-of-the-mill operation, Mrs. O'Shea." His shrug was unconcerned. "Find Zachary Law. With luck he leads us to the kid. Then we all pack up, and I go home to my place in the mountains. In and out."

She looked at him as if he'd just told her the South had won the Civil War. "But you need *me* to find Zach."

"Sugar thinks we need you. I don't." He pictured the bloodless face of the young woman who had died so needlessly under his watch in Kandahar. *Not again.* "Do you really believe Zachary Law is alive?"

Speaking to the sky, she said, "It's possible he didn't die in that bombing. He was injured, he may have lost his memory." Talking too fast, she added, "Or perhaps he simply found another life, another woman."

*Right*, thought Beckett. Maybe if Beirut had left the guy blind and deaf. And impotent.

"I hate secrets," she said. "I hate not knowing the truth."

"You've fallen into a world that's all about secrets," he admitted. "Did Sugar ever tell you about the husband who reported to work at the CIA and discovered that his boss was his wife?"

The faint, brief smile rewarded him. "What's *really* bothering you, Mrs. O'Shea?"

"In my heart, I think Zach must be dead. Maybe he didn't love me any longer, but he would never have abandoned his music. *Never*! It was the very blood coursing through his body." She gazed toward the clouds. "Life without music would be unbearable for Zach, impossible. If he were still alive, I would have heard his music—on the radio, in a concert hall, somewhere. I would have known..."

"But there's more, isn't there?"

"Yes. Zachary Law composed the concerto that was on the disc he sent to his father, I'm certain of that. But he is *not* the person playing that piano."

"If you think Law's dead, Mrs. O'Shea, then why the devil are you here?"

"Maybe this is part of the answer." She was staring down at the grave of a French officer killed in WWI. The inscription on the worn blue stone implored the soldier's wife not to forget him. Two words had been added later: *I remember*.

In the green stillness, Beckett watched the lost, bewildered expression shadow her face. The bright, hurt look in her eyes. "Stirring up the past like this can't be easy for you."

"People die, Colonel, and the rest of us just have to get on with it. Maybe I'm here because the past won't rest until I know the truth." She hugged her shoulders, and he wondered suddenly whether she was talking about Zachary Law—or her husband.

\* \* \*

Just ahead of them on the path, an old veteran with caved cheeks and lieutenant bars on his worn uniform sat on the grass. Maggie watched as the colonel stooped, spoke softly, then gently pressed several folded euros into the soldier's palm.

He scares me, she thought. But he gives money to a homeless man when most people I know would just walk on by. He tries to ignore that beautiful Golden—but there is something in his eyes when he looks at that dog. She said, "You're not what I expected, Colonel Beckett."

"People are always more than one thing, ma'am."

They walked on without speaking.

At the end of the path, they stopped, struck by the cemetery's powerful memorial to Holocaust victims. "Evil isn't just an abstract concept, Mrs. O'Shea," he said, staring up at the emotional sculpture.

Maggie gazed at the skeletal stone figure, breaking the grip of his barbed-wire prison and rising into the bright morning sky. "There was an orchestra of prisoners at Auschwitz, did you know that?" she said suddenly. "Music composed by Jews was found at Thereseinstadt and several other camps." She turned to him. "How is it possible? Why do we let things go so far?"

"Maybe because we can't imagine such evil." Beckett squinted into the distance. "No man knows how he'll behave until he hears the sound of boots on the stairs, the knock on the door in the dead of night. The Jews were stripped of all human dignity. And yet—"

"And yet these same people somehow found the courage to make music, to love and have faith. To keep the human spirit alive. *Defiance.*"

Maggie looked up at the memorial, stark and anguished against the cloudless sky. "When Winston Churchill was asked to cut arts funding in favor of the war effort, he simply replied, 'Then what are we fighting for?'"

Beckett nodded. "I was in Jerusalem last year, witnessed a suicide bombing in a café," he said quietly. "Fifteen dead, including two children. The next morning, I went back with the investigating team. The café was filled with people, drinking their coffee. Defiance. It's the right word. I guess that's why some of us keep fighting. For them, and for ourselves."

They turned uphill once more. "Fighting the good fight," Maggie said suddenly. "That's finally the truth, isn't it? Why you're really here in Paris?"

"Seems to me there are three kinds of people in this world, Mrs. O'Shea. The creators, the destroyers, and the maintainers." He glanced down at her. "You—you are a music maker. A creator. You search for beauty in a harsh world."

She felt herself go still, listening.

"Me, I seem to be one of the maintainers." He scowled down at her. "The creators need protectors, it seems. And I don't want the bad guys to run the world. So, yes, ma'am, I guess that's why I'm here."

"And you think Victor Orsini is one of the destroyers."

"I know he is."

She saw the darkness at the back of his eyes, and grasped his sleeve. "Then don't ask me to leave! You want Orsini. I need to find Zachary Law. We can help each other."

"Your elevator keeps missing the penthouse, ma'am. I work alone. I walk my own night patrols."

Her hand dropped from his arm. "I'm going to bring my godson home, Colonel. Help me or don't help me, but don't try to stop me."

"And if we don't find the boy? What then?"

She looked at him as if he'd hit her. "I have to do this, Colonel. If I'm ever going to be free."

A sudden, distant booming sound.

Beckett paled, spun around, his body thrust in front of hers. The Golden gave a high, frenzied whine as he crawled beneath a bench.

"My God!" cried Maggie. "What was that?"

Beckett shook his head, crouching to reach gently for the dog. "Nothing good, ma'am."

# CHAPTER THIRTY-TWO

Sirens in the distance.

Beckett watched Maggie brace herself against a low stone wall and extend her left leg behind her to stretch the calf muscles. She was getting ready, once more, to run. Not a chance.

In that stance, with those graceful, muscled legs, she looked like a dancer. "Are you sure you're a pianist?" he asked her.

"Pretty sure," she said with a faint smile. She turned toward the Gambetta gate.

His eyes narrowed. "And just where do you think you are going, ma'am?"

"To find my godson."

A faint buzz filled the air around them. He pulled the cell phone from his jacket and listened without taking his eyes off her. "Be at the Gambetta gate. Ten minutes."

"The explosion?" she asked. "The Secretary of State is in town—"

"I've got to go. But I've arranged safe transportation for you."

"I don't need your car. I'm neither innocent nor frail. I can pay for my own hotel. I speak passable French, and I know Zach was last seen at the Café de la Paix."

"I don't want to have to pull rank on you, Mrs. O'Shea."

"I'm not afraid of you, Colonel Beckett."

He smiled grimly. "Your nose is growing longer, ma'am."

Beckett pulled an airline ticket to Boston from his pocket and thrust it into her hand. "Go home, Mrs. O'Shea. Go home to your family and your music. You live in the normal world, but I live in a darker place. A world of shadows. You don't want to look at the world through my window."

"But I've got the perfect reason for being here—and it's the truth! I'm a widowed musician trying to get on with my life. No one suspects me of anything. There won't be any danger as long as I'm careful."

He remained silent, with his arms folded, eyes appraising.

She searched his eyes. "I'm afraid we're both just going to have to do the right thing, Colonel. And that includes naming your dog."

"You are one damned exhausting woman, Mrs. O'Shea. And he's not *my* dog."

"What I am is a soloist. I'm accustomed to working alone. I believe that I am the one who does not need *you*, because I have my husband's calendar book. That's all the information I need." She turned and jogged deliberately past him toward the tall cemetery gates.

"What calendar?" he asked.

She stopped, turned slowly. "Simon Sugarman must have told you that my husband began searching for Zach Law last summer—without my knowledge. I found Johnny's date book just before I flew to Paris. A diary, with all of his notes. Names, places, phone numbers, appointments. He uses codes, abbreviations. I have no idea what all of it means, but he was on to something."

"I need to know what's in your husband's book, Mrs. O'Shea. I'll keep you updated—"

"I don't buy it," she said. "You need me and it makes you furious."

"I need the calendar book, ma'am, not you."

She folded her arms and locked her eyes on his. "Do you have a gun, Colonel?"

"Excuse me?"

"Because the only way you're going to get rid of me is to shoot me."

He swore under his breath and rubbed his jaw wearily. "All

right," he sighed finally. "We'll try it. But at the first sign of danger, you're on the first flight home. Count on it."

A spark flared deep in her eyes. Beckett found himself thinking of October leaves glinting in the evening sun, back home in Virginia.

"I have a meeting with Vanessa Durand today at noon," said Maggie. "You're welcome to join me."

"Durand? Who the devil is she?"

"An art gallery owner. My husband discovered that she had a connection to both Sofia and Victor Orsini. I found her initials, VD, in his calendar, along with the phone number of her gallery here in Paris. I called the number, asked for the owner. *Voilà*, Vanessa Durand. Johnny met with her just two days before he died."

"Just where is this meeting of yours?"

"Her home. The quai, Right Bank side of the Pont Alexandre III."

"We should see her before we go to the Café de la Paix," said Beckett. Then, "Do you ever play by the rules, Mrs. O'Shea?"

"Music is all about rules, Colonel. Knowing those rules makes me a schooled musician." Her smile flickered at him. "But *breaking* the rules...well, then you have *jazz*."

He took a deep breath, as if counting to ten, and gestured toward the taxi waiting at the gate. "Okay. That taxi is driven by Lieutenant Henri LeBlanc of the French Sûreté. He'll be working with us. Go back to your hotel, and I'll meet you at the bridge just before noon."

"Whatever you say, Colonel."

"I say you're more than I bargained for, ma'am."

She flashed a smile over her shoulder as she jogged toward the gate. Beckett scowled down at the Golden. "If a beautiful woman ever drops out of the sky in front of you, run for the hills!" The Golden snorted beside him.

He watched the cab disappear around a corner and felt, suddenly, as if the light had gone out of the morning. Admit it, he told himself grudgingly. You admire her determination to search all of France alone to find her friend's kid. *In another time*, he thought, *it would have been nice to get to know her better.*

"Round one to you, Mrs. O'Shea," said Michael Beckett quietly, touching a finger to his forehead in salute.

He looked down at the Golden, who was gazing off toward the trees. "Come on, Dog. Miles to go." The Golden sat still, gazing up at him. Beckett rolled his eyes. "Please."

At that moment Beckett's phone rang again.

# CHAPTER THIRTY-THREE

The deck rocked gently beneath her feet as Vanessa Durand stood alone on the small boat, gazing down at the gray waters of the Seine. Today the river was as restless as her thoughts.

At forty years of age, she was tall, willowy and elegant in her white silk suit and pearls. Hair the color of summer wheat curved softly against her pale cheeks, framing eyes of a startling blue. Only the tightly clasped hands betrayed her tension.

The houseboat was moored on the quai just below the ornate arch of the Pont Alexandre III. Across the Seine, rooftops glowed pink in the afternoon light.

So beautiful on the surface, she told herself. Until a bomb outside a bistro shatters a peaceful morning and turns it into a nightmare.

\* \* \*

Simon Sugarman sat hunched over a crossword puzzle in the driver's seat of a taxi parked outside the Relais Odette. Only Beckett and the Admiral knew he was in Paris.

He filled in 21 Down—"Synergy," hell of a word—and thought about the woman he was waiting for. Full of surprises, that was for sure. Who knew the Doc would arrange her own meeting with Sofia's closest friend in Europe? But that was Maggie O'Shea for you, determined to do it her way.

He thought about Vanessa Durand. Why couldn't he shake

the feeling that the art gallery owner was involved in this mystery up to her pretty little neck?

Sugarman hadn't seen Vanessa since just after Sofia's death—some ten months, now. When he'd questioned her, she had been shocked, grief-stricken, angry. Blamed herself for not finding her friend in time. But as far as Sugarman was concerned, too many questions had never been adequately answered.

Who had helped Sofia escape from Rome? Who followed Sofia to that remote island? What had happened to her boy? What had been rolled up in that empty canister? And the million dollar question, what happened to Victor Orsini's journal?

Sugarman tapped his pen thoughtfully on the newspaper. Sofia Orsini and Vanessa Durand had been friends since Fee's early days in Italy. Vanessa was an art dealer with galleries in Paris and Rome who had been hired to catalog Victor's collection at the villa. After Sofia's marriage, the women continued to see each other at Embassy parties, art gallery openings, the cafés and theatre. Sofia never suspected that Vanessa could be anything more than a beautiful Renaissance art dealer.

No doubt his old pal Beckett would believe Vanessa's innocent, wide baby-blues, too. But one question kept nagging at him. The person Sofia had trusted to help her escape to the island was the only one who knew where Fee and Tommy had gone to ground.

*That person had betrayed Sofia Orsini to her killer.*

Sugarman rubbed the back of his neck to ease the grip of jet lag. At least the shark had taken the bait. Someone had broken into Maggie's music shop, injuring her friend Luze Jacobs.

Sugarman stared thoughtfully across the courtyard at the elegant entrance to the Relais Odette. Beautiful Maggie. His sweet lamb. His lure. Yeah, here's the stake and the rope, angel. I'll just slip this around your beautiful neck and send you out there, so I can smoke out the bad guys.

Maggie appeared in the hotel doorway.

Dropping the newspaper to the seat, Sugarman leaned out the window. "Yo, Doc! Taxi, Mad-moi-zell-ee?"

"Simon!" Maggie smiled with surprise as she moved toward the car.

"Back seat, Doc, quickly!"

She slipped into the Fiat, and he pulled out into the narrow Rue Christine, eyes on the rearview mirror. She leaned forward to touch his shoulder. "What are you doing here in Paris?"

"Checking on my team." Sugarman wagged a dark finger at her in the rear-view mirror. "Beckett says you're a loose cannon already."

"I am not loose."

He grinned. "You're forgiven, if you know a five letter word for 'northern hemisphere.'"

She thought for a moment, then smiled. "Igloo."

"Igloo! I'll be damned." He turned toward the Seine. "Almost there. Ready to meet Sofia's friend? She's a real knock-out."

"Simon..."

"What's bothering you, Doc? Second thoughts about Vanessa?"

"It's Colonel Beckett. I met him this morning. He made it very clear that he wants to work alone."

"Trust me, Maggie, we need your help. Mike is here to take over after you find Zachary Law. Okay, his people skills aren't the greatest." He grinned at her as he maneuvered the Fiat onto the Alexandre Bridge. "He's always been a loner. He's a good man in a bad world, a moral man caught in an immoral life. Too damned noble for his own good sometimes."

"You like him."

"Oh, yeah. West Point, Special Forces, handful of medals hidden in the back of a drawer somewhere. Won't talk about it. Took a barrage of bullets in Afghanistan one time. He could barely walk, but he stood up to draw incoming fire so his men could get the other wounded away." He glanced back at her. "Ever notice that when all hell breaks loose, most people run away as fast as they can? But there are always a few who run toward the screams, the smoke. To help. That's Mike Beckett. Hell, I'd want him guarding my back any day."

She had noticed the Colonel's limp in the cemetery. But he'd told her he was just a paper pusher. "But this is Paris, Simon, not some war zone."

"Some of us are always at war, Maggie. And sometimes it gives us a dark soul."

*A dark soul.* Maggie thought of the colonel's dark, wintry eyes.

"Give him a chance, Doc. He's driven by a sense of justice. Doesn't always do everything right, but he wants to make it right." Sugarman pulled over at the end of the bridge. "Time to boogie!"

\* \* \*

Beckett could hear Sugarman's laughter lingering in the air as the Fiat pulled back out into the bridge traffic. Once again, looking down at Maggie O'Shea, he was struck by her eyes—large and luminous as emeralds in the sunlight. He much preferred blue, himself.

He stared at her and her slight smile disappeared. Taking her elbow, he cocked his chin at the Golden, and steered them both toward the stone steps that led down to the path along the river. Her subtle perfume reminded him of spring in Virginia.

"Wait." Maggie hesitated at the top of the steps, pulled back.

"What's wrong?"

She glanced uneasily down toward the dark water of the Seine. "I don't see her..."

"She must be inside." He gestured toward the line of gently rocking barges and houseboats as he began to descend the narrow steps. Maggie stopped abruptly, and the Golden hesitated beside her with a low whine.

"Where is she exactly?" Her husky voice was strange, tight.

Beckett raised an eyebrow impatiently. "Waiting for us on the third houseboat."

"No!"

"Excuse me, ma'am?"

"No. I said no, Colonel. I won't get on that boat."

"What is it, Mrs. O'Shea? The boat is very private. We can even take her down the Seine toward—"

She pulled away from him. "I can't do it! I'm sorry, but I just—cannot. The boat, the water..." She was shaking her head from side to side, backing slowly away from the steps.

Boat? What the devil? Suddenly he remembered a line in Sugarman's file. "Husband killed in a boating accident." *Beckett, you idiot.*

"Mrs. O'Shea. Just give me a moment to make other arrangements. Wait for me here. Please." He looked hard at the Golden. "Stay with her."

\* \* \*

Shocked and embarrassed by her unexpected reaction, Maggie sat down on the ancient stone steps, hugged her elbows tightly, and took several deep breaths. The Golden pressed against her knee and whined softly.

That's it for me, she thought, watching the colonel limp angrily up the gangplank. Disgraced by an innocent, flower-decked boat on a sunny river in Paris.

*Fight it*, she challenged.

A deep breath. Stand up. One step toward the river. Another. Her body began to shake. Fight the nightmare, damn you. You can do it. More steps, quickly, across the stones. The edge of the river, and now the water was dark and swirling. She felt dizzy, sickened, and closed her eyes tightly. Get on the boat, damn you. *She felt herself tilting forward.*

Loud barking. Then a hand grasped her elbow roughly, swinging her around, away from the water. She opened her eyes. Beckett was standing in front of her.

"Vanessa will meet us across the river at the Musée d'Orsay."

His eyes were splinters of gray ice. "I trust you'll find no demons in an art museum?"

"Please understand, Colonel—"

"It's time for *you* to understand, Mrs. O'Shea. Beauty has wandered into the Beast's garden now."

# CHAPTER THIRTY-FOUR

"Magdalena O'Shea is in Paris."

Far to the south, Victor Orsini heard Dane's words and gripped the phone to his ear. *She is in France*!

"What do you want me to do?" asked Dane.

"I'll get back to you."

Orsini disconnected.

Magdalena O'Shea. What did she remember? What did she want? *What did she know*?

He paced slowly back and forth across the antique Aubusson carpet in his bedroom like a caged prisoner, his heavy features indistinct in the half light.

Back and forth. Back and forth.

He stopped, finally, before his favorite Lippi panel. *The Annunciation*, with the Archangel Gabriel on bended knee. As always, he appreciated the irony of the artist's story. Lippi, an orphan raised in a priory, had taken his vows as a Carmelite only to discover, too late, that he was better suited to earthly pursuits when he eloped with a nun who bore him a child.

Orsini bent closer, examining the fine, nuanced brush strokes, the richness of the colors. The *emotion*. Orsini shook his head. He had given up on his own emotions years before, deliberately closed the door on every feeling, every response. The only emotion he allowed himself now was the fierce hatred that fueled his need for revenge.

Once more his eyes swept over the Lippi. There had been a

Lippi in the collection he'd been admiring on the afternoon he met John O'Shea. At an Old Masters exhibit at the Galerie sur le Port in Hyères, he'd been standing in the midst of a huge, noisy crowd, drinking *Moët et Chandon* and studying Carravagio's *The Lute Player...*

"Not bad, I guess. If you like Carravagio."

Orsini turned from the magnificent oil to stare into eyes the color of the Mediterranean Sea just beyond the gallery windows.

"Victor Orsini, right?" said the blue-eyed, red-bearded American behind him.

"And you are?"

"John O'Shea. I've been looking for you."

Orsini shrugged, not recognizing the name.

"My wife is Magdalena O'Shea."

Orsini stared at him. "What do you want?"

"The answers to a few questions."

"About?"

"The usual. Art. Music. Your business." A tilt of the head. "Your wife's death."

"Perhaps you should reconsider, Mr. O'Shea. These are dangerous topics. You wouldn't want anything to happen..."

The man gazed around the crowded gallery. "You can't hurt me, Mr. Orsini."

"I wouldn't think of it, Mr. O'Shea. But I could hurt your wife."

* * *

Orsini opened his eyes, gazed around the shadowed bedroom. Now, he knew what to do. He reached for his cell phone. When Dane answered, Orsini spoke only seven words.

"Find Magdalena O'Shea. Bring her to me."

# CHAPTER THIRTY-FIVE

Vanessa Durand wandered slowly through the sky-lit gallery of the nineteenth-century building known as Musée d'Orsay. Once a dark, abandoned railway station, the renovated art museum now had an airy atmosphere of space and sunlight. Pausing to enjoy the changing light on Monet's gardens, she saw Michael Beckett in the next gallery.

The colonel looked hard and cynical. And very angry about the change in plans.

She stopped in the doorway, suddenly glad she was meeting with the colonel instead of Simon Sugarman. Sugarman was too unsettling, always looking at her with a question in his dark eyes. And now he'd brought another woman into his investigation.

It had to be the woman gazing at a luminous Pissaro, unaware of the colonel's eyes on her. She's quite lovely, thought Vanessa. Slender and raven-haired, Magdalena O'Shea reminded her of Sofia Orsini. But smaller—and far too casually dressed for Paris. Really, wherever did one find a French-cut t-shirt emblazoned with the words *Piano Power*?

She sat down next to Maggie O'Shea and crossed her silken knees as her jeweled hand motioned toward a darkly beautiful Van Gogh. "You are enjoying our collection, yes? I am Vanessa Durand."

Maggie turned to study her. "They are exquisite." Lowering her voice, she said, "I'm Maggie O'Shea. I've come to find Fee's son. My godson."

"She spoke of you often. How can I help?"

"An old friend, Zachary Law, may know where Tommy is hidden. Do you know him?"

"No. Is he the reason Simon asked you to meet with me?"

"Meeting you was my decision."

Vanessa raised a surprised eyebrow. "Then perhaps Simon has met his match. But Simon *always* has his own agenda, I think."

"So do I, Ms. Durand."

* * *

Steps away, Beckett pretended to study a Sisley—no pretense needed, actually, it was quite beautiful—while leaning against the narrow archway to discourage curious tourists. Impressionists and classical music, he thought. *How the devil did my world suddenly become so cultured?*

He shook his head and moved closer to stand behind the two women.

* * *

"I found your phone number in my husband's calendar," said Maggie, suddenly surrounded by Vanessa's spicy, expensive perfume. "You met with him last fall, here in Paris. John O'Shea?"

Vanessa stared at Maggie. "Yes, of course, he was looking for information on Fee and Tommy. I met with him at my gallery on Rue du Bac. Didn't he tell you?"

Maggie's voice dropped. "No. He...died very suddenly, in the South of France."

"*Mon Dieu*! I did not know. How did it happen?"

Maggie shook her head, unable to speak of it. "I need to know what you told my husband."

"He wanted to know about Sofia and Victor. Fee and I became friends when she moved to Rome. I have an art gallery there as well, on the Via Veneto. Fee introduced me to Victor."

Maggie watched her thoughtfully. "After my husband left

you, he went on to the Mediterranean coast. Hyères, just east of Marseilles."

"I sent him there. I explained that, several months before Fee died, Victor hired me to catalog his art collection. He also commissioned me to search for an oil that he was most interested in possessing. A Lippi. Victor had given me a special postal office where I could contact him."

"Hyères."

"*Oui*. I also gave your husband the name of an art dealer in Hyères who might have had some dealings with Victor."

"Yes, Jacques Racine, at the Galerie sur le Port. It was in my husband's notes. I called, but no one answered."

Vanessa looked down at her hands. "You know, don't you? If Victor didn't hold the knife to Sofia, then he gave the order. Either way, Victor Orsini is a murderer."

"You and I, we were her friends. Why didn't we stop her from marrying him?"

"I don't think we could have. You know that Victor is a seductive, charismatic man. She was Catholic—and already pregnant." Vanessa hesitated. "He could be very cruel." Vanessa glanced around. "But Victor is a powerful man, with powerful friends. He refused to divorce her without custody. She stayed because of her son."

"A mother will do anything to protect her child," said Maggie. "It was all in her letters." She shook her head. "I should have insisted that she leave him."

"We can only go forward." Vanessa turned away. "I want to help you find Victor, for Fee. Since one of his passions is art, I'm concentrating there. A gallery owner heard a rumor that Victor was seen in the South of France. I'm driving down to Cannes this weekend."

Something in Vanessa's words caught at Maggie, like an unexpected arpeggio in a melody.

"Vanessa. You said that art was *one* of Victor's passions. What are the others?"

"Music. He collects rare, autographed scores. He owns sever-

al rare violins as well, including a Gradoux-Matt and a del Gesù."
Maggie felt something click into place in her head.

She stood and held out her hand. "Thank you for your help.
I'll stay in touch." She turned toward the arched exit.

"Just where the devil do you think you're going, Mrs.
O'Shea?" said Beckett from behind.

"A lecture at the Conservatoire de Musique," began Maggie,
but Beckett put his big hand on her shoulder. None too gently,
she noticed.

"They're expecting me. I'm a visiting pianist, remember?
Mozart? Debussy?"

"What color is the sky in your world, Mrs. O'Shea?"

# CHAPTER THIRTY-SIX

*Come in and close the door.*

Returning to the Left Bank hotel, Maggie had turned to Beckett in the tiny lobby and offered to show him her husband's calendar. Together they had ridden in the narrow lift, with the Golden wedged between them, to her room on the third floor.

The clock on the mantel was chiming the eight o'clock hour when they entered the garret room with its view of the rooftops of Paris.

Beckett watched as she flipped the lamp switch, and the room flowered with light. Beyond the arched window, he glimpsed a silvery curve of river and a sky streaked with purple above dark-angled rooftops.

"Come in and close the door, Colonel."

He and the Golden watched as she crossed the room to the closet, spun the dial on the small steel safe. Then she handed him a thick leather book and a vellum envelope. "Johnny's calendar. And my research. Read it all tonight. We can talk about it in the morning. I'll want his calendar back, of course."

He looked down at the worn ebony leather. "Of course."

Her eyes stayed on his. "Do you trust her?"

"Who?"

"The art gallery owner. Vanessa Durand. I know she was Fee's friend, but she sent my husband to Hyères. I had the feeling today that she knew more than she told us."

"I'm beginning to trust your instincts, ma'am. I'll talk to Sugar."

She nodded and turned toward the window. He watched her in silence as she gazed out at the glimmering dusk, twisting the golden wedding band on her finger. Silhouetted in the half-light of the window, she was as beautiful as one of the paintings he had seen in the Musée D'Orsay that afternoon. But lost, bereft.

He turned away, unsettled by her quiet, raw emotion. The unexpected moment felt too intimate, making him feel like an intruder.

"The morning, then," he said, giving the Golden's leash a gentle pull. "Good night, Mrs. O'Shea."

* * *

Alone in the small room, Maggie turned on the radio, kicking off her heels as the strains of classical guitar filled the intimate room. Two balloons of brandy were set out on the low table by the window. *Two.*

Maggie reached for the brandy, folded herself back into the cushioned window seat and watched the night gather its dusky cloak around the city. Edges blurred, lamps burned gold in narrow windows, a Bateau-Mouche strung with gay lights sailed slowly up the river toward Notre Dame. Above the steep rooftops, the Eiffel Tower was a glittering tracery of light against the deep cobalt sky.

It had been a long, exhausting day, beginning with her sunrise run. And ending just an hour earlier, with a sunset concert in Sainte-Chapelle. *It's where a visiting musician would go, Colonel.*

In the tiny Gothic chapel, as the last light fell like jeweled rain through the high stained-glass windows, she had listened to the small orchestra play Haydn's Symphony No. 45. *The Farewell Symphony.*

Each musician lit a candle fixed to his or her music stand, until the whole chapel flickered with candlelight. As each instrument reached the end of its score, that musician rose quietly, blew out the candle and left the chapel, until the last violinist played alone. When he played the last note, he, too, blew out his candle.

*Farewell.* In the sudden, silent darkness, she'd felt Beckett's eyes on her.

Maggie refilled her brandy glass as night turned the rooftops blue. She was so tired of drowning nightmares and maddening colonels and vast empty beds. The guitar suite ended and Ravel began his sensuous, slow beat in the air.

Music swirled like smoke around her, stroking and teasing. When she closed her eyes, the music became phantom lips on her skin. Desire stirred, then leaped with sudden flame deep within her body. *Johnny. I miss you so...* The Bolero beat quickened, matching her pulse.

A sudden and passionate grief jolted through her. Here in Paris, Johnny was everywhere she looked. The book stalls, the outdoor cafés, the narrow cobblestoned streets. She could see his face reflected in the dark waters of the Seine. Hear his voice, sighing in the shifting leaves outside her window.

*Johnny?* she tried.

She waited. Only silence.

Maggie touched the empty seat cushion beside her. Hugging her knees tightly to her chest, trying to hold herself together, she looked down into the empty brandy glass as if she were looking into a crystal ball. Her husband had discovered something in France. Something important. Something that had led to his death? She felt like the violinist in Haydn's symphony. Blowing out the last candle, sitting alone in the dark silence.

*Farewell...*

Oh, God. Will I ever remember what it's like just to be happy?

* * *

The red soccer ball sailed through the air. A flash of sleek golden fur. The thin legs of the boy, pumping like pistons across the dusty square. The sudden gleam of sunlight on metal...

*No, Farzad!*

A deafening roar. Blood. Blood everywhere.

Beckett flung out his hand, searching for his weapon. Soft damp sheets beneath his fingers.

A bed. He was lying on a bed. Still dressed, his head on a down pillow.

Breathe.

He squinted, eyes settling on a bureau in the dim light, a mirror. A jacket flung over a chair. There, the double window. A smooth golden head, still as a carving, silhouetted against the cobalt square of night beyond the glass.

"Hey, Dog. You awake, too?"

The Golden remained motionless. Okay. You're in Paris, he reassured himself. Two doors down from Magdalena O'Shea. He allowed himself a small smile, remembering Sugarman's aggravation over the last-minute change of hotels. Not to mention the expense. Score one for the piano player.

Okay, breathing back to normal. Almost.

His fingers searched, found his glasses on his chest. Must have fallen asleep while he was reading. The calendar! Where was it? He twisted, saw it had fallen to the floor.

Long day, longer night. He thought again of Maggie O'Shea, of the sunset concert in the tiny chapel across the Seine. Colored lights falling like rain through the high stained glass windows, touching her skin with jewels. While he sat watching her, listening to...Haydn, she'd said. A long time since he'd listened to classical music. Then the violinist had blown out the last candle, leaving them in shadows and silence. A long time since he'd known a moment of such beauty and peace.

In the vast empty bed, he felt a sudden, inexplicable sense of loneliness. Glancing over at the Golden, he snapped his fingers. "You lonely tonight, too, fella?" Beckett gently patted the bedding beside him. "C'mon, boy. Come here."

The Golden turned away, dark eyes glistening and scars burning like long thin swords in the light of the streetlamps.

Beckett nodded. "Two strays in this world, you and me—two lost souls—who somehow found each other." He sighed, closed his eyes. "Afghanistan," he whispered into the darkness. "It never goes away."

Beckett breathed deeply, searching his mind for a kinder memory, a moment—a quiet, undamaged place. His cabin, shining like a lantern through the pines. Fishing on the lake with Red. A woman sitting quietly in a pool of jeweled light, the last notes of a Haydn symphony lingering in the air. He felt himself drifting down into sleep.

Just for a moment, in the split second before he fell, he thought he felt the mattress dip with weight, a settling, a warm breath near his face.

Peace.

# CHAPTER THIRTY-SEVEN

It had rained in the night, but now the morning was brilliant with early sun that edged the old Paris Opera House in gold.

The dark Peugeot pulled up to the corner of the Boulevard des Capucines. Maggie O'Shea stepped from the car and dropped lightly into one of the cane chairs under the green and white umbrellas of the Café de la Paix.

The man leaning back in the chair had his eyes half-closed. He was dressed in boots, jeans, a navy turtleneck, and a camel jacket. Light played on the strong, rough planes of his face. An unlit cigarette was jammed between his lips. Maggie studied him from behind her dark glasses.

"Tough night, Colonel Beckett?"

Without opening his eyes he quoted, "Of all the gin joints in the world, Mrs. O'Shea, you had to walk into mine..."

So he, too, liked old movies. "Sitting with your back to the wall...watching for me?"

Beckett opened his eyes and the corners of his mouth moved.

"Be careful," warned Maggie. "You almost smiled." She bent to pet the Golden curled warily behind his chair. "Didn't he, fella?"

Beckett slid a dish toward her across the small marble table.

"What's this?"

"Egg, sausage, and Brie on a buttered croissant."

"I'd rather die."

This time he laughed.

\* \* \*

He had been in the café for twenty minutes, listening for the dusky voice, a sound a man couldn't forget. And he'd known the minute she'd arrived. She was boyishly dressed, with a faded blue sweatshirt tied around her hips and a bright yellow NYPD cap on her head. Her long hair was caught back in a braid. No make-up, silver hoops dangling from her ears, sunglasses so big they covered half her face.

"You look like a teenager," he said. "Exhausted and scruffy."

Maggie ignored him and gazed out over the swirling traffic toward the old Opera House, shining like an antique jewel in the sunlight. Behind the sunglasses, her face was unreadable. The smell of coffee and baked bread drifted from the café. "It's so beautiful here," she said.

"Too much traffic."

"The outdoor cafés," she went on, "the ancient churches..."

"*Le Big Mac.* All those damned nervous little dogs." He looked down at the Golden and raised a bushy eyebrow. The Golden raised his chin, seeming to agree.

Maggie tossed her cap on the table, lifted the dark glasses to the top of her head, and stared at him. "Why are you so growl-y?"

"Growl-y?" He reached for his old lighter, flicked the flame, and glared at her over its flare. Then he tossed the unlit cigarette into the ashtray, his eyes still on Maggie.

Warm from running, she closed her eyes, arched her neck, and held a glass of ice water to her cheek.

He dropped his eyes to the small print on her fitted bright red t-shirt, reached for his glasses, stopped and lifted his coffee cup instead.

"It says," offered Maggie, "When the Going gets Tough, the Tough go Chopin."

He crossed a booted foot over his knee and regarded her. "You are a piece of work."

"Is that a compliment or an accusation?"

"Not sure yet," he told her honestly.

"Why do you keep staring at me like that, Colonel?"

"Just tryin' to figure out why you're still here, ma'am. What makes you tick?" His silver brow spiked. "I understand about your godson. But I can't help thinkin' you've still got a few prize heifers locked in the back barn."

She looked at him as if he'd read her thoughts. "I'm private, Colonel. Perhaps you're just not used to women who don't like to talk about themselves." She leaned toward him. "I'd rather talk about that explosion yesterday. Did it have anything to do with why you're here?"

"What makes you think so?"

"The look in your eyes this morning. I know the Secretary is safe, but—one more anti-US attack, so close on the heels of that bombing in Amsterdam. I read that the CIA's Chief of Station in Paris was at that meeting at the bistro as well. They *named* him—"

Beckett frowned. "He'll have to be pulled out now, for his safety. One more dangerous, embarrassing leak."

"All these recent attacks. They seem so personal."

"There are men and women who hate America. Too often their mothers, sisters, children are collateral damage in war. If someone they love is harmed, they will fight us forever."

"How do we stop them?"

"It's too damned easy to hurt people. We have more satellites and drones and high-tech weapons than we can use, and it still comes down to a faceless man in a wired truck or plane who's not afraid to die. So the best way to stop them is to cut off their funding. Don't give them the chance to train and grow strong, to travel and communicate, to wire that truck."

Beckett reached down to touch the Golden, but the dog shied away. "Have you ever loved someone—or something— enough, Mrs. O'Shea, to do *anything* for them?"

Her eyes locked on his. "I hope I never have to find out."

He nodded slowly. "Back to our mission, then. I'm here to

help you trace your godson, ma'am. Not a terrorist. We need to find Zachary Law."

She glanced around the café. "And this is where he was seen last."

Beckett reached for her husband's calendar book on the small round table and tapped it with the palm of his hand. "Your husband was damned close to finding Law. These notes of his—two libraries, a cathedral, the city of Vienna. Most of the information in this calendar circles back to one connection."

"Music." She gazed across the busy square at the Opera House. "It's music."

She was too damned quick, her thoughts as unsettling as the scent of her hair. "I agree with you. But help me understand why your husband started his search in Vienna."

"It's the *city* of music. It was Zach's dream, to go there. I told Johnny that, once. And Johnny said that we all have that one special place we'd go to hide when our lives are falling apart." She looked down at her wedding ring. "For me, it was Martha's Vineyard."

Beckett regarded her in silence. True enough, he thought. When he'd been released, finally, from Walter Reed, he'd only wanted to go to ground in his cabin in the mountains.

"But I'm sure Johnny had other sources as well," smiled Maggie, "considering he drank whiskey every Friday night with most of the Pentagon brass."

He returned the smile before he could stop himself. "Okay. So Zach Law survives Beirut, eventually makes his way to Vienna, and goes to ground. Gets himself a new identity. Then..."

"Music," she repeated. "A musician can't live without music, it's as simple as that. So, if he felt he couldn't play the piano publicly, then he would have chosen some other kind of musical life. Composing, teaching, writing about music, studying—oh, my God." She turned so quickly that her cup rattled. "Vanessa Durand said that she was hired by Orsini to catalog his art collection. And that Orsini also collected rare musical scores.

What if Orsini hired Zach to authenticate the pieces in his music collection?"

He looked up sharply. "You may be on to something. And that would connect with the research you did on those two libraries your husband mentioned."

"The Morgan in New York and Israel's National Library. Yes."

He pulled on his glasses, squinted down at the papers in his hand. "According to your research, The Morgan has an extraordinary collection of illuminated music manuscripts, letters, printed scores."

She smiled. "The library is beautiful, filled with priceless cultural treasures—original sheet music by Haydn, Liszt, Chopin. Letters from a thirteen-year-old Mozart. Best of all, an autographed manuscript of Beethoven's Violin Sonata in G. My God, seeing—touching—the very same pages Beethoven touched! Can you imagine?"

"No," he said honestly, trying to keep a straight face.

She laughed. "Okay. But there's a connection."

"To the Israeli National Library." He tilted his glasses, read aloud the caption of the newspaper article she'd copied. "Stolen manuscripts plague Israeli Archives in Jerusalem. Hundreds of items missing from the music collection, including manuscripts and letters by Yehudi Menuhin, Jascha Heifetz, Pablo Casals, Mendelssohn, Strauss..."

He took off his glasses, leaned toward her. "It fits. Your husband saw it, you see it, too. Orsini is not simply a collector of rare music. His collection must include *stolen* music."

Her eyes flashed at him. "Yes. And that's why Johnny was interested in Spain's Las Palmas Cathedral. Four hundred music manuscripts stolen from its archives, still unsolved. All those priceless cultural treasures—Victor Orsini is a *thief* as well as a murderer."

He tilted back in his cane chair and nodded at her. "Your husband must have found this link months ago. He was searching for

Zach Law and your godson, and somehow he stumbled on something even bigger—"

"My husband was too smart to *stumble* on anything, Colonel. He had to be investigating Orsini as well. But why?"

Beckett's fingers tightened on his coffee cup. Beyond her, the buses and cars swept around the Place de L'Opéra in a bright, frenetic blur.

Above the blaring horns in the square, a sudden, whomping sound.

Louder.

They looked up. A helicopter, coming in quickly, low, over the rooftops.

The Golden snarled, fur bristling.

"Incoming!" shouted Beckett, throwing his arms around Maggie and knocking her to the ground as the Golden let out a howl of fear.

As the helicopter roared overhead, a stunned Maggie struggled from beneath Beckett's body and saw the Golden, teeth bared in terror, tear away to stagger blindly out into the swirling traffic.

"*No!*" She leaped to her feet and dashed after the dog.

# CHAPTER THIRTY-EIGHT

PARIS. MORNING, JULY 7

Screams. Horns blaring. The screech of tires and blasts of hot air as bicycles, cars, trucks, buses careened around her. Someone shouted her name. The world blurred.

God, God. Where was the dog? A flash of golden fur. There!

A huge truck, hurling across the square. "Watch out!" she screamed, lunging toward the terrified animal.

She threw out her arms, flung herself toward the Golden.

All sound stopped. And then she felt him, a body almost her own size, fur and muscle wrapped in her arms.

A moment of horror, the giant spinning wheels of the truck so close she could touch them.

She was tackled from behind.

They fell to the pavement. Hard.

She opened her eyes. Looked into the deep brown, glistening eyes of the Golden. "Are we alive?" she whispered.

Sound came back.

The Golden barked, once.

The Colonel's voice, low, fierce.

Blackness.

\* \* \*

"Of all the crazy, bloody damn fool things to do..."

"Please, Colonel. I'm just glad we're all okay." The coffee was strong, hot, stinging her mouth. They were back at the café table, the Golden once more safely curled behind the Colonel's chair, quivering but unhurt, with a huge beef bone and a fresh bowl of water. Traffic had resumed speeding around the square, the crowd of concerned onlookers dispersed.

Maggie untied the sweatshirt from her waist and pulled it over her head.

Beckett shook his shaggy head back and forth. "I'm supposed to protect you, damn it!"

"The only thing broken is a pair of sunglasses. And the only thing bruised is my ego. I can't believe I fainted." She tried a small smile. "I've suffered more stress on the stage at Carnegie Hall."

She reached out, covered his large hand with hers. "But I wasn't in any danger. That was a traffic helicopter. Your dog has post-traumatic stress, doesn't he?" She refused to add, *and so do you.*

"Afghanistan." He pulled his hand away from her. "The doc calls it Battle Fatigue. Nightmares, flashbacks, startling, insomnia. We're working on it," said Beckett, his tone angry. Raw.

"I know you're angry, Colonel, but—"

The silver brows bristled at her. "Angry? You ran into eight lanes of speeding traffic to save a damned dog with three legs, Mrs. O'Shea!"

"But you were right behind me. You're the one who pushed us away from that truck."

* * *

She'd refused to return to the hotel, insisting on staying at the café while Beckett spoke to the staff. Thirty minutes later, he sat down across from her once more.

Cocking an eyebrow in surprise, he stared at the dog, whose large head was now resting in Maggie O'Shea's lap. The dog hadn't looked that peaceful since...well, never. "*Et tu, Brute?*" he murmured.

She smiled as she stroked the sleek fur. "Any luck?"

"Everyone has been questioned," he told her. "No one remembers the people in the photograph or the day the photo was taken. I'm afraid it's a dead end, ma'am."

She gazed past him toward the Opera House. "There has to be *something* more we can do besides drink coffee and stare at every man who enters the café."

He took another slow, thoughtful drink of coffee. "Einstein said that if you have one hour to save the world, spend fifty-five minutes thinking about how and five minutes doing it."

She raised an eyebrow, sat back. "Okay, then, we think. Zach was here, we know that from the photograph. Someone must have talked with him, served him a drink...what?"

He was looking through the café doors at a large, hard-looking woman with bleached hair and dark armpits who polished wine glasses behind the café bar. "That woman," he said. "The one who looks as if she could tear the New York telephone book in half? There was something in her face..." Beckett stood up. "I'll talk to her again."

Maggie laid her hand on his arm, stopping him. "Let me." She gave the Golden a gentle nudge, and stood. "*I'll* talk to her."

"Mrs. O'She—"

"My friends call me Maggie, Colonel."

"Professional boundaries, Mrs. O'Shea. Under the circumstances, it's better to maintain a strictly professional relationship."

She stepped back as if he'd pushed her and walked away from him into the smoky café.

* * *

Maggie slid onto one of the round stools along the zinc bar of the Café de la Paix.

The woman called Yvette eyed her with suspicion. The arched, darkly-painted eyebrows gave her a look of perpetual surprise.

"Madame," said Maggie, "I need your help." She spoke slowly in French, her voice soft and confidential. She nodded toward Beckett, who leaned against the doorway. "That gentleman only told you part of our story." She beckoned Yvette closer.

Unlike many of her countrymen, the Frenchwoman seemed

to appreciate the polite attempt to speak her language. She leaned her rough elbows on the bar and waited.

"You're the crazy American who ran into the square after the dog," she said suddenly, in English.

"That would be me," admitted Maggie.

"I love my little Papillon," said Yvette. "What help do you need?"

"My friend thinks this is an official matter. But no, Madame. Woman to woman, this is...*une affaire d'un coeur.*"

"Ah," murmured Yvette knowingly, turning a baleful glare on Beckett.

Maggie caught the colonel's eye in the long mirror over the bar. Then she held out the photograph and pointed to Zach. "Please, Madame," she implored, searching for the words that would reach this cynical, weary woman. "I'm searching for my son's father. Thirty years ago, I was going to marry this man. We were very much in love." Maggie saw a tiny spark of response in the tired eyes. *You, too, once upon a time, Yvette?*

"But then he went to Beirut. There was a bombing..." Now the words came quickly, in English. "All these years, I've believed he was dead. Until now. The man in this picture is so much like him. Like my son..."

Yvette had not taken her eyes off the photograph.

"If you know this man," whispered Maggie, "tell me where I can find him."

Yvette's eyes were bright with some indefinable expression. Finally she said, "*Alors.* I remember the one you seek. American, *oui*? The handsome one with—" She stopped abruptly. "You say you haven't seen him in thirty years, *chérie*?"

"*Oui, Madame.*" *What was she going to tell me?*

Yvette looked at the photograph again, this time more carefully, then something darkened her eyes. "I will tell you this," she said. "He came in two, maybe three times in the last few months. He always liked to sit outside in the sunshine. His companions called him Gid." She pronounced it "Geed."

"Gid," said Maggie aloud. "Gideon?" The name meant nothing to her. But then a small cymbal sounded in her head. Something she should remember... "A last name, Madame?"

"But who can be sure?" Yvette held out her hands, reddened palms up. "So many people come to Café de la Paix. *C'est impossible.*" The Frenchwoman tilted her chin toward the old Opera House across the square. "They always came before the performances. He teased me, eh, because I said I would rather spend the evening with Monsieur Mozart than with my husband." She chuckled at the memory.

"I've spent many evenings with Monsieur Mozart myself," smiled Maggie.

"Then they went off to the Opera House and left me to polish my glasses." Yvette turned away.

"Please, just a moment more." Maggie held out the photograph again. "What about the other faces?"

Yvette pursed her lips. "The girl was quiet. Always—" she glanced at Maggie—"touching your Gid. He called her—Celene? Cecile? The older man standing behind Gid, I don't remember him at all."

Maggie glimpsed the colonel's grim face in the mirror above the bar. "What about the man in the sunglasses?" she asked quickly.

Yvette spat on the floor. "Him, I remember. Handsome, yes, but there was something—bad about him. I am not easily frightened, *petite*, but he frightened me."

Maggie looked down once again at the menacing, wolf-like face. "Oh, I believe you, Madame," she said. "But I need a last name, an address?"

"I am sorry. Perhaps, if they lived here in Paris..." A true Parisian, Yvette raised a hand in dismissal of all imbeciles who chose to live anywhere else. "You say Gid is your son's father, eh? Then—perhaps there is something."

"Oh, please! Anything that would allow me to hope."

"*Alors...*" Yvette searched Maggie's face for a long moment, making up her mind. Finally she nodded and reached beneath the counter for a large black handbag. Maggie watched in fascination as Yvette pulled out make-up, brushes, a heavy coin purse. Rolls of candy. Two thin books of...poetry? Then she extracted a small notepad from the clutter and studied the crowded script.

"*Eh bien*! Here it is." There was a look of triumph in her eyes. "Across the way, at the Opera House. An usher named Jacques. Your friend said that if I ever wanted to hear Monsieur Mozart, I should go to Jacques, and he would find me a ticket."

Maggie leaned across the countertop and kissed the rough cheek. Yvette blinked in surprise. "But I do not understand, *petite*. It is only the name of an usher."

And a memory of a stranger with the face of her son, who loved music. "You have given me hope, Madame."

Yvette rolled her heavily mascaraed eyes. "Hope is for the very young, *chérie*."

Maggie fingered the clasp of her own small purse. "How can I thank you?"

The rough red hand came down with strength on Maggie's wrist. "Between women, eh? Come back with your handsome Gid one day and tell me how your story ends." She eyed the colonel standing by the door. "More handsome than that one, eh?"

Maggie touched the older woman's hand and slipped from the stool.

Yvette was looking at her with an odd expression. "Wars change people, *petite*. Just be careful."

Again, there was that fleeting shadow of sadness in the woman's eyes. *Wars change people*...the words echoed for Maggie like the last haunting notes of a Debussy nocturne. "What is it, Yvette? What else do you remember?"

The French woman only shook her head as she shuffled slowly toward the far end of the bar.

# CHAPTER THIRTY-NINE

Dane entered Room 18 in the Relais Odette.

It had been ridiculously easy to gain access to the small hotel. He'd found the staff entrance in the deserted alley near the kitchen. Then he had waited, just off the tiny lobby, until the lone concierge had gone in search of a taxi for a guest. It was a simple matter to glance at the register. Magdalena O'Shea, *Chambre* 18. The clerk at the Ambassador Hotel had told the truth.

He was in the elevator before the concierge returned. The ancient lock had given easily under his knife.

He scanned the hotel room with care. Antique bed, oak armoire, window seat, Chinese dressing screen in one corner. The perfect stage setting for a Molière farce.

The bathroom was empty, scented with powder and roses. Dane prowled around the room, stopping to touch a hairbrush, a small CD player, a biography of Leonard Bernstein. He lifted a pair of gold hoop earrings and held them up to the light.

He found the two photographs hidden beneath silken lingerie. A worn picture of a young man in a relief worker's uniform, face shadowed by sunglasses and the brim of his cap. And a photo of a smiling red-bearded man with an arm around O'Shea's brat. There was something familiar about both men. A young aid worker. And a father with his son. Dane examined the faces more closely. *What was it?*

Had he seen these men before? Let it be, he told himself. It will come to you. He slipped the photographs back into the drawer.

A pianist... Who was she, really? Why was Victor so interested in her?

In the armoire he found a green silken scarf that held a subtle scent of her perfume. He slipped the silky square into his jacket as he pressed the Play button on her CD player. Bolling's Jazz Piano Suite filled the room. Whoever she was, she had good taste in music. And perfume.

A maid had draped an ivory satin nightgown on the bed, pinching the gown at the waist and then fanning the skirt over the quilt. Dane lifted the thin fabric and held it to his face. Like the scarf, it smelled of her. He closed his eyes as he rubbed the nightgown slowly against his lips. The scent of her filled his nostrils.

*I want you*, he thought suddenly. He dropped the gown back to the bed.

He found what he was looking for behind the Chinese screen in the far corner of the bedroom. A utility closet. Opening the door, he saw a dark, narrow storage area filled with linens and cleaning materials. He froze, jarred by a searing flash of memory.

*A frightened young boy, locked in a small, suffocating closet with no light.*

He fought for breath, then saw the small window high on the wall. Light. Breathe, he told himself, as he stepped slowly inside, leaving the door ajar behind him. He would be okay, as long as he controlled his breathing. As long as he could see. As long as the door wasn't locked.

*As long as he had a way out.*

In the quiet shadows, waiting for Magdalena O'Shea, Dane wondered once more why Victor wanted her brought to him.

*But Victor will have to wait, my angel.*

# CHAPTER FORTY

"His name is Gideon."

"Gideon who?"

"This is not a knock-knock joke, Colonel. Yvette said that Gideon is a music lover who befriended an Opera House usher named Jacques." She gestured toward the Opera House across the busy square. "Let's go find Jacques."

Standing on the sidewalk just outside the Café de la Paix, in the bright sunlight, Beckett looked down at Maggie O'Shea. Blessed are the Cracked, he thought, for they shall let in the Light.

"Admit it, Colonel. I discovered something important from Yvette this morning."

He glanced down at the Golden, crouched but alert, against Maggie's leg. "Even a blind dog finds a bone once in a while, right, fella?" he muttered. "Okay." He raised a hand to signal Henri, the French Sûreté Lieutenant working with Beckett, who now waited by the Citroën parked illegally at the curb. "Can you take the dog for awhile?"

The Golden gave a soft whine, strained away, pulling against the leash as if he didn't want to leave.

"Go," said Beckett firmly. The Golden limped away with the lieutenant without a backward glance.

Beckett gestured with his chin, and he and Maggie turned toward the Opera House doors.

* * *

Dane was half-asleep in the shadowed closet. Fragments of images whirled like a kaleidoscope in his mind, settling finally on the photographs he had found in Maggie's room.

Maybe the tall red-bearded man was the O'Shea kid's father...

Dane's thoughts spun to his own father, who also had been a big man. They'd lived in small dark rooms, close to the docks where his father worked. In his memories, it was always dirty in Hamburg, always raining. He couldn't remember ever celebrating a birthday. Or Christmas.

When he was very young, in the years before his mother disappeared, his father would lock him in a closet with no light, much smaller than this one. He would curl up for hours, his hands over his ears, trying not to hear the sounds in the next room. His mother's cries in the darkness.

*He was still terrified of being locked up.*

And then one day she just wasn't there when he came home from school. He'd known she was gone. The rooms had been so still. They didn't even smell the same. He'd run from room to room, calling her name. *Don't leave me.*

She hadn't even said goodbye.

After his mother left, there were other women, other cries in the lonely night. More and more, Dane escaped into his books and imagination. Until his father began to turn his drunken violent anger on the quiet bookish boy who was his son.

Dane stopped going home after school. Often he stayed down the lane at a female neighbor's home. It was Greta who'd introduced him to sex when he turned eleven.

Somehow, his father always found him.

Then, at fourteen, a drama coach had drafted him against his will for the part of Lucio in a school production of Shakespeare's *Measure for Measure*. Sweet God, the surprising glory of it all! Not to be himself. To wear another man's clothes, speak words not his own. To be called by a different name, and live another life, as if suddenly he had been reborn in the dark and magical world of the stage.

His father showed up at the school on opening night, drunk, dislocating Dane's arm as he pulled him off the stage. He'd awakened at dawn to find his father like a maddened ape in his room, eyes glassy, hot breath stinking of whiskey, thin fisherman's knife sharp against his son's throat.

*I'll teach you a lesson you'll never forget.*

His father had pushed him back down on the bed, torn off his pants, held him down. Shock. Pain. Revulsion. And then—

In the shadows of the closet, Dane rubbed the scar on his neck, remembering.

*There had been so much blood.*

By noon that day he had been fifty miles out to sea on an Italian freighter.

A sound jerked Dane awake.

Creaking gears. Someone was coming up in the lift. He shifted his position. If he cracked the door just a bit more, he could see a sliver of the shadowed room beyond the Chinese screen. He smiled. His palms still tingled with the feel of her smooth satin nightdress. Does your skin feel as soft, Magdalena O'Shea?

He flexed his powerful fingers, wanting to touch her.

The lift came to a halt, and Dane kept his eyes on the crack of light. He imagined her opening the door, sitting down on the bed, taking off her stockings.

He thought about the ivory gown laid out on the coverlet and wondered how she would look in it tonight. How her face would look at him if he raised her arms above her head, used his knife to slash the gown's thin straps so that the satin would slide down her body to crumple on the floor at her feet.

A knife was so much more personal than a pistol.

The sound of a door opening down the hall. Not her. He rubbed the smooth scarf against his lips. "Come home to me, Magdalena O'Shea," he whispered. "I'm waiting for you."

# CHAPTER FORTY-ONE

"That's it, then. No Gideons. Another dead end." In the small Opera House office, Beckett pulled off his glasses in frustration and tossed them onto the useless stack of computerized ticket orders and mailing lists.

"But we have the information from Jacques, Colonel. Isn't that enough?"

The old usher had been more than helpful. *"Ah, oui, mon ami Gid."* After a brief search of his pockets he'd resurrected a half-used matchbook advertising a café in Southern France. *Les Deux Garçons. A café in Aix-en-Provence, Gid said, where everyone loves la musique. He said he would look for me there, at his favorite café, this summer.*

"Aix-en-Provence," repeated Maggie. Her hand ran down a bright poster advertising the summer's music festivals. "Festival de Musique, Aix-en-Provence. It opened last night. And look, Colonel. Tomorrow night is a gala performance of Tchaikovsky's Piano Concerto. Zach loved that concerto." She stopped, swung around. "Gideon. Could he be Johnny's G. Black?"

Beckett's head came up. "G. Black?" He thought, then remembered. "Right, the name in your husband's calendar. Good catch." He reached once more for the computer lists.

Fifteen minutes later, they found the name on a mailing list: G. Black, Aix-en-Provence.

"Aix-en-Provence," said Maggie.

"Aha!" said Beckett.

"Aha?"

"All the famous detectives say that when they find a clue."

Maggie smiled. "Zach's *there*, in Aix. And Zach wouldn't miss tomorrow's concert. Or should I say Gideon Black. We've got to be there."

"We'll leave for Aix first thing in the morning." Beckett handed her a card. "My cell number, if you have to reach me. Lieutenant Henri will pick you up for tonight's concert at seven."

They were walking down a long hallway crowded with statues. Now Maggie stopped at the foot of the magnificent Grand Staircase.

"I came here once for Tchaikovsky's Romeo and Juliet," said Maggie.

"When it comes to composers, ma'am, I tend to think of John Lennon."

"Lennon's good. But nothing can compare to a Mozart concerto."

"The closest I've come to classical music," he grinned, "was making love on an Asian beach to a blond violinist with the USO tour."

She took a step up the broad marble staircase, so that when she turned to face him their eyes were on the same level. "I think we can do better than that."

His eyes met hers, glinting at the challenge, and he watched her cheeks grow pink. "I listened to Zach Law's CD last night," admitted Beckett. "I liked it. But you're looking at a man who hears The William Tell Overture and thinks of the Lone Ranger."

She laughed, a silver chain of sound. "You see, Colonel? Music can seduce anyone, even you!"

He sat down on the broad step. "Teach me, then. Exactly what is a concerto?" He gestured to her to join him.

She dropped lightly to the step beside him. "A concerto is a drama in music. There's a soloist—and an orchestra, like the chorus in a Greek tragedy."

"Ah. So a continually changing balance of power?"

"Can't take the soldier out of the man, I see. Let's say a competitive spirit." She shifted casually to put more space between them. "A concerto typically has three movements. The first is highly dramatic. The orchestra introduces the theme while the soloist reflects upon it."

*Not unlike this mission*, thought Beckett.

"The second movement has the slower, more personal melody of the soloist."

*That's you*, he told her silently.

"In the finale, the tempo picks up. Soloist and orchestra join together, pressing on to a triumphant conclusion." He saw the heat brush her face once more as she heard the unintentional sensuality of her words.

"I could hear the passion in Law's concerto. Somehow he changes the notes and goes from wonder to sorrow..."

She stared at him. "You really should give Mozart a try, Colonel."

"You talk about Mozart the way I talk about a beautiful woman." Suddenly intrigued, he flashed a look at her. "I'll listen to Mozart, ma'am, if you'll spend a night with B.B. King."

"Blues?"

"The best. His albums are at my place in Virginia."

She rose gracefully and held out her hand to him. "B.B. for Mozart. You've got yourself a deal, Colonel Beckett."

They shook hands solemnly.

She said, "You remind me of my son. He's classically trained, but loves jazz and blues."

"A kid with taste. I'd like to meet him."

"He'd like you, too." He heard the sudden surprise in her words.

A sound from the balcony level caught their attention as an usher unlocked the theatre doors.

"Don't even *think* about it, Mrs. O'Shea."

But already she was running up the steps.

His eyes darkened as he followed her. Damned knee was already killing him. It was all uphill with Maggie O'Shea.

* * *

In the shadows of the storage room, Dane illuminated his watch. After three! Where was she? He stretched his legs, then clenched and unclenched his fingers. *He needed to get out of this fucking closet.*

Concentrate on the woman. It was always more exciting to balance on the edge. To hunt, to play a game with his prey, torture it, then perhaps let it think it was free.

* * *

Maggie and Beckett stood alone on the shadowed, dusty stage of the darkened theatre. Behind them, the balconies and courtyards of sixteenth-century Verona waited to come alive for the star-crossed young lovers. Beyond the dim footlights, the sumptuous horseshoe-shaped auditorium glinted with opera-red silks and velvet and five levels of gilded boxes.

Beckett's breath whistled in appreciation as he raised his eyes to the color-swirled ceiling adorned by Chagall. "Beautiful," he murmured.

"The larger operas are performed in the Bastille now." Maggie gestured towards the great crystal chandelier. "But this theatre was the inspiration for *The Phantom of the Opera*. His river is still here, beneath the theatre, five levels down." She stopped. "Why are you looking at me like that?"

"I was just wondering what it's like to perform in a place like this. How do you make something so beautiful out of thin air? Where does it come from?"

"Mendelssohn was inspired by a ruined Edinburgh chapel, Villa-Lobos by birds in a Brazilian jungle. Beethoven composed the Emperor Concerto while the French bombarded Vienna. Mahler added drums to his Tenth Symphony after weeping at a funeral cortege..."

"I meant *you*," said Beckett. "Where does music come from inside you?"

She was quiet for a long moment. Then she said, simply, "Music chose *me*, Colonel. My body pulses with music. I wake up with rhythms singing in my head. Music is the last sound I hear before I sleep."

"Tell me," he said. "Tell me what it's like."

She was still as a painting—remembering. Then she gestured toward the velvety box seats high in the shadows. "They're empty now. But imagine the moment of darkness before the curtain goes up, the moment when anything can happen. The theatre is full of expectant faces, like stars across the night sky, anticipating the magic."

Her low voice took on a dreamy quality. "You stand in the wings, waiting. The only sound is your heart beating in your ears. Then the heavy curtain slides open. You walk out onto the stage—always from the left, of course, the way one reads a book." As she spoke, she walked slowly, head high, back straight, toward the front center of the stage. "Applause echoes around you. Then the bow—just an acknowledgement, really—and perhaps a small gesture toward someone in the box seat above you."

Unable to take his eyes from her face, Beckett watched as Maggie raised a hand to her braid and shook her hair free. Caught in her memories, she bowed slowly, regally, from the waist toward the empty seats. Her hair fell forward like shining water.

He looked at her, a tiny figure in jeans and a faded blue sweatshirt on the vast empty stage. For a moment he imagined her standing in the spotlight in a long, flowing gown, with roses strewn at her feet.

"Beautiful," he murmured once more.

Her dark eyes were dreamy, turned inward, as if she was listening to some far-away music. "He always sat in the left box seat, close to the stage," she explained. Her hand stroked the cotton of the large sweatshirt that engulfed her. Beckett realized, suddenly, that it was a man's shirt. Her husband's.

"My husband was brilliant and passionate and larger than life, an Irish rogue with big gentle hands." Her voice dropped an octave. "Death swooped down on him just like some tragic last scene of grand opera. One second, and all that incredible energy and life force suddenly disappeared." Her words died in her throat. "He was only fifty-seven when he died. We never had a chance to say goodbye."

"I'm..." Becket stopped, painfully aware that no words could take that look from her face.

She spun in a slow circle, as if she wanted to drink in the sight and smell and feel of the dusky stage one last time. Stopping abruptly, she moved away from him. *Now what the devil?*

An old practice piano, scarred and stained, keys yellowed with use, stood in the far corner of the dim stage. She seemed helpless against the force that drew her. It was as if the instrument called to her in some ancient siren's language, drawing her to the keys the way the moon draws the tides. Inexorable. Inevitable.

Once more, her words echoed in his head. *For a musician, music is essential as air.*

He watched as she stopped, smoothed her hand over the wood, hesitated, finally pressed one narrow finger on an ivory key. The middle C note sounded, loud and unnerving as a scream in the silent theatre.

"It's out of tune," she murmured to herself. She sat down on the scarred bench and let her fingers rest on the silent keyboard. "The last time I performed in concert—it was New York, early October—I played Liszt's Hungarian Rhapsody No. 2. The C-sharp minor. Johnny was there, and my son." She closed her eyes. "The lights dim. You arch your hands above the keys, let everything flow out of you except the music."

He had to will himself not to reach out and touch her.

"Sometimes, in a darkened concert hall like this, the magic takes over. It's just you and the piano. The ceiling floats away, and the music takes you."

Her hands dropped to her sides and she sat, still and stricken, staring at him.

"Music expresses what is too deep for words," she said, so softly he could barely hear her. "It's the language of the soul. The piano was my anchor, Colonel. Now I'm...adrift. There is no music for me now."

"The music is still there, waiting. Tell me what you'll play," he demanded, "when the music comes back."

"Beethoven!" she flashed at him. "The Emperor Concerto, the Eroica, the Appassionata." He could hear the raw hurting in her voice. "Beethoven gave us anger in music. Chopin was a poet, Schumann was mad, Mozart lyrical. But Beethoven gave us rage and pain. He bared his soul. He gave us desolation."

She bowed her head, overcome.

"Keep talking," he urged.

"He lost *his* music, too." Her eyes were stricken. "Beethoven turned completely deaf before the age of forty. Yet he insisted on conducting his own music even when his wild gestures threw the orchestra completely off course."

Pain shimmered and broke in her voice. "When he conducted his Ninth Symphony for the first time in Vienna—his incomparable Choral—he kept conducting long after the orchestra finished. The contralto had to grasp his sleeve and direct his attention to the wildly clapping hands and waving handkerchiefs."

"It won't be like that for you."

"I was playing the piano while my husband was dying. I chose my *music*—"

The shock of her words hit him like a fist. "Your husband died because he was looking for your godson."

She shook her head. "Maybe it's not possible to have both art and love. A soloist is always alone." Abruptly, she turned her back on the piano.

He watched her walk away from him, across the darkened stage toward the wings.

# CHAPTER FORTY-TWO

The key turned in the lock and instantly he was alert. She was back.

Very quietly, Dane moved closer to the hidden door, tense and ready to spring. If Magdalena O'Shea was an American agent, she would be cautious, inspecting the room carefully.

"*Merci bien,* Lieutenant Henri."

A man's murmured farewell, the sound of a door closing. She was alone. Suddenly she moved into his line of sight. A small crystal lamp illuminated her face.

*It seems she hangs upon the cheek of night like a rich jewel in an Ethiop's ear.* The words suddenly swirled in his head. He was Romeo once again, seeing his Juliet for the first time at the Capulet feast.

Juliet moved out of vision.

A click. Faint music. The Madrigals, arriving at the hall for the Capulet's banquet.

He shook his head to clear his thoughts. It was Chopin, not Madrigals. No London stage, no darkened theatre, but a hotel room on the Left Bank. Sounds of movement. Drawers opening and closing. Packing, fair Juliet?

Her voice, placing a call to a Boston hospital in the United States. Asking for Lucinda Jacobs' room. The woman had survived? A mistake. It won't happen again.

A sigh of frustration, a door opening. The sound of water. He closed his eyes and saw her small, boyish body in the shower. He imagined her, slippery with scented soap, hot water running in shiny rivers down over her flat stomach.

He crushed her scarf tightly in his fingers. It would be so easy. Grab her from behind, slip the scarf around her mouth to keep her from screaming, take her right there on the tiled floor. Or perhaps he would take her in the shower, standing up, under the hot stinging water. Yes. Tiny, pointed breasts pushing against his skin. Lifting her, slippery and struggling, impaling her against the wet tiles. She was so small.

He smiled at his body's quick response to his fantasies. Huge and aching and ready for her. He moved silently into her bedroom.

*Yes*, he thought. *Why not?*

He stopped in front of the bathroom door.

The blade of the Laguiole pressed against his hip, as hard and demanding as the erection in his loins. She would tell him what he wanted to know. He could make a woman say anything.

His hand closed on the brass doorknob.

# CHAPTER FORTY-THREE

"Aix-en-Provence?" In the small CIA office near the Louvre, Simon Sugarman turned to Beckett. "I knew Maggie would come through for us. When do you leave?"

"Tomorrow, early. Henri took her back to the hotel."

Beckett lifted the soft blue sweatshirt Maggie had forgotten when she returned to her hotel, then tossed it onto the chair. "Or so she promised. She's like a long-tailed cat in a room full of rocking chairs." He gazed at the Golden, who was curled, shivering and panting, beneath the desk. "I'm leaving the dog here with you, Sugar. He wants nothing to do with me."

"No way, Mike. I'm outta here. Got the team focused on finding a 'G. Black' now, thanks to la Maggie. And I'm headed south to Hyères, to follow up on that art gallery where Vanessa Durand sent John O'Shea."

"Something doesn't feel right about that story, Sugar. About her..."

"You don't think she's just an innocent art gallery owner either?"

The phone on the table jangled. The skittish Golden jolted, backed further under the desk as both men reached for the receiver.

"Beckett here. What's going on?" He listened with absolute concentration. "Okay, I want you guys to stay on her family like a June bug on a hot mare." He hung up the telephone. "Luze Jacobs gets out of the hospital today."

Sugarman's eyes were hooded. "She doesn't know how lucky she is."

"Her surgeon said she was wearing some kind of stiff corset that deflected the knife."

"A knife..."

Their eyes met.

"A Laguiole. The team finally got to question her. Congratulations, Sugar. Your quarry has taken the bait."

Sugarman waved a dismissive hand. "What about Maggie's kid?"

"Brian O'Shea and his wife are safe on Cape Cod. I assigned a unit to guard them as soon as I heard about the attack on Jacobs."

"Did Jacobs give a description?"

"He wore a stocking over his face. But he called her Titania."

"Shakespeare!" Sugarman snapped his fingers. "Come to Mama, baby."

"Goddamn it, Sugar, he's a cobra and Maggie O'Shea is his rabbit! He's after her. And he's had more than enough time to fly to France. If he knows she's in Paris..."

"Sometimes in this work, the innocents have to get hurt so that we can stop the bad guys. You know it, Mike. Who's to say what's right and what's wrong?"

Beckett looked over at the Golden as he reached for his cell phone. "I know," he muttered. "You think I'm Gepetto tossing sweet Pinocchio into the wood chipper."

*Damned dog wasn't wrong.*

\* \* \*

In the Left Bank hotel room on Rue Christine, a cloud of hot steam surged over Dane as he inched open the bathroom doorway.

The sharp buzz of the telephone sounded behind him.

His hand dropped from the doorknob. Another ring. The shower stopped.

He moved quickly across the bedroom carpet and disappeared behind the Chinese screen.

Dashing footsteps. "Luze? Hello? Oh. Yes, Colonel. Sorry, I was hoping for another call." Dane could hear the disappointment in her voice.

*Colonel?* Intrigued, Dane pressed closer to the crack of the screen. She was so close that he could breathe in her flowered scent. He'd taken his mirrored glasses off, and he smiled, knowing his strange golden irises glowed dangerous as tiger's eyes.

"...pack after the theatre so I'll be ready to leave for Aix first thing in the morning."

*Aix.* Dane froze. She was going to Aix with a colonel?

More words, too low to understand. Speak louder, he cursed her. Then her voice, clear and shocking. "If we find Gideon..."

*Gideon.* Dane's face hardened with shock. That was why the picture in her dresser was so familiar. Why Victor wanted her. *But why was she searching for Gideon?*

"Meet you now? But I need to..."

A meeting? Speak louder, my angel.

"...bags will be with the concierge." Her voice was angry. "Two hours. Yes, fine, I'll lock the door and stay put!" There was a crack as she disconnected the call.

"Like hell I will," she said aloud to the empty room.

Dane heard the bathroom door close once more. So, she was going to meet this mysterious colonel. Someone Dane wanted very much to see. She would be easy to follow. Then...Aix-en-Provence. *Closer to Victor. But why?*

No time for games now. He had to identify the colonel. And determine their business in Provence. He moved quietly toward the door, then stopped to look back at the ivory nightgown draped over bed.

"Don't forget to pack that bit of satin, fair Juliet," he whispered. "You and I still have unfinished business together."

The mirrored glasses dropped like a silver curtain over his eyes as he disappeared into the empty hallway.

# CHAPTER FORTY-FOUR

Maggie stood in the Jardins du Luxembourg on the Left Bank. At the end of a narrow pool, the Medici Fountain dripped under a leafy arch of green. Soft sunlight spun down through the trees, and she watched the water shine and darken like a Monet painting in ever-changing patterns of light and shadow. Today, the calm water held no nightmare images of jagged rocks or shattered sailboats.

The colonel would be furious with her for going out. But his warnings sounded so unbelievable in this quiet, sunlit glade.

The hell with Beckett's rules. She needed to be doing something other than hiding away in a garret bedroom grieving. Just for a little while, she needed to see people involved in the everyday unfolding of their lives—buying bread, reading to a child by the Seine. A stolen kiss in an outdoor café. Not worried about missing children, phantom lovers, lost music. Or a bomb in a crowded square.

The colonel's car would be pulling up to her hotel soon. Use the time. She hurried across the sweeping terrace, past the gardeners pruning the orange trees, past the blank-eyed French queens carved in stone.

Just ahead, a tangle of young French school children squealed and clapped in delight. The Théâtre des Marionnettes, Maggie realized with pleasure as she saw the colorful slapstick action of the puppets.

"*Guignol!*" cried a little boy with a high-pitched voice to the most famous puppet in France. "*Prenez-garde!*"

The cry of the child followed her, a warning note sounding in the flute-like voice. "*Regardez! En arriere...*" Look behind you! Maggie swung around.

A bright puppet waving a huge club advanced on the unsuspecting Guignol. At the edge of her vision, a man in the crowd turned his head quickly away. Tall, with long, wheat-blond hair under a brimmed hat. A sudden, vague sense of alarm washed over her. The man moved again. For a brief instant the sun flashed on mirrored glasses.

"Oh, God." Fear leaped at her. The wolf-faced man in the photograph. Her stomach contracted into a tight hard knot. She dropped her eyes and somehow had the presence of mind to remain still. When she raised her eyes again, the face was gone. Had he seen her?

She took a deep breath. Imagination? No. Get out of the park, quickly! Call the colonel. Where the hell was her cell? Back in the hotel room.

She forced herself to turn her back on the theatre. Was he behind her? Dear God, where could she hide? She gripped the card with Beckett's phone number, deep in her jeans pocket. Her eyes searched the open garden. Marionette theatre, playground, carousel, waffle stand. No public telephone, no help from the colonel now. She was on her own.

*Just hide, get out of sight.* Get away from this dangerous, open garden.

Bright painted horses slid past her. The gay organ music flowing from the carousel was speeding up. Without thought she jumped onto the spinning merry-go-round. Quickly she ducked down behind a moving horse.

Faces whirled by her, distorted, threatening, like grinning masks glimpsed from a rushing train.

There he was! A tall blond man, moving past the women who smoked and gossiped on the long benches. A bell rang. The horse beneath her hand lurched, stopped.

What now? She scanned the park, saw the pale globes that marked the Luxembourg Metro entrance. The trains! Her fingers searched for a Metro token. *Hurry.*

She jumped off the merry-go-round, ran across the slippery grass toward a group of Sorbonne students in tight black t-shirts. She slipped among the backpacks, moved with them. With one last backward glance at the crowded garden, she clattered down the Metro stairs.

\* \* \*

Dane stared after her hurrying figure as she disappeared down the Metro steps.

He hadn't expected her to turn so suddenly. Did you see me, Juliet? Did you recognize my face? He pulled off the bush hat and moved toward the Metro entrance.

\* \* \*

The down escalator carried her deep underground.

Maggie ran down a long tiled corridor, twisted through the turnstile, felt the trembling of the tunnels beneath her feet. The screeching of a train tore into her, then vanished into the subterranean maze. Her mouth was dry with fear.

What now? The bright route map was on the wall in front of her. Where was Beckett's office? Near the Louvre, he'd said. She heard the rumble of an approaching train. Lights swept across dark tracks. She ran down the steep stairway and boarded the train.

The doors slid closed and the train pulled from the station. Strangers closed in around her, locked with her now in the rushing steel tube. Blurred faces stared blankly at her, frozen for an instant in the harsh glare of station bulbs, then disappearing as the pitch-black tunnel swallowed the light.

Maggie realized that she was holding her breath. She raised her eyes to the crowd of faces. No tall blond man in sunglasses.

She felt a hand on her shoulder, whirled. An old woman, off balance by the rocking train. Maggie looked into the tired eyes. What would you do if I told you that a man is chasing me? Insanity.

They were slowing into a station. She studied the Metro map. She was on the Orange Line. Gare de St. Michel, Cité, then the big exchange at Châtelet. She could get to Beckett's office from there. Bright lights flashed by as the train picked up speed again, sped through the dark tunnel. She hated being trapped under the ground.

She turned her head. And saw the fair hair, heart-stoppingly unmistakable, reflected in the train's window at the far end of the car.

*Oh God, he was on the train.*

He raised his head and looked directly at her. He knows I recognized him! A sob escaped her throat as she pushed behind the safe broad shoulders of a fat muttering Frenchman.

When she looked again, the face was gone.

The train rumbled into the Cité station. *Get off the damned train!*

Ducking her head, she moved toward the sliding doors. She forced herself to stand still, staring at her own reflection in the dark glass, while riders hurried from the train. Eyes huge in the small white face. Wait, wait. A wave of people surged into the car. Almost... Just as the doors began to close, Maggie bent low, darted from the train, rudely pushed past the people standing by the door.

Now where? She was disoriented by the noise and shadows, the thick crush of people. She was surrounded by a sea of broad backs and shoulders.

The train began to pull away. She turned to search the moving car for a tall blond head. Oh God, where was he?

She swung her head, searching for a gendarme. High on the tiled wall she saw the "Sortie" sign. The exit.

"*Je m'excuse. Excusez-moi.*" The crowd closed in around her. She raised her voice. "*Pardonnez-moi*! Let me through, damn it!"

Over there. The escalator to the street. Maggie's heart sank when she saw the people crowded together at the base of the moving stairway. Then, to her left, the doors of an elevator slid open. Without thought she ran into the metal box, wedging herself into the far corner behind a thick Frenchwoman wrapped in a stained white jacket.

Close the doors, close the doors. More people crowded into the elevator.

Above the open doors, a message flashed on and off. Maggie stared at the words. *"Dans huit secondes prochaine departe."* In eight seconds the elevator doors would close. Eight more seconds? Oh God.

Six, now. She kept her eyes riveted on the flashing number under the sign. Five. More bodies crowded into the box. She heard a shout from somewhere out on the platform, to the left. Him? Four. Three.

Running footsteps. Two.

A voice. Low, angry. *"Arretez!"*

No, don't wait! She pressed her back hard against the wall. The whine of a motor. Eyes riveted to the flashing numbers. *One!* The elevator doors began to slide closed. A man's hand grasped the edge of the metal door.

# CHAPTER FORTY-FIVE

Sugarman hung up his cell phone and turned to Beckett with an odd expression in his eyes.

"Isn't she ready yet?" asked Beckett.

"Henri says her luggage is in the lobby. But she's nowhere to be found."

"Jesus, Sugar! Where the hell was Henri?"

"She asked him to get coffee for her. Take it easy, pal. She probably stepped into the courtyard."

"And I'm the bloody tooth fairy!"

"She told the concierge that she just needed some air and to tell Henri she would be back by four." Sugarman glanced down at his watch, then reached for his *International Tribune*. "Relax. Henri will find her. And it's only ten to four. Doc's a smart woman, she knows what she's doing. Give her a chance."

Beckett turned away to look at the Golden. "Something's not right," he murmured.

* * *

The hand clutched the elevator door. Maggie saw a flash of sapphire as she closed her eyes. The mechanism lurched. She heard a guttural curse. The heavy doors slammed shut. The elevator began to rise.

Only moments of safety, she knew. He would run to the stairs. She kept her eyes on the closed doors. The elevator shuddered, bumped to a stop. Would he be waiting? She was propelled by the crowd out into the bright sunshine.

The air vibrated around her with high, unexpected sound. A small plaque nailed to a tree told her that she was in the tiny marketplace of Louis Lepine. The piercing sounds were *birds*!

Birds everywhere. The air was quick with their cries. She froze, surrounded by cages of every size, stacked like giant blocks ten feet high. She was in the bird market.

The cages were arranged in a maze of dark narrow aisles, stacked higher than her head. Quickly she hid behind a wall of screeching jays. *God, why had she forgotten her phone!*

She turned left, then right, deeper into the fluttering maze. The high leafy trees blocked the sun, trapping her in sharp-edged, shrieking darkness.

Disoriented, Maggie ran down the dark paths. She looked frantically around, her instincts primitive—she needed a safe, covered place. A place to hide.

*There.* Above the treetops to her right, she saw the spire of Notre Dame. *The church,* she thought. *I can hide there.* With a last backward glance, she ran past the high stacked cages.

* * *

She'd gone off the grid.

Beckett paced angrily back and forth in the small CIA office. The argument had been fierce but swiftly decided. Four o'clock had come and gone, with no Maggie O'Shea. Something *was* wrong. Sugarman had gone to Maggie's hotel, Beckett staying in the office to wait for her call. Hadn't he given her his goddamned cell number? Could the office phone be their only link to Maggie? Dammit, he had to do something!

He stared down at the silent phone. Call. Just call me, Maggie.

But what if she couldn't? What if she was in trouble? It would be so easy. A car coming forward, a voice saying "The Colonel sent me," a hand reaching out to grasp her wrist—

His eyes fell on the blue sweatshirt. He grabbed it, shoved it toward the Golden's nose. "You're a Retriever, damn it! This is her scent, you like Maggie. *Find* her!"

The dog raised his head, sniffed, fur rippling. Then he began to pace, lurching back and forth in front of the window with a low, rumbling growl.

Beckett stared at the distressed Golden, then let the blue shirt fall to the floor. "Christ, what's the matter with me?" He blinked at the telephone. Ring, damn you. Ring!

\* \* \*

It was dark and cool among the bird cages. Dane moved slowly through the screeching maze, searching each shadowy aisle. The market wasn't very crowded. He would find her.

Had she recognized him? He still wasn't sure. Maybe she'd thought he was just some French thug. He bent to search under a table of cages. She had to be here somewhere. He turned a corner and looked down into the frightened eyes of Magdalena O'Shea.

\* \* \*

Maggie cried out in fear, twisting away, but iron fingers shot out, gripping her shoulders and spinning her around to face him. She looked around wildly, searching for help, pulling against him. But the aisle of cages was empty.

"Let me go!"

"Don't scream again, Juliet," said the man with the wolf's face. "I don't want to hurt you."

The quiet words, spoken in English, chilled her. Maggie looked up into the glasses and saw her own eyes, dark with fright, reflected in the mirrors. A sudden warning flashed in her head. *Don't let him know you recognize him!* She forced herself to look at him blankly. "Who are you?" she whispered. "Please—My name's not Juliet! You have the wrong person."

He only smiled and dragged her back into the shadows. Hard arms closed around her in a terrifying mockery of a lover's embrace, locking her against his chest.

Her arms were trapped against him and she felt the scream of panic coming. "What do you want with me?"

He lowered his head until his lips were hot against her ear. He smiled as he told her, slowly and deliberately in a silky whisper, exactly what he wanted. "I'll tie your hands behind your back and touch you the way you need to be touched."

"No! Oh God, you filthy..." She began to struggle frantically against him.

He held her effortlessly.

Terrified by his strength, she fought to free her hands, but his left arm held her in a painful, unbreakable grip. His right hand dropped to her waist, moved up under her t-shirt to close over her breast. The rough fingers hurt her. She cried out again with the unexpected pain and kicked out with her legs.

Brutal fingers covered her lips before she could scream again. A large ring flashed blue in the light. Then his mouth covered hers, insistent and demanding, forcing her mouth open, crushing her lips against his teeth.

She bit him.

He cursed, hit her hard across the face.

"Help," she screamed. "Help me!" Maggie felt herself spun around with such tremendous force that she crashed into the wall of cages. Hot black pain stabbed through her.

*Voices, coming closer*!

Her attacker turned, loosened his grip. Suddenly free of his arms, she flung out her right hand. She felt the glasses spin from his face. Then her knuckles smashed into a cage. Some inner musician's voice screamed, *Your hands, watch out for your hands*! No hope for it. She locked her fingers through the wire mesh and pulled with all her strength. He reached for her wrist.

Two women appeared at the end of the aisle just as the precariously stacked cages shifted, tilted. She felt them give and pulled harder, frantic now. This time several of the huge, top-heavy cages dislodged and came crashing down on the man. The iron hands fell away from her as the birds shrieked in terror. She felt a sharp edge graze her cheek and doubled over as a small cage hit her shoulder. *Protect your hands*! A latch snapped and dozens of small bright birds whirled and beat around her head. She heard the man growl with pain.

For a brief, terrifying moment she looked at her attacker.

Then she turned and ran.

Above her head, the freed birds lifted into the high clear sky over the towers of Notre Dame.

# CHAPTER FORTY-SIX

Beckett stood at the window of the small office and stared down at the cars inching along the narrow Rue des Halles. No taxi pulling to the curb. No dark-haired woman in jeans and a music t-shirt hurrying along the sidewalk.

*Why did I leave her alone? What the devil did she think she was doing? She'll be on the next plane home if I have to carry her to the airport myself. Damn the woman!*

He fixed his gaze on the Golden. *If only—*

His cell phone rang, and he lunged for it. "Beckett."

"Colonel! Thank God. He's here, in Paris!"

His breath whooshed out as the Golden gave a low whine and hopped toward him. "Whoa, Mrs. O'Shea. Where are you, and are you hurt?"

"I'm in a souvenir shop"—she hesitated, and he pictured her glancing around—"across the square from Notre Dame. I've borrowed a phone, I...it's him!"

Her fear hammered at him across the wires. He shouted, "Who, Maggie? Who?"

"It's the blond man, Michael! The one with the sunglasses—in Simon's photograph! He followed me here, he—"

*Oh sweet Christ.* Some part of him registered that she'd used his first name. "Listen to me, Mrs. O'Shea. I'm coming for you right now. Just stay where you are. Wait for me."

"No! I'm too exposed here. I'm going to hide in the church."

"Not Notre Dame, Maggie! It's the first place he'll look—"

A harsh, ragged breath. And then, "The gargoyles, Michael! I'll be—"

*Gargoyles?* "Stay away from the tower, Maggie!" he shouted into the receiver. "Don't get trapped up there—"

The dial tone buzzed in his ear.

\*\*\*

The blond man was only yards away from the souvenir shop, walking slowly across the Square du Parvis toward the small row of stores.

She slammed down the phone and sank to the floor behind a tall stand of post cards. Quickly she pulled off her bright sweater, dropping it behind her. She pulled a cotton scarf from around her neck, struggling to tie it over her hair. *Hurry*. She took a ragged breath and inched toward the door.

He was entering the souvenir shop.

She hunched down, praying that no one would look at her. He was headed toward the rear of the shop. She waited a heartbeat, then, staying low, ran out into the open square.

She looked around wildly. One hundred feet above the crowded square, she saw people moving among the gargoyles on the high carved gallery that linked the two gothic towers of Notre Dame.

The tiny square, dominated by the great stone face of Notre Dame, was congested with tourists. Head down, she ran to the base of the north tower. Moving under the shadowed portal, she turned to look back, just as the man appeared in the souvenir shop doorway. Something bright orange was in his hand. Her sweater. He dropped the cardigan to the cobblestones and moved with quick strides across the square toward the cathedral.

She stood frozen in the tower entrance, watching him come towards her. A laughing group of Italian tourists crowded past her up the steps. Without conscious thought she turned and followed them through the stone portal of the north tower into the cool sheltering darkness.

The small white sign said Five Euros. Maggie dropped the coins into a gnarled hand, passed beyond the gate, and began to climb the steep circular stairs.

She hesitated once, looking back down. The tower's curved stone steps were so narrow. Would she be trapped? More women crowded behind her, calling out in Spanish, pushing her forward. Too late now. She ran up the stairs.

Several hundred steps later, breathless, she emerged into the hot sun and wind high above Paris.

The gallery was a narrow, fenced-in walkway across the roof of Notre Dame to the south tower. There was no place to hide, and no exit behind her—only the graceful spire and the huge, intricate flying buttresses that supported the cathedral's roof.

She forced herself to move out onto the walkway. Perched at intervals along the balustrade, protected from falling by meshed netting, were the ancient, fantastic stone figures of Notre Dame—the birds, demons, and monsters who for centuries had guarded the cathedral while gazing out over the rooftops of Paris. Up close, the twisted gargoyle faces were agonized and evil.

The gallery was crowded with tourists. For the first time in an hour, among all these smiling ordinary people, Maggie felt safe. Moving to the edge of the carved balustrade, she peered cautiously over the edge. One hundred feet below her, the Square du Parvis ebbed and flowed with people. Too far down to see faces clearly. She glanced toward the exit. Should she take the stairway down the south tower? *Where was he?*

She watched the gallery entrance. What if he had seen her enter the tower? She touched her throbbing cheek, surprised to find a trace of blood on her fingertips. She shivered as she remembered his hands on her body, the filthy words he had whispered in her ear. Movement in the doorway. *Oh please no.*

Several tourists stared openly at her, and she raised her hand to hide the blood on her cheek. Quickly she moved behind a large, hideous stone bird and shrank against it.

"Not my day for birds," she said under her breath.

Fifteen minutes later she saw him emerge, squinting, into the sunlight. She took a deep shuddering breath and stepped out from behind the gargoyle to face him.

# CHAPTER FORTY-SEVEN

"Colonel!" The whisper came from the far end of the parapet. "Over here."

He limped slowly toward her in the hot white light, winded, leaning heavily on his cane. Then he stopped and looked down at her, at the cut lip and purpling bruise on her cheek, at the blood on her hands and face and the torn knee of her jeans. Her whole body was shaking.

His hands closed gently over her shoulders. "Mrs. O'Shea. You're okay now. I've got you." The tight anger in his voice was barely controlled. He hadn't realized he'd been so afraid until he looked down at her.

She gripped his arms with surprising strength. "Forget about me, did you get him?"

"My first job is to look after you, ma'am."

"Then he's still out there."

Her eyes were dark with fear, her skin ashen and slashed with crimson. Christ, when was the last time he had been this frightened for someone? Afghanistan. He shook his head. "Just what the devil did you think you were doing, Mrs. O'Shea?"

"I found the man in the photograph for you. I...he..."

She was close to hysteria. He bent toward her the way a father might comfort a frightened child, and spoke slowly. "You got away from him. You're safe now."

"Not safe. Scared." She shook her head back and forth. "I saw his eyes. Yellow, like antifreeze." She shivered. "He quoted Shakespeare, he called me his Juliet..."

Very gently, Beckett reached out to slip the ridiculous scarf back from her tangled hair. "Did he hurt you?"

She took a deep breath, and he could see the effort for control. "No, not really, I'm fine." Now the low voice was restrained, almost indifferent. But the huge eyes gave her away.

He had to will himself not to touch her face. "Your cheek is bleeding."

She raised a hand to hide the bruises. Forcing a weak grin, she said, "I guess I went ass over teakettle."

*Who says that?* "Tell me," he said.

"He hit me. He...put his hands on me. He had a knife, he said he wanted to...he put his mouth on mine. I didn't think anything could frighten me so much."

*He'd hit her.* Very deliberately, as if to erase the other man's touch, Beckett's thumb traced her swollen lips. "He won't hurt you again. Count on it."

She shook her head, dizzy and disoriented in the hot sunlight. She tilted toward him.

He caught her, felt the trembling of her body beneath the thin fabric of her shirt. "I've got you," he said.

She pulled away. "I've been a damned fool," she whispered. "I thought I could take care of myself. But I ran *away* from him, I didn't fight. I was so scared. I wasn't brave enough. Just once, I want to be able to *run toward*, like you do."

He looked down at her. How could she not know how strong she was? "You ran into eight lanes of Parisian traffic just hours ago to save a dog! Now you've poked a sleeping tiger, Mrs. O'Shea, and you're still standing. That's saying something."

"But I didn't..."

"Courage isn't the absence of fear. It's understanding that there is something more important than fear."

"Like finding my godson." A smile flickered, and she took a

deep breath to regain control. "So, Colonel, are all your investigations like this?"

His laughter startled them both. "I rescue Yankee piano players from cathedral spires at least once a month, Mrs. O'Shea," he said.

"You laughed. And your face didn't break! You should try it more often."

"Come here, dammit, you're still shivering." He drew her out of sight, into the shadows, then removed his jacket and dropped it over her shoulders. "What is it?"

"The gun." She was staring at the 9mm Beretta automatic in the holster beneath his arm.

"I've been trying to tell you, Mrs. O'Shea."

"You've killed people."

"Yes."

She nodded bleakly. "Oh."

"Bad people." He scowled down at her. "I've never hurt anyone who didn't deserve it. I try to save lives, not take them. But, sometimes it's hurt or be hurt, kill or be killed. And when you kill someone, anyone, you still have to carry it with you for the rest of your life."

She looked away. "I shouldn't have asked you that."

"The life you choose has a way of becoming who you are. I told you, I live in a world of shadows. Cold, black shadows. And you're surrounded by light."

She drew a sharp, quick breath. "Now here's the part where you say 'Go home' again."

"Because I want you away from the darkness."

"The decision to stay or go is still mine. I refuse to be a victim."

That damned defiance again. "But your physical well-being is my business." He thought of the young girl he'd lost in Kandahar. "If you're going to let your heart rule over your head, Mrs. O'Shea, then you shouldn't be here."

"Okay, got it. Head, not heart."

He shook his head. "That bastard tracked you, found you to-day. He could find you again. He's let you know he can reach you."

"But *why*?"

"Because he knows you can identify him now. Somehow," Beckett lied, "he knows you've seen that photograph." *Damn you, Sugar.* "Now you know he's connected to Orsini—and you've seen his face. That makes you a problem. His problem. So he's af-ter you."

"I won't let him stop me. It's not right."

*Right*? I don't know what the devil's right anymore, he thought. Finding that kid is right. But—she didn't get that she still wasn't safe.

"You know the danger is real. I've got to get to Aix. If you come, there'll be no turning back. I won't ask again. Are you ready to go home?"

"This search has given me a reason to get up every morning. Until now, all I wanted was to hide in Boston, curled up in a tight little ball." She touched her bruised mouth. "I know this is not a game, Colonel. But I won't change my mind."

"Things could get worse in Aix," he warned her.

"There's an old newspaper photograph framed on the wall in my shop. It shows the crumbling, bombed-out city of Sarajevo in 1992, shells of exploded buildings everywhere. An old man in for-mal evening wear is sitting outdoors on a folding chair in a square that's been reduced to rubble. He's holding a cello between his knees, playing Albinoni's Adagio in honor of the dead. Humanity, in the midst of violence."

"You do have a way," Beckett murmured, "of finding beauty in a brutal world."

"Music demands that we remember," she whispered. "Some-times you just have to keep going, remember what's important." She looked out over the Seine. "I know now that I need to do this. Not just for my son and my godson. For myself."

He stared at her for a long moment. "Then we need to leave Paris immediately. We'll drive through the night."

"Aix marks the spot."

Just shoot me, he thought. "But from now on, Mrs. O'Shea, there will be no running off. I'm the soldier. You are the piano player."

She stood in front of him, small, back straight, bruised and smiling grimly. Brave as hell.

"What am I going to do with you?" The blinding honesty in his voice stunned them both.

"How about you finally start calling me Maggie?"

"Boundaries, remember? *I'm* the professional."

She looked at him for a long moment. Then, "Right. Boundaries. Okay, *Colonel*. Then how about finding me a hot bath and a brandy? At least..."

"At least, what?"

"We'll always have Paris, Colonel."

She was the damndest, most complicated woman he'd ever known. "Do you come with instructions, Mrs. O'Shea?"

* * *

Dane stood outside a small patisserie near the cathedral, punching numbers into his cell phone. He'd lost her. She was probably with that colonel of hers. But not for long. He'd find her. He'd find them both.

The little bitch had outfoxed him. He fingered the gash above his eye. The next time they met, she wouldn't be so lucky.

The phone rang six times. Then a female voice came on the line. "*Oui?*"

"Lapin."

"Dane? Where are you?"

"Paris. I want you to go to Ménerbes. I should be there before dawn."

Silence. Then, "Tonight? Please, you know I can't—"

"I want you, Lapin. In the bedroom, waiting for me."

Once more he touched the gash above his eye and thought of Magdalena O'Shea. The boyish body, the silky nightgown. The feel of her under his fingers.

"Wear the red silk, Lapin. And the stockings."

"No, Dane. I won't be there."

"Yes," he told her. "You will. You don't have a choice." He clicked off his phone and walked out into the bright square.

# CHAPTER FORTY-EIGHT

The dark bar at the Four Seasons Hotel on Pennsylvania Avenue thrummed with the voices and secrets of Washington's pre-dinner crowd.

In the corner near the fireplace, the CIA's Deputy Director of Operations sat hunched in the shadows like a vulture waiting for its next victim. Alone on the deep-cushioned sofa, he drank one hundred-year-old brandy and watched the shifting faces from beneath his hooded eyes. The silver wheelchair was folded on the carpet beside him.

He raised his hand in greeting but turned away to discourage conversation. Two senators, several congressmen and one congresswoman, a high-profile judge, White House aides all dressed alike in the blue blazer uniform, a few would-be Woodwards from the *Post*. All trying to save the world. Or sniff out its secrets.

And the biggest secret of all was right under their clueless collective noses...

He glanced at the *Post* reporter who'd broken the story of the attack near the French bistro where the Secretary of State was holding his meeting. You missed your Pulitzer by not digging deeper.

Orsini had struck again. The Secretary was safe—no great cause for celebration there—but a group of Japanese tourists by the fountain had not been so lucky. And that damaging leak of the name of the CIA's Paris Chief of Station—damn Orsini for firing one more shot across the CIA's bow.

And then there was the murder at the Kennedy Center Opera House.

Victor Orsini was becoming a huge problem, a rogue elephant in the circus. The Admiral smiled grimly at the metaphor and scraped a hand across his jaw. His leathery palm made a whispery sound against his whiskers.

He had to have the names in that journal Sofia Orsini had hidden. Then he could take aim and destroy the rogue.

It had to be all over by his granddaughter's wedding day.

His hand shook as he drained the last inch of brandy. Fire ignited in his stomach, but he ignored the pain and signaled for another. The whole damned operation hinged on an innocent concert pianist who was no bigger than a minute. Hunched in the shadows of the fire-lit bar, the Admiral knew, suddenly, what he had to do.

A full brandy snifter was placed in front of him. He drank slowly, moving the chess pieces carefully in his head. Then he nodded and punched a number into his cell phone.

\* \* \*

Several thousand miles to the East, in Southern France, it was almost one a.m.

In the darkened bedroom, Victor Orsini was still awake, pacing.

The bombing in Paris had gone successfully. Worth the money he'd spent, one more move in his intricate game of chess. It would not be long now. He pictured the Admiral's face and smiled.

Victor slipped a CD into the Bose player, and the notes of Tchaikovsky's Violin Concerto in D spilled into the room. He heard the violin enter in its lowest register, and waited for the storm. His sister had always insisted that the fiendishly difficult solo was "un-violinistic."

But she had managed it.

He resumed his pacing. Back and forth. Back and forth.

Now the brilliant cadenza, the intensity, building to the great dash in double time for the finale. He turned up the volume and the huge notes tumbled like roaring thunder into the room.

People who spent so much time alone always filled the silence with music.

The lighted glass case in the corner of the bedroom drew him closer. Two rare music manuscripts rested on a deep blue velvet background. Pages from an authenticated Paganini Concerto that had been lost for three hundred years, and an original score of a Piano Concerto by Bach. His eyes moved to the third space, in the center of the case. Empty now. He stared down at the blue velvet lining. Months earlier, it had held his most important possession. A musical score, very old. Stained, marked. *Signed.* A violin concerto that had never been played. A concerto lost for centuries. *Meant for his sister...*

But his wife had stolen it. He turned away with an oath. Spiteful bitch. She had taken the concerto to hurt him. What had she done with it? Did you send it to your closest friend, Sofia? Did you send it to Magdalena O'Shea?

And that was not all Sofia had stolen. He glanced back at the darkly-glowing Rubens on the far wall. Behind it, his wall safe—found almost empty after Sofia disappeared. Did she know the value of what she had taken? The damage that the information in his journal could do?

Just beyond the case, on a small table deep in shadow, lay the del Gesù violin and bow. One of only two hundred del Gesù violins still remaining, the instrument was as beautiful and curved as a woman. He still could see a pale, narrow hand on the bow, still hear the notes that fell into the air like a silver river of sound...

That del Gesù was meant for you, *il mio amore.* He closed his eyes as the old pain, never far away, sliced sharply into him once more. Don't think of that night. *Don't think of her.*

He turned, forced his eyes to rest on the small, exquisite Monet on the far wall. One of the artist's studies of *The Street at Argenteuil.* A village street, bare tree limbs, huge flakes of swirling white snow. The image triggered a long forgotten memory, and he closed his eyes and let himself fall. It was 1985, *the year that changed everything*. He was in a small office in DC. It was snowing...

* * *

He stood by a bare desk looking out the one narrow window. Outside, on K Street, the snow swirled wildly. The calendar on the gray wall behind him, with its photograph of the Lincoln Memorial, showed the month of February, 1985. The newspapers were calling it "The Year of the Spy." Revelations of John Walker, Ronald Pelton, Edward Howard.

Washington was tense during the last days of CIA director William Casey. Orsini was deeply involved in Veil, the code name for the covert action compartment in the Reagan administration. Iran-Contra, Middle East assassination attempts, behind-the-scenes election upheavals in Europe, paramilitary worldwide operations. Secrets hidden under a veil. The list was endless.

Orsini paced back and forth in the small office, waiting to meet the new hotshot assistant deputy who would be taking over several of the Veil operations. The man rumored to be an aggressive operative, known only as The Admiral, who would push to expand the "off the shelf, secret runaway missions" that ran deep in the CIA bloodstream. What did The Admiral want with him?

Back and forth. Back and forth.

Outside, the snow whirled through the barren branches, turning everything to white. *Like a veil.*

Behind him, the door opened. Orsini turned. A man of perhaps forty entered, tall but stooped, with prematurely white, long hair secured at the nape of his neck and heavily hooded eyes.

"Orsini." The voice was deep, raspy as wet sand scraping over rocks.

"Admiral. What can I do for you?"

"I want to meet your sister."

# CHAPTER FORTY-NINE

Beckett drove well, but very fast. Already the black Fiat was two hundred miles south of Paris. The air was deep blue with the memory of twilight. The dog was asleep, twitching and occasionally whining in the rear seat. Nightmares.

*I get it, Dog.*

He glanced once again in his mirror—the headlights were still there, half a mile back—then down at the woman by his side. Her eyes were closed, the lashes dark fans against skin that was bruised and pale as bone. The long slim legs were drawn up beneath her in an innocent, vulnerable way. But tonight the words on her t-shirt carried a stark challenge. *Don't Shoot the Piano Player.*

Right, this *was* all about music. But it placed the beautiful pianist next to him at the very center of the storm. Not for the first time, he found himself wondering if it had been someone's plan all along to get her to Provence.

Damn it all. Why couldn't he shake the image of Maggie O'Shea on the rooftop of Notre Dame, those bright eyes blazing with defiance, caught against the glimmering sky.

He accelerated into the next curve.

* * *

Maggie was awake. She couldn't get the wolf-like face out of her mind. Couldn't stop the chilling voice from echoing in her head.

*I'll tie your hands behind your back and touch you the way you need to be touched.*

The Fiat swerved, braked, and her eyes shot open. Beckett had pulled the car off the road, into the shelter of a dark stand of fir trees. Out on the highway, headlamps speared the darkness, probed, moved on.

The Golden started, jumped to his feet, and thrust his head into the front seat between them. Maggie smiled as Beckett offered him a treat, then tossed an orange at her. "Dinner is served, ma'am."

She searched in her purse, found the small red army knife she'd taken from her checked luggage, and began to peel the fruit. "My son gave this to me when he was an Eagle Scout," she murmured, waving the shiny blade at him as she handed him a slice of orange. And then, "Don't you think it's time you tell me what's been worrying you since we left Paris?"

The first rays of moonlight slanted through the high pines in bars of soft, cloudy light. He glanced at the dog, opened the door. "Break time. Don't go far."

The Golden jumped awkwardly from the car and loped for the trees.

"Damned dog doesn't know he has only three legs." Then Beckett looked down at her. "You're right, Mrs. O'Shea. There *is* something you need to know."

"You're scaring me."

"The monster who attacked you today. Sugar and I think he's a professional killer. And the same man who hurt your friend Luze Jacobs."

"Luze," whispered Maggie, "was hurt because of the photograph I saw?"

"Yes."

"My God!" Her eyes flew to his, her voice urgent with new fear. "Brian?"

"Your son is fine. I swear it."

"You're certain?" She gripped his arm so tightly that her fingers turned white. "Colonel, if anything happens to my son...I couldn't bear it."

"He's safe, ma'am. I've had two men on the Cape since the attack."

She searched his face and saw something she needed to see. "But, that man today. He *had* me. He could have—"

"You're too useful running free," he told her. "And he may think you have something he wants." He waited.

"If I do have something, I don't know it." Her head came up sharply. "But as long as I stay here in France, that blond monster will stay here, too. Brian and his family will be safe."

Beckett stared at her. "You're making yourself the bait. He'll come after you."

"Isn't that what you really want?"

He looked at her as if he'd been punched. Without speaking, he whistled to the dog and turned on the engine. In moments they were driving south once more into the gathering darkness.

* * *

The Jaguar gleamed like liquid mercury in the moonlight.

Dane downshifted as he headed into the long curve that edged a dark copse of pines. Once more his eyes left the road to scan the dark countryside. His Juliet was on her way to Aix. He would find her there. And bring her to Victor.

When he was ready.

His foot pressed down on the accelerator. Soon he would reach Ménerbes, where another woman waited for him.

"One fire burns out another's burning," he murmured.

* * *

The music came from the grand piano on the edge of the beach. The night was black, flickering with rain. A ringing phone. Roaring waves. A pale hand breaking the water...

The Fiat swerved and Maggie jolted awake. Indigo shadows concealed the face of the man beside her. Large hands shifted on the steering wheel.

*Johnny? Is that you?*

Fine hairs on his knuckles glinted silver in the shadows and brought her wrenchingly back to the present. Strong scarred fingers. No wedding band.

*Not Johnny.* God, she hadn't thought of her husband once since—when?

Only silence in the dark Fiat. She moved restlessly.

"Having trouble sleeping, Mrs. O'Shea?"

"Your hands," she said simply. "I was dreaming. I saw your hands move in the shadows, and for a moment I thought..." She turned away. "I know my husband is dead. The moment I open my eyes each morning, it hits me. He's *gone.*"

"And you grieve all over again."

"Yes. Every damn morning, it's a stunning new loss. *Why am I alone in this bed?* And then I remember."

"*I wake and feel the fell of dark, not day,*" he quoted.

Her breath caught. "Whose words are those?"

"Gerard Manley Hopkins."

She nodded. "He understood. I glimpse Johnny's face in a crowded room, smell his cologne, hear his voice behind me. I dream that he's with me in the night, and reach for him..."

"You must have loved your husband very much."

"I still do, Colonel."

"In Iraq," he said, "I would dream of home." His eyes flicked to the rearview mirror, then back. "Those blue Virginia hills, an old hound dog named Red, fishing on a summer mornin', peaches big as fists piled on the grass..."

His easy drawl was soothing, the big hands strong and steady on the wheel. In the shadowed intimacy of the car Maggie was very aware of the man beside her. Dark antagonist—and gentle protector. Suddenly she wanted very much to tell him about the nightmares. Wanted him to take her in his arms and hold her so tightly that the dreams couldn't touch her.

*I've got you,* he'd said.

He made her feel safe.

She pulled her eyes away from his hands, cracked the window, and drew a deep breath. The air smelled of grapevines and wood smoke.

"I was never able to cry after my husband died," she said into the silence. "I'm full of unshed tears. Choking with them. But I can't cry."

"Numb," he murmured. "I know what it feels like to lose your way—and to not be real interested in finding it again."

She stared at him as if he'd just read her mind.

"But you've got to learn to live with loss. Because the ghosts will come no matter what." Beckett's gaze fixed on the Golden and he stopped speaking.

"I should have known Johnny was dead," she said. "You would think you would just *know*, when you love someone so much, that exact moment they draw their last breath."

"When you're ready, Mrs. O'Shea, you'll cry. Then, very slowly, you'll stop crying." He reached out as if to touch her. "Love runs deeper than grief."

"I don't know who I am without my music," she said bleakly. "I don't know who I am without my husband."

"Ready or not, one of these days life will come roaring back. You won't forget your husband. Those ghosts, they're a determined lot." The glimmer of a smile. "You've got to remember, it's not about death. It's about piecing your life back together after the unthinkable happens. You will move on. You will heal. You will play the piano again. And you will learn to love again."

She watched him shift down for a curve, then keep his hand on the seat between them. There was a disturbing sense of intimacy in the dark car. The air electric. His hand, so close to hers. She could almost feel the sparks leaping off his skin.

*Johnny, I need you tonight. Where are you?*

\* \* \*

The crush of her pain hit him hard, and he turned to her. He flexed his fingers, so close to hers, and sighed with frustration.

This physical attraction to Maggie O'Shea was so unexpected, so...disconcerting. Beckett looked down at her in the darkness and felt the faint, unfamiliar stirring of his heart.

It was the very last thing he wanted.

# CHAPTER FIFTY

SOUTH OF FRANCE. DAWN, JULY 8

Hidden by dense pines, the stone house on the hillside could not be seen from the Provençal village of Ménerbes.

A young woman stood by the open window, waiting for the dawn. The fire was in embers. Next to the silk-covered bed, candles guttered in a pair of candlesticks made of a stag's horns. A gilt-edged mirror reflected the flickering flames, the waiting bed, and the portrait over the fireplace, an oil of a woman in a golden gown whose hair glowed with black fire.

Somewhere out in the darkness a night bird sang a last song before the sunrise, but the young woman found no beauty in the sound.

She hated this room and the degrading, painful things he did to her here. The last time she had spat in his face and, in her rage, sworn to kill him. Her fury had only excited him. He had hurt her.

And yet she returned, again and again, when he called. Because he knew her secrets. Because he could take away the one thing she loved.

Behind her a door opened and closed softly. "Dane," she whispered.

Still she did not turn around. She heard his duffel bag drop to the floor, ice against crystal, the sound of pouring liquid, then his footsteps, coming closer.

A hand brushed the feathery hair on her neck. She felt the soft mustache rub against her skin.

"You're not wearing the scarlet nightgown, Lapin." Dane stood behind her, his chest pressed to her shoulder blades. His voice was as smooth as the silk of her shirt.

She looked down at her blouse and trousers. "I can't stay. Gideon wakes up so early..."

"Tell him you went for a sunrise walk." He laid long fingers lightly on her arm. Slowly, he rubbed them back and forth on her skin. Their intricate, sexual dance had begun.

"I shouldn't be here," she said.

He lifted his other hand and tangled his fingers in the short black hair, pulling her head back. He began to stroke the tight arch of her neck with his thumb.

Tense and wary, she tried to ignore the sensations he was arousing in her body. She wanted to pull away but felt powerless under his touch. Each time, her intense hatred became inextricably bound with desire.

The fingers moved down her neck, very slowly. Down the soft rise of her shirt to the hidden nipple. Now she did make an effort to pull away, but he only gripped her more tightly. "You know what I need, Lapin," he murmured hoarsely.

"Yes."

He squeezed her nipple beneath the silk. "There is a woman searching for Gideon. I want to know why, Lapin."

She twisted in his arms as his fingers continued to tease her. She could feel his arousal, thick and hard, rubbing against her. "What woman?" She gasped, tormented by his bruising fingers.

His hands stopped. "All in good time."

She tried to pull away. "Please."

"I want you to keep Gideon away from the festival."

She looked up at him with surprise. "Why? Don't make me think about Gid. Not here..." His right hand slipped under the silk and moved to circle a tingling breast. She moaned, grasped his hand, brought it to her mouth.

Dane smiled. "Tell me," he whispered, "does Gid ever send you flowers?"

"Flowers? Why do you..."

His fingers moved to her lips, silencing her. He pushed his thumb into her mouth, moving it slowly. "Don't question me, Lapin. Just answer."

Her teeth closed hard on his thumb and he wrenched her head back. "Bitch!"

Without warning he slipped a steel arm around her waist and lifted her roughly against his body so that her back was pressed against the hardness of his chest. No match for his great size and strength, she writhed against him helplessly. "Let go of me!"

He carried her, struggling, across the room until they stood in front of the full-length mirror. "Open your eyes," he commanded in his low, sensual voice.

She watched as he tore the silk shirt off her shoulders, down past her breasts. She stared at the nipples, hard and dark and wanting in the flickering firelight, as if they belonged to someone else. She wanted to shut her eyes, but his hand mesmerized her.

Imprisoned by the steel grip of his arm, she watched as the fingers caressed her waist and stomach, watched as they moved lower still, slipping beneath the waist of her slacks. She turned her head away from the mirror as he began to stroke her. Her narrow hips arched frantically against him.

"No, not like this—"

"Yes, Lapin, exactly like this. Until you give me what I want." His voice changed, grew harder, breath hot against her skin. "Tell me," he demanded, "what flowers does Gideon send you?"

She twisted in his arms, but there was no escape from the brutal hands. "Daisies," she gasped finally. "Gid likes daisies."

The long fingers caressed her in approval. "Good, Lapin, very good." He swept her up and carried her toward the bed in the dark corner of the room.

"No, I must get back to Gideon."

"It's not yet light. And you are pleasing me tonight."

One powerful hand pushed her roughly down onto the great high bed.

The last candle guttered, flickered, burned out.

# CHAPTER FIFTY-ONE

"Provence," murmured Maggie. "I'd forgotten that there is still such beauty in the world."

She stood transfixed on the small balcony, totally still, as if stunned by the sun. The Provence stretching before her was a land of light and texture and primary colors. Golden sky and ocher earth, blue shadows on pink rock. Emerald cypresses keeping watch over houses of rough silvery stone, twisted purple vines on a dusty hillside. The very earth seemed to glow from within, as if the land drew its light from the vast opalescent sky.

They had driven up a long, misty driveway to the ivy-covered inn just before dawn. "Intimate enough for you this time, Mrs. O'Shea?" the colonel had asked with cynical amusement.

She had been charmed by the simple beauty of her large, airy room. The carved antique bed. A sofa draped with a paisley shawl. Ripe plums in a shallow bowl. Tall French doors, left open to a narrow balcony, flooding the room with sunrise. And a small cat the color of old pearls, asleep on a silk cushion by a window filled with blue.

Maggie had called Brian immediately—to hell with the time zones. *No, no baby yet, Grandma, but all's well. Any news of my father?* I still haven't found him, Bones.

Then the call to Luze Jacobs in Boston. *I've gained two pounds on* hospital *food, Maggs! There's no justice!* Finally reassured, she'd gone running with a young Aixois policeman.

Now, drawn by the siren song of the cicadas, she stood on the small balcony.

Below her, in the small courtyard, scarlet geraniums spilled from earthen pots, their scent spicy and sharp as wood smoke in the air. Beyond, like a painted canvas, the Provence immortalized by Paul Cézanne rose and fell toward the distant Mont St. Victoire in an ocean of lavender.

The pearl cat appeared and rubbed against her ankles. Gathering the tiny creature to her breast, Maggie gazed into the sky.

"I don't think we're in Kansas anymore, Toto."

* * *

"Welcome to the monk's cell."

In the old town of Aix, Simon Sugarman gestured Beckett and the Golden through an arched doorway.

"Used to be a convent," said Sugarman. "Martin Luther slept here." He closed and locked the door, then bent to rub the dog's head. "How's la Maggie?"

"Obstinate, headstrong, and impossible."

"Admit it, pal. She's getting to you."

"Dammit, Sugar," growled Beckett, "Maggie O'Shea is a target for a brutal killer. Thanks to us. When she finds out the truth..."

"It's one thing to believe in truth, Mike, another thing to live with it."

"Just when a man thinks he's done with women," Beckett muttered. He looked out the mullioned window as if the sky held the answer he sought. "She's just—not like anybody else. She's got a way about her—"

"Yeah, yeah, Billy Joel, *and a smile that heals me.*" Sugarman grinned down at the Golden, who'd settled on the carpet in a square of sunlight.

Beckett shrugged. "She makes me think about things I don't usually think about, dammit. Feel things I don't want to feel."

"So let her in. What's the worst that can happen?"

Beckett stared at him. "The worst. Seriously? Life is easier in a combat zone." Beckett shrugged and turned away. "Back to work, Sugar. Did you find anything at the art gallery in Hyères?"

"Place cleaned out, doors locked tight. Guy next door said the owner just disappeared in the middle of the night."

"Disappeared? Vanessa Durand sent John O'Shea there to look for Orsini. And now the gallery owner's missing. I don't like it, Sugar."

"Bingo. Vanessa and I are going to have a little talk about that as soon as—"

The computer on a bare table sprang to life, and Sugarman squinted at the screen. "From my team in DC. Check this out. Security cameras caught the bastard who knifed my informer at the Opera House. It's not good, Mike." He tossed a photograph at Beckett.

The colonel stared down at a handsome face with long, pulled-back hair, hawk nose, strong hard mouth. Diamond earring. Tinted glasses stared blankly back at him. *Like a wolf,* Maggie O'Shea had said. Recognition sparked. "This guy has a mustache and darker hair, but your killer is the man in the Café de la Paix photograph." *The man who hurt Maggie.*

"Bingo. We also know that he boarded a flight from Boston to Paris the next day."

"He's followed her here."

"Maybe that means Orsini's close, too. We'll get them both." Sugarman looked out the window toward the tiny square as if he expected Orsini to saunter past the fountain. "Amah," he murmured.

"New code word?"

"Funny. 'Amah' means 'Indian servant'. It's in every crossword there is." He shook his head. "The journal Sofia Orsini stole from her husband. That's our 'amah.'"

Beckett nodded. "All those clients, bank accounts, investors. That intel should indict Victor and God knows how many others."

"Yeah, the Admiral wants those names bad, pal."

"If only it didn't hinge on Sofia's little boy."

"The kid was there when Fee died. The kid was with her that whole time, he has to know where she hid it. And Maggie's the one who can find him."

"Sometimes I hate this business."

"*You do what you gotta do*, my daddy always told me," said Sugarman. "He taught me to use my head, not my fists. A black man can't show anger. And he did what *he* had to. Worked on the trains all day and drilled me in history all night."

"My father"—the colonel struck a match and stared at the flame—"Big Jack Beckett, was military all the way. Discipline is the stuff of men. Honor, Duty and Fearlessness." He blew out the flame. "Called him 'Sir' from the moment I could talk."

"And here you are today, pal, honorable and dick-fucking-fearless."

"You learn fear when you have someone to lose," said Beckett, gazing down at the Golden.

Sugar's voice drew him back. "So, are you in or out, pal?"

"You dance with the one that brung ya, Sugar. Isn't that what you always say?"

"Because of the kid."

"Yeah, you subtle bastard. Because of the kid."

"It's hell being a good guy." Sugarman zipped up his windbreaker to hide the gun. "Time to rock n' roll. I'm outta here." He tossed his newspaper at Beckett. "I got Maggie's name into the morning papers. She won't play the piano, but even a small rumor of her appearance at the concert tonight can't hurt. It's a Tchaikovsky Piano Concerto. No way Law won't come if he thinks she'll be there."

"Damn you, Sugar. You also just told the killer who attacked Maggie where she'll be."

"You're ridin' that white horse again, pal! We're here to find Zach Law and Orsini's journal. You protect Maggie O'Shea. I'll do what I gotta do."

"That's what worries me."

# CHAPTER FIFTY-TWO

"Her name is Toto," said Maggie to the Golden, gesturing toward the small watchful cat curled on the seat pillow. "She's the chef's cat. Play nice."

The Golden, visiting from Beckett's room, approached the cat slowly, sat down and sniffed her outstretched paw. Maggie watched as they eyed each other thoughtfully, unblinking.

Smiling, she turned away. Morning light flooded through the open terrace doors, falling onto the animals, her open laptop, and the bowl of plums that glowed like amethysts in the light. Back to work.

The Golden gave a sudden growl as a soft footstep sounded on the balcony.

Maggie's stomach clenched in fear. She clutched her son's pocketknife and spun around. "Who's there?"

The figure in the shadows leaned one shoulder against the terrace door, thumbs hooked in jean pockets. Then he sneezed and reached out to tip the pearl cat from her pillow. The Golden followed her, both settling on the hearth rug.

"Ma'am." He raised a brow at the Golden, nestling against the tiny cat. "Seriously?"

"Colonel Beckett. What are you doing on my balcony?"

"Why the devil are these doors unlocked?" he countered. Uninvited, Beckett moved into the room. He eyed her mannish, loose white shirt, the baggy trousers over bare feet. "And, Mrs. O'Shea, that little-bitty knife wouldn't dent one of these plums."

"Not funny. I can't get that wolf-faced man out of my head..."

"When you're in danger, there are no rules. Run, scream, blow a whistle, use hairspray. Use fingernails, a pen, car keys. Thumb in the eye, knee in the groin. Could you shoot someone?"

"Absolutely not! I wouldn't even buy my son a toy gun when he was little."

Violins swelled insistently from her radio, and Beckett raised his head. "What music is that? I like it."

"Bartok. Asymmetrical phrasing—it's like you—odd, but oddly appealing."

"Thank you. I think."

He peered down at her and reached out as if to tip her chin into the light. But he stopped without touching her, dropped his hand. "Something's different."

*I'm coming back to life, Colonel.* Whether I'm ready or not.

She lowered her lashes and sat on the edge of the desk. "You're the one who's different. No cane this morning."

He bent toward her, so close that the scent of him—rock, sun, a hint of lemons—was like a warm breath against her skin. "Stronger every day. I came to tell you that several folks at Deux Garçons recognized Law's photo. But no last name or address. No record at all of a G. Black in Aix. I'm sorry."

She was quiet, bare foot swinging back and forth like a metronome. "Don't be," she said. "He won't be the man I knew."

His eyes were on her foot. "Is that good or bad?"

"Zach was like his music," she said. "Passionate and tempestuous and enchanting as a wizard. So brooding and intense, he never once smiled on stage." Her voice caught. "He was reckless and alone and extraordinary."

"Sure trumps 'oddly appealing,'" he said.

"Why would I want a man like that back in my life?"

"Why wouldn't you?"

*Because he promised to come home, but he never did.*

"If he's alive," she said, "then he hurt me, Colonel. And he robbed my son of a father." Her cell phone rang. She held up her hand, signaling him to wait.

"Magdalena O'Shea. Yes. Is there a photograph of him? Oh. Well, thank you so much, Herr Westoff."

She disconnected and turned to Beckett. "That was the President of the University of Music and the Performing Arts in Vienna, Austria. A man named G. Black was a student there, in the mid-eighties. No photograph available, but he earned a doctorate in Musicology. Then he just dropped off the face of the earth. Again."

Beckett was staring at her. "You know the President of a university in Vienna?"

She smiled. "I soloed there, with the Vienna Symphony."

His gaze rested on her face. "Musicology. I think you could be right about Law working for Orsini. A musicologist could authenticate rare scores, you said?"

She nodded. "Absolutely."

"Good for you. I'll tell Sugar." And then, "I brought this for you." He reached for her hand, and she started at his touch. Their eyes met. Just for a moment, there was a sudden blaze in his, like lightning in a mirror. He dropped a length of emerald ribbon into her palm.

"It's got a radio transmitter. A miniature GPS tracking beacon."

"Why do I need a transmitter?"

"In case you need the posse at Deux Garçons. Wear that green ribbon in your hair."

"Are you expecting trouble?"

"If you want to make God laugh, ma'am, just tell him your plans. But two gendarmes will always be at your elbow."

"The next thing I know," she teased him, "you'll be telling me I have a code name."

The ghost of a smile touched his mouth. "You're Concerto."

\* \* \*

In a farmhouse in the Luberon hills, just north of Aix-en-Provence, the man who called himself Gideon Black was thinking of Deux Garçons as he entered the French doors. Slipping off muddy boots, he imagined himself sitting in the sunlight at one of their tiny café tables, sipping a glass of Pinot, talking music with friends. Looking forward to the festival. But there was much to do before he could leave. Fix the tractor, give the dogs a run, pay the bills, call Victor with his report on the Chopin manuscript.

He checked his watch. After nine already. Through the open kitchen window, he could see the pines, pale gray against a square of glowing blue. He gazed at the rows of vines, twisted and green, that climbed the hillside.

He could feel the tension in his shoulders, the restlessness he'd been feeling for days, waiting for tonight's festival gala. Now the day called to him, like the sirens of ancient Greece had called to Odysseus. But Odysseus, he reminded himself, found nothing but trouble.

He reached for his second cup of coffee of the morning, took a deep swallow, and returned to the bedroom.

Celeste was still asleep. He touched her shoulder. Her skin was smooth and cool as water under his fingertips. Not feverish at all, but then he knew she wasn't really sick.

This tender, fragile woman. There'd been some bad times here in Provence, when the painkillers weren't enough, and she'd been there for him.

Gideon slipped off his work clothes, then caught his reflection in the mirror as he turned. Unrelenting light played on a tall, bearded man with long dark hair and intense eyes. His naked body was lean and scarred, the scars white slashes on the sunbrowned skin.

He turned away from the image. Today, he needed time alone in his music room. He wanted to think about tonight's concerto.

Behind him, Celeste stirred in the massive bed.

She hated what she called his "*l'addiction pour la musique*." But he had to have a place of his own, with a stereo and a grand piano, where he could be alone to think, to listen, to compose. To study, to work. To remember.

Sometimes he locked the door. He knew it hurt her. But it was a part of his life he couldn't share. *Would not* share.

He turned to look at the lovely figure curled in the bed. The white sheet draped across the bone of her hip, exposing one lovely, high breast. His breath quickened. Why couldn't she understand that his need for the world of music was so intense that it was fiercely physical. An aching, longing desire. His drug. And his punishment.

Her soft sigh drew him back to the bed. It would be so easy to drown in her. But tonight Tchaikovsky's Piano Concerto No. 1 headlined the festival. His heart quickened. No way he would miss it. He'd gone to the vineyards early, so that he would have time to drive into Aix and drop in at Deux Garçons for that glass of wine.

The day, bright gold, waited for him. And the morning papers, full of festival news.

He reached for his robe, dropped a gentle kiss on the woman's brow, and went down the hall to wake the child.

# CHAPTER FIFTY-THREE

Sugarman tossed his file on the table and moved to the window to stare down at the narrow courtyard and alleys of Aix. He'd meant what he'd told Beckett. Orsini was close, he could feel it. But he was missing something. What?

Too many things just didn't add up. He went over the questions in his mind once more. There was always a damned trigger.

His thoughts kept spinning back to Yale. Why had Victor joined the CIA in the early eighties when he'd been so committed to art, to music? It made no sense. Victor had been looking forward to taking his rightful place in the arts world, and then everything changed on a dime. What had been different in those last weeks before graduation?

He closed his eyes. Dinners. Thesis. Those late-night talks about the future, in their suite, in front of the fire.

An image took shape. Sugarman sitting in their suite, gazing into the fire. *Alone.* Where had Victor been? He stiffened. Of course. Victor's mother had died. Victor had gone to New York for her funeral. But he'd been gone a long time. Five, six days? Too long. Where had he gone, what had happened? Could his mother's death have set everything else in motion?

* * *

The wall safe in the quiet, book-lined library stood open. Victor Orsini sat at his desk in the light of a single lamp, gazing down at the letter in his hand. On the smooth ebony desktop, a huge old-fashioned key glittered in the light.

Thank God Sofia had not known about this safe. He shook his head, lifting his mother's letter to the light.

His given name, Vittorio, was written across the pale vellum envelope. His mother's spidery script brought back vivid memories of long-ago summers spent in the gardens at the villa in the hills above Florence. The cool sharpness of lemonade on the lips, shifting shadows of the umbrella pines, the scent of late summer roses on the breeze. And the sounds—his mother's melodious voice, the scratch of her fountain pen in the lovely old notebook, the chords of a violin shimmering across the lawn.

He had been called Vittorio then. He and his sister had been born and raised in New York City, where his father owned several art galleries and his mother taught music on the Upper West Side. But every summer they'd returned to their mother's villa, while his father stayed in New York.

Then one night, when they were away in Florence, his father died alone in New York, the victim of a gunshot wound when he'd tried to stop a random mugging. His father had been hailed a hero. He'd always believed that the pain shining so brightly in his mother's eyes was because she hadn't been able to say goodbye.

In 1978, when he'd gone off to Yale to study philosophy, music, art, he'd been convinced that his future was ordained. To walk in his father's footsteps, running the successful global art business inherited from his father, having perhaps a second home in Southern Europe, a wife, children. Concerts at Carnegie Hall...

When the men in dark glasses and suits had come to his Yale suite that first time, in the fall of his senior year, with their invitation to join them in Washington, he had laughed in their faces and turned away.

But then his mother had died the month before he was to graduate. And he was given the letter by her lawyer, and the key to her villa in Florence, at the funeral. He had read his mother's letter—her confession—and in that sickening instant his life was claimed by darkness.

Orsini slipped the letter from its pale cream envelope, gazed down at the black, spidery script.

*My Son,*

*I have been keeping a terrible secret from you and your sister. Now you deserve to know the truth. Your father was not a hero, not the man you believed him to be. The crimes he committed, they are horrific, beyond understanding. But you must know. You must make amends for all of us.*

*You cannot imagine how it was for us in Florence in 1943, the year of the German Occupation. My beloved Firenze, I never could speak of it to you. Before the Germans came I had my home, my friends, my music. Your father, a friend of my cousin's, ran a small art gallery not far away. We all had a modest life, even with Mussolini in power. Then Hitler invaded. We were occupied, and life changed forever.*

*One of my family's friends was Signore Felix Hoffmann. An Austrian Jew, he left Vienna with his wife and young daughter when the war began, to open a gallery near the Duomo. He had many beautiful paintings, but he specialized in rare music—old scores, autographed manuscripts by the great classical composers, beautiful handmade instruments.*

*I often took his daughter, Rebekkah, to the park. Signore Hoffmann knew I played the violin, and one day he invited me into the back of his shop, where he showed me a signed Vivaldi score, a Stradivarius violin, and an original Bach concerto. On the table was an inlaid wooden box, engraved with his name— The Felix Hoffmann Gallery. I can still see it. Inside was the most beautiful del Gesù violin I had ever seen, once played by Paganini. Imagine.*

*"Come next week," he smiled, "and I will show you my greatest treasure, a violin concerto I found in an attic in Vienna. The most beautiful concerto ever written."*

*I counted the days, but when I returned to his gallery, the windows were smashed. Huge yellow swastikas were painted on walls now bare of paintings. The safe broken open, empty. There was no sign of the del Gesù, no sign of Signore Hoffmann, no sign of my gentle friend Rebekkah. Nothing was left. And then I knew that our friends were lost, along with "the most beautiful concerto ever written."*

*I later learned that the Hoffmanns had been taken to the trains, in the middle of the night. I never saw them again. I never discovered what happened to the del Gesù or the violin concerto Signore Hoffman had found.*

*In the weeks that followed the Hoffmann family's disappearance, hundreds of Jews were deported. Friends and neighbors. Artists and musicians. Bread lines were commonplace. We all lived in fear. Our beautiful bridges and churches and homes blown up.*

*And then the soldiers came one night to your father's gallery.*

*Do you know that Hitler, at one time before the war, was a practicing artist? He actually dreamed of building his own art museum in his home town of Linz. And so he gave his orders. My God, the looting, the confiscation, the destruction. Canvases, sculpture, music, religious treasures. Priceless pieces hidden, auctioned, sent out of the country, or burned.*

*Hitler believed that the Impressionists, the Modernists, were morally degenerate. Your father had a Murillo, a Picasso, a gorgeous Cézanne in his gallery. They would have been destroyed, along with so many other confiscated, beautiful pieces, and he couldn't bear it. He made a deal with the Germans.*

*Your father became a collaborator.*

*He stored and auctioned pieces for the Nazis, bought Old Masters and whole collections at the very lowest prices from our Jewish friends when they fled. Or from those who were under unspeakable duress to sell. And in return, he was allowed to keep most of the pieces in his gallery. I suspect he stole the occasional piece from a confiscated collection as well, before it was sent on to Germany. Stealing from the thieves. Stealing from our friends.*

*I did not know any of this, when I married your father just after the war. Or even after we emigrated to America. I found out just after he died.*

*This is the key to my villa in Florence, closed for years, where he hid so many priceless pieces of art, so many rare musical scores and books. The treasures that allowed him to build his business empire in the US, on the backs of so much suffering. The continuing source of money that paid for our home, and Yale, and your sister's education and competitions as well.*

*I cannot bear to tell Bianca. Please, protect your sister from this terrible legacy.*

*Now, only you can make restitution. You must do the right thing.*

*I love you still, Vittorio mio. Always take care of your sister,*

It was signed, simply, *Your Mother.*

Victor Orsini's breath was harsh in the quiet library, remembering. Feeling the guilt stir once more, he gazed down at the huge, ornate metal key shining in the pool of lamplight on his desk.

After the funeral, he had taken the key and flown to Florence in a haze of disbelief and horror. And there, hidden in the dusty attic of his mother's villa, he had found a fortune in missing art and music. Shocked, sickened, overwhelmed, he'd known he needed help. Who could he call? Who could he *trust*?

An hour later, he'd dialed two numbers in the United States, spoken at length to two people from his past. People he trusted with his life. Then, with their guidance, he'd rented a truck and, in the dead of night, moved all the canvases and manuscripts to a safer place. And then he had flown home to graduate.

Guilt-ridden, frightened, desperate—with no idea what he was going to do—he was only sure of one thing on the flight home. There was only one person left in all the world that he loved now. He would protect her, and their terrible secret, with his life.

But that first night after he'd returned to Yale, the suited men from Washington had shown up at his doorstep once more. And this time, he was not given a choice.

# CHAPTER FIFTY-FOUR

Pretending to read the newspaper at a rear table in Café des Deux Garçons, Beckett gazed at the ancient city of Aix-en-Provence. The Golden sat quietly beside him, wary but calm, brown eyes fixed on the sidewalk violinist. Beyond the musician, rows of high leafy plane trees shaded the fountains and exclusive shops of the Cours Mirabeau.

"American concert pianist Magdalena O'Shea is in Aix-en-Provence for tonight's concert at the Palace of the Archbishop." Beckett looked down at her photograph. Law couldn't miss the *International Herald Tribune* article. If he didn't show up at the café, they'd find him tonight.

"*Mon Dieu!*" exclaimed the young Frenchman sitting to Beckett's right. The colonel raised his head. Maggie O'Shea was walking toward the flowered entrance to the café.

"Easy boy," whispered Beckett. "We're not supposed to know her, remember?" The Golden gave him a considering look, but remained blessedly still.

Maggie's hair and eyes were completely hidden by a wide straw hat with a massive brim, trimmed with a green ribbon that fluttered down her back. Long earrings dangled like wind chimes from her ears. Her skirt was long, loose, and honey-colored, swinging softly with each step. Today, when every other woman in sight wore a "*Festival de Musique*" t-shirt, Maggie's shirt proclaimed "ETUDE, BRUTE?" in bold yellow letters.

Something about the way she looked in the dappled sunlight,

and the way the silvery chimes danced when she moved, caused more than one head to turn.

\* \* \*

Beneath the broad-brimmed hat, Maggie's eyes were focused on the Café des Deux Garçons. Zach's café. She was certain every passerby could see the thumping of her heart beneath the thin t-shirt.

She'd spent the late morning like every other tourist, exploring the cobbled squares and shuttered eighteenth-century homes of Cézanne's city. Now, it seemed perfectly natural to stop for a glass of wine at one of the outdoor cafés strung like bright beads along the broad, tree-shaded avenue. She remembered the words of the usher at the theatre in Paris. Deux Garçons, Gideon's favorite café.

A white-gloved hand stopped her.

Maggie stared into the white-painted face of a mime. Suddenly, magically, he produced a huge bouquet of scarlet poppies. Pleading broadly, whistling a popular French love song, he postured for the tourists in the café.

Maggie began to whistle a Mozart melody and returned a single bright poppy to the mime before presenting the bouquet to a startled passerby. Then, to the smiling applause of the café patrons, she moved to a just-vacated table.

\* \* \*

Beckett raised the newspaper to cover his face. Damn if she doesn't whistle better than I do, he thought. In classical, no less. If Law was in Aix, he'd damn well know Maggie O'Shea was in town. The mime had more than earned the fifty euros Beckett had paid him.

He watched her lift her face to the scattered sunlight.

\* \* \*

The glass shook in Maggie's hand. She took a long swallow of wine and forced herself to glance casually around the noisy brasserie.

Several men sat alone or in small groups under the bright umbrellas. She eyed each one carefully. No one looked familiar. She turned to search the faces behind her and saw Beckett's eyes on her.

A woman nearby was relating an amusing story about a snapped cello string, a man's low voice answered.

She fingered the green ribbon blowing across her cheek, and drank her wine.

Three men entered the café. One, talking to his companions, had his face turned away from her. He was tall and broad-shouldered, with the dark, curling hair she remembered. Suddenly unable to breathe, she willed him to turn toward her.

He swung around as if he'd heard her thoughts, and she caught her breath.

His eyes touched hers, paused admiringly, moved on. Light eyes. Not Zach.

Dear God. She stood abruptly, dropped too many euros on the table, and left.

# CHAPTER FIFTY-FIVE

THE LUBERON HILLS. EARLY AFTERNOON, JULY 8

"Goddamn it!"

Gideon stood in front of an oak armoire in the bedroom of the Luberon farmhouse. An empty envelope dangled from his hand.

The dark-haired woman, curled in a chair by the window, watched him tensely. "What is it, chéri?"

"First no newspapers delivered this morning, then the trouble in the winery. And now—where are the tickets, Celeste?"

She looked away. "Dane came by. When you were in the vineyard."

"Dane's back? He was here?"

"Yes. He said he needed tonight's gala tickets for Victor."

"So you gave him the tickets, just like that? Without asking me?"

"Please, Gid. I'm sorry. You weren't here and—you know how Dane frightens me."

Gideon turned angrily from her. It wasn't her fault. But to miss tonight's concerto... Suddenly he stiffened. "Celeste. What about the abbey tickets for tomorrow afternoon?"

"He took all the tickets."

"Damn him to hell! Where is Dane now?"

"He left hours ago." She raised a delicate hand to his chest. "Gid—"

Gideon pulled away from her. "Then I'll find him."

"No!" She gripped his arm. "Please, Gid," she whispered. "You're scaring me. It will be dark soon, chéri, it's too late. Don't leave me." Her hand moved down his chest to his flat stomach. When her fingers reached the brass buckle, his hand closed over hers, stopping her.

"Please," she pleaded. "Just for tonight. We'll go to the abbey tomorrow, I promise you." Her hand loosened the narrow belt. Warm fingers slipped lower, lips moved across his breastbone. Her tongue was hot and quick, the small fingers demanding.

He sighed and moved against her.

"Gid, let me love you. We will make our own music tonight, yes?"

She took his hand and sank to the floor as the setting sun turned her skin to gold.

*I'm going to that performance tonight, Celeste*, he told her silently. I can call in a favor, get another ticket. No matter what you say. Or do.

He bent over her.

# CHAPTER FIFTY-SIX

In the intimate inner courtyard of the eighteenth-century Palais de l'Ancien Archevêché—the Palace of the Archbishop—the stage lights dimmed. A hostess dressed in white showed Maggie to her tenth row center seat just as the first violinist of the Orchestre de Paris strode onto the stage.

The open-aired courtyard was small, steep, and bowl-shaped. Maggie had arrived early to wander the aisles of the roofless theatre in search of Zachary Law. To her surprise and pleasure, she had spoken to many old friends and colleagues in the music world. But not the man she sought. Now, one final time, she searched the expectant faces around her. No bearded, sensitive face, no dark brooding eyes in the dusky light.

She turned to scan the upper tiers behind her. There, off to the side, was the colonel. He touched his forehead in salute and folded his arms across his chest.

Maggie smiled and returned her eyes to the stage as the oboist tuned the orchestra with the oboe's long one-note A. The program in her hand announced that the evening's All-Tchaikovsky program was a Gala Benefit for the Performing Arts of Provence. Surely Zach would never miss the Piano Concerto No. 1? Not when it had consumed him—possessed him—that long ago Boston summer.

*He's here*, she thought. *I feel him.*

Applause broke into her thoughts. The conductor was taking his bow, then sweeping his arm toward the wings to welcome the French soloist. Like an expectant child, Maggie crossed her fingers and held her breath.

A tall dark-haired man strode forward. Her heart skipped in her chest. *OhdearGod...*

A stranger's face turned to the audience. She exhaled slowly. Foolish, to hope Zach might have walked out onto the bright stage.

The young soloist settled himself at the Steinway grand piano. Just for a moment, Maggie was eighteen again, breathless and blinded by the searing spotlight, sitting at the newly tuned Baldwin on the stage of Boston's Symphony Hall. Trembling hands clasped in black silk lap, unable to control the wild beating of wings against her ribs. Trying like hell to remember the opening notes of the Rachmaninoff Concerto No. 2 in C minor.

*You won't forget the opening passage, Slim.*

And Zach had been right. You won't forget, she told the soloist now.

The conductor raised his baton for a beat of silence. Then the huge introduction of Tchaikovsky's B-flat minor concerto, which critics still insisted was in the wrong key, began with the call of the horns. The pianist's hands descended into an ocean of sound. Maggie wondered again why Tchaikovsky had never repeated this haunting opening theme anywhere else in the concerto.

\* \* \*

From a seat high to the left of the stage, Dane watched Maggie move down the steep aisle. Tonight her hair, lit by the full moon, shone with dark fire. "Gideon's woman," he said softly, tasting the words.

Dane fingered the engraved invitation to the reception. It would be so easy to watch her, see whom she met, follow her to her hotel. And if she wanted to find Gideon, he would surely help her. *You will hear from your sweet prince tomorrow, fair Juliet.*

He looked up at the star-strewn night sky. "By yonder blessed moon I swear."

\* \* \*

"Not bad," murmured Beckett.

The candlelit Romanesque cloister of the cathedral of St.

Sauveur, adjacent to the Archbishop's Palace, was an arched, roofed passage around an open inner courtyard. In his opinion, the perfect setting for the gala reception.

Beckett leaned against one of the columns that supported the low roof and watched the flow of faces carefully. No light-eyed man with long, fair hair. But too many darkly bearded faces that could have been Zachary Law.

He tried to imagine twelfth-century monks wandering in the peaceful garden, lost in reflection. Tonight, the cloister's atmosphere held a far more worldly beauty.

Flickering candles were scattered among the monks' carefully tended roses, while waiters in tuxedos poured champagne for elegant women in long gowns. In one cloistered corner, beneath a sculpture of St. Peter, a woman sang of love and heartbreak. Couples swayed slowly on a circle of smooth stones under the stars. The high parasol pines were lit by fireflies.

The reception was By-Invitation-Only for festival benefactors, musicians, and their guests. What am I doing in a place like this? Beckett tugged at the too-tight black silk bow tie. A job, he reminded himself—and that "job" was right over there across the courtyard, having her hand kissed by no less than the conductor himself. Then she walked across the courtyard toward him.

Her gown shimmered like shadows, leaving her throat and shoulders bare. A fringed shawl, knotted loosely around her hips, swayed as she walked. Then she was standing in front of him. In spite of her high-heeled sandals, he towered over her. Under the bright moon, her hair was full of light. Tonight, it was swept up from her neck, caught high with tortoiseshell combs.

"Am I disturbing you, Colonel?" she asked.

"You disturb me very much, Mrs. O'Shea."

Her eyes held his as his fingers pulled at the offending bow tie until the knot gave. Once again he scanned the crowd as he unbuttoned the neck of the starched shirt.

"Do you ever get the feelin', ma'am, that the whole world's a tuxedo and you're a pair of brown shoes?"

She smiled up at him.

There was something in her expression, and he decided that he must look quite dashing with the open bow tie hanging down the snowy shirt front.

"Would you like a drink?"

"I'd kill for one."

"I think there's an easier way." He signaled a waiter with a silver tray of wine bottles and crystal glasses balanced on his shoulder.

* * *

Gideon stood alone, out of sight beyond the shifting swirl of dancers, watching the guests. The air was heavy with the scent of jasmine, and the last chords of the concerto were still singing in his blood. It was a night made for music. He damn well wasn't ready to leave.

A woman's low, throaty laugh cascaded to his left, beyond the roses. His head came up. It was a sound he still heard sometimes, in his dreams. A long-forgotten memory stirred in his chest.

He swung around.

# CHAPTER FIFTY-SEVEN

Beckett's hands closed around Maggie's waist and he lifted her to sit on the cloister's low stone wall.

He saw her hands trembling as she smoothed the silky dress over her knees. Her eyes were smoky and flickering, filled with green shadows. *Slow down*, he warned himself, intensely aware of the feeling of her body, hard as a diamond, under his fingers.

He let his hands fall and they were both silent, listening to the night song of the cicadas.

"Van Gogh was convinced the cicadas spoke ancient Greek," she told him.

"Van Gogh was mad," he reminded her. *Don't look into those eyes.* He turned away to look out over the crowd. "Have you seen anyone who could be Zach Law?"

"No. No one. Zach loved that concerto, he chose it for his New York debut. He would have been here tonight, if..." Her voice trailed off uncertainly.

He felt her exhaustion. "There are more performances tomorrow. You need some rest."

"When are you going to stop treating me as if I'm made of glass, Colonel?"

*When the haunted look is gone from your eyes.* "We'll stay, then."

She looked up at the stars and said, "Do you ever wish that life could stand still, just for a moment?"

"I suppose I have known, once or twice, that quick feeling of fear that comes when you are so damned happy that you cannot conceive of wanting anything more but this moment to last."

He felt her studying him.

"Tell me more about those blue mountains of yours," she said.

* * *

The sound of the woman's voice echoed in his head. *Where was she?*

Gideon's eyes searched the crowded cloister. There, by the roses, a tantalizing flash of night-black hair.

He moved across the stones.

A hand came down hard on his shoulder, stopping him. A curse in his ear, low and angry. "*Nique ta mère*, what are you doing here?"

Gideon turned his head and looked into Dane's light eyes.

"Take your hands off me."

Just for a moment, Dane tightened his grip. Then his hands fell away. "You shouldn't be here."

"Because you stole my ticket, you bastard? Don't you *ever* take anything of mine again."

Dane looked at him with an unreadable expression before turning away. "You shouldn't be here because Celeste needs you at Le Refuge. She called my cell when she couldn't reach you."

Gideon's chest tightened and he clutched Dane's arm, his fingers crushing. "What's wrong? Is it TJ?"

"A fever, a nightmare, nothing more. She coddles the boy, you both do." A shrug of powerful shoulders. "But I could go to them if you want to stay—"

"Like hell you will." Gideon was already moving toward the exit. He could feel Dane's eyes on his back. With one last disappointed glance toward the cloister, he ran through the high stone arch toward his car.

# CHAPTER FIFTY-EIGHT

Dane watched Gideon disappear through the arched exit. He waited several minutes, while, across the garden, Maggie O'Shea gazed up at an older, broad-shouldered man. When he was satisfied that Gideon was gone, he dropped the mirrored glasses over his eyes and moved deeper into the shadows of the cloister wall, watching them from behind a stone pillar.

A handsome young musician stopped to speak with her, then moved on. Dane kept his eyes on Maggie. He wanted to get closer, listen to her voice. But it was too dangerous. He studied the older man with the loosened bow tie. A hard face, eyes that watched the crowd too carefully. Eyes that seemed to burn when they looked down at Magdalena O'Shea.

Watching them, Dane remembered hiding in Magdalena's hotel room in Paris. The ringing telephone, her voice arranging to meet someone she called "Colonel."

*This is her colonel*, thought Dane.

The man bent and whispered. Dane saw the sudden smile light her face.

He pressed back against the cold rough stone and watched them together.

* * *

Beckett watched a tall fair-haired man move slowly among the guests. Then the man swept an older woman onto the dance floor. Not the man he was looking for.

"Tell me about your mountains," prompted Maggie.

Beckett kept his eyes on the dancers. "The Blue Ridge Mountains of Virginia, ma'am. Born and raised in their shadow. Dad still lives there."

"And you live in Washington."

"I did, for a long time. But I couldn't seem to get the country out of the boy. So I bought a place in the foothills of the Blue Ridge."

"What is it you do in those Blue Hills, when winter comes?"

It was a long time since he had talked about himself. "Sour mash whiskey," he said finally, "fast cars. And a good book to get me to sleep." That was safe. "Go fishing. Light a fire, cook, see friends. Until last winter I had an old hound dog. Found him as a puppy by the roadside, covered in mud. Named him Red."

"You miss him."

"I do. But I fill the quiet nights with music. *Real* music. Country, jazz. Blues—rough and smoky."

"You promised to introduce me to B.B. King."

He pictured her curled on the easy chair in his cabin. "I haven't forgotten. I give Mozart a chance, and you have to spend a night with B.B."

"Does your offer include dinner?"

"You expect me to cook?"

"Do you?" She smiled.

"We'll take Shiloh, then, and catch our dinner in the lake."

"Who's Shiloh?"

"The Golden." He gazed down at her. "Okay, you were right. Dog needs a name. He's got a brave heart, was injured in a bad war. Needs a home, a safe place, like all of us, I guess." *Light, not darkness.* "Shiloh just seems fitting, somehow."

"Oh, Colonel. I'm glad. He's going to love your mountains."

"Watching the light change on those blue mountains, ma'am, you feel alive." He looked around the glittering cloister. "I'm a long way from home tonight."

* * *

Maggie liked the deep, easy sound of his voice. "Music and nights by your fire..." she encouraged him.

"Those winter nights staring into the flames, a man gets to thinking. About the men who've fought beside him, the friends he's lost, the women he's known." Beckett flashed a look at her. "The roads not taken. Hopes and dreams. The times he's hurt someone."

The wavering candlelight caught the hard planes of his face. "How did such a country boy ever get into this line of work?"

Wine swirled like smoke in his glass. "My family fought in every war since the Civil War," he said. "To an idealistic kid in a military prep school, West Point was honor, bravery, patriotism—and escape, in a way—all wrapped up with a big red, white, and blue bow like a giant gift under a Christmas tree." He shook his head, as if amazed by the innocence of youth.

"Then all of a sudden I was a scared-shit lieutenant in Vietnam, and every day I saw a new bunch of children ripped to pieces." He stopped. "I don't talk about those days."

"You can trust me, Colonel."

He was silent before taking a deep swallow of wine.

"One night patrol, there was an explosion, just ahead of us. Running through the smoke, I found a bleeding kid. He'd stepped on a land mine. He asked me to take him home." He took a harsh breath. "Christ! Walking into that hospital tent, with a dead kid slung on my back—I knew it was time to get out."

His dark, desolate anger frightened her. But the yearning to comfort him frightened her far more. "You took care of him."

"Tell that to his mother. We took baby-faced boys from their parents and put M-16s into their hands. Told them to aim at other kids. Other mothers' sons." His voice was like cold stones. "They come to war as bright-eyed kids, and then they see every horror. Their eyes grow hard and haunted. They write messages on their helmets that break your heart. We give them medals, and then we bury them."

His voice changed. "One Christmas Eve, there were no

bombs. It was so quiet. A homesick soldier started singing 'Silent Night.' Then my men joined in, until the words echoed over the hills." He looked at her. "It's the only moment of solace I can remember in that desolate place."

"And then you came home..."

"To an America I didn't know. A woman in a black armband spit on me in the airport when I landed. The people and places you left behind aren't the same. All of a sudden, home is more baffling and tormenting than war."

She knew what his next words would be. "You turned around and went back."

"Someone had to take care of all those green kids. Libya, Iran, Iraq. Afghanistan. So many damned wars. In Afghanistan, there was this one kid..." He stopped.

*What had happened to him there?*

"Is that why you're still watching over kids in trouble?"

"Maybe. But finding Tommy Orsini will be the last song for me." He gazed down at her. "You are dangerously easy to talk to, Magdalena O'Shea."

He poured the last of the wine into their glasses. Once more he studied the faces of the guests drifting through the cloistered garden. Then he turned to her.

"Now it's your turn," he said.

* * *

Dane moved slowly toward them, keeping well within the shadows of the columned cloister. What were they talking about, that seemed to close them away from the rest of the glittering night?

He needed answers. He needed to talk to her. He had to get her away from her colonel. *He had to get her to Orsini.*

# CHAPTER FIFTY-NINE

The breeze rocked the pines as Maggie gazed at the dancers in the candlelit cloister. "You already know more about me than I want you to know, Colonel."

"Not why you decided to become a concert pianist."

"I couldn't play the cello."

"Van Cliburn didn't play the piano for eleven years. *He* came back."

"How did you know that?"

He shrugged. "Tell me how you found music."

"My mother, Lily," said Maggie. "She was a pianist, too. Her piano was the first sound I heard in the morning, the last lullaby as I fell asleep."

Lost in early memories, Maggie said, "When I was four or five, I would nap on a pillow beneath the piano while my mother rehearsed. She taught me how to sit at the piano, move my arms, position tiny fingers. All those hours of exercises. But then Mozart practiced so much that all the cartilage crumbled in his fingers."

"Ouch." He gazed down at her hands. "But it was what you wanted?"

"More than anything. I still remember the first time I wrote 'Pianist' on a form. I don't regret those missed dances. The piano was my choice, from the time I could reach the keys. Music was all I ever wanted."

"And so you became a concert pianist."

She almost choked on the last swallow of wine. "Good God,

Colonel, it took *years*. Brian's homework and swimming lessons and PTA took precedence over the piano for a long time."

She felt the memories light her smile.

"Imagine a gleaming nine-foot monster made of sitka spruce and eighty-eight keys, and there you are with only ten fingers. Polish the repertoire at dawn, feed my little boy, press the black dress while you recite nursery rhymes. And practice—my instructor told me I only had to practice on days when I'd eat." She laughed. "Even when you think you're ready, still you need to learn how to listen to an orchestra, get along with the prima donna conductor, relate to an audience, overcome stage fright." Her hands fluttered gracefully in the air. "I had to learn how to walk on and off a stage."

"I think you've got the walk down, ma'am."

"I've been given a profoundly precious gift, Colonel. I've always believed it's an artist's responsibility to share that gift." She shook her head. "But now..."

"You'll play again. Just remember Van Cliburn."

"Thank you," she said. "You've reminded me why I got into music in the first place. Mozart, Chopin, Liszt, Beethoven. The great pieces. This is music I love, music I still want to share."

Beckett flexed his fingers and broke a white-globed rose from the tangle of blossoms on the wall. "*Mes hommages*," he said with a bow.

* * *

In the deep shadows of the ancient cloister wall, Dane's hands clenched and unclenched around the icy glass of Evian as he watched them together.

He could still feel her nails in the bird market, sharp against his skin. She would find a way to meet him alone. If she had good reason.

He watched as the man held a pale flower out to her. Saw how she lifted her face to his. You like flowers, my Juliet?

*I know how I will get to her.*

# CHAPTER SIXTY

"Rachmaninov," murmured Maggie, holding the rose to her cheek, "received white lilacs from a fan before every concert in St. Petersburg." Her eyes held his. "I always secretly hoped someone would send me white lilacs before a performance."

"I'd bring you the whole damned bush if it would help you."

"It's been months now since I've touched the piano. After my husband drowned..." She faltered. "Have you ever been given a choice, Colonel—and made the wrong one?"

"Yes." And then, gently, "Your turn to trust. Tell me what happened."

She closed her eyes. "On the day Johnny drowned, I was home, totally absorbed in the Grieg concerto. I'd asked him to go to France, to look for Tommy..."

Her hands clenched, bone-white in her lap. "That day, when the phone rang, I kept playing. I didn't even answer." Her eyes flew open, desolate, inconsolable. "My husband was calling me, and I didn't answer the goddamned phone."

"Maggie..." The longing to take her in his arms was overwhelming.

"The next morning, there was a knock at the door. There was a vase of tulips on the Steinway. I have no memory of that officer's face. But I remember falling to my knees... and I can still see the sunlight shining on those damned yellow tulips."

"Bad things happen fast, ma'am, but you live through them slow."

She stared at him. "It's not just the dying. It's the way he died." She shook her head back and forth. "I wasn't there for him. My husband drowned alone, in a terrible storm far from home. My life froze inside of me that night," she whispered.

Her eyes burned at him, fiercely alive. And suddenly, he understood. "Until now," he said.

"Until now. Here in Provence, something is happening to me. It's as if I'm composing a new life. But..."

"You still have music inside you. Focus your pain, dammit, and put it into the piano. Turn it into something beautiful. Don't let your husband's death take away who you are, Mrs. O'Shea."

He set down his wine glass. "Dance with me."

"Dance?" Apprehensive eyes flew to his. "Oh, no. Please. I can't."

He was looming above her, lifting her down off the wall. "Your body needs to feel music again."

He caught her wrist with strong, demanding fingers. Slowly, inexorably he pulled her toward the tiny dance floor.

* * *

She hadn't danced with a man since her husband died.

He caught hold of her waist and pulled her against him. She raised her hands between them as a barrier, her neck arched back, away from him.

They stared at each other, not speaking.

He moved his hand up under her hair and carefully, slowly eased her head forward to rest against his chest. They stood stiffly, scarcely moving.

"*Quand on n'a que l'amour*," sang the chanteuse. If we only have love.

Maggie was aware of the soft cotton of his shirt against her cheek. She felt his heart hammer against the hollow of her palm. He smelled like tobacco and red wine. The steely arms felt good, safe after the terrors of Paris.

"Only one person can lead, Mrs. O'Shea," he said against her hair.

She allowed her body to soften against his. Very slowly, she began to respond to the music. She thought, I've had too much wine. But I want to be held. Just for a little while.

"You told me in Paris that you hate dancing," she murmured into his shirt, "but you hold a woman as if you like dancing very much."

"I guess it depends on the woman I'm holding."

"*Je ne regrette rien*," crooned the chanteuse. I regret nothing.

She closed her eyes, very aware of the hard body against hers. The faintest touch of his hand on her bare back. Deep within her she felt the smallest quiver. She thought she felt his lips brush her hair.

She lifted her head. Looked up at his face, gripped his shirt. Legs closer.

"I've got you," he whispered, holding her close.

The music quickened.

They swayed together, barely moving, in and out of the shadows.

* * *

She was all sharp angles and resistance. He trapped her hand against his heart, astonished by this feel of her in his arms. And suddenly, without warning, felt the whispering begin, deep in his bones.

He was acutely aware of her legs pressed against his, of the way his hand fit the curve of her spine. Only days ago, he'd wanted her to leave. Now he just...wanted her.

Holding her, moving with her, he felt the almost imperceptible softening of her body. He could feel her need, stirring beneath his fingers. He looked down at her. She raised her head slowly. The candlelight threw her eyes into deep shadows, but he saw the sudden flare in the green depths. His hand tightened on her back.

Bright tears starred her lashes, and the truth hit him like a punch. Dammit, Beckett, what's the matter with you? Haven't you learned anything? *It's her husband she wants, not you.*

* * *

She saw the spark, deep in the wintry eyes, and pressed against him. And felt his gun, hard against her ribs.

She had forgotten the gun. *Oh God*, she thought, *he scares me so.* How could she be attracted to such a dark, dangerous man?

He moved a finger to her chin and slowly lifted her face.

"Maggie," he said hoarsely. "You can't go on loving a dead man forever."

"Why not?"

They stopped dancing and stared at each other.

With a rough thumb he brushed a single tear from her pale cheek. When she began to tremble, he dropped his hand. "I wanted you to leave," he told her, his eyes conflicted. "I don't *want* to want you."

They were standing very close to each other, her skin burning where he had touched her. "I can't do this," she whispered, shaken by this betrayal of her body, this unexpected, powerful response to this man's touch.

"Don't be afraid of me," he said.

"Don't you understand? I'm afraid of what I see in your eyes." *I'm afraid of what you see in mine.*

She turned and fled across the cloister.

Beckett ran after her.

They did not see the tall, fair man in the far shadows of the cloister, who swallowed the last of his ice water and followed them into the darkness.

# CHAPTER SIXTY-ONE

The child's bedroom door was open. The light from his small lamp spilled across the curled shape in a fuzzy, diagonal band. A worn stuffed bear was clutched in the boy's arms. Gideon stood by the bed, keeping watch, and reached out to smooth springy curls off TJ's forehead. Then he touched his lips to the child's cheek. Cool skin, a peaceful sleep.

"Sweet dreams, TJ," he whispered.

He walked back to his own room, undressed, and slipped under the sheets. The woman beside him made a small sound but did not wake up.

The window was filled with stars. Tomorrow, he vowed, I'll find a way to get to the abbey. And this time Dane won't stop me.

He lay on his back for a long time, watching the starry night and listening to the sounds that echoed in his head—the swirling notes of a piano concerto, and the low, haunting notes of a woman's laughter.

* * *

Her glass of brandy was almost empty.

Almost midnight. Maggie stood on her small balcony, staring up at a sky the color of grapes. The warm night wind washed over her, scented with night-blooming jasmine, and the tall pines shifted against the glimmering sky.

Movement down to her left caught Maggie's eye. A lone man stood on a darkening rise, hands in pockets, a stark figure against the canvas of stars. Michael Beckett. The Golden sat a few feet away from him, still as a statue, staring out at the hills.

Maggie watched a match flare as he turned toward the distant black shape of Mont St. Victoire. There was a core of darkness in this man, a frightening sense of violence and danger about him. Are you lonely tonight, too, Colonel? she asked the silent figure in the blue light. But there was only the red glow of the cigarette, arcing like a falling star against the night sky.

Did he know that, when they were dancing, he'd called her by her name? Somewhere in the hills, an owl cried out. It was a cold, lonely sound. Desolate. Maggie shivered and pulled her thin sweater tightly around her shoulders.

Not even grief stays the same, she thought with despair. Today there had been no time for private sorrow, no time for thoughts of her husband. And tonight—tonight, she had danced with another man and wanted him to kiss her.

*What is happening to me?*

"Johnny?" she whispered into the night.

Silence.

"I don't want to lose you, Johnny."

Maggie drained her glass and turned to lock the French doors against the terrors of the night.

\* \* \*

The night was all black and silver. The clock chimed two a.m., but Beckett was not asleep. Dressed in a navy turtleneck and jeans, he had been sitting on his balcony, smoking and watchful, for over an hour. Only two cigarettes left. The Golden was snoring in the bedroom behind him.

Once, he thought he saw a slight movement in the shadows. There, to the right of the garden. A deeper blackness, shifting against the dark pines. But all remained quiet. "Damned eyes," he said aloud.

He stared at the dark trees and listened to the faint classical music coming from Maggie's room. Lonely people fill their rooms with sound, he thought. I ought to know.

She had to be asleep by now. He touched the gun tucked into the waistband of his jeans. Once again, he climbed across the narrow gap onto her balcony.

He settled into the wicker chair just outside her French doors. It was cooler than he had expected for a summer night in Provence, and he shifted awkwardly on the small seat. The devil with comfort. He was going to stay close to her, after that attack in the bird market.

Beckett watched the stars wink uncertainly through the shifting pines. What would happen if they found Zachary Law? Christ, how could any man walk away from a woman like Maggie O'Shea? He pictured her face when she'd spoken of Law. Would she fall in love with Zachary Law all over again, now that her husband was gone? Beckett didn't want to know.

Face it, he told himself. The Maggie O'Sheas of this world do not end up with the Michael Becketts. Just concentrate on the work and—

The cry, low and desperate, jolted him from his thoughts. Someone was in her room! In an instant he was on his feet. The lock was forced quickly and easily under his strong hands, and he entered the room in a crouched position, gun drawn.

"Maggie!"

Faint moonlight bathed the room in ghostly light. His eyes searched the shadows. There was no one else in the bedroom. All he could see was Maggie, small and lost in the great four-poster bed. She was on her knees, her nightgown a floating blur of white veils. The dark hair was wild, loose and long, tangled about her face and shoulders. Once more she cried out desperately. He moved swiftly toward her.

The faint light was behind him. In the shadows, she would see only the broad shoulders and the dark, indistinct face. Don't scare her...

She reached out to him.

Somehow he was in her arms.

"You're here," she whispered. "Oh, God. Hold me. Hold me, please. Don't let me go."

Her rough pain tore at him. He put his arms around her and folded her gently against his chest in the velvet dark.

As he smoothed back her hair, the soft scent of her seemed to fill his head. Roses. "I've got you," he said softly.

Trembling, she turned blindly towards him. "Love me," she whispered, and kissed the dark hollow of his neck.

Astonishing, the feel of her lips on his skin.

Desire, hot and strong and totally unexpected, washed through him. Suddenly he was intensely aware of her slim nakedness under his hands. Heart hammering, he tilted back her chin and lowered his head as his mouth sought hers.

Caught in the dream, she whispered into his mouth, "God, yes. Love me, Johnny. Love me."

Beckett froze. The realization was sudden, shattering. *She's been dreaming. She thinks I'm Johnny O'Shea. I should have known better.*

With an intense effort of will Beckett forced down the roaring flood of his need.

Very gently, he eased her back against the pillows and tucked the quilt around her trembling body. "Go back to sleep, Mrs. O'Shea," he whispered. "You were dreaming. But you're safe now."

*I've got you.*

# CHAPTER SIXTY-TWO

Sunrise spilled gold over the rocky hilltop and lit the silver-gray Jaguar XJ12 parked in the still-quiet marketplace in the village of Ménerbes.

This morning the square was eerily silent. Dane was the only customer in the café. He finished writing, slipped the note into an envelope, and leaned back in the chair to wait. Light glinted off the mirrored glasses as his eyes caressed the smooth, sensuous curves of the Jag. Dropping a hand to his thigh, he felt the reassuring pressure of the knife against his leg.

He watched the small flower stand across the marketplace, where an old woman with withered skin worked in the sunlight. Yes, old one, he thought, choose your best.

He glanced at the new Rolex. Soon, down in the valley, his beautiful Juliet would wait in the abbey garden. He pictured her sitting alone in a purple sea of lavender. Waiting for Gideon.

The coffee was hot and strong and very sweet in his mouth. He looked out over the ochre valley and thought of the bedroom in his house on the cliffs. The wide antique bed, the thick stone walls that muffled all sound. Tonight he—not Gideon—would have her. She would tell him everything he wanted to know.

Dane stared blindly out at the sunlit hills. Would she tell her colonel where she was going? It was a risk. But if her protector followed her to the abbey—Dane flexed his muscular shoulders—so be it. You won't stop me.

"*Je m'excuse, Monsieur.*" The old woman stood in front of

him. "*Vos fleurs.*" She handed him a huge bouquet, dewy and fragrant in the morning air.

Dane pressed a handful of francs into her hand and adjusted the mirrored sunglasses over his eyes. He was ready.

Sliding into the Jaguar, he drove south through the quiet countryside. The motor purred softly as the powerful car responded instantly to his touch.

He glanced down at the bouquet. Only once, years ago, had he given flowers to a woman. His beautiful Viola, in Twelfth Night. It had been snowing all day, but still he had managed to find the small nosegay of spring flowers. When the curtain came down, she had slipped her arms around his neck and kissed his rough cheek. The only woman who ever really loved him.

*Until she discovered his secret life.*

He accelerated past the ruins that stood over the red roofs of Ménerbes like a sinister ghost town on the skyline. When he returned, he would not be alone.

His gloved hand slowly rubbed back and forth against the soft black leather of the passenger seat. Gideon's woman...

It was time for Magdalena O'Shea to tell him exactly why she was in Aix. He needed to know, before he delivered her to Victor.

Anticipation only fueled his excitement.

\* \* \*

Gideon hung up the telephone and moved to the Bechstein piano. "No problem," the conductor had said. "Always a ticket for you." Gideon stared down at the ivory keys. No one could have kept me away from Sénanque Abbey today, he thought.

A small hand touched his knee.

"TJ, good morning." He hugged the child, kissed the top of the dark curls. "Did you have your breakfast?" A vigorous nod. "Celeste is still asleep," Gideon said to the boy. "We could have a quick lesson now if you'd like." The child settled himself on the piano bench and smiled up at the tall man beside him.

Gideon looked past the child, through the open French

doors. The day, luminous amber now, was waiting for him. He could already hear the music in the abbey.

"Okay, TJ," he said. "Let's begin with the F-sharp cadenza."

* * *

Maggie stripped off her sweat-stained running clothes and dropped them in a damp pile on the bathroom tiles. She had needed the morning's run, needed to hear the sound of her feet hitting the shaded cobblestones, the beat as regular and reassuring as a Scarlatti sonata.

And maybe, she admitted to herself at last, to crush last night's mutiny of the body with grueling physical exertion.

The full-length mirror caught her attention, and she looked closely at the face in the glass. Familiar...and yet unfamiliar. Was there more color in the pale skin this morning? Less shadow across her eyes?

She kicked off her Reeboks and stepped into the shower. No time for such thoughts. There was an open-air jazz concert scheduled for noon, then Gounod and Bach at St. Sauveur Cathedral. Also, she remembered, there was a small classical performance in an abbey in the countryside north of Aix. She would have loved that. But Simon Sugarman wanted her here in town.

You're here to find Zach, she told herself. *Nothing more.*

She lifted her face to the tingling water, and memory washed over her. The first time she and Zach had made love, it had been in the tiny shower stall in his Cambridge apartment after a performance of La Boheme. *I'm falling in love with you, Slim.*

She stepped from the shower and wrapped herself in a thick white robe. The memories of Zach were sweet, but they were also part of another life. She was no longer eighteen. She was no longer afraid of an old love.

A knock sounded at the door. "Madame O'Shea." It was the voice of the concierge. She unbolted the door.

"*Les fleurs. Pour vous, Madame.*" The small man beamed at her.

Wildflowers and daisies like huge white stars with fiery

hearts. "How beautiful!" breathed Maggie. She buried her face in the blooms. From the colonel? She reached for the small envelope tucked inside the shiny green leaves.

A festival ticket was enclosed within the note. The Sénanque Abbey, one p.m. Vivaldi's Nisi Dominus. Charpentier's Te Deum. And a new concerto—the Piano Concerto No. 1 in D minor—by a local composer. Quickly her eyes dropped to the printed words of the note.

"*Les fleurs sont belles, comme tu.*" The flowers are beautiful, like you. Oh, Michael, thought Maggie. Then she saw the next words. Her heart stopped.

"I saw you last night in the cloister. Meet me this afternoon, in the lavender garden of the abbey, after the performance. If you want to see me, you must come alone."

Suddenly weak-kneed, Maggie sank to the cushion on the window seat. Dear God, she thought. It could only be Zach. Zach, who had always given her daisies.

*You're alive, Zach.*

Her son's father was alive. She felt numb, gladdened, terrified. She knew only that she wanted to see him. After all these years, he was somewhere in the Luberon hills, waiting for her.

Just as the colonel had hoped. Her eyes sought the ribbon with the tiny transmitter. The bright bit of emerald, forgotten among the bottles on the vanity table, would lead the colonel, like a shimmering green road, directly to her. And to Zach.

*If you want to see me*, the note said, *come alone.*

But after the attack in Paris, Michael would never agree to let her go to Zach on her own. Maggie lifted the bit of ribbon thoughtfully. The wolf-faced man couldn't possibly know she was here—couldn't know about the abbey. She'd come all this way to find Zach. And he would never hurt her.

Before she could change her mind, she called the concierge for a car, dressed quickly, and scribbled a message on the hotel stationery. At the last minute, she fastened the green silk to her hair.

Then she edged into Beckett's shadowed room, using the extra key he had given her.

He was there, sleeping soundly, one arm flung across his eyes. A bare, muscular shoulder was just visible above a fold of white sheet. The Golden, curled on the bed next to him, raised his head to gaze at her. She raised a finger to her lips, smiled, and whispered, "Shh. I'll keep your secret if you'll keep mine." Seeming to understand, the Golden put his head back down on his paw but kept his eyes on her.

Her gaze returned to the colonel and her hand moved without conscious thought, as if to smooth the sheets over the broad shoulder. Her fingers stopped in mid-air, remembering the feel of him as they'd danced. *Don't even think about touching him.*

Very quietly, she moved the tumble of books on his nightstand to one side. *The Average Joe's Guide to Classical Music.* No wonder he'd known about Van Cliburn. She smiled, touched, glancing at the other titles. The new Winston Churchill biography, Neil Sheehan's *A Bright Shining Lie.* Dark heroes, World War II, Vietnam, Afghanistan. And there, tossed over a nearby chair, a worn gray t-shirt with the words, *Got Freedom?*

She left the message on the nightstand. "I hope you will understand, Michael," she whispered as she closed the door behind her.

* * *

Gideon pulled the Fiat over to the side of the hairpin road and walked to the edge of the cliff. It felt good to be out of the confining car, good to breathe the valley air and feel the sun warm his neck.

He was on a hilltop just beyond the town of Gordes. Now, before dropping down into the deep valley, he wanted to enjoy this view of Abbaye de Sénanque. Below him, solitary and austere and veiled in white light, the twelfth-century Cistercian abbey waited tranquilly in a sea of lavender. In a few hours the church would be alive with music, but for this moment it belonged only to him.

He stood for a long time, savoring the beauty and serenity

of the old abbey rising out of the purple wilderness. Pure light on red cliffs, and the valley carpeted with flowers. This place spoke to him. There was a spirit here, like the spirit in his Luberon vineyard. Inspiration...a passage of new music was forming in his mind, like swirling crystals arranging themselves into intricate patterns against the bright sky. A passage that spoke of sunlight and chimes, lavender and prayer.

A sudden breeze carried the scent of distant rain. He lifted his head and felt on his face the faintest breath of a Provençal thunderstorm, the kind that broke suddenly, wildly across the hills and then just as quickly was gone.

The pattern of crystal notes broke, rearranged, found a stormy new intensity on the phantom piano in his head, as Gideon climbed back into the car and drove down into the valley.

* * *

Beckett groaned and sat up, shielding his eyes against the glare of sunlight. His head felt thick and fuzzy. He fumbled for his watch and glasses on the small table beside the bed. The white envelope fell unseen to the floor.

He squinted at his watch. After ten already.

Dropping back to the bed, he lit one of the last two cigarettes left in their crumpled package and watched the blue smoke swirl lazily toward the spinning ceiling fan. The Golden was sitting by the French doors, waiting for him.

Dark dreams still swirled in his head. He couldn't shake the strong sense of danger, the sense of being followed, last night after the reception. Maggie had been driven back to the inn by an Aixois policeman. He'd taken a more circuitous route, watching a parade of changing headlamps catch his rearview mirror. Twice he'd glimpsed a dark compact, once a jeep, once a low-slung sports car—maybe a Jag or a Zee—glinting silver in the moonlight. He thought he'd lost them, but—damn. His instincts were rarely wrong.

After Maggie's nightmare, he'd stayed watchfully awake. A bad case of JDFR, Sugar would call it. *Just Didn't Feel Right.*

Half sitting up in the bed, Beckett pulled the hotel phone over and balanced it on his chest. He dialed the concierge. "Have you made the arrangements I requested last night?" he asked.

"*Mais oui*, everything is in readiness. We will take care of Madame O'Shea's surprise this afternoon, while she is out," answered the young concierge, who enjoyed satisfying the unusual requests of his guests. "This one is quite a challenge."

Beckett left a message for Sugarman, then moved naked to the bathroom. The face that stared out at him from the mirror was tired and troubled. He rubbed the gray-flecked jaw as he looked into the flinty eyes. How does she see me, he wondered.

A girl's voice, high and slightly off-key, reached him from the open balcony doors. "Now, what the devil?" muttered Beckett. He pulled on a pair of jeans and moved barefoot out onto his balcony.

He leaned around the leafy partition. The tiny maid, dwarfed by a frilly white uniform, was singing as she rubbed lavender scent into the flowered carpet.

"Mademoiselle," he called. "Where is Mrs. O'Shea?" The singing stopped abruptly. The girl turned with a smile, then saw the dark look on his face. "But she is not here, Monsieur Beckette," she said. "Madame left over one hour ago. She asked me to tell you that she left a message for you, by your books."

He found it on the floor, the first words turning him cold. "Heard from Z."

*Zachary Law.* Bloody hell. Somehow, she'd been in touch with him. His heart thudded like cannons as he read the words. "Meeting him at Sénanque Abbey. Please give me today. I need to see him alone. Forgive me. M." Beneath the words, a scrawled postscript: "It's not like Paris. Z won't hurt me."

"Goddamn it," shouted Beckett, lunging for his Nikes. She didn't know the danger. He should have told her last night.

He was still buttoning his shirt as he raced down the stairs, Shiloh loping behind him. He was almost out the hotel door when he stopped in the lobby and turned to the young concierge.

"Did you rent a car for Madame O'Shea this morning?" he asked.

The young Frenchman smiled. "*Mais oui, Monsieur.*"

"What make?"

"A yellow Renault." He shook his head in bewilderment. "She did not like your flowers, Monsieur?"

Beckett halted, halfway through the door, and swung around. "What did you say?"

"The wildflowers, Monsieur." The concierge stared at the rigid body and shook his head. "Daisies. You did not—"

"Who delivered them?" Beckett demanded through clenched teeth.

"A tall blond gentleman, Monsieur. In sunglasses. It was odd, now that I think of it—a delivery man, driving a silver Jaguar. But then, in Provence—"

Last night. Moonlight glinting silver on a sports car in his rearview mirror.

Beckett and the dog were already out the door.

# CHAPTER SIXTY-THREE

Sugarman gazed down at the file in his hand. Vanessa Durand. On paper, the beautiful art gallery owner was a successful, innocent businesswoman. A friend of Fee's, a woman trying to help them find Orsini. So why didn't he trust her? She'd worked for Orsini in Rome. She sent John O'Shea to Hyères. Okay. No crime there. Unless...

His cell phone jangled, scattering his thoughts. Sugarman pitched wadded balls of yellow legal paper toward a wastebasket as he answered. "Yes, sir, good morning."

The Admiral's voice rumbled in his ear.

Sugarman listened, pitched, and scored. *Swish*!

"Nada. Yet. But Maggie O'Shea's attending more performances today. My gut tells me Zachary Law and Victor Orsini are close. We'll find them."

He sent another paper ball sailing across the room. I just need time, he told himself, and a major dose of seren-fucking-dipity. "I know, I know," he murmured into the receiver. "Three more days 'til the twelfth. If we're right, then we're running out of time. I say we cancel the President's plans."

The answer did not surprise him. This President refused to give in to fear. And he was, after all, asking to alter the schedules of the world's most powerful leaders.

"This guy has a world-class knowledge of explosives, sir," warned Sugarman. "He's a master of disguise, he can get a weapon past any airport or embassy security, he can patch into iPhones and computers—"

The words in his ear were sharp and final.

"Yes, *sir*," said Sugarman. So, he told himself, we protect The Man and his guests, like it or not. Level four cover. An attack in New York would be—shit! He said, "We still don't know for sure if the President is the target."

Sugarman listened, then sat up, paper basketballs forgotten.

"They *can* get into a big reception, sir," he warned. "Especially a man who's faceless. I guarantee it."

Sugarman moved to the window and looked down into the small courtyard. "One man's terrorist is another man's freedom fighter."

A new note of urgency in the answering voice.

"Yeah, I hear you. We need Victor Orsini. Yesterday. But I have an idea, sir. If you're willing. May be crazy, but I think it's worth a shot..."

Ten minutes later, Sugarman clicked off his cell and stared unseeing at the floor. "All hell's gonna break loose," he said. "It's on your shoulders now, Maggie O'Shea. Babe, you have *got* to find Zach Law."

\*\*\*

Maggie stood quietly in the back of the soaring arched nave in the Abbey of Sénanque, captivated by the simplicity and the harmony of line. The church was a great tunnel of light and shade, a place of austere beauty devoid of paintings, sculpture, and stained glass. The only richness, thought Maggie, was the grand piano, lit by bands of dusty light that poured through three high arched windows.

Beyond the windows, the lavender garden waited. Was Zach waiting there for her now? Standing in the silent shadowy nave, a curious calm settled over her. Zachary Law felt very close.

Would it be Zach who strode onto the stage?

The small orchestra of men and women sat quietly, hands on their instruments, waiting. The conductor entered, followed moments later by the soloist. But the pianist chosen to premiere the concerto was a young Asian. *If you're not playing, Zach, then where are you?* Once more, her gaze swept the crowd.

The baton came down. The piano's opening trills fell around her like the golden light that rained from the high stone walls. Chords that were hauntingly, achingly familiar.

She recognized the music immediately. It was Zachary Law's concerto.

And then she turned her head and saw him.

# CHAPTER SIXTY-FOUR

"Don't even think about it."

Dane had just locked the Jag when he heard the low voice behind him. He turned. It was Magdalena O'Shea's colonel, pointing the black barrel of a gun at his heart.

His hand hovered near his knife, the Laguiole's blade newly sharpened.

They stood, not moving, at the edge of the small field where visitors parked. The faint sound of violins and piano echoed toward them from the abbey.

"Over there," said the man, motioning him toward the offices behind the abbey. "The French authorities have some questions for you. And so do I."

Behind the mirrored glasses, Dane's eyes swept the field. The abbey, straight ahead. Two buses, some eighty or ninety cars. To the left, a wall of rock and gorse leading out of the valley. To his right, the field dropped off into a steep rock-filled ravine. "You will get no answers from me," he said.

"Shut up and move," said the man. He took a step closer.

Dane coughed, raising a hand to his mouth. The man recognized the danger just as the knife slipped into Dane's fingers, but he reacted just seconds too late. Dane dropped to the earth and lashed out with his boot at the man's bad knee, smashing him into the hood of a parked Fiat. His pistol arced into the air.

Dane flung himself toward the gun. Then the man was on top of him.

Locked together, they rolled over bone-grinding rocks toward the edge of the ravine.

A wild barking, from the parking lot.

A hard knee to the groin, a harsh scrape of breath. The flash of the knife. A brutal fist, numbing the arm. Now the bright blade, skittering across silver rock.

No gun, no knife. No rules. A shuddering kick, smashing into ribs. A muttered curse, a sickening blow to the kidneys. A sudden dark burst of blood from Dane's nose, splattering their faces with streaks of crimson.

Dane's hands closed around the man's neck. Gasping for breath, his opponent slammed a savage blow to his skull. They crashed backwards together, tumbling toward the edge of the ravine.

A thumb, digging into an eye. A chopping blow to the temple.

A fist to the back of the neck.

They both saw it at the same time. Through the red mist, a glint of half moon, caked in earth and rust. They threw themselves at the scythe.

Dane reached for the blade, but the man's fingers closed around the wooden handle and hurled it out of reach. Dane slammed his boot into the man's back. The man grabbed Dane's leg and twisted. Somewhere, a dog was howling.

The scythe was just feet away from them. They rolled together, locked like lovers, toward the blade.

It was Dane who gripped the steel beneath his fingers and dragged it closer.

* * *

Beckett felt the heavy blade press against his neck. There was a roaring inside his head. Golden eyes smiled down at him.

*No way, you fucking bastard.* If he could just reach—his fingers tore at his pocket, searched, clutched, locked on cold metal. His lighter.

He gripped his adversary's wrist with savage brutality. The orange flame shot high, moved closer. Beckett forced the fire against the man's palm as he looked into the glowing eyes. "This hand hurt her," he whispered.

The man roared, as flame seared flesh.

Fingers torn away. Ragged, gasping breath.

A sharp kick, sending the scythe sliding down into the ravine.

A rock held high, blocking out the sun.

Beckett twisted away, toward the edge of the ravine.

Over! Falling, falling.

Blue sky, then red darkness.

* * *

She saw him first in profile, his left side toward her, a bearded man in a camel sports coat leaning against a stone pillar in the back of the nave. His fingers drummed his thigh to the rhythm of the music in a gesture she remembered immediately. He was alone.

Classical jazz notes swirled around her.

She could not breathe. He was taller than she remembered and very thin, with the high brow and the jutting, bony nose above the bearded chin. His skin was darkened by the sun. Black hair, still much too long, fell over his forehead and curled behind the ears. The way his shoulder curved into the muscular back. Oh, God. He was so much like Brian.

He swung his head around and looked directly at her.

The music faded, all sound stopped.

*He's alive.*

The abbey seemed to blur around the edges of her vision. Dazed and lightheaded, Maggie was unable to move. She simply stood and stared at him. He's older, she thought with shock. The gentleness was gone from the dark, sensitive eyes. A jagged scar ran from his temple down the side of his face. The man who looked down at her was still disconcertingly handsome, but now the face was hard, and scored by pain.

A rush of memories, dizzying. She took a step toward him, holding out her hands. "Zach?"

He was looking at her as he would a stranger.

"Zach," she said again.

She saw the shock jolt his body. "Slim?" he said, in the voice she remembered. The old endearment seemed to rise unbidden to his lips.

But then the dark lashes lowered over his eyes, like the shadow of wings on bright stone. He turned fully to face her. The empty right sleeve of his coat swung gently toward her as he moved.

Zachary Law no longer had a right arm.

# CHAPTER SIXTY-FIVE

Her denial was immediate. "No! Oh dear God, Zach. Not your arm—"

Her words sounded as if they echoed toward him through a long tunnel. But the words didn't matter; he couldn't seem to take his eyes off her face. She was much thinner, but startlingly beautiful. Her hair was still long, caught back at the nape of her neck with an emerald ribbon. He had forgotten how green her eyes were. Eyes that still, after all the years, gazed at him in his dreams.

The notes of his concerto crashed around him. He raised a finger to touch her cheek. "You still look like a girl," he said.

* * *

Maggie looked at his empty jacket sleeve. All in an instant, she saw him the way he had been. Alone on a spot-lit stage. The sensitive hands, long-fingered and strong, flying across the keys; the power and passion of Tchaikovsky and Beethoven and Chopin, flung out into the far corners of the dark theatre; the wild, tumultuous applause. The exultant look on his face.

The true extent of his loss hit her with sudden, devastating brutality. A great rush of pain and rage surged through her.

"Zach. Your music."

They stared at each other, not breathing, like two lost children.

His breath came out as he grasped her arm tightly with his left hand. "Get hold of yourself, Slim," he said, unconsciously using the old nickname again. The concerto was approaching the end of the first movement, and several pairs of curious eyes in the back rows already were focused on them. "Come with me."

He dropped his hand and hefted a cane that had been resting against the pillar. *Not his leg, too.* She watched him move haltingly, favoring his right leg, toward the door.

She followed him out into the purple valley.

\* \* \*

Dane opened his eyes and saw that he was bleeding on the black leather seat. *Merde!* His hand was on fire.

There was sharp pain and a thick, wet stickiness above his left eye. Forehead, he thought groggily. What else?

Slowly, carefully, he took a mental inventory of his body. Finally he was satisfied. The eye, his ribs, his left leg. *The burned hand...* Fury gorged his throat as he tore the sleeve from his shirt and tied the cotton around his palm. Raising his head painfully, he looked out the Jaguar's window.

Off to the south, great gray clouds raced toward the valley.

Very carefully, Dane shifted his body and turned the key in the engine. Pain shot through his fingers as the motor leapt instantly to life. Go easy. He slipped the car into reverse and backed slowly out of the field onto the road.

His foot slammed the brake. *Go back for her!*

She had told the man she called Colonel to come to the abbey.

Dane stared at the abbey doors, then down at his charred hand. The need to punish her was overwhelming. *Take her now.* He grasped the door handle. *Think,* his thoughts hammered. She was in the abbey, surrounded by hundreds of people. He pulled the saturated crimson cloth tighter around his throbbing fingers.

Blood was pooling on the Jag's leather seat. Magdalena O'Shea would have to wait. But only for a little while.

He eased the car forward, not even glancing at the ravine.

The colonel had disappeared over a steep ledge. He was no longer a problem.

*  *  *

Zachary Law led Maggie through the garden. Clouds rolled toward them like great black ships, driven by the wind. She kept her face turned away. The quickening wind loosened her hair, lifting it in dark ribbons behind her.

Finally he stopped by a small wooden bench and turned to her. "I like your Leonard Bernstein shirt," he said. "Do you remember the night we—"

"Stop it!"

"Maggie. Look at me." His left hand lifted her chin, and he stared down into her face. Not the face of the girl he had loved. He was struck again by the change in her, wary and thinner. "You're even more beautiful now," he murmured.

"Don't." She tried to pull away, but still he held her chin in his strong fingers, forcing her to face him.

"Why, Zach?" Shock shimmered in her voice. "How could this happen? To such a brilliant pianist..." She could not finish.

His fingers traced the lines of her jaw. "Do you have any idea how many nights I've tried to recapture the sound of your voice? The nights I've heard your laughter in my dreams, imagined this face next to mine?" His fingers moved to her lips. "My beautiful Slim..."

She twisted away from him. "Don't call me that! You let me think you were dead." Years of anger and pain trembled in the words as thunder echoed toward them from the blackening hills.

"How could you do that to me?" she cried. "Zach. Look at me. I need to know why."

Zach kept his eyes on the flickering sky. "My name is Gideon now."

"Gideon." She said the name, trying to connect it with the bearded, sunburnt face and the long, curling hair. He's suffered, she told herself. She could see it in the eyes, just as she'd heard it in his concerto. *You really are another person now. I don't know you.*

"I loved you," she said. "But you never came home to me. The arm wouldn't have mattered, Zach—"

"I left a lot more than my right arm back in that desert, Maggie."

"You pretended to be *dead*. I have a right to know why." She thought of their son Brian. "Why didn't you come home?"

Thunder rumbled over them, lightning flashed over the black hillside. "I don't want to leave you, but I have no choice. The storm..." He looked down at her. "I can't lose you again, Maggie."

"Then don't walk away from me, Zach. I have to know the truth."

"I know," he said, "but I have to go." His voice was filled with urgency. He rushed on recklessly, gesturing toward the south. "Spend the day with me tomorrow, Maggie. I've made my life here, just over those hills. A small vineyard in the Luberon. I'll tell you everything."

Maggie looked south, beyond the purple rain-swept cliffs.

"I have a family now," he said. "It's the storm—I *must* get back to them."

Family. I have a family, too, she thought. A son, Zach. *Our* son. But she was not ready to speak of Brian. Not yet. Maybe not ever. And—he did not ask.

"Please," he said to her. "Where are you staying?"

"Aix," she whispered. "But—"

Zach's next words were swallowed by the wind. "—and I've got to leave *now*! Driving these roads in a storm is hard enough with two arms." He held out his left hand to her. "I'll take you to your car."

She stared at him, wanting desperately to grasp his hand, to go with him. *Don't leave me again, Zach...* "Just go," she told him.

"Maggie! Come to me tomorrow."

She closed her eyes against the pain. Just do it, damn you. Do it for your godchild.

"Yes," she whispered. "Yes, I'll come to you."

He gave her the sweet smile that was Brian's, and her heart twisted inside her chest. "Come early," he told her, turning toward the cars. "Le Refuge, we call the vineyard. Just south of Lourmarin, on the D943. No more than forty-five minutes from Aix."

She watched him hurry away from her, the limp more pronounced now, as the immense black sky above the valley trembled with thunder. He was leaving her again. And still, she had no answers.

For an instant, a flash of light lit his diminishing figure. She thought her heart would break with the pain.

This stranger was her son's father. They had been so young when she loved him. But he was no longer that boy. He was a man now. With a new name, a beard, a broken body. A different look in the eyes. He belonged to another country, another life—another woman? No, he was not the man she remembered.

The truth was there all along, she thought. All the unsettling moments—the unfamiliar handwriting on the note to his father, the look in Yvette's eyes in the Café de la Paix, the incredible left-hand passages in his concerto—all fell into place for her now like notes completing an unfinished symphony.

Maggie raised her face to the wildness of the day. She felt as storm-tossed as the cypress trees around her. You've lost so much, Zach. Your arm, your music, your dreams. Your son.

Only then did she remember the morning's daisies, and the note. *But it had not been Zach who asked her to meet him in the garden...*

The first drops of rain hit her upturned face.

And then, over the thunder, she heard the distant howling of a dog.

# CHAPTER SIXTY-SIX

Shiloh's howls brought him back to consciousness.

Rain stabbed his face with icy needles. Beckett groaned and rolled over. Shiloh? Thank God he'd locked the Golden in the car with the windows cracked. No telling what he would have— images of the fight came roaring back. Where is the damned gun? And where in bloody hell is Maggie?

Pain shot through his head, threatening unconsciousness. You're too mean to die in the rain, he told himself. Slowly, he pulled himself to his feet. Fire ignited in his knee, seared up into his groin. He took a deep breath and squinted up into the driving rain.

A flash of lightning lit the wall of the ravine. Rocks, gorse, trees. And fucking steep. He grasped a tree trunk and hauled his body upward. Pain hammered at him as fear for Maggie drove him on.

Reach. Grasp. Pull.

Reach higher. Drag. Haul. Breathe.

Slip back, lunge upward.

*God, he had to get to her!*

One final lunge and he rolled onto the field. How long had he been unconscious? His eyes passed over the wildly blowing cypresses, the parked cars, the lights in the abbey. Thunder rumbled overhead, but then, in a beat of sudden silence, he heard the sounds of violins, faintly, in the darkness.

He stood up, swayed, forced his mind to focus. Through the

curtain of rain he saw an empty rectangle of grass. The silver Jaguar was gone. *Where are you, Maggie?*

He fumbled for the small transmitter. She was close!

He limped to his car, ignoring the pain that seared through his leg, and freed the Golden. Shiloh lunged out into the rain, leaped up, slammed against his chest. Beckett staggered, started running toward the great abbey doors. Be there, Maggie. "Come, Shiloh!" he shouted.

But the Golden held back, barking, his gaze fixed beyond the abbey walls.

Beckett stopped, turned. A flash of lightning turned the ancient stone to silver and for an instant lit the garden beyond the cloister wall. Was someone out there? He stopped, squinting through the pelting rain. Only blackness.

"Find her, Shiloh! Find Maggie." The Golden loped away into the veil of rain, and Beckett ran blindly after him through the gates. *Let it be her...*

"Mrs. O'Shea! Maggie!" His voice was drowned out by the wind and the sound of rain pelting the stone.

He felt her before he saw her. Then a shadow shifted, moved. Lightning flashed, illuminating the pale, rain-streaked face framed by her wild and glistening hair. She was on her knees, arms wrapped around the dog while the rain streamed over them.

He ran up to her. Her eyes glittered with profound shock.

"My God," he said. "Did you find Law?"

"He's alive, Michael." Her voice trembled with disbelief.

He bent, put his arm around her, drew her to her feet. "Of all the crazy, dangerous things to do!" He pulled off his jacket and dropped it over her shaking shoulders.

Another roll of thunder as she pulled the jacket around her, the Golden pressing close against her. In the flashing darkness, she did not seem to register his battered face and mud-streaked clothing. "Zach," she whispered, shivering uncontrollably. "He's—"

"We'll talk about Law when you're warm. Let's go home now, Maggie."

"Home?" She turned to him and clutched his sleeve. "There is no turning back for me now!"

A jagged bolt of lightning lit the great dome of black sky. The wind ripped at the green ribbon and her hair blew free, whipping about her face. They faced each other, breathing rapidly, in the hurling rain.

She tried to pull away, but still he held onto her. "What happened to you, Maggie?" he yelled above the howl of the wind.

She broke from his grasp and whirled away from him.

"Tell me," he demanded.

She raised her face to the rain and threw her arms toward the electric sky. "*Zachary Law is alive!*" she shouted into the wild dark.

She stood before him in the driving rain, a burning, vibrant figure, defiant and fiercely alive against the immense violent sky, with the Golden pressed against her side.

It was an intensely elemental image. Beckett stared at her, shocked by his primitive response to this woman in the storm. She was so damned...valiant. He reached to push the wet hair from her eyes.

"No," she said, turning away from his touch and walking away from him through the dark rain.

A woman scarred by death. And a man scarred by life.

He let her go.

# CHAPTER SIXTY-SEVEN

PROVENCE. NIGHT, JULY 9

"What's the matter with you, Gideon?"

Zachary Law stood at the window of the music room, watching the storm roll over the vineyard in great roaring waves of dark and light.

"Gid?" Celeste's voice was frightened. "You've been so edgy since you got home. So distant. Please..."

He turned to her. "It's the storm, Celie," he lied. But it wasn't the storm, or the long-awaited premiere of his concerto, that gripped him. Tonight his thoughts swirled around Maggie O'Shea.

So many memories crowded his mind. The rehearsal room in Boston. The long walks, the secrets whispered late at night. Her beautiful, giving body. The piano, always the piano.

He hadn't even asked about his father. All memories from another life, a life when he could still play a keyboard, shake hands, knot a black bow tie, applaud—when he could make love to a woman, balance above her. Maggie, too, was a part of his concerto. He would tell her that tomorrow.

Celeste's arms slipped around his waist from behind. "Come to bed, Gideon. Let me make you forget."

"No, Celie." His left hand dropped to the silent keys of the Bechstein. "You go on. I'll be along in a while."

His fingers caressed the piano as she reached to touch the back of his neck. She waited, letting her hand linger on his skin. When he did not respond, she turned and left the room.

\* \* \*

At the inn on the edge of Aix-en-Provence, the tiny old-fashioned lift clanked slowly upward in the shadows. Outside, the rain still fell.

They'd dropped Shiloh off with the concierge and Maggie and Beckett rode pressed together in a silence vibrating with tension.

She had told him about Zachary Law on the drive back to the inn. Only twice did her voice flicker. Once, when she told him that someone—not Zach—had lured her to the abbey with a note in a bouquet of flowers. And once when she told him about the loss of Zachary Law's arm. And then—

*He asked me to come to him tomorrow, to Le Refuge.*

*No way in hell.*

*I'm going, Michael. You won't stop me.*

Silence.

The ancient lift trembled to a shuddering halt. She caught Beckett's wince as he slid the metal gates open. In the dim light of the hallway bulb, the bruises on the side of his face were garish.

"Why won't you tell me what happened to you today?" she demanded.

He closed the gates with a clang. "Took on a scythe, ma'am. The scythe won."

"A scythe! At the abbey?" Suddenly, with sickening clarity, she knew. The man from the bird market had been waiting for her at the abbey. And found the colonel instead.

"The man who sent me the flowers—he did this." Without conscious thought, her fingers brushed Beckett's face. He smiled grimly, as if trying to hide the impact of her unexpected tenderness.

"I hope you hurt him." And then, a bare whisper, "Who have I become?"

"Age and treachery overcome youth and skill, ma'am. I hurt him, all right."

"And what about you?"

"I hurt *him*, ma'am. That's what counts."

"What do you do after a day like this?" she asked him.

"Drink."

\* \* \*

They walked down the dark, carpeted hallway, past the French policeman on guard by the lift, to her door.

Beckett stood behind her. Somewhere below them, a buzzer sounded. With a clanking motion, the lift began its slow descent.

She found the key and fumbled with the lock nervously. "Fit, damn you."

"You can't keep running away from me, Mrs. O'Shea."

She turned slowly. "Say my name, Michael."

He stared down at her, his eyes burning.

"*Say my name!*"

"Maggie."

He caught her hand in his, raised it to his lips. "Maggie," he said again, his mouth against her skin.

His large hands gripped her shoulders, and she closed her eyes and leaned against him. She'd pinned up her wet hair, and his fingers caressed the bare skin of her neck.

Far below her, she heard the faint click of the lift's door.

The lift began its slow, grinding ascent.

"Take down your hair," he murmured into her ear.

"Michael. Please..." Her whole body was quivering with exhaustion and the overwhelming shock of finding Zach. She had no control, no defenses left. Only need. *If he touches me again*, she thought, *I'm lost*.

He took the key from her trembling fingers.

She was trapped between his body and the room's door. She knew he wanted to come in. She was afraid to ask herself what she wanted.

*Who have I become?*

The ancient machinery of the lift hummed louder.

He looked down at her and pressed her back against the door, then his thumb brushed slowly across her lips.

"You need to get out of these wet clothes," he told her.

They were the sexiest, scariest words a man had ever said to her.

He turned the key in the lock. "I'll check your room." Swinging the door inward, he turned on the small lamp by the door and stepped inside.

She stood absolutely still, staring after him. Suddenly, sharply, she wanted—

The small elevator whirred to a halt.

A sharp clang as the gate opened. Low voices.

Soft footsteps, coming toward her through the darkness.

In an instant, Beckett was in front of her, shielding her with his body.

A man's voice in the quiet hallway.

"*Mon Colonel, c'est moi.*" It was the young concierge. "A message for you, from the States." He handed Beckett a folded slip of paper. "'Urgent', I was told, Monsieur. From Madame Beckett. Your wife."

*Wife...* Maggie stood frozen, watching the look of concern leap into Beckett's eyes.

He read quickly, then looked at her. "Life is a comedy for those who think," he murmured, "and a tragedy for those who feel."

"You're...married?"

A brusque nod. "There's a problem at home. I've got to make a call." He waved to the policeman standing near the lift. "Stay by her door," he ordered, and headed toward his room.

Beckett turned once more. She stood motionless in the dark hallway, hugging his jacket to her shivering shoulders. "Get out of those wet clothes," he repeated. "And promise me you won't go to Law without me."

Then his own door closed firmly behind him.

Blindly, she entered her room. Unable to move another step, she leaned her forehead against the oak door and closed her eyes.

Zach is alive. And Michael Beckett is married.

*He has a wife...*

And yet, when they'd stood alone in the dark hallway, she'd seen the longing in his eyes. And she'd known that he wanted her.

God help her, she'd almost let him stay.

She caught her breath in a harsh sob. The scent of lilacs filled her head.

Her eyes flew open. The light from the small lamp cast wavering shadows across the room. At that moment she sensed, rather than saw, the looming dark shape in front of her. Her heart seemed to shift in her chest. Slowly, disbelievingly, she moved forward.

Someone had removed the sofa. Watery moonlight fell in a silver path through the French doors to illuminate an enormous bouquet of white lilacs. *White lilacs, sent by a loving fan to Rachmaninoff...*

"Oh, Michael," breathed Maggie.

The flowers rested like tiny stars on a glowing baby grand piano.

Like a sleepwalker, Maggie walked forward. She laid her palms on the beautiful, polished instrument. A Mason and Hamlin piano—they didn't make these anymore. How, when had he arranged this?

Very gently her fingers touched the smooth ivory and ebony keys. Slowly, she depressed the middle C, heard the note, pure and true, felt the familiar vibration move through the bone and muscle of her arm. Tonight, her need for release from all the pain was overpowering. Somehow, Michael had known.

Maggie shook her head back and forth like a broken metronome. Nothing makes sense, she thought. My husband dies. Zachary Law is alive. The colonel is married—but he gives me a piano. It was too much. So many feelings locked deep within her trembling body, so many unshed, frozen tears. Suddenly she felt ready to shatter into a thousand brilliant shards of glass.

\* \* \*

It was very late. The crisis with his wife had been handled. For now.

Beckett poured a stiff drink and he and the Golden moved haltingly out onto his balcony to stare unseeing over the black hills.

Maggie O'Shea had done the impossible. She had found Zachary Law. Tomorrow, he and Sugar would know about the Orsini boy, one way or another. If only...

He couldn't forget the look on Maggie's face in the dark hallway. How could he betray her trust?

The rain had blown off. He looked up at the stars winking through the clouds.

He deliberately had withheld the location of Law's winery from a euphoric Sugarman. Couldn't trust Sugar not to charge in tonight, take the place by storm. No, they'd do it right.

He could still give Maggie time to tell Law about their son before all hell broke loose. After all the lies, he owed her that much.

He glanced once more toward her bedroom. Tonight, when he'd left her, her eyes had been too hard, too bright. *I didn't want it to be this way.* Try to sleep now, Maggie. You've found the father of your son. The last act begins tomorrow.

He listened to the quiet of the night. High above him, in the deep silence, the silver clouds raced across the face of the moon.

Suddenly the silent night was shattered by a crashing, violent storm of piano chords. The tumultuous notes flung themselves out into the dark tempest of the night, fearsome and blistering, smoldering and swirling and full of fury.

"Jesus," breathed Beckett. His hand sought the dog and held on.

He stood very still, bombarded by the fierce, turbulent music that burst like fireworks around him. Trembling, dropping, then soaring higher. What had she told him she would play? The hurtling, searing rage of Beethoven.

For a long time, Beckett and the Golden listened in the darkness as she played wave after wave of savage, agonized notes.

Played as if her heart, her very breath, were the notes that hurled like bullets through the air. It was the most aching music he'd ever heard.

Then, finally, she struck the fearsome opening chords of music he'd never heard. The Grieg? The music she'd been playing when her husband died? Beckett felt as if the notes were being torn from deep within her haunted body.

On and on, the music soared into the blackness.

Suddenly there was an exhausted, final crash of chords, chords that spiraled up towards the shadowed moon and echoed out over the listening hills. The air rang and rang with the fading music until, at last, there was absolute silence.

Beckett whispered, "Brava, Mrs. O'Shea."

And then her agonized, wrenching sobs filled the night.

# CHAPTER SIXTY-EIGHT

Victor Orsini swirled the wine in his mouth, then swallowed the rich, crimson Brunello. A good year for wine, he thought, lifting the glass to toast himself in the mirror. The man staring back at him was bull-faced and dark-visaged with a sheen of silver over the heavy jaw and eyes black and deep as agate. Burning like coals, yet without light. The large cross around his neck glittered gold against his skin.

The book he had been reading lay on the table beside him, still open, but facedown. It told the true story of an ancient Italian family in Sicily, one in which the father had ruled his family with an iron hand. Orsini had remembered his own father, slapping him hard across the face because he had not respected his mother. He'd been only seven or eight, and no longer had any idea what his act of disrespect had been.

But he could still see his mother's shocked face if he closed his eyes, hear his younger sister's frightened wails, feel the sharp, bright sting of his father's huge hand. "You will learn respect, Vittorio. Discipline." He had slapped his *own* son, hadn't he, in the garden in Rome, just before Sofia left him.

*Respect. Discipline.*

"The sins of the father..." he murmured. He took another deep swallow of wine, fingering the heavy cross at his throat. What would have happened that day if he had not slapped his son? If he had not threatened Sofia, but told her the truth? That he had to go into hiding. That he was afraid.

*What if he had told her about Ravello?*

He shook his heavy head. Would she have understood? Stayed with him? Or would the ending of their lives together have happened no matter what?

*I loved you once,* he told her silently. *But I loved another more. The truth is, I should never have married you.*

The sins of the father.

He rubbed his cheek slowly, remembering. As a boy, as a young man, he'd had a powerful love for his father. Followed him, emulated him, revered him. Until he learned the shocking, unspeakable truth.

His father's intolerable secret.

Orsini's fingers tightened on the glass until his knuckles were white. His father's blood ran in his veins. Tonight, he could feel the ghost of his father standing behind him. Feel the heavy hand on his shoulder.

He turned sharply. No one there. Only shadows.

He drank quickly then, finished the wine, poured another glass. And there, in the depths of the crystal, he watched the memory swirl and take shape.

* * *

*His mother's villa, pine shrouded and very old, stood at the end of a long, curving lane, on the edge of a hill high above Florence.* From the blue-stoned terrace, you could see the lights of *Firenze* flickering in the distance.

The old villa was totally dark, with an air of long abandonment, a looming black shape against the starless cobalt sky. Below the hillside, the lights of Florence flickered in the distance.

Just one day after his mother's funeral, Victor Orsini stood on the curving drive. Tall Tuscan pines surrounded the house, close together, silent and still as sentinels. The light from his flashlight played over the ancient gold stone with its rusting barred windows, the broad marble steps that led up to tall double doors. How many times had he run up those steps with his sis-

ter those long ago summers? Now a thick iron gate protected the
doors, locked against intruders. The heavy, ornate metal key was
in his hand.

*I don't want to go in. I don't want to find what I know is hid-
den there.*

He climbed the steps slowly, slipped the key into the lock.
A scraping of metal, a push. The gate folded back, doors swung
open with a protesting creak.

Huge round foyer, smelling of must and decaying flowers.
And, for just an instant, a faint breath of his mother's perfume.
*Emeraude.* A powerful surge of longing. Then it was gone.

He knew, intimately, every room, every window, every door,
every hallway. He turned to play his small light over the high
foyer, the glassed conservatory to the left, the arched doorway to
the formal living room. He glanced into the room. Hulking white
shapes, covered in dusty sheets, forgotten. He turned away.

His steps took him toward the high curve of staircase. Twenty-five steps to the landing, he remembered. Worn down over two
centuries by his ancestors, his grandparents, his mother, his sister,
himself.

Down the long dark upper hallway. Somewhere to his left,
the sound of dripping water. He walked like a man in prison to
the end of the hall, where a floor-to-ceiling antique cherry bookcase held gilt-framed photographs of happier times and his mother's dusty collection of colorful, never-used Tuscan pottery. Cor-
tona, he remembered.

He set the flashlight down, used both hands to grip one side
of the case. He was a strong man, determined. Slowly, slowly, he
angled the heavy case away from the wall. One large potter's bowl
tottered, crashed to the floor. He ignored it, continued to shift
the bookcase until he'd exposed the narrow door behind it.

He took a deep breath, inserted the key once more. Left,
then right. The stairs led up into an opaque, musky blackness.

He hesitated, unsure. He could not remember ever entering
the locked, hidden attic.

Fuck, he said to himself. Just do it.

The stairs creaked beneath his weight. Cobwebs, tiny drifting filaments in the shine of his flashlight, brushed over his face, his hands. Now he could smell, very faintly, wood. And something else...

He shined his light around the low attic space.

They were there, in the corner, under several white sheets. He tore at the sheets, closing his eyes against the dust that rose like clouds of insects.

He caught his breath. Stacks upon stacks, the canvases facing in against the wall, leaning against each other. And boxes, large and small, one on top of the other.

Reaching out his hand, he gripped the ornate golden frame nearest to him, turning the canvas so that he could see it in the light. The glow of huge spinning snowflakes...

*Jesus God.*

Monet. *The Street at Argenteuil? Jesus God.*

Quickly now, one canvas after another. Murillo. Klimt. Michelangelo's *Madonna of Bruges*. Dalí, Titian. Christ on the Cross. Botticelli... A flash of a red vest. Cézanne?

*JesusGodJesusGodJesusGod.*

He reached for the Murillo, best known for his religious works. Two saints—sisters, potters, martyrs. Facing each other, holding a small tower between them. Rufina and Justa? He vaguely remembered reading about this piece. Very slowly he turned the canvas over. The back of the frame contained the number R1171. He froze, knowing, from his studies at Yale, that it stood for the Rothschilds—the 1,171st object stolen from the family by the Nazis during the war. My God, it had to be worth ten million dollars.

He shook his head back and forth, sickeningly aware that he was looking at millions and millions of dollars' worth of looted art. Overwhelmed, barely able to breathe, he turned to the boxes. Tipped the cover off the first one. Shined his light over the contents.

An instrument case of beautiful inlaid wood. Engraved with

the letters *The Felix Hoffmann Gallery*. Pain, knife-sharp, speared through his chest. He sprang the latch, raised the lid slowly.

A violin. A del Gesù? He lifted it gently, checked the label in the frail light. A Roman cross. My God, he thought. Felix Hoffman's del Gesù. He thought he was going to be sick. Then he thought of his sister, and how she could make such a beautiful instrument sing. With reverence, he placed the violin back into its case, re-set the cover and turned to the next box, also labeled *The Felix Hoffman Gallery*.

He held his breath as he lifted the cover.

*Music.*

Scores.

He'd never come close to having the concert quality brilliance of his sister, but he could read music, play the piano with fair competence. Enough to recognize Benjamin Britten. Bach. Chopin, an autographed Vivaldi. But also sheaves of music he could not recognize at all.

Old, stained. Some with signatures or writing too faded to read. Manuscripts, dozens of pages of musical phrases, notations. Very carefully, he shifted several pages, searching deep into the box. Lifted one fragile, ink-marked score to the light. Covered in hand-written notations, blotched with ink. Cracked, faded, the edges browned. But—

He squinted, bent to examine the signed manuscript closely.

*No. Impossible. Jesus God.*

# PART III

## Found

*...for the touch of a vanished hand...*
—Alfred, Lord Tennyson

# CHAPTER SIXTY-NINE

It was just after midnight in Virginia, the air still and swollen with heat, when the eyes-only email account in the seventh floor CIA office hummed to life.

To the Deputy Director, 7/10, 12:01 a.m.

From S. Sugarman

Re: Operation Bright Angel

ZL alive. Concerto seeking child today.

They were in!

The silver-haired Admiral swung his wheelchair to the tall windows behind his desk. Just dawn in France, he thought. Sugar's photo hadn't lied. Zachary Law was alive. The O'Shea woman had found him. Now she just had to find the boy.

And if she did? A Commando-style abduction wouldn't work in a quiet French village. He could just hear the Special Prosecutor's rant over that one.

But if he knew Sugarman, he'd find a way. You're between a rock and a hard place, he told himself. *Orsini's client names and accounts are the key to your political survival.*

And the key to your destruction.

He had to get his hands on Orsini's journal before anyone else saw it.

Orsini's organization had been "extremely helpful" to America's interests in the past. But now alarm claxons clamored in his head, reminding him of the days when he'd commanded his own sub. Take action. *Dive!* The beast, so useful to him in the past, had broken out of its cage.

The Admiral's call to Vanessa Durand had been frustrating enough to cause a blistering argument. Orsini had gone to ground, and the art gallery dealer did not know how to reach him. Time was running out. Only forty-eight hours until the reception in New York. The President's guests arrived late tomorrow.

Somehow, he had to stop Orsini. He lit a cigar and closed his eyes as a cloud of smoke enveloped his head.

*I can't wait any longer.*

The wheelchair spun back to his state-of-the-art computer terminal. He thought for a moment. Then his hands began punching the keys.

Ninety seconds later, new instructions were received and acknowledged in a small office in Geneva. And in the blink of an eye, over three million dollars were transferred from one private Cayman bank account to another.

* * *

"Don't go, Maggie."

It was dawn in Provence. Beckett stood on her balcony, Shiloh sitting on guard by his side. They were surrounded by a watery mist that locked them in a silent gray world.

She was very still. Then, "You've started calling me Maggie."

"I gave you lilacs," he said. "I wanted to kiss you. I'd say that crossed the professional boundaries line, wouldn't you?" He held out his hands.

She thought about the night before and gestured toward the grand piano with its huge bouquet of flowers. "No one has ever given me white lilacs."

"Now that's a shame, ma'am."

"Thank you, Michael. For the piano. For the music."

"You're crazy talented. *You* brought your music back. Not me."

"I can't help wondering, who is this man standing in the mist on my balcony?"

"What I do is who I am. I'm just a man, Maggie. Not a hero. I get beaten up. I make mistakes..."

"Was last night a mistake, Michael? Was I wrong about you?" She looked away. "About us?"

The silvery eyes locked on hers. "No. We surely did open up something between us. And I don't know how to close it."

"Do you want to close it?" *Do I?*

"All I know is that I can't take the place of a ghost for you."

"It doesn't matter. You're married. I will not be 'the other woman.'"

"It matters, all right. But because you're not ready. Yes, I'm married, I never lied about that. But I don't park my car in that garage anymore. Haven't for fifteen years."

She watched his face, confused. "So you live alone?"

"I am alone. But this isn't about my wife. This search—it isn't over for either one of us. I'm not the man you think I am. The reality of my profession is that you hurt the people you love."

"What has hurt you so much?"

He was quiet for a long moment. Finally he said, "My wife and I, we'd been through...a really horrific time." His eyes turned black, remembering. "After my wife became withdrawn, depressed, full of anger and blame. Then all of a sudden, she was going out again in the afternoon, coming home late. All perfumed, with gin on her breath. Her eyes secretive.

"I didn't know what to do, so I brought her flowers. Yellow, her favorite color. She began to sob. Flowers couldn't fill the emptiness, she said. *I* couldn't fill the emptiness."

He looked away. "But apparently other men could. Men and booze. After a while, she just crawled inside a bottle. Then one day I came home and she was gone. Never gave a woman flowers again. 'Til you."

"What counts to me, Colonel, is that your wife can still count on you. You're there for her."

"I have to be. Because too much of it was my fault. Jeannie and I live separately, have for a long time. But she still needs someone to take her to AA, hold her head when she gets sick. She keeps promising to change, Maggie, and I want to believe her."

"You still love her."

"Yes. But the way I would love a hurting child. Not a woman." His eyes held hers. "I just never had a reason to go beyond our separation. Until now."

"Don't blame yourself for loving her."

"You can't be my damned bandage, Maggie."

"You're right, of course." She took a step away, looked out over the gauzy hills. "Zach is waiting for me. I should be leaving soon."

"Don't go, Maggie," he said again. "I don't want you to do this."

"I have to do this."

He handed her the green ribbon with the GPS device. "Then I'll keep you safe," he said.

# CHAPTER SEVENTY

"Please wait here, Madame." The housekeeper gestured to a cushioned chair shaded by a trellis of tangled wisteria vines. "Monsieur Gideon will return from the vineyard shortly."

It had been an easy drive, only forty minutes. Now, alone on the flagstone terrace, surrounded by huge bushes of wild rosemary and fragrant mimosa, Maggie turned in a slow circle and took a deep breath. The air was hot, dry, aromatic.

Scarlet geraniums spilled from ochre-colored pots, flaming hibiscus climbed a small fountain that shimmered with sunlight. In the shifting shade of the vines, a table set for two was laden with juice, fruit, and bright yellow cheese. She felt as if she had stepped inside an Impressionist painting.

Mindful of Simon Sugarman's instructions, Maggie's eyes searched the terrace carefully. But there were no toys, no torn candy wrappers, no ball and glove. No forgotten sneaker, no sudden shout of laughter. No sign at all that a small boy lived in this beautiful old farmhouse. Only the musical splash of the fountain and the drone of bees broke the stillness.

She moved to the edge of the patio. The rambling gold stone house called Le Refuge—Zach had described it as a Provençal "mas," a farmhouse—was set on a hillside strewn with fig trees and sunflowers. The land fell away to a deep azure pool, still as a mirror. She forced her eyes away from the water, toward the rows of green grape vines that flowed toward a high stone wall. Beyond the road, the red-rocked hills rose again, steeply.

A white spire and tiled roofs were just visible through a shifting forest of pines.

It was Beethoven's Pastoral Symphony come to life. And yet...

The vineyard was oddly guarded. Was Le Refuge really a haven from the world? Or a place to hide? She stared thoughtfully at the high walls surrounding the property. When she'd arrived, a man had been leaning against the huge locked gate, his hand resting casually on his hip. Too casually. And what about the Doberman by his side, an ugly brute with dark bristles and eyes the color of onyx? Leashed, certainly. But tense and watchful. Like the man. Were there more dogs? She shivered despite the heat.

Where was Zach? And where the hell was Michael?

Maggie poured a glass of orange juice from a tall pitcher. Shading her eyes against the bright Luberon sun, she searched the pines that curved along the vineyard's high wall. Michael had promised, in his exasperating way, that he would be "all over her like a cheap suit." But as her eyes swept the boulder-strewn hills and the stand of firs so green against the sky, there was no protector in sight.

Still exhausted from the long, emotional night, Maggie thought about how much her life had changed in these last weeks. For months she'd been totally alone and now, suddenly, *two* men were in her life. Closer than she wanted them to be.

Just concentrate on the reason you're here—Zach, and Tommy. But somehow her thoughts kept returning to the man who had walked into her life in an ancient cemetery, given her laughter and a piano and whispered into her hair in a dark hallway. The man who had given the music back to her.

In one night I found Zach and my music, she thought. And I lost someone to a wife I never knew existed.

*But Michael Beckett was never mine to lose.*

She held her wrists under the cooling water of the fountain and closed her eyes, giving herself up to the drone of the bees and the faint sound of music on the breeze.

Music? *A piano.*

Her head came up. She was absolutely still, listening. Yes. Piano music, coming from somewhere deep in the back of the farmhouse.

She moved toward the sound. The terrace extended beyond the trellis wall and disappeared around the corner of the house. Again she listened. No ominous footsteps approaching, no growling dog. Just the notes of the piano, calling to her like a lost friend. Glancing once more over her shoulder, Maggie moved cautiously to the rear of the terrace.

She rounded the corner and stopped just outside the open french doors, listening. It sounded like Zach's concerto. But a very simplified, childlike version, halting and uncertain. Long, white curtains billowed like a cloud around her, and the music beckoned. In the distance, a dog barked sharply.

Without looking back, Maggie stepped through the open doors into the room.

# CHAPTER SEVENTY-ONE

Maggie stood absolutely still in the doorway.

In the slanting light that poured through an arched window, a slight boy of five or six sat at a grand piano. He wore a striped t-shirt and shorts, exposing bony knees, and his bare feet strained to reach the pedals. He had black hair, sun-browned arms and legs, and he was as thin as an oboe. He was too engrossed in the music to notice her.

She stared at the child. Zach's boy? He had the look of Zach, certainly, with the dark hair and skin. And that intensity! But he resembled, too, the child in Sofia's most recent photograph of her son. This child's hair was much longer, the face thinner, older, and very solemn. She couldn't be sure.

She stood still for a long time, watching the boy and listening to the haunting melody. In spite of the hesitation, he played quite well for one so young. Someone had given him expressive dynamics. Already, he had a real feel for the keys. Inherited talent? she asked herself. This very intense child could well be Zach's son. His *other* son.

The music stopped abruptly and Maggie found herself looking into eyes that were black and very large in the thin face. Frightened eyes. All of her instincts came alive with warning. No child should be this afraid.

"Hello," she smiled gently. Without thought, she spoke in English. "My name is Maggie. I was waiting on the terrace, but your music was so beautiful."

For an instant, the boy froze. Then, eyes wide with uncomprehending terror, he slipped off the bench and ran to crouch behind the piano. Just like Beckett's Golden.

"Please," she said softly. "I'm not here to hurt you. I've come to visit Zach—no, Gideon," she amended quickly. She saw the tiny spark of interest flare like a struck match in the wary eyes, and pressed on. "You understand English, don't you? Did Gideon teach you to play the piano?"

The barest nod.

She took a step closer. "He taught me a piece of music, too, a very long time ago." The black eyes widened and lost some of their fear. "It was the Prelude in C, by Bach. It was one of—Gideon's—favorites, and became one of mine."

Very slowly, she moved to the piano, sat down, and touched the keys lightly. He stood slowly, keeping his eyes on her.

"Would you like to hear me play it for you?"

The child shrank back. She could tell by the set of his shoulders that he was ready to run.

"Please don't go." She reached for a thick stack of sheet music on top of the piano. "Maybe we could find the Prelude here? Then you could begin to learn it." She smiled again. "So perhaps one day you could surprise Gideon?"

It was this suggestion that won the small, heart-clenching response. The boy took a step toward the piano, searching her face for reassurance. His eyes met her own, silently beseeching. What is troubling him so, she asked herself?

"It's okay," said Maggie to the small, stiff figure. "Ah, here's the Prelude."

The child perched on the far edge of the piano bench, tense and ready to flee at the least sign of threat. Maggie looked into the desolate eyes with growing concern. She shifted slowly, careful not to touch him.

"I'm very rusty," she confided as she ran her fingers over the keys. "This music always made me think of bright colors. And running barefoot in the grass." She began to play.

When the last notes still trembled in the air, Maggie turned to the dark-haired boy. "I haven't played that piece in a very long time. Did you like it?"

A cautious nod.

"Me, too. But too many wrong notes. I need to practice. My son calls practice the P-word." Another wordless nod, and the first faint glimmer of humor in the expressive eyes. Maggie felt her heart trip in her chest. The silent appeal of this child was very great. She reached out to touch the boy's shoulder. Immediately he shrank from her.

"Maggie!"

Zach stood like a dark Greek god in the doorway. A bristling black Doberman with eyes like burning coals strained at the leash by his side.

"Zach." Maggie rose from the bench, surprised by the anger in his voice. The dog growled, low in his throat.

"Quiet, Bartok," said Zach.

"Bartok? You never did like his music." She tried a small smile.

Zach turned to the boy. "Go to your room, TJ."

The child jumped to his feet and stood behind the piano, rigid and resistant. Maggie smiled at the child. "Your name is TJ? Cool name."

The solemn face stared back at her.

"Maybe I could come back later," she tried again, "and we could work on the music some more?"

This time she thought she saw the barest of smiles tug at the corners of the boy's mouth.

"What's going on with you two?" said Zach. The anger no longer burned in his voice as he turned to the boy. "Sorry, TJ," he said. "I'm not angry with you. Why don't you try out that new kite of yours? We'll be outside in just a minute."

With a final, questioning look at Maggie, the boy slipped past Zach and disappeared through the double doors.

Zach looked down at her. "How long have you been here?"

"Your dog is scaring me."

"Sorry." He bent to unclasp the leash. "Go, Bartok," he said. "Go with TJ." The huge animal bounded from the room.

"Zach!" cried Maggie.

"Relax," said Zach, as he took her elbow and guided her toward the open French doors. "The dogs would give their lives for that kid." He turned to face her. "How long have you been here?" he asked again.

"Long enough to play the Prelude in C for a new friend. Not very well, I might add."

"So I heard. Bach's Prelude..." He looked down at his left hand. "It's been so long since I played that piece."

"I understand now," she said.

He swung around. "Understand what?"

"Your concerto," she said. "The one I heard yesterday at the abbey. So much of the music written for the left hand. It reminded me of Ravel's Concerto for the Left Hand. But I didn't make the connection."

She'd remembered, just in time, that Zach couldn't know she'd been searching for him. He had no idea that she had seen the note to his father with the unfamiliar handwriting, heard a CD of music not played by his hands, watched the sadness touch the eyes of a woman called Yvette in a Paris café. Yet all the clues had been there for her.

The watchful look dissolved in Zach's eyes. "Yes, the Austrian pianist, Paul Wittgenstein, commissioned Ravel after he lost his own arm in World War I."

"Tell me more about your concerto."

"Still unnamed. But it's good, isn't it? Actually, I was inspired by several pieces for the left hand. Saint-Saens, Britten, Strauss. Felix Blumenfeld's Etude in A-flat, and Prokofiev's Concerto No. 4." His fingers moved over the keys of the Bechstein. "Now I'm working on improvisations for Mozart's Coronation Piano Concerto No. 26, the one where he never wrote down the left-hand part." He looked down at his left hand. "Music for one hand that creates the sound of two."

Questions crowded against her lips, but the past would have to wait. You need to know about the child. He's what's important.

She took a deep breath. "Tell me about TJ. Does he speak English?"

"TJ understands French, English, and Italian," said Zach. His voice vibrated with anger and frustration. "But he didn't answer you because he can't."

"I don't understand."

"The boy suffers from traumatic speech loss, Slim. He doesn't speak at all. He's been mute for almost a year."

# CHAPTER SEVENTY-TWO

Dane awakened alone in the great bed, his naked body cold and glistening with sweat. A terrible scream still echoed in his head.

For a long moment he lay very still, trying to sort out the reality from the dream. Who had screamed his name? Sofia Orsini? The boy?

The kid can't speak, he reminded himself. I'm safe—*as long as he doesn't speak.*

He had been dreaming. About Sofia. He had been with her in the darkened chapel on the island. She had looked into his eyes and called him a murderer.

Dane shifted painfully in the bed, still caught in the dream. He had pulled her hard against him. "Where, Sofia?" he'd whispered. "Where did you hide the journal?" Her face was so pale and beautiful in the flickering darkness. He could still feel the sting of her palm as she slapped him. The scrape of her fingernails on his cheek. That was when he had drawn the knife.

He hadn't meant to kill her, only to bring her home. But he had lost control.

He pictured her brushing her raven hair in the firelight of her bedroom, before she'd left Rome. Just as his mother had done so many years ago.

"Sofia," he murmured into the quiet shadows.

But when he closed his eyes again, it was Magdalena O'Shea's face that he saw.

The yellow eyes flew open. Fully awake, Dane smiled slowly.

Sofia Orsini and Magdalena O'Shea. Two black-haired, beautiful women.

Both wanting to hurt him.

Dane reached for the empty Absolut bottle that lay cradled on the silken pillow beside his head. Hot pain shot from his injured hand up through his arm and shoulder. *Merde.*

He steeled himself against the pain and rolled over until he could see the clock on the mantel. Almost noon. He had been sleeping—passed out?—for more than fifteen hours. The vodka, he thought groggily. Alcohol and drugs.

Never before had he failed so badly. *You gave up control.*

The memories flooded back in a whirling rush. The abbey, the colonel, the fierce struggle. The scorching fire on his palm. The fury and strength of that man were so fucking unexpected. But he'd disappeared over the ledge. Had to be dead.

He sat up with a groan. The vodka chaser for the painkillers had been a mistake. No more drinking, he told himself. Take back control.

First, take care of the hand. Then find Magdalena O'Shea. He would begin the search at Le Refuge. If she had come for Gideon, then Gideon would have the answers.

The kid would be at Le Refuge, too. Watching him, as he always did, with those frightened, dark eyes.

Dane blinked, remembering that night on the island. Finding the terrified boy crumpled on the cliff ledge. It had been so easy to threaten him, slide the knife along his cheek, demand that he never, ever speak of what he'd seen in the chapel.

He knew the boy wouldn't stay quiet forever.

It had been a mistake to let him live. But the kid had to know where Sofia had hidden Victor's journal. And, he was Victor's son.

Dane felt the fear rise in his throat. *His* name was in that journal, his name, and all the crimes he'd committed. For Victor. But he would not go, *could not go*, to prison. His hands fisted tightly as he remembered the dark, terrifying closet of his childhood. The ominous scrape of the key in the lock. No. He would never survive being locked up again.

Forget the fucking journal, he told himself. The moment Sofia died, his bridges were burned with Victor. As soon as he completed the hit in the US, he would be gone. "Dane" would no longer exist.

But first...he had to take care of the kid.

Dane smiled in the darkness. The boy had to be silenced for good. Then, finally, he would be safe.

The line from Richard III came to him suddenly, and Dane spoke into the shadows. "So wise, so young, they say, do never live long."

Once more, he was in control. I have forty-eight hours before I have to be in the US, he told himself. More than enough time to take care of the kid. And Magdalena O'Shea.

*I can't let anyone stop me now. I will not be locked up. Never again.*

\* \* \*

Beckett lowered the powerful field glasses and sat back on the heels of his boots. Dressed in dark jeans and a black t-shirt, he was almost invisible in the dense tangle of pines that clung to the steep hillside.

Below him to the south, Le Refuge shone gold in the midday sun.

Once more his eyes scanned the valley, the road, the vineyards climbing toward the rocky hills, then came back to the house. From his vantage point he could see the curving terrace and the entire rear of the property. Quiet—almost too quiet. Even the dogs had disappeared somewhere. He should have expected the dogs.

He squinted at the tall curtained windows at the back of the house. Where was she?

He'd been in place when she'd arrived at Le Refuge and watched as she waited alone on the terrace. He saw her wander across the stones and hold her wrists under the cool water of the fountain. What had she been thinking?

Then she'd lifted her head to listen—what the devil had she heard, anyway? Squaring her shoulders, she'd walked with determination toward the rear of the house.

Don't do it, Maggie, he'd pleaded, understanding her destination. Heart hammering in his chest, Beckett watched the billowing white curtains envelop her. Like a malevolent magician's trick, she was gone.

In the shadow of the parasol pines, Beckett squinted down at his watch. He spat the cold coffee to the earth and once more raised the powerful binoculars to his eyes. You've got five more minutes, Maggie.

Beckett shifted his position with an oath as his injured leg began to cramp. You're too old for this shit, he told himself. A burned-out soldier on a mountainside, searching for a terrorist, a kid, and a one-armed musician. Not to mention hand-to-hand combat in a ravine with a guy some thirty years younger. Somewhere along the line, he'd surely pissed off the gods of irony.

Make that *seriously* pissed off, he amended. Because here he was, smitten by a piano player still in love with her dead husband.

Today Maggie's t-shirt had said, "Support the Arts. Kiss a Musician." Why couldn't he get that reckless honesty, those eyes so full of thought and hurt, out of his mind?

Damn! Everything about his life was so predictable. Except for the way she made him feel.

You're still married, he told himself. He gazed down at the now empty terrace. If only he could walk away from it all, free to love again.

He sighed as he re-focused the field glasses. The terrace of Le Refuge sprang into view.

A tall one-armed man strode across the stones with a vicious-looking Doberman and vanished through the curtained doors. It was the man in Sugar's photo—Zachary Law.

Beckett punched his cell phone. "I'm going in."

He was running down the hillside when a small boy burst from the house and headed directly toward him across the vineyard.

# CHAPTER SEVENTY-THREE

Zach and Maggie wandered slowly along the waist-high rows of purple grapes. A short distance away, the child darted like a wild thing through the vines.

"How did you find me?"

The vehemence of the question took her by surprise. She looked up at him, searching for the youthful Zach in the face of this bearded, brooding stranger.

"I need to know, Slim. Did someone send you here? What do you want from me? It's important."

What had Michael told her? *Always tell as much of the truth as possible.*

"Musicians attend music festivals," she began. "No. The truth is...seeing you in the abbey was a terrible shock. Like seeing a ghost. I thought you were *dead*, Zach!"

He searched her face. "It's what I wanted you to think."

Pain ripped through her. Use it, she told herself. Now is the time. You've got to know the answers. You've come so far, for this moment. Just say the words.

*You abandoned me. You weren't there for our son.*

She felt the tears sting her eyelids, and she turned away to blink at the rows of bright vines climbing the hillside. This is about your godson, she reminded herself.

"Thirty years," she murmured. "I'm looking at a man I loved thirty years ago with my whole heart, and then he died. How did a dead man end up here, Zach, in a French vineyard so far from home?" *With a little boy who cannot speak...*

His eyes were on the child, running and leaping through the vines. "Short version. Beirut almost killed me. The rehab was long, agonizing. After I was finally released from the hospital, I just wanted to disappear. Then I remembered our dream of Vienna." He looked down at her, smiling faintly. "You know musicians are a tight, small community. The Viennese welcomed me, no questions asked. I became friendly with a young violinist, in Vienna for a series of concerts. God, she played like an angel. Beautiful, brilliant. Her signature piece was the Paganini..."

Maggie raised a brow, knowing how impossibly demanding Paganini's Caprice could be.

"Yeah, she was that good," said Zach, raising his hand to wave at the boy. "It was Bee who encouraged me to go to the university, study music. And one night, just before she left to go on tour, she told me about her brother, a music lover who owned a Provençal vineyard called Le Refuge. *Le Refuge*...the name spoke to me." He rubbed his left hand across his eyes. "I never saw her again. But several years ago, when I was going through a really bad time and needed a place to recover, I remembered her brother—and a place called Le Refuge."

"And the violinist?"

Zach let out his breath. "Just after she left on her tour, there was a horrible accident. She—"

A high, sweet cry from the vines. They both turned toward the sound. A bright red bird soared and dipped across the sun. Maggie's eyes followed the cord to the troubled little boy who flew his kite alone in the windy vineyard.

She was here because of this child. The fate of the violinist and her brother would have to wait. "Let's go to him," she said, walking toward the child in the vines. When he fell into step beside her, she said, "Zach. Tell me about TJ."

Zach pulled off a ripe grape and tossed it into the sky.

"Something bad happened to him last fall. He hasn't spoken since. He just...retreated into a wall of silence."

She saw the pain on his face.

"Are you his father?"

Zach stared at her, his eyes considering answers that raced like clouds across the sky. "No," he said finally, "I won't lie to you, Slim. TJ isn't my son. But I wish he were."

Again the pain in her chest, sharp and desolate as keening violins.

"I'm TJ's legal guardian," said Zach. "I live here with a French physical therapist I met in the hospital here in Aix. Celeste LaMartine. Celie and I, we're...friends of TJ's family. We care for him as if he were our own. The people in the village think he's my son."

*Your son.* She swallowed. She believed he was being honest with her. Suddenly she felt very dirty. *I'm so sorry, Zach, sorry I have to use you.* "Where are his parents?"

His expression grew darker. "I really shouldn't be talking about this. The answers to these questions could only hurt TJ."

"What about his mother?"

"Let it be, Maggie."

"You love him very much."

"Wouldn't you?"

She looked at the child who ran and leaped, small and wild and out of control, across the vineyard. "He's found a way to express what he can't say," she said.

"A beautiful kid in a silent world. It's so damned unfair."

"What happened to him?"

Zach squinted into the distance and shook his head. "I don't know."

"What do his doctors say?"

"The vocal specialist, the pediatrician, or the shrink?"

Maggie winced at the bitterness in his voice.

"Sorry. I just get so fucking tired of the same mumbo jumbo. Psychosomatic Mute, Elective Mutism, Traumatized Speech Syndrome. It sounds even worse in French." Zach turned to her.

"Then there's my personal favorite, APTSD. That's Acute Post-Traumatic Stress Disorder, the same thing affecting guys who came home from Vietnam, Kosovo, the Gulf, Afghanistan. In World War I it was shell shock. You experience a horrible event, and you can't handle it. It shocks the mind. The body shuts down."

His eyes followed the red slash of the kite against the deep blue sky. "Something frightened TJ very badly. Physically, there's no reason why he can't speak, according to the docs. But emotionally, we just don't know what's going on inside his head, how much can be brought back. Hell, it might be better for him if it just stays locked away. But the docs say he won't talk until he's ready. Or until he's not scared anymore."

She thought of the man with the wolf's face. "No one should be so afraid. Especially an innocent child."

"You should have seen him when he first came to us, last September. Surly, uncooperative, filled with resentment. Fearful."

Her godson had disappeared on the first day of September. "And traumatized," she said. "This child saw or heard something he desperately wants to forget."

"He ran away the first week. Jesus, what a nightmare. Found him the next morning, sleeping in those pines up there." He gestured toward the rocky, tree-strewn hillside. "I had to start locking his room at night like a damned jailer." He rubbed his hand across his eyes. "He was so lost, Maggie. Sometimes it seemed as if we'd never reach him."

She thought of the urchin-like child, sitting at the grand piano, absorbed in playing Zach's concerto. "But you *are* reaching him, Zach. You've been good for him."

"At least I don't have to lock him in his room anymore. Hell, Maggie, I just decided to give him everything I would have given my own son." She turned away so he wouldn't see the sudden flash of pain in her eyes.

"Sports, games, books," he went on. "Hard work outdoors with the grapes. Animals like your friend Bartok." He flashed a brittle smile. "He needed safety and tenderness. And he needed a *voice*. That's when I turned to music."

"Music was always my inner voice, too."

"I remember." This time Zach's smile was real. "You and I always understood the healing potential in rhythm and melody. The piano has been wonderful therapy for TJ."

"And for you, too. You finished your concerto."

"Loving TJ gave me back my music," he said simply.

She stared at him. *Love*. Ultimately, was it as simple as that?

Zach paced away from her. "But love can't give TJ what he needs. I can't take away the fear in his eyes, Maggie."

"Surely the key lies in what happened to him?"

Zach watched the boy race like a wild creature with the wind. "I don't know what happened. I wasn't there. I've tried talking to him about it, but he just shuts down. So it's all locked in his head. I don't know what he remembers—or what he's had to forget—God help him."

Maggie's eyes, too, were on the little boy, but her thoughts were on Simon Sugarman's terrible story of the island. Mother murdered, child disappeared, killer never found. Once more she thought of the guard at the locked gate of Le Refuge, the high walls, the watchful Dobermans. "Zach," she said slowly, "TJ is still in danger, isn't he?"

In the distance, a bell rang somewhere in the farmhouse. They both turned to see TJ running toward them through the vines.

"Time for lunch," said Zach. He held out his left arm, and TJ ran full tilt into his body. Zach grunted, staggered, and hugged the child tightly. Maggie stood to one side, watching the tall man bend to the silent child, with the sunlight dazzling behind them. And she knew.

I've found your son, Fee. I've found my godson.

Oh God, what am I going to tell Simon? How do we take this child away from you, Zach? How do we cause this boy any more pain?

With a heavy heart she followed them across the vineyard back to the house.

# CHAPTER SEVENTY-FOUR

"Try a bit more con brio here," said Maggie, marking the sheet music with a pencil. "Do you know what that is?" She stamped her foot, hard. "With *fire*!"

TJ stamped his foot. Hard. Then, nodding with satisfaction, he settled back on the bench, and the notes of Bach's Prelude tumbled from his fingers as he attacked the penciled passage with far more energy.

"Absolutely! Well done. Gideon has taught you well, TJ. You must be very proud." She gestured at the Doberman, who sat, black ears alert and listening, on guard beside the piano. "See, even Bartok approved."

Was that the barest of smiles on the waif-like face? She wanted to smooth the dark curls back from his forehead, but she caught herself just in time. "It's warm in here, isn't it?" she asked, as she pulled the green ribbon from her upswept hair and tucked it in her pocket. She shook her head from side to side so that her hair fell about her face.

The little boy's eyes widened with shock as he stared at her.

"What is it, TJ?"

Very slowly, as if mesmerized, the child reached out to touch the dark halo of hair.

"TJ?" whispered Maggie. The grief she saw flooding the boy's eyes broke her heart. "Can you tell me, sweetheart?"

Only silence, louder than words in the quiet room, and eyes shining with desolation. As if from a great distance, Maggie heard

Simon Sugarman's voice. "Sofia had that beautiful black hair framing her face. You have the look of her."

*I remind TJ of his mother.*

The child's eyes met hers with a silent cry of despair. Unable to speak, the small fists began to pound the piano keys in frustration.

The lost expression on the boy's face was unbearable. You focus on your own grief until something bigger happens, she thought. This child's suffering was far greater than her own.

Desperate to stop the hurt in his eyes, Maggie pulled back her hair and secured it close to her head. "Do you know," she said, "that when my son was your age he used to memorize music by whistling the melody." Maggie began to whistle the first bars of Bach's Prelude.

Still the dark eyes followed her, searching for one more glimpse of his mother. But the spell was broken, and one small hand rubbed the tears away. With a sigh the boy inched toward her on the piano bench, close to, but not touching, her knee.

I've been forgiven, thought Maggie gratefully. Very deliberately, she stopped whistling in the middle of a phrase.

Intrigued, TJ pursed his lips and began to whistle the next phrases of the music. The sight and flutelike sounds of the child, eyes closed, lips communicating in his own special way, caught at her.

Maggie sat in the sunlit music room watching the whistling boy and felt it begin, infinitesimal but distinct. The healing of her heart.

When he ended the prelude with a difficult trill, Maggie broke into pleased applause. "You whistle better than I do! My son Brian would be very impressed."

The child moved closer and lifted his chin, waiting.

"Would you like to know about Brian?"

A definite nod.

She laughed. "It's amazing how clearly you make your wishes known. Does anyone ever deny you anything?"

The eyes locked on her face, waiting. Everyone anticipates his needs, she realized, everyone speaks for him. Including me. There's no need for him to speak.

She sighed. "When Brian was about your age he was always bringing home stray animals. Dogs, turtles, injured birds, and later, a one-eyed cat named Gracie, who still lives with me in Boston and sings along when Brian plays the piano." She smiled down at the child. "Do you think we could teach Bartok to accompany you when you play for Gideon?"

Pleasure sparked in the dark eyes.

"One time Brian found a family of rabbits at his Boy Scout camp and he...wait a minute." Maggie grabbed her purse. "I know it's here somewhere," she murmured. "Ah! Here it is. I gave this to Brian when he became a Scout. Every little boy loves these."

In triumph she held out her hand. Brian's Swiss army knife was folded in her palm. The boy peered closely at the mysterious red object.

"If you promise to be very careful, and if Gideon approves, of course, I'll leave this with you for your own adventures. See? It opens this way." Her fingers slid over the handle. The small blade sprang forward, flashing silver in the slanting sunlight.

The little boy flinched as if he'd been struck. A high, keening sound erupted from his throat. He jumped to his feet in terror, wordlessly backing away from her. Instantly the Doberman was in front of the child, growling a warning at Maggie through knife-sharp teeth.

"TJ! Honey, what—"

With another tortured sound the wild-eyed child spun around and ran from the room with the dog at his heels.

"Wait. TJ!" She ran to the doorway.

Boy and dog ran through the vines toward the high red

rocks. Maggie stared helplessly down at the knife in her palm, then raised her eyes.

In that moment, watching the frightened little boy and the dog named Bartok running away from her through the fading light, Maggie knew that she would do anything to keep the child safe from harm.

"What the hell is going on here?"

The woman from Simon Sugarman's photograph stood in the doorway.

# CHAPTER SEVENTY-FIVE

"Spend the night here."

It was a soft evening, with a sky like the inside of a shell. Zach sat across from Maggie on the terrace of Le Refuge. Mozart played from a hidden speaker as they watched the feathery sky turn to gold. Down the stone steps, a now calmer TJ splashed in the pool while Bartok paced back and forth along the edge of the water, silent and watchful.

Maggie watched the boy with concern. The woman with the very short hair—Celeste LaMartine, as she was later introduced by Zach—had found TJ in the vineyard and brought him home. Together, finally, they had managed to quiet the distraught child. The small red knife—the cause of TJ's fear, Maggie was certain—was once again safely hidden in the depths of Maggie's shoulder bag.

Now Celeste, clad in a bright orange bikini, sat in a chaise lounge by the pool. Every few moments, her eyes would leave the boy and rest, with a speculative expression, on Maggie.

Maggie turned her back on the watchful eyes and looked at Zach. "You're *sure* TJ's a good swimmer?"

Zach shook his head, cocking a crooked black brow. "Still afraid of the water, Slim?"

"Even more so now."

When she added no explanation, he shrugged and said, "I was asking you to spend the night."

She gazed at this man she no longer knew, his face far more

compelling than that of the boy she remembered. But it was the boy's face she had loved.

"I can't stay, Zach. I need to get back."

"Why? We have more than thirty years to share, Maggie." He leaned toward her. "I want to drink wine with you, talk music until dawn." He watched her face. "I think TJ would like it if you stayed."

Maggie looked over at the child in the pool. "Your little charmer's quite a swimmer. I'd like to spend more time with him, too. But I have no clothes, no—"

"You never wore nightgowns."

After all these years, he still had the power to make her knees weak. It was her first glimpse of the youthful Zachary in the man he had become, this dark, grown-up stranger.

She looked at the father of her son, dressed in jeans, an old sweater and an army jacket, so tall and brown and intense in the glowing pink light. And she thought, yes, we need time. I need to understand why this man let me believe he was dead. I need time to tell him about his son.

"Say yes," his familiar voice urged.

"Yes."

"Ah, but which woman has agreed to stay? The youthful lover or the intriguing stranger?"

She looked away, no longer sure herself.

"I saw you play, you know. In Austria, seven, maybe eight years ago."

She swung around, shocked.

"I read about you coming to the Mozart Festival. Drove to Salzburg. Thought maybe..." He shook his head, sighed. "You played his Piano Concerto number—"

"Number 21," she whispered. "The Andante section—"

"Was spectacular." He smiled. "You had a good mentor. I remember rehearsing it with you." He reached out to touch her cheek. "You were luminous that night, Slim. Astonishing."

"But you didn't come backstage."

He gazed at the distant hills, melting now into the sunset. "The program said you were married, with a son. You had moved on, had a family..."

She stared at him. *Your* son, Zach. Tell him now. But she was still unable to say the words.

She simply shook her head and turned away from him.

And so they sat together without speaking, while the light fell from the sky and the clatter of the cicadas surrounded them, each lost in their own thoughts of what might have been. The air turned cooler, chasing Celeste and TJ into the house to shower before dinner. Maggie waved to the child, then turned to the man who had loved her so long ago. It was time.

"Zach. I need to know."

"Why I lied to you. Yes." He took his jacket and dropped it over her shoulders. His left hand came up slowly and cupped her chin. "You are more beautiful now than that day you barged into my rehearsal room, Slim," he said, leaning toward her. "Do you re-member our first kiss? Leaning against that piano?"

Without warning, his mouth found hers.

Shock arced like a lightning bolt through her body. Just for a moment, she remembered the taste of him, the scent of his skin, the hardness of his chest beneath her fingertips.

Then she pulled back.

"Don't." The boy's lips were soft, she thought, but the man's lips were hard. She pushed his hand aside. His beautiful hand, once so sensitive and erotic. Her voice trembled. "If you want me to stay, then don't."

His hand dropped to his side. "Sorry. I gave up my right to touch you a long time ago."

"I thought you loved me, but you pretended to be dead!" The stark pain splintered the air between them into shards of glass. "You promised to come home to me, Zach. You *promised*."

"I did love you, Maggie." He gazed toward the vineyard. "Probably still do."

She looked at the scarred, bearded face, familiar and yet

unfamiliar. "The woman you loved no longer exists, Zach. The woman you knew is gone."

"I tried to forget about you for thirty years, Slim. I woke up thinking about you every morning. I fell asleep missing you every night. Why did you come back, dammit? To break my heart all over again?"

"What about my heart, Zach? It was thirty years for me, too. All the endless questions. Looking for you in the subway, in the market, in the concert hall. I'd see a man...and my heart would stop. But it was never you. I knew if you were alive, you would have called." Her breath caught. "But you were in Austria. And now you're here, with a child."

Maggie swiped at the tears that ran down her face. "You say you loved me, so *why*? You look me in the eye and tell me how you could let me think you were dead, how you could be so damned heartless. So cruel." She locked eyes with him. "Maybe *you* didn't die, Zach, but a big piece of *me* did."

He looked down at his body. "A part of me died, too, Maggie."

"Your arm wouldn't have mattered to me."

He turned his right side toward her, so that the empty sleeve of his sweater swung across his chest. "Half a man, coming home to make love to his girl?" he asked brutally. "What a fucking joke! I couldn't piss without a plastic bag, Maggie. Is that what you deserved? A one-armed fucking piano player who couldn't even balance his body over yours?"

"Don't, Zach."

"Why not? You were so perfect. I was...a broken, impotent junkie. Afraid to sleep. Or if I took drugs to sleep, I'd wake up crying. Screaming. All I could give you was rage."

"I wouldn't have turned away from you," she whispered.

"It was so complicated," he said. "After all those months in the rehab hospital, I was strung out, big time, on rum and dope. And the PTS—I'd hear a car backfire and I'd shout 'Down!' and hit the sidewalk. I wore sunglasses all the time because my eyes had seen so much death." His voice took on a new edge. "Then there were the nightmares, that no drug or double whiskey could kill. How could I have been there for you? I couldn't take care of my own damned life."

"We could have taken care of each other."

He went on as if she hadn't spoken, staring at the toe of his boot. "I went over there to prove something to my father. My dad, the war hero." His voice faltered. "I never told you about the last time I saw my father."

She waited wordlessly.

"He told me that the piano was a hobby, not a real man's job. That I would never put food on the table." He took a shuddering breath. "Called me a coward and a failure. Said I'd never be a real man."

His devastation thrust at her. She wanted to say, *Your father misses you. He adores our son.* But she couldn't. "I didn't know," she said.

"That night I went to a bar, ran into a high school friend who was headed to the Middle East. Told me about a peace-keeping program over there." He turned to her. "Dad wanted a hero, goddamn it, and I was going to give him one. I'd go, do something for my country, make Dad proud, and come home to you. But, Jesus, it was so much worse than I expected."

"Oh, Zach—"

He rubbed his hand over his eyes as if he could wipe away the images. "War changes you, Maggie. You become somebody else."

The words touched Maggie's cheek with a cold ghostly breath.

"Beirut, so hot you could smell it." Zach's words broke into her thoughts, halting, his eyes unfocused, locked on the distant hills. "The first thing the guys said to me was, 'Just don't show me any pictures of your sweetheart back home.' They understood."

He shook his head. "I was living with them in the Marine barracks. They were my *friends*. And then—"

She winced. "Maybe you shouldn't—"

But it was as if a solid wall of rock had blasted open and Zach's words rushed at her in a flood of wild water.

"It was just after dawn. Already hot. I couldn't sleep. I was outside, sharing a smoke with a Marine. Quiet, so quiet all I could hear was the guy's breath. I remember that I wondered why there were no bird sounds."

"I saw the truck coming at us. The explosion came out of nowhere, so loud and close your eardrums burst, and suddenly the morning was alive with fire, and I was flying through the air. One minute you were joking with a buddy, the next minute you were scraping him off your skin."

He closed his eyes. "I saw the bomber's face, Maggie, just before the truck blew. He was *smiling*."

Zach gazed out into the blackness of the vineyard as if it held the answers he sought. "My pal didn't make it," he said, "And I was left for dead, buried beneath a pile of bodies. A medic found me. Or what was left of me."

She leaned toward him in the shadows. "I would have come to you in the hospital," she said.

"I didn't *want* you, dammit! I was halfway around the world in a stinking hospital with kids just like me, trying to cope with lost limbs and burned bodies and pain. It was no place for someone like you. The music in my head changed. It became all shrieking alarms and black, horrible sounds."

Yes, she told him silently, I know how that feels.

"I don't remember too much about the months after the bombing. Just pain. Pain and drugs and fog. But it was much worse when the truth finally hit me. I could never play the piano again." The dark, haunted eyes held hers. "I wanted to die, Maggie."

He looked up at the purple sky. "To be honest, sometimes it still feels as if I *did* die. The music was gone. And I didn't have you. I had nothing."

"Oh, Zach," she whispered.

"Thirty years ago, the piano was my whole life. I looked at the other guys in that hospital—we were all kids. Jesus, I was so goddamned angry. They hadn't lost their one reason for living. Even if they'd lost an arm or their legs, they could still go back to college, sell insurance, practice law. Manage a restaurant, run for mayor. But the piano was all I had."

She wanted to say, you had me, Zach. You had us. But she knew it wouldn't have been enough for him.

His hand found her fingers in the darkness. "Of all people, Slim, you understand. The other guys, they made plans, called home. Just two of us—the high school basketball hero and the fucking piano player—just the two of us would lie awake in the dark and talk about dying."

"No." There was denial in the shake of her head.

His voice was a low growl. "I couldn't go home, don't you see? The music was lost somewhere with the arm and pieces of my gut and groin in a stinking burning desert." It was a flat, unemotional recital. "I lost a lot more than my right arm in that bombing, Maggie."

She reached out and touched his empty sleeve. "I know, Zach. I know what you lost. I just wish you had told me. I wish you had come home."

"And dragged you down into hell with me? 'Hi, honey, I'm home!' Strung out on heroin, having terrible flashbacks, sleeping with a loaded gun under my pillow, wanting to use it on anything that moved. Maybe myself. Or, God help me, maybe you."

"You would never have hurt me, Zach."

"You think so? There was a grand piano at the rehab center, a gorgeous Bechstein. As soon as I could walk, use my left arm, I found myself a mallet. And in the middle of the night I bashed that damned beautiful piano to splinters." His fingers raked through his long hair, sweeping it back from his face.

"I tried to commit suicide that night in the hospital. But I was so drunk that I blew it. For men like me," said Zach, "suicide is always there, lurking like a dark monster in the wings."

"Listen to me," she demanded. "You've carried this for so long. But it's over now, Zach, it's time to let go. You've made a good life here for yourself and TJ and Celeste. You've written that extraordinary concerto."

"But I'm not the man you loved."

She watched him in the soft darkness, unable to answer. If he had not disappeared so many years ago, would they still be together? Ultimately, the answer could have been *no*. She would never know...

"Fucking injuries," sighed Zach, turning away. "I can't play the piano. And I can't ever have children, Maggie."

*You have Brian.* "Zach..." she began.

The child called from inside the farmhouse, and Zach stood up. "It's getting late."

"Please, just a moment more. I need to tell you—"

But Zachary Law silenced her with her son's dark eyes. "Smiling-fucking-bomber..." he whispered. "The Gulf never goes away, Maggie. If you were there, no explanation is necessary. But if you weren't, no explanation is possible."

* * *

"She's *what*?"

"You heard me, Mike. Maggie is spending the night. She just texted me."

"She wants to stay with Zach Law?"

Sugarman let out his breath. "I haven't known what she really wants since I met her. Haven't been able to change her mind, either. All I know is, she's staying."

"Over my dead body," muttered Beckett, disconnecting his cell with an angry snap.

Beckett stared down at the lamp-lit house, shining like a beacon in the black expanse of vineyard. He closed his eyes and once again saw that kiss on the terrace.

As he stood up and checked his gun, the words of an old country song slipped unbidden into his head. *If tomorrow never comes...will she know how much I loved her?*

Damn. It took him by surprise, how much it mattered. Shook him badly.

Didn't matter now. Never did. It was time. Knowing full well what was about to happen, Beckett began to make his way quietly down through the pines and across the black hillside toward the house.

*What will she think*, he asked himself in the lonely darkness, *when she discovers your betrayal*?

# CHAPTER SEVENTY-SIX

Dressed entirely in black, Dane stood in the shadow of the pines, just steps away from the terrace of Le Refuge. It was pitch dark, just before twelve-thirty a.m.

He slipped the key to the French doors from his jeans pocket as he scanned the shadows. No sign of the Dobermans. But he could take care of any problems.

The long blade of his knife pressed against his thigh as he moved silently across the stones.

\* \* \*

*Something was wrong.*

Restless, unable to sleep, Maggie couldn't get Zach—or the child sleeping just down the hall—out of her mind. Was that a sound? Somewhere in the house?

She slipped out of bed, moved quietly to the door, checked the long, shadowed passage, listened. All quiet. Just her imagination, working overtime. Too much had happened too quickly.

She turned toward the tall antique mirror.

*Johnny?*

Silence. Her own reflection stared back at her from the sepia glass.

Okay, then. She turned on the bedside lamp and reached for the glossy magazine on the bedside table. Provençal recipes, French politics, the latest fashions on Rue Faubourg... She flipped the pages, listening for sounds from the hallway.

Somewhere in the house, a clock chimed the half hour. Twelve thirty already? Just one more article, she told herself. Concentrate. She turned the page and found a story on Europe's top classical music festivals. Intrigued, she scanned the list. Aix-en-Provence, of course. London's Handel Festival. Music in Bonn, Istanbul, Dubrovnik, Ravello, Salzburg... She stopped, her eyes coming back to Ravello.

*Ravello.* She remembered very well the tiny Italian hill village perched high above the Amalfi coastline—so heart-stoppingly beautiful, it had inspired Richard Wagner to compose his opera, *Parsifal.* And over the years, it had become the site for one of Europe's most spectacular classical outdoor festivals. She had been invited to solo there one summer—when?—a decade ago, with the San Francisco Philharmonic. It had been an "All Chopin" concert, set in the gardens of the ancient Villa Rufolo, with the tuxedoed orchestra arranged behind her on a huge, natural stone ledge high above the coast.

In the quiet bedroom, Maggie closed her eyes and saw herself seated at a grand piano in a long, fitted black gown, bathed in moonlight. The stage was lit by small, winking lights. Above her, the grand expanse of glowing Mediterranean sky. And beyond the terrace, the steep, dramatic fall of tall pines, rooftops, olive gardens and flowers, down to a deep blue sea.

The air was summer warm and smelled of roses. The notes of Chopin's Ballade No. 4 in F minor—her all-time favorite piece—flew from her fingers.

That night, she remembered, there had only been the beauty of the starry night and the music. There had been no sign of the tragic explosion so many years earlier that had taken the lives of several musicians and guests during a performance of Tartini on that very stage—

Maggie's eyes flew open. The long-ago explosion in Ravello...

Zach's earlier words clicked into her head. *My friend Bee, the brilliant violinist. Her brother owned a vineyard called Le Refuge. There was a terrible accident. I never saw her again.*

"Oh, my God," whispered Maggie. Was it possible?

She slipped quickly out of the bed, reaching for her shoulder bag. In a large zippered pocket, she retrieved her husband's calendar diary and searched for his last entries.

In the last months of his life, he'd been to Rome, Brittany, Vienna, Hyères... And there it was, in his bold script. Naples/BF. She'd had no idea what the notation meant.

But now—when she had traveled to Ravello with the symphony orchestra, she had flown into Naples. Ravello was only an hour's twisting ride by car to the north. Johnny had gone to Naples. To Ravello? Because of someone with the initials BF?

*Bianca Farnese.* Maggie's heart was hammering like steel piano strings in her chest. Bianca Farnese had been one of the world's leading young violinists. Could she have been Johnny's "BF," Zach's "Bee"? She'd been destined for such a bright and glorious future in the music world. But then she had died, shockingly and far too soon, in a horrible terrorist firestorm when a bomb exploded on stage during a classical performance of Tartini's *Devil's Trill* in Ravello.

Maggie closed her eyes, trying to remember details. It had happened sometime in the mid-eighties. A special classical performance, in honor of the newly elected Italian Prime Minister and the US Ambassador to Italy. So many had died. And, in the end, chaos for the Italian government, and crippling distrust of the Americans. Just the kind of story her husband would have investigated.

Maggie looked down at the leather calendar clutched in her hands and thought once more about Zach's words. *Bee's brother owned a vineyard, Le Refuge.*

But Victor Orsini had owned Le Refuge.

Was Bianca Farnese the sister of Victor Orsini?

# CHAPTER SEVENTY-SEVEN

*Come with me, Vito*!

Just an hour's drive to the south of Le Refuge, Victor Orsini stood alone by the night-filled window. The notes of Paganini's Caprice No. 24 flew like a tempest through the dark bedroom—complex, ferocious, impossible.

He raised his head, eyes closed, listening. The Paganini—considered by many to be the most difficult of all violin pieces—had been his sister's signature piece. "The music flowed through you like some wild rushing river, *il mio amore*," he whispered.

His sister's voice answered, spinning like silver above the notes—high, young, musical. "Come with me, Vito!"

"But you have not finished practicing. Father will be furious."

"I've been practicing since sunrise! Look, my fingers are bleeding! It's my birthday, Vito, finally thirteen! I want to celebrate!"

"We will all celebrate tonight. After you've practiced."

"No, now! I want to climb over the wall, run through the woods, have a picnic with you by the lake. Cook will make us sandwiches—"

"No, no, *mio*. Think. Father will—"

"You will protect me from Father, Vito. You always do. Hurry, come with me."

She had taken his hand. And he had followed her out the door and over the garden wall.

*But I didn't protect her...*

Orsini shook his head and gazed down at the CD of music gripped in his fingers. A young woman, raven-haired and beautiful as a Botticelli, stared back at him from the cover.

He turned the CD over and read the list of titles he knew by heart.

Paganini, Vivaldi, Beethoven, Shostakovich, Tchaikovsky. Tartini. By her early twenties, she'd mastered all the great violin pieces.

She'd had two degrees in Music, been compared to Perlman, Heifetz. Won the prestigious international competitions, the Menuhin Competition, the Sibelius. Even the Tchaikovsky in Moscow. His sister had been one of the very few who could hit that high note at the end of Tchaikovsky's Violin Concerto in D major and give it that amazing vibrato... in just one fifth of a second.

Orsini's eyes dropped to the reviews. "Hair-raising pizzicato and bowing passages. Grueling, double-stop trills. Marvelous tonal quality. Technical artistry."

The Paganini notes spun in the room around him, making him sick and dizzy.

He dropped the CD to the table as if it burned his fingers. Yes, it was all so beautiful. Until it all went wrong.

Ravello, 1985. So many years ago. A soft summer night. His sister only twenty-five, radiant, standing on the starlit stage, lifting her beloved Stradivarius—given to her by their father before his death—to her shoulder. The beat of hesitation, and then the storm of notes.

His boss, the Admiral, had arranged the performance. He could still hear the words, spoken so long ago in the small CIA office, in that scraping voice. *I want to meet your sister.*

I did it all for you, *il mio amore*. For your music.

Orsini fingered the heavy gold cross that hung from the chain around his neck. She'd been supposed to play the Paganini, it was printed in the program.

But at the last minute she'd substituted the Tartini. The *Devil's Trill*. Why? Who had told her to make the switch? Was it a signal?

As he'd stood, listening to the opening chords, the unthink-able had happened. He had looked across the theatre and seen the tense, familiar faces. Faces that should not have been there. A hand signal. Two men hurrying away from the stage.

*Away.* Not toward.

The flash, the terrible thunderclap of the explosion, the sear-ing heat, black smoke. The smell. His body, thrown violently backwards into the seats.

The keening sounds of a man screaming her name over and over.

*Bianca.*

# CHAPTER SEVENTY-EIGHT

Dane made his way past the ticking grandfather clock down the shadowed, quiet hallway of Le Refuge.

Access to the well-protected vineyard had been ridiculously easy. He'd stolen the keys from Celeste's purse some months before, copying and replacing them without her knowledge. He'd waited for the guard at the gate to complete the hourly rounds. The dogs, of course, knew him. But where, he wondered again, was Bartok? Probably with the kid.

His fingers clenched around the knife. He was prepared if the Doberman gave him any trouble.

His gloved hand eased open the door to the master bedroom suite, just an inch, and he stood, listening. Darkness, and faint breathing. Sleep well with your Gideon, little Lapin.

The boy's room was at the far end of the hall. He moved toward it.

A sound!

Dane stopped. A crack of lamplight appeared beneath the door on his left, and he pressed himself against the wall. The guest room. Are you sleepless tonight, too, my Juliet?

Bedsprings creaked in answer, then settled.

He stayed pressed against the wall, listening in the shadows, picturing her ivory body on the bed, her beautiful hair on the silken pillow. Not tonight, but very soon, I promise you.

Tonight, he had to take care of the kid.

Soundlessly he moved down the hall toward the last doorway.

\* \* \*

Maggie stood at the open window, gazing into the scented darkness. To the south, black clouds sailed across the heavens like great ships, promising more rain, but now the room was lit by the last curve of moon that dropped like a silver scythe from the vast night sky. Cheshire Moons, her son called them.

When the sun rises, she told herself, I'll wake Zach and tell him about Brian. He deserves to know about his son. He *needs* to know. And so does Brian.

Before anything else happened. Because she had called Simon, and now he knew she was certain that the child called TJ was Thomas James Orsini. Her godson.

"I'm so sorry," she whispered into the shadows. For once it wasn't dreams of her husband that kept her sleepless, but worries over an urchin-faced little boy.

Her head came up. Another sound in the hallway? She waited, body very still, listening. Only silence. Then, a footstep. TJ? In the quiet of her room, Maggie was overwhelmed by an inexplicable sense of urgency.

She was reaching for her robe when the voice, as soft as the whisper of the pines outside her window, stopped her.

*Maggie.*

She swung around.

*Johnny?* Desperately her eyes searched the shadows for her husband's face.

*Take care, Lass...*

Was that a door closing? She turned her head toward the hallway, straining to listen. TJ can't cry out for help, she thought. She had to go *now*.

*Johnny, I don't want to leave you, but TJ needs me.*

She opened the bedroom door, losing the connection to her husband as she spoke.

*Maggie-mine...*

His voice was fading with the night, barely audible now in the shadows. She ran into the hallway, flinging the words over her shoulder as she ran. Knowing she was losing him.

*I will always love you, Johnny.*

A sharp bark, somewhere in the house. Then silence.

Something was wrong. She ran faster, down the long, dark hallway. *Away from her husband.*

The door to TJ's room was closed.

The doorknob turned under her fingers, and she moved into the stillness of the room.

"TJ?"

No movement. In the dawn's half-light, toys and clothes and the bright red kite were strewn on the floor. The bed was empty.

Don't panic. She forced herself to search the room.

The closets and bathroom were dark and silent.

Another sound, this time from the direction of the music room. Thank God!

She ran across the hall and swung open the door. "TJ?" Her breath caught.

The long lace curtains caught the moonlight and billowed like silver sails through the wide open French doors that led to the terrace. On the floor by the grand piano, surrounded by scattered sheet music, the dog Bartok lay crumpled and still.

There was no sign of Tommy Orsini.

# CHAPTER SEVENTY-NINE

Dawn, but dark with billowing clouds. Another storm was coming.

Maggie glanced up at the slate sky as she ran through the cloistered courtyard of Simon Sugarman's hotel in the old town of Aix. Soon hard rain would sweep down from the mountains to thrash against the ancient cobblestones.

Zach and Celeste were still at Le Refuge, frantically searching the house and grounds for the child. But she'd known TJ was gone.

What if he was all alone, somewhere, when the storm hit?

There had been no answer in Michael's room when she'd called. Nor did he answer his cell. Now Simon was her last chance. She ran up the narrow stairs, unwilling to wait for the lift. She couldn't get the fear on Zach's face out of her mind.

Fourth floor. Her eyes searched the gloomy hallway for Room 41. There, on the left. She rapped sharply with her fist.

"Simon!"

She knocked again, harder. "Simon," she hissed. "It's Maggie. Open the damned door."

The door opened and Beckett stood facing her.

Confusion and an unexpected sense of safety flooded through her. "Michael," she whispered, "what's going on?"

One hand touched her lips gently for silence while his other hand closed over her arm and drew her into the shaded room. Quickly he locked the door behind her.

"What is it?" she whispered, suddenly afraid of the expression in his eyes. "Why is it so dark in here?"

"Try to understand, Maggie."

"Understand what?" Over his shoulder, she saw Sugarman, head bent and powerful shoulders bunched with tension, talking quietly into the telephone.

"You're both scaring me. Why—"

She stopped speaking as she became aware of the soft breathing behind her.

Knowledge hit her like a sudden punch, and she took a step back, away from him. "Not you," she said, looking into Beckett's unflinching eyes, suddenly knowing what she would find when she turned her head.

In Sugarman's large bed, Shiloh was stretched lengthwise on the blanket, his wary eyes keeping watch over the tiny body pressed up against him. With one thin arm curled tightly around a small stuffed bear, Thomas James Orsini was deeply and peacefully asleep.

\* \* \*

"They have your son."

Dane's voice.

Victor Orsini gripped the phone. "Tell me what you know."

He closed his eyes while Dane described Maggie's visit to Le Refuge and his suspicions regarding the colonel.

"Where is Gideon now?" interrupted Orsini.

"Out with the dogs, searching the grounds."

"TJ won't be there. Gideon would have no reason to suspect the O'Shea woman, but I know she is responsible for this." Orsini's voice rasped with rage. "Taking my son is her own wild justice."

"What justice, Victor?" asked Dane. "Why is she a threat to us?"

"All you need to know is that Magdalena O'Shea has family on Cape Cod, Massachusetts. Use that against her, make the calls, do whatever you have to do. Just find my son."

Orsini disconnected and then, very slowly, walked across the room to the violin stand where the del Gesù, stolen by his father decades earlier and now so beautiful in the light, still waited to be played.

Grasping the neck tightly, he raised the instrument high above his head and slammed it against the wall.

* * *

"TJ! Thank God he's okay."

Maggie moved to the edge of the bed and looked down at the sleeping child. The Golden raised his head to her, but refused to leave the boy's side. She turned on the two men. "He *is* all right, isn't he? Simon?"

"Of course he is," interrupted Beckett. "I would never risk harming a little boy. Lucky for us he's a deep sleeper." There was an expression she'd never seen in the gray eyes.

"You've kidnapped a child, Colonel!"

"We've saved a child, Maggie. It was the right thing to do."

She touched the soft bear cradled in TJ's arms. Michael kidnaps a child, she thought—and takes the time to bring a stuffed animal along. None of it made sense. "And Bartok?"

"Who the devil is Bartok?"

"The Doberman."

"The kid's dog?" For the first time, Beckett smiled. "Animal tranquilizer dart. Right now he's happier than a beaver dreamin' of a pine forest."

She shook her head in weary disbelief and dropped to the edge of the bed. TJ stirred beneath the bedclothes, and she put a gentle hand on the child's back. She fixed her eyes on the two men towering above her.

"Just what the hell is going on?" she demanded.

Beckett wore his "I warned you I'm no damned choirboy" expression as he leaned against the wall with his hands pushed deep into his pockets. She deliberately turned her back on him.

"Simon? Talk. You got me into this."

"Okay, Doc. You've earned the right to know. We're not the bad guys."

"You lied to me, Simon. Right from the beginning." The anger shivered like glass in her voice.

Simon began to pace. "Not true, Maggie. I just never told you all of the truth."

"Then tell me now. Or I leave this room and go straight to the authorities."

"We *are* the authorities. We've been working with the French all along. It all comes back to terrorism, Maggie."

Suddenly sickened, she waited in silence, watching his face.

"You know Americans are the target of choice for terrorists these days," said Simon. "Your husband was writing about it when he died."

Maggie winced, then nodded. "Go on."

Simon moved to the window, stared down at the shifting treetops. "So many terrorist groups," he said. "But they all have one thing in common, Doc. They need money. Explosives, weapons, false identities, inside information, traveling expenses, ways to communicate. Those services don't come free." He turned to look at her. "That means financing. We're talking millions. Hell, billions."

"You need to know where the money comes from."

"Money is a weapon, the one thing indispensible to terrorists. It's the financiers—the Money Guys—who are the most dangerous terrorists of all. They call themselves facilitators—a nice, innocuous word. But they finance the bastards who plan and commit the violence."

"Johnny called them 'The Orchestrators.'"

"Your husband understood. He wrote that terrorism is a monster. He was right. But to kill a monster, Doc, you gotta strike at the heart of the beast. Or cut off the head, so the body will die." Simon locked eyes with her. "These financiers are not ordinary men. They have wealth, ambition, power, connections. Hurting innocent people means nothing to them. It's my job to go after them. To stop them."

"And Victor Orsini is one of your monsters." Her voice was barely audible as another piece of the puzzle fell into place.

Finally, Beckett spoke. "Orsini is especially dangerous to us because when groups come to him, asking for help, he's been deliberately choosing the terrorists who focus on American targets. He's been supporting groups that want to embarrass the US, especially the CIA. The attacks not only hurt Americans, they're planned to make us look guilty in the eyes of the world, to create distrust among our allies. Destroy our relationships. Orsini knows all the players. The high rollers, the clients, the bank accounts, the investors. The extent of the networks, the identities of terrorists planting the bombs. And where they plan to strike next."

"So it's these names and accounts you've wanted all along."

"Quite a list, huh, Doc?" said Simon. "And Sofia found it all. In her husband's journal. It's why she died. Now only the kid knows where his mama hid that evidence. And he ain't sayin'." He looked down at the sleeping child. "This kid is sitting on one enormous friggin' secret and if we can just—"

Simon's cell phone buzzed. He took the call and listened without saying a word. "Gotta go," he announced, terminating the call and heading for the door. "Mike can tell you the rest." The door closed behind him with a firm click.

Beckett and Maggie looked at each other across the blanketed shape of the little boy. He stood very still, with his hands in his pockets, waiting and watching her. The bed was like a vast unbreachable river between them.

"I trusted you," she whispered. "I can't believe that you deceived me."

Beckett's eyes asked her to understand. "I had no choice, Maggie. Orsini is an animal. He's financed attacks all over the world. Hundreds dead, including kids. Like Sugar said, he's focusing on Americans." He shook his head. "It's so damned personal. I can't help but think it's about vengeance. But whatever it is, something else is going to happen soon. There's a brutal killer out there and you—"

"You think I know him." She finished the sentence for him in a low, dead voice. A man with a wolf's smile and frightening yellow eyes.

"You and I *do* know him, Maggie. Not his name. But we've seen his face."

It hit her all at once. Her body began to tremble.

"You should have told me."

"Dammit, Maggie, do you think I wanted to hurt you? Every time I look in the mirror, I ask myself the same impossible questions. What is right, what is wrong? Do I risk one life to save many? What is the honorable choice?"

"Michael—"

But he rushed on. "I've seen a little girl sobbing outside her burning house. But *we* bombed that village, Maggie, not the enemy. I've put a bullet in the throat of a man who aimed a machine gun at my men. But I see that man's wife in my dreams. I see his kid. Knowing mine was the bullet that left them alone."

His breathing was harsh in the quiet of the room. "Like Sugar says, you do what you have to do," he said at last. "You just need to find a way to live with it." Beckett looked at the sleeping child on the bed. "How the devil do I live with myself if I just walk away?"

It was the fierce grief in his voice that reached her, somehow, through the shield of her anger. She stared at his face, at the dark, frightening core of him that burned in his eyes, and, finally, she understood.

She moved slowly around the edge of the bed until she stood in front of him.

"You've lost a child of your own."

His hand was over his eyes. "You asked me once if I'd ever trusted anyone enough to get really close, to get inside."

She nodded, unable to speak.

He took a jagged breath and looked down at the little boy. "I had a son. Sam. Sam Houston Beckett. He was four. I was in South America on assignment, and he got sick." The deep-set eyes glistened blindly down at her. "I was in a remote part of the world, caught up in the thrill of the chase. I didn't make it home in time. My wife was never able to forgive me."

"But illness is no one's fault," whispered Maggie.

He blinked at her. "I should have been with him," he said. "I should have held my son in my arms and said goodbye."

She took his hands and held them tightly. The tears ran unheeded down her cheeks. "We both have to learn how to forgive ourselves," she said.

Beckett looked down once more at the sleeping child. "I just wanted to be able to protect somebody's kid," he said.

"I know, Michael."

His hands moved to grip her shoulders. "Sugar has his agenda, but I have my own. I won't let anything happen to you or TJ. I swear it."

She pulled away from him. Beyond the window, the sky changed color all of a sudden, and rain clattered against the windowpane.

The phone jangled once more on the desk, and the child whimpered in his sleep.

"Don't answer," said Maggie.

He reached for the phone.

* * *

"Beckett here."

"Mike!" Sugarman could barely contain the excitement in his voice. "Orsini's made his move."

Beckett turned his back on Maggie. "Where are you?"

"At your hotel, in Maggie's bedroom. He's been here."

"You're sure?"

"Hell yes. He killed a bird. Broke its neck and left it here in the middle of her pillow, with a message."

Beckett felt his stomach turn over. "Jesus," he breathed. "Read it to me."

"Bring the boy to Cézanne's studio at one p.m., or there will be no music on Cape Cod tonight." There was silence for a heartbeat. Then Sugarman read the chilling last words of Victor Orsini's message.

"Your son for mine."

# CHAPTER EIGHTY

It was six hours earlier on the northeastern coast of the United States.

A thin ribbon of gold was just edging the horizon when two men in black track suits quietly closed the doors of a mud-splattered Honda parked behind a row of tall sea grass. They ran across the deserted Cape Cod beach toward a silver-shingled cottage half hidden in the dunes.

On reaching their target, they disappeared behind the dunes and merged with the dawn's gray shadows by the windows at the back of the house. A small penlight, shaded by a gloved hand, blinked on and off.

"The O'Shea's kid's in there," said the taller man under his breath, gesturing toward the corner window. He studied the screen door. "It's an easy lock."

"Then shut the fuck up and do it," said the second man. He pulled a silenced Luger from beneath his jacket and reached for the doorknob.

\* \* \*

The scent of oil paint and dried flowers sickened her.

On a hillside just outside Aix-en-Provence, Maggie stood alone in the art studio of Paul Cézanne. Preserved as a small museum, the unsettling studio was as it had been at the time of the artist's death. Palette, beret and cape were scattered about. An unfinished canvas leaned against the far wall. Plastic fruit was laid out in a still life on a wooden table.

The museum was closed for the day, and Maggie was alone. Rain slammed like bullets against the tall north window, screened now by trees grown taller over the years to block the view of Cézanne's most famous landscapes. Maggie stared at a tender sketch of the artist's son, asleep. *I'm going to be sick*, she thought. She leaned her forehead against the cool rain-slicked glass and bit her lip to keep from crying out.

She was shivering uncontrollably. Please God, she pleaded, over and over like a litany. *PleasekeepBriansafe.*

"Maggie." Zach stepped into the room and stood looking at her in the splintered light. "Where is TJ?" His voice was as stony as his eyes.

"Zach! He's fine, waiting in a black Fiat, just across the square—"

Zach spun toward the door, and Maggie cried out as she reached for him. "No! Where's my son? The *trade*, Zach!"

Zach turned. "*Your* son? What the hell are you talking about?"

"You know I have a son, you told me so, last night on the terrace—"

At that moment Celeste LaMartine entered the room. In her hand was a pearl-handled automatic aimed at Maggie's chest.

"Celie!" Zach moved in front of Maggie. "There's been enough trouble. Give me the gun." Zach put his hand, very gently, over Celeste's, and took the gun away from her. "Now go check the Fiat across the square and see if she's telling the truth."

Celeste twisted away and ran through the door. As Zach turned to follow her, Maggie clutched the sleeve of his jacket. "No! It's Brian who needs us now!"

Zach stopped. "God help you if Celeste doesn't find TJ."

"TJ is out there, I swear it! This is about Brian. Victor Orsini has taken my son." Her voice shook with exhaustion and terror. "It's a *trade*, Zach! I return TJ to you, and you make the phone call to release my son."

"Victor said nothing about any trade, Maggie. Nothing about your boy."

"No." She shook her head, raw with fear. "You've got to get to Victor, you've got to make him tell you—"

"I'm leaving. TJ needs me." He pulled away from her.

"Wait!" Her agonized cry tore the air. She gripped his arm, held tight.

"Brian is *your* son, too."

Zach froze. "What did you say?"

"Brian is *ours*, Zach. Born just after you disappeared in Beirut." Her voice caught and broke. "Don't let them hurt him. Don't let Victor hurt our son."

\* \* \*

Some four thousand miles to the west, the dawning sun struck the silvery shingles on a quiet beach house and turned them to gold fire. Light sparkled on the frothing green sea and painted the underside of the gulls' wings a deep rose against the high blue sky.

When the sound of gunshot shattered the serene morning air, it was as shocking and obscene as a shouted blasphemy in a silent church.

The shot echoed for a long time over the dunes, drowning out the sound of the car telephone that rang and rang in the vacant Honda hidden beyond the sand.

Then there was nothing but the sound of the surging waves crashing on the empty beach and the cries of the frightened gulls as they whirled against the newly bright sky.

\* \* \*

Beckett looked down at the little boy curled in the rear seat of the black Fiat and reached out to tousle his hair. The child gazed at him sleepily, then turned away to rub Shiloh's fur. Sweet kid, thought Beckett, as he gazed through the pouring rain at the museum across the square.

Where the hell was Maggie? What was going on in there?

Rain slammed against the hood of the car, falling in a thick gray curtain.

A figure, running across the square toward him through the rain. A woman. Maggie?

He opened the car door, jumped out, ran to meet her. "What—"

The woman drew closer. Not Maggie. He stopped, braced. *Protect the child.*

The woman shouted, raised her arm.

Fuck me, she has a gun!

A bright flash.

A loud, frenzied bark. He was back in Afghanistan. *Farzad, no!*

She was closer now, he could see the mouth of the pistol pointed at his heart. He held up his hands.

A frantic snarl. Another flash!

The Golden smashed into him, sending him crashing to the cobblestones.

Protect the boy... A sharp wet pain as he tried to raise his head. One more shot. *Not Shiloh!*

Darkness.

* * *

In Cézanne's studio, the sudden roar of gunshots echoed above the battering sound of the rain.

"Oh, God, what was that?" Maggie spun around.

"TJ!" Zach ran toward the exit. Maggie was only steps behind him.

She saw the scene in the rain-lit square as if it were enclosed in a bright bubble. Michael, gray eyes glazed with shock, leaning against the side of the Fiat, trying desperately to stay on his feet. A scarlet stain obscuring his left eye and cheek, splashing onto his rain-soaked sweater. The Fiat's back door hanging open, leather seat empty.

Maggie stood as if caught in a nightmare. Someone had *shot* him? No. Please, no.

A small crowd had formed a tight circle around the car. One woman screamed, a man's voice shouted for help, others just stood silently in the pouring rain, confusion on stunned faces. Someone had phoned for an ambulance, and the distant sirens grew louder and louder.

Pushing through the crowd, Maggie tore off her silk scarf and pressed it hard against Beckett's temple. "Michael," she cried, "talk to me, damn you. What *happened*?"

At the sound of her voice, Beckett blinked. "Shiloh?" he whispered, trying to see past her shoulder. "Woman aimed a gun at my heart, crazy dog saved my life..." Then he saw the empty Fiat.

"She took the kid," he said in an odd voice. "Blew it." A deep, shuddering breath rasped in his throat. "Should have known better. Beautiful women, nothing but trouble."

Zach looked at Maggie. "Celeste. She must have had a second pistol."

"Michael—" She tore his blood-soaked collar open to ease his breathing, saw the glint of a badly damaged medal against his skin. Had the bullet glanced off the medal?

"Dammit," groaned Beckett. "There's no time! Heard her tell the boy—taking him to his father. Call Sugar. Go after them." He shook his head back and forth. "Shiloh!" he shouted. "Where are you, boy?"

Maggie gazed past Beckett's shoulder, saw the golden body lying so still on the wet cobblestoned street. "I can't leave you like this," she whispered.

"You never hear the shot that kills you, Maggie. I'm okay." His cold fingers gripped the medal. "St. Michael," he murmured, "protector of cops and...dogs." His breath caught. "Just get TJ. You can do it! I'll protect"—his eyes began to close—"your son. Promised...you."

The fingers fell from her arm just as the ambulance lights turned the rain to flickering crimson. "Go," he whispered.

"Michael—"

"Come *on*, Maggie!" Zach's voice, urgent through the curtain of rain. "He's right. We've got to go. Now!"

"Wait. Law—" Beckett's voice, rasping up at them. Zach bent

until his ear was very close to Beckett's lips. He listened, nodded, and whispered an answer. Then the medics ran over, and Zach grasped Maggie's arm.

"Damn you, Michael Beckett, don't you dare die on me!" she shouted. "I won't have it, do you hear me?" The tears were hot, running with the rain down her cheeks, as she reached out to touch his face. God, he was so cold.

"He's going into shock!" shouted one of the medics, pushing her aside.

Crazy with fear, she struggled toward Beckett, but Zach put his strong arm around her and dragged her through the rain toward his car.

As they drove away, she saw the Golden stagger to his feet and take a wild running leap into the ambulance just before two men in white slammed the doors. Twin taillights flashed in the darkness like small red eyes. Then she saw nothing but the rain.

# CHAPTER EIGHTY-ONE

"What in blazes is going on over there?" The Admiral's voice rasped across the miles.

"Tommy Orsini has been grabbed, taken to his father," said Sugarman. "Mike Beckett was shot. He's in the hospital. Zach Law and Maggie are on their way to Cassis to find the kid."

"Did you get Orsini's journal?"

Jesus, thought Sugarman, *lives* are in danger here.

"No, no journal. But I'll get Orsini. He must be in Cassis."

"Where the hell is that?"

"Fishing port just east of Marseilles, surrounded by cliffs. I'm leaving now."

"Just find that journal, Sugar."

A knock on the door. Sugarman disconnected, swung open the door.

Vanessa Durand stood before him. The art gallery owner reached out to touch his arm. "I'm here to help you find Victor Orsini," she said into the silence.

* * *

Zachary Law sped south through the narrow streets of Aix in the pouring rain while Maggie shouted into her cell phone. Finally she dropped her phone into her lap and turned to him. "Sugarman will meet us in Cassis."

She turned to face him, and he saw that her eyes had lost

their hopelessness. Two bright flames burned in the sheet-white face. "Maggie?" he said.

Fiercely, she wiped the tears away. "I won't be used anymore," she said in a voice that trembled with rage. "I'm fighting back, Zach. Hurry! Victor Orsini has the answers. We've got to help Brian."

"I know Victor. Let me handle it."

"How far?"

"An hour, less."

"Hurry, Zach. Our son needs us."

*Our son...*Zach gunned the engine and turned the car toward the outskirts of Aix. "Then start talking. I want the truth this time, Slim. All of it."

"Everything, I promise. Just hurry, please." She took a deep breath. "What did he say to you?"

The car sliced across the rain-slicked road. "Beckett? He told me to watch out for you, because you can be an obstinate—" He shook his head at her. "He needed to know where Victor is hiding."

"You told him?"

Zach nodded as he pressed his foot to the accelerator. "Of course. He's convinced that TJ is in danger," he said. "I believe him. Now I want you to tell me why."

"Because Victor Orsini is responsible for his own wife's death."

"Victor murdered Sofia?" His voice shimmered with shock. "That's impossible."

"Why?"

"He was nowhere near that island, Maggie. He loves his son. And he's been more of a father to me than my own father ever was."

"Zach—"

"I told you. I went to him at Le Refuge several years ago. Damned heroin had me in a vise, I had nowhere else to go. Told him his sister had been my friend. Victor was good to me. Stood by me during my recovery, hired me to authenticate his collection of music manuscripts, sold me the vineyard. He trusted me with his son's *life.*"

"Victor Orsini is not the man you think he is," she insisted. "There's a blond man who works for Victor, a man with mirrored glasses—"

He swung toward her with shock. "You know Dane?"

"Dane." She said the name out loud, slowly, as if it tasted like bile in her mouth. "Yes. I know Dane." And she told him then about Simon Sugarman's photograph, and the murder of Sofia Orsini, while they sped south into the dark heart of the storm.

\* \* \*

Zach's face was like a stone in the silent car.

He's thinking about TJ, thought Maggie, hurting for him. TJ, innocent witness to his mother's unspeakable death. Locked in his silent world because of it.

As oncoming headlamps outlined the hard planes of Zach's face, the burning rage leaped in her chest. She knew with certainty that she would do anything to fight for TJ and her son. *Anything*, she repeated in the darkness.

She peered out the black, rain-swept windshield. *Hurry, hurry.* She turned to Zach. "How much longer?"

He gestured with his chin toward a blurred road sign. "Cassis. Thirty more kilometers."

The car swerved sharply as a sheet of rain slammed into the windshield, and Maggie caught her breath. Zach's foot eased off the accelerator, and the Mercedes steadied under his strong hand. For the first time he turned his head to look directly at her.

"Tell me about my son. How old? Thirty? After Beirut, I was told I'd never father a child, and now... Jesus, Maggie, how the fuck am I supposed to feel?"

"I don't know, Zach. You're the one who chose not to come home."

He shook his head. "What did you tell him about me?"

"What I believed to be the truth, damn you! That you died in Beirut, working for peace."

"And now?"

"He knows I've come to look for you. But I had to be sure..."

He was silent for a moment, thinking about her words. "Of what?" he asked finally. "That I won't abandon him this time? Or that I'm not a murderer?"

She looked down at her fingers, clasped tightly in her lap. "That you wouldn't hurt him."

"Do you believe it?"

"You're not...one of them. I know it."

His face changed. "Thank God for that."

"I tried to tell you last night," she said. "In the garden at Le Refuge. But then TJ called to you, and you went to him..."

"It wouldn't have changed anything, ultimately. What does he look like?"

"You. You and your father. The same bony face, the same long hair, the same dark, expressive eyes. But Brian's taller than you are. And not quite so...intense."

The lights of Marseilles blinked through the fog. "Not long now," he murmured. "He's into music?"

She nodded. "Studied music and history at Penn. He's an amazing classical pianist, but now he's into jazz and blues."

Zach's head swung toward her, and she saw the pleased surprise flash in his eyes. "You taught him to play?"

She smiled for the first time in hours. "Worse than teaching him to drive."

Zach chuckled. "He any good?"

"The best."

When she remained silent, he said, "Brian. A strong name."

"Brian Zachary Sophocles," she corrected. "Who is now married and going to be a father in a few months."

"I'm going to be a *grandfather*?" His breath came out in a long, disbelieving whoosh. "I should have been there for you, Maggie. For both of you. I never meant to hurt you."

"But you did hurt us, Zach. You weren't dead. You made a choice not to come home. You missed all those sweet unfurling moments of his life. The smell of his damp cheek after a bath. The singing of a lullaby..." Her voice caught.

The small sign for Cassis appeared out of the fog. He took the exit ramp too fast and remained silent.

Suddenly, after all the years, her anger was uncontainable, rushing from her like the hot tears that slid unchecked down her face. "I saw every day how much he missed having a father. Where were you when Brian took his first step, hit his first home run? Where were you when he broke his arm, discovered girls? When he played Basie and Bach on a stage and heard his first applause?" Her voice broke. "You weren't there, Zach, when I found my grown son crying alone in the garden because he'd blown his audition at Juilliard..."

Zach pulled the car over and turned off the lights and engine. Now the only sound in the car was Maggie's sobbing. When he turned to her, there were tears in his eyes as well.

"He's going to be okay, Maggie. I'm going to meet my son."

She wiped the tears from her cheeks with the back of her hand. If it's the last thing I do, she swore to herself. She said, "We're wasting time. Where is Victor?"

"He's here. That's Celeste's car parked next to us." He turned to pull at some clothing in the back seat. "There's an old sweatshirt here somewhere, maybe a wool hat. This storm is really battering the coast. It will be cold out there on the water. You'll need—"

"Water?" She could hear the note of panic in her voice.

His look was questioning as he handed her the warm shirt. "I told you, Victor's here at Cassis harbor." His hand waved toward the wet darkness. "Over there. He's been living on that yacht for the past year, since his wife died."

"He's on a *boat*? Sweet Mary, I didn't think..." Her voice trailed off as she clutched the clothes to her chest and pressed her forehead against the cold window glass. Squinting through the heavy rain, she could just make out the small red lights shift-ing and blinking on a huge black shape that was darker than the night. Huge. It had to be half a football field in length.

*A boat.*

Black, wet fear engulfed her.

Then the night came alive with the throttle of powerful die-sel engines.

"He's leaving!" cried Zach, throwing open the door and run-ning from the car. "Let's go. *Now*, Maggie!"

Maggie looked up at the ship. It was black and huge against the sky, rocking dangerously in the angry sea. She froze, heart hammering in her chest. *I can't*, she thought in terror. Then, *I have to.* For TJ.

And for Brian.

Without another thought she dropped the clothes to the seat and followed Zach into the storm.

# CHAPTER EIGHTY-TWO

The afternoon sky was midnight dark. Rain and seawater blew in crashing curtains across the harbor, driving the crew below decks. Under cover of this curtain, the two crouching figures made their way up the short gangplank and dropped down to the deck.

She felt his cold lips and the scratch of his beard against her ear. "Are you okay?"

"I'm scared to death!" she hissed back. "What now?"

"Come here." Zach pulled her across the deck into a dark and blessedly dry passageway. "They'll be casting off any minute. We've got to find TJ."

"And Victor." She turned toward the stairs.

His hand shot out to grip her sleeve. "Where the hell are you going?"

She pulled away from him. "I'll make him tell me where Brian is." Her voice was ragged with fear, on the edge of hysteria.

"Get hold of yourself, we've got to split up. I'll go to Victor, he trusts me. I'll find out about Brian, I promise you. Just find TJ. Bring him to—"

The sound of booted footsteps on a metal stairway.

A moment later, when the crewman on watch glanced through the doorway, the dark passageway was empty.

\* \* \*

Feet apart for balance, Victor Orsini stood in the center of *Le Destin's* grand salon. With every roll of the ship, brass lamps swung slowly above his head, casting shifting shadows on the polished teak walls. In the trembling light, the darkly textured faces in the Lippi and El Greco oils glowed with an eerie life.

"Stop your damned crying, Celeste." Orsini handed her a full crystal snifter.

He felt the shudder of the massive engines under his feet as the yacht pulled away from its moorings. As he raised his glass to his lips, a huge wave hit the starboard bow, crashing seawater against the windows and sloshing brandy against his shirtfront. Celeste staggered, crying out in fear.

The storm was worsening. The new stabilizers would be tested tonight.

He turned to her. "Calm down, I said. We will get to Cannes and ride out the storm in the harbor. Then we will worry about Gideon."

"I don't think so, Victor," said a low voice from the doorway.

Orsini swung around.

Zach walked into the salon and stood in front of the man who had changed his life.

* * *

It was very dark in the narrow hallway as Maggie moved down the passageway, gripping the handrails for balance. At each door she stopped and turned the knob. Most of the rooms were locked.

She was midway down the passage when the deck shifted under her feet. She froze, listening in panic to the ominous throbbing of engines somewhere deep below her.

The ship was pulling away from the dock!

Immediately the nightmare's images assaulted her. The broken boat, whirling black water, the white hand reaching for her. Fight! she told herself fiercely. You're not in the water, you're not drowning. Fight for TJ. Fight for Brian.

Her hand closed on another doorknob. "TJ," she called. "TJ, it's Maggie. Where are you?"

She listened, knowing how well he could communicate.

Unless... Don't think about it. "Bang on the wall, honey, I'll find you!" she said, as loud as she dared, against the door. She held her breath. But the only sound was the growl of the engines and the slam of water against the boat.

Then, over the whine of the wind and engines, she heard it. A whistle. Toward the end of the passageway, someone was whistling the opening bars of Zach's piano concerto.

* * *

"I want the truth, Victor," said Zachary Law. "Did you order your wife's death?"

"She took my son from me. I sent Dane to bring them home." The heavy bull-like face stared at him. "You think I killed her?"

"I don't know what to think anymore." Zach's head came up, eyes pleading. "You took me in, Victor, when I was strung out. Gave me work. Trusted me when I was beyond trusting. Sat with me late into the night, when sleeping was too dangerous." The words caught in his throat. "Took the gun out of my hand that night..."

"Then you should trust me now," said Orsini.

"You've been more like a father to me than my own father. Where is TJ, Victor?"

"You must try to understand, Gideon. I only—"

"Your son is mute because he witnessed his mother's murder."

Orsini's eyes blazed in the shadows. "The O'Shea woman told you that?"

"Please, Gid," cried Celeste, moving to stand between the two men. "She lied to you! TJ is here, safe with us." A wave crashed with shuddering ferocity against the hull. Celeste cried out again as the lights blinked off, then on. Zach steadied himself against a heavy oak table.

"You've got TJ back," said Zach in a strange voice. "What about the trade? What about Maggie's son?"

"So you know about him?" Orsini's powerful shoulders

tensed with sudden anger. "And now you've come to corner the bull in his labyrinth." Orsini stared at the rain hurling like silver daggers against the yacht windows. "You fool. Magdalena O'Shea betrayed you, too. Why do you care what happens to her son?"

Zach's arm shot out to grip the neck of Orsini's silken shirt. "The betrayal is yours, Victor. Where is her boy?"

"Let it be!" cried Celeste. "Let Victor take care of that woman."

"That 'woman', Celeste, is the mother of my son." Zach ignored her gasp of shock as he locked his eyes on Orsini. "Maggie was used, too. Just like the rest of us. She didn't come to France to find you, Victor. It was me she wanted to find, all along. The father of her son."

"She was married to Johnny O'Shea. She's here because of him."

"She's here to tell me I have a son, damn you. Where is Brian, Victor?" His strong fingers tightened on Orsini's shirt. "*Where is my boy?*"

"It's too late," said Orsini.

* * *

*Hurry.* Maggie eased the bright blade of her son's army knife against the latch. The whine of the engines changed, and she fell against the wall as the deck pitched beneath her. The breakwater, she thought in panic. We're leaving the harbor!

*Hurry.*

Just a little more...

Click!

The door swung open and TJ flung himself into her arms.

She snapped the knife shut and pushed it out of his sight, deep into her jeans pocket as she hugged him tightly. "It's okay, honey," she whispered. "Gideon is here. I'll take you to him."

The boy shook his head back and forth frantically and began to pull her toward the stairs that led up to the main deck. His eyes were huge and frightened in the thin face.

Was he so afraid of his father? Something was very wrong.

"What is it, TJ?" Her heart was pounding as loud as the waves against the hull. She ran after him up the narrow stairway.

The heavy door at the top of the steps swung open. Cold wet air rushed down at her.

The boy made a sound like a cry.

She raised her eyes.

Dane's head and shoulders were silhouetted against the rain-black sky.

# CHAPTER EIGHTY-THREE

"You!" Maggie stared into Dane's cold eyes.

TJ turned to her with a cry. She flung her body toward the terrified child.

But Dane was closer. His hand shot out of the darkness, caught the boy's shirt, and pulled him through the narrow doorway.

"TJ!" Maggie ran up the stairway and out into the storm.

Dane stood against the pitching rail, holding the struggling boy against his body. Beyond the railing, the sea crashed in white-foamed anger against the jagged cliffs. She could see the orange harbor lights, big as moons through the fog. Close, she registered, through her shock and fear. *We're dangerously close to shore.* The wind and water were forcing them inland.

Toward the rocks.

Dane, watching her face, smiled in the stormy light. "You are right to be afraid, Juliet. I told you that we would meet again."

TJ made another sound, high-pitched and fearful.

She locked on the yellow eyes. "Let him go, Dane."

"You know my name?"

His silky voice made her blood run cold. There was no Michael, no Zach to help her now. *What am I going to do?* Beckett's words swam toward her. Find a weapon, create a diversion.

As if he'd heard her, TJ began to thrash in Dane's arms. "Mmm...Mmm..." His lips worked frantically to communicate.

Dane's eyes dropped to the boy. "You want to speak, Thomas

James?" he murmured. "I see that I've waited too long to take care of you."

Maggie seized the moment to move closer. Now she was positioned within reach of—what? Her frantic eyes searched the deck. Rope, life preservers, a fire extinguisher, a long metal pole with a hook on the end of it...

"TJ!" she shouted.

The child focused on her and she stamped her foot. "Con brio!" *With fire.*

The child twisted in Dane's arms and crashed his foot into Dane's shin.

"Fucking brat!"

*Now!* She flung herself toward the fire extinguisher.

Everything happened in slow motion.

Dane lifted the child into the air just as the yacht shuddered and pitched abruptly to starboard.

In the shattered light she saw Dane fling out his arms.

She watched in horror as the child arced over the railing with a silent cry and disappeared into the churning blackness.

"No!" screamed Maggie.

Dane cursed and lunged toward her.

She slammed the heavy metal canister into the side of his face with every ounce of her strength.

Blood splattered across her chest. She saw his body falling backward.

*Fee gave her life for her son.* Her hand reached out blindly to clutch one of the life vests.

*I will not let this child drown.*

Then she was over the railing and hurtling down into the blackness.

* * *

"What was that?" cried Zach. He lifted his chin, listening intently. "Someone screamed. Who else is on board?"

"The crew. TJ—"

"Dane! Is Dane here?"

Victor shrugged. "We had some business."

"Oh God damn," shouted Zach, running toward the door.

* * *

*It was the nightmare!*

Spinning blackness closed over her head. Cold, numbing. Paralyzing.

Blind terror washed over her.

Her arms and legs fought the choking darkness.

Churning salt water pounded in her ears and seared her burning lungs.

She clawed at the water in terror. Suddenly the sea flung her out into the wild night, and she felt the air on her face. Gasping for breath, she fought to stay on the surface.

"TJ!" she screamed.

Could he hear her above the roaring of the storm? *Find him. Please God.*

The whirling water sucked at her clothing, dragging her down. She held the orange life jacket in a death grip against her chest, flinging out her free arm to search the heaving blackness. "TJ!"

He could swim, she knew he could swim, she'd seen him in the pool.

A towering wave lifted her high, dropped her, then crashed over her in a thundering burst of silver needles. Foaming seawater poured into her mouth, down her throat, burning her stomach. She choked and gagged and went under.

Plummeting, whirling darkness. The crushing black weight of the sea.

*I won't die, dammit.*

Not in the sea.

Not like Johnny.

Orange moons shimmered above her. Harbor lights! She thrust toward the moons.

Air! She retched into the darkness.

"I'm coming, TJ."

*A hand!*

She twisted sideways, groping, clawing, reaching out.

Gone.

*Johnny, take my hand...*

No, this time the hand of a little boy. There! Fingers!

She gripped with inhuman strength and dragged him against her.

"TJ," she gasped against his cold cheek.

"Mmm." He clung to her, sucking in great gulps of air.

"I've got you," she said into his ear.

Somehow, she forced the small stiff arms into the life jacket before the hungry water could suck him away from her. It was too big for the child, and he slipped down, sinking like a stone into the blackness.

*Hold him!*

Her frozen fingers reached into the sea, locked onto his pants. She groped for the life preserver straps, secured them around the small chest. Then she pulled him tightly against her heart as they tumbled together in the wild raging water.

*Whatever happens, I will not lose this child.*

*Unless...* She thought of the hand in her nightmare.

*Unless I'm pulled down. If I'm pulled down, I'll set him free.*

*Please, please let me be brave.*

Then she heard it. A sound like drums under water.

*What?* She clutched the child against her, straining to see through the crashing sheets of water.

Another wave caught them, lifted them high. There! Just past the harbor lights. A phosphorescent foaming, a massive blackness, glistening against the wild sky.

Her ears throbbed. It was so hard to think. What was that sound?

A deep thunder, like being caught inside a giant, roaring shell.

Her heart lurched as an avalanche of white spray swept over them. Breakers!

And then they were caught in a frothing cauldron of water, falling, foaming, tumbling, spinning out of control. A great drumming sound filled her head.

The rocks! The cliffs of Cassis...

\* \* \*

"He's taken the motorboat!" Zach leaned over the rail, searching the white-capped water through the dark curtain of rain. "TJ and Maggie must be with him! Hurry, Victor! Bring the yacht about! We've got to follow—"

"Not you, Gideon."

"No, Victor!" Zach heard the terror in Celeste's voice. "Don't hurt him!"

Zach turned and found himself staring down the black barrel of a Luger.

"Don't do this," said Zach.

"I will not let you take my son," said Victor.

"TJ and Maggie are in trouble," said Zach. "I'm going after them."

Orsini raised his arm. Celeste screamed and threw herself at Orsini.

\* \* \*

A mountainous wave, black and shimmering in the broken light, hurled them up into the foaming sky. Then they fell, plunging down, tumbling wildly, spinning toward the shining wall of rock.

The churning water dragged at the child like a hungry animal. She thought her arms were being torn from her shoulders. "I won't let you go," she gasped.

Somehow, she held on to him.

A sound like a battering ram, and a rushing vortex of water.

*We're going to die.* She closed her eyes and held on to the child and felt the raging sea suck them down into the darkness.

Hold him up, her heart cried. *Just hold him up. Do it for Fee, let me be as brave as she was.*

She held her breath, lungs burning in her chest. A surging crescendo of sound. Body falling into blackness.

It was the nightmare. She was going down. *She was drowning...*

Desperate to save the child, she jerked her arms from the jacket straps. She thrust his small twisting body toward the surface, holding him above the water, pushing him toward the precious air.

*Help me, Johnny! I know you're here with me. Help me save this child.*

A sudden pressure against her back propelled them up, up through the black water toward the dark night sky.

Cold air on her face!

Lungs bursting, she gulped a breath. Another.

A sound like a rushing freight train.

A wall of black rock hurtling toward them. She screamed.

A giant fist slamming into her chest.

A small body torn from her arms.

Darkness.

# CHAPTER EIGHTY-FOUR

THE MEDITERRANEAN COAST. JULY 11

There was sand in her mouth.

She tried to lift her head slowly and felt a shooting pain in her arm.

She opened her eyes and stared at a bright orange life jacket. Memory flooded back.

"TJ!" The small body lying next to her was inert.

GODGODGOD. "TJ, honey?" She touched his wet face.

The child whimpered and stirred slowly. She tried to shift her body and saw that his fingers were locked in the loose knit of her soaked sweater.

An icy wave washed against her bare feet.

She tried to sit up. What mattered now was getting TJ to some warmth. The rain was lighter, almost gone, they would be able to—

The sound of the engine reached her over the surge of the sea and a new fear lurched in her chest.

Dane!

Coming for them.

No time to think.

She ignored the pain in her arm and jumped to her feet.

Hurry.

Her eyes searched the darkness.

Down the coast, less than half a mile, flashing lights. The harbor. Behind her, a massive wall of shining stone and jagged boulders. In front of her, the churning sea.

Not the sea. Not again.

The engine was louder, closer.

She thought she saw a shape, lighter than the darkness, on the crest of the wave.

Do something.

She turned to the child, whispered, helped him to stand.

Together they stumbled toward the rocks.

He fell in the darkness and began to whimper.

She picked him up and tried to run across the sand.

A scraping sound behind her.

The boy was so heavy. Her legs were too slow, like in a child's dream, and she couldn't run. She staggered and fell to her knees and began to cry.

TJ's fingers touched her cheek and pointed. They'd made it to the rocks. She gripped his fingers and wedged him behind a rain-black boulder.

"You'll be okay," she told him. "Just stay here. Don't make a sound." The irony of her words struck her and she pressed her lips together.

The child's frightened eyes held onto hers.

In the darkness, a small boat engine whirred, coughed, and stopped. A louder scraping sound. Silence.

She looked down at the child. Dear God, she thought, *I can't lead him to you.*

She had to get Dane away from her godson.

She whispered into the boy's ear. Then she crouched down and crawled away from him, as quickly as she dared, over the rocks.

Slippery, sharp, slicing into her feet. *Just don't make a sound.*

When she was twenty yards away from the child, she pressed against a boulder and waited.

Very slowly, she shifted until she could see the beach.

Nothing.

And then a hand. Ten feet away.

She smothered a cry.

Then she heard the voice. Sinister, whispery, yet finding her over the sound of the sea.

"Juliet."

She pushed her knuckles into her mouth.

A click. The beam of a powerful flashlight speared the night like a searchlight in a prison yard.

Stay down, TJ, she prayed. He won't find you if you just—

*The life jacket.* TJ's fluorescent orange jacket.

The beam crawled like a terrible creature over the rocks, blinding, hunting her, moving inexorably toward the boulders where the little boy crouched in fear.

Any second now, Dane would see the orange jacket.

She stood up and walked toward Dane.

The yellow eyes locked on hers. The side of his face was grotesque with dried blood.

She was shaking so much she could hardly move, but she forced herself to stand directly in his path.

"Goddamn you to hell, you bastard." Her words hurled at him. "I won't let you take him. You'll have to kill me first."

He dropped the flashlight to the sand, plunging them into uncertain shadow. "I have more pleasurable plans for you, my Juliet." His hand shot up and gripped the tangled wet hair at the nape of her neck.

She cried out in fear and tried to twist away. He hit her hard across the face. Pain exploded in a bursting light behind her eyes. She kicked out blindly, but he caught her foot and swept her legs from under her so that she fell to the sand.

Then he was on top of her, huge and hard, the heavy body hurting, pinning her down.

Her scream was silenced as he caught her jaw in his vise-like fingers and forced her chin up.

"I'm going to hurt you, Juliet," he whispered, his face close to hers.

She tried to turn her face away, but his lips found hers, brutal and demanding, forcing her mouth open. She tasted blood on her lips.

Somehow her arms were free and beating against him and his hands were on the waist of her jeans and she felt the material tear and then his strong fingers were moving down over her stomach.

"Please, please," she sobbed. "Don't do this."

"We must hurry," he said against her skin. "My priestly vestments await." His voice was strange and frightening.

Frantic with terror, she struggled beneath him, clutching for his hands.

Something hard against her hip. Brian's army knife!

Dane's breath was coming in hoarse gasps. With every ounce of concentration she pushed her hand into the tight jeans pocket.

She felt the shock of his fingers invading her, searching and brutal. "You are mine now, Juliet," he whispered. "I will dance barefoot on our wedding day, and lead the apes in hell."

She screamed again, trembling with revulsion.

Her frantic fingers, slippery with blood, found the knife. Closed over it.

Pulled it free.

He made a sound, slamming her face sideways into the sand with a sickening impact and knocking the breath from her lungs.

Somehow, she managed to hold onto the knife.

There was a great roaring inside her head. Locked in his deadly embrace, she heard his voice as if from a great distance. "I will be your last lover."

She shouted and twisted desperately beneath him, hitting out wildly until she felt the knife rip into his body.

"Bitch!" Iron fingers grasped her wrist, tearing the knife cruelly from her grip.

She struggled to face him, dimly aware that he was on his knees above her, arm raised, the small steel blade flashing silver in the wavering beam of the flashlight.

"*Mama! No!*"

The child's cry pierced the night air, clear and sharp as the rain.

Dane's arm froze in the air.

Frantic barking tore the night. Sudden shouts from the left. "*Ici*! Over here!"

"It is not finished between us, Juliet," he whispered in her ear. Then the terrible weight sprang from her body as beams of light cut like bright swords through the darkness, searching, finding her.

She sat up, shielding her eyes. Pulling at her jeans, she tried to stand.

Somewhere on the water the sound of an engine filled the blackness.

She blinked, struggled to focus through the blur of her tears.

The Golden was loping toward her across the wet sand. TJ and Beckett were running just behind him.

Michael? She must be dreaming.

She took a step. Fell to her knees.

She held out her hands.

The Golden was the first to reach her. "Shiloh," she whispered, tangling her fingers in the warmth of his coat, burying her face against his body.

"Maggie." Beckett dropped to his knees in front of her. Her eyes registered the white bandages across his left eye as he pulled her roughly against him.

"Michael, stop him." Her voice was scratchy with confusion.

She was shivering violently. Beckett gripped her shoulders.

"Maggie, listen to me. Brian is okay. *Your son is safe.*"

A small body slammed against her legs, almost knocking her over, and wrapped wiry arms tightly around her.

"Mag-gee," said the little boy into her sweater. The small halting voice scraped from the long-dormant throat muscles. She thought it was the most beautiful sound she had ever heard. She forgot everything but the sight and feel of the boy, alive and reaching out to her. She simply wrapped her arms around him and rocked him back and forth. The tears welled, and something broken inside her finally began to mend.

"TJ, my hero," she whispered.

"Her-o," rasped the exhausted but satisfied child.

Beckett took her face in his hand and tilted her chin until she was looking into his eyes. "Your son is fine," he said. "His wife, too. And the baby, still safe in his mama's womb. They're at the Hyannis police station, waiting for you to call."

"Brian," she murmured, as the words penetrated the cold fear that still gripped her like a black vise.

Beckett helped her to stand and stepped back. They stared at each other, while the boy and the Golden pressed tightly against her body. She swayed, holding them close. Beckett smoothed the wet dark hair back from her forehead. "Bad hair day," he said.

"Michael..."

And then he was folding her into his arms, and she felt herself silenced by his mouth. His lips were cold and tasted of rain. She could feel the wild thudding of his heart through her soaked sweater. "Oh, Michael," she murmured, and clung to him like a child just rescued from a nightmare.

"I've got you," he said into her hair.

She was vaguely aware of Shiloh's nose, pushing against her leg. Then her knees gave way and Beckett caught her as she collapsed against him. Ignoring his own injuries, he gathered her in his arms and, with the little boy in the bright orange vest and the three-legged dog walking beside him, carried her as if she weighed no more than a seashell across the storm-swept beach toward the flashing blue lights of the police cars.

*I've got you.*

# CHAPTER EIGHTY-FIVE

"Yes, Brian's fine, Luze. Truly. I just spoke with him for twenty minutes. The Hyannis police are all going to his club tonight. Knowing that you and Brian and TJ are okay means everything to me."

*Except for Zach...*

Her friend's voice was warm and comforting in her ear. "Yes, I'll be home late tomorrow." She glanced at the bolted connecting door to Michael Beckett's room. "There's no reason to stay here now."

Safe once more in her hotel room in Aix-en-Provence, Maggie sat with her legs curled under her in front of the fire. In spite of the warm white robe wrapped around her body, she continued to shiver uncontrollably. Don't think about Dane.

She looked across the room. The rain had blown away as suddenly as it had come. Late moonlight shone through the French doors, spilling in a silvery river over the glimmering grand piano. Just three hours ago, she had been on the beach in Cassis...

"No, Luze, Michael Beckett is not *my* colonel. But the Hyannis detective told me that 'some army fella from south of the Mason-Dixon' had agents guarding Brian and Laura around the clock since the beginning."

She stopped speaking. Where was he?

The jangle of Lucy's bracelets sounded clearly across the ocean. Maggie sighed. "Of course Bones asked about his father. I told him the basics but I want to tell him about Zach in person."

She closed her eyes and felt the fire's heat on her eyelids. "Luze, the last time I saw Zach, we were on Victor's yacht. What if I've found Zach only to lose him again?"

A sharp knock at the door interrupted her, and her heart skipped sickeningly beneath her breast. Dane? No, it had to be Michael. Please let it be Michael.

"I think the answers are knocking at my door. Yes, love you too, bye."

She leaned her forehead against the door and whispered, "Michael?"

"His better half." Simon Sugarman's voice. She opened the door.

Immediately she found herself enveloped in a huge bear hug. "Can't stay, Doc, gotta get to the airport. But I couldn't leave without saying goodbye to my favorite lady." He looked down at her. "This hotel gives you these great robes?"

"Simon!" Her hands pressed on his solid chest, pushing him away.

"Still angry with me, huh?"

"I thought we were friends," she said.

The dark eyes studied her. "We are friends, Doc. But—" he shook his cannonball head—"I always told you, in my business, you do what you—"

"Gotta do," she finished for him. "Why didn't I see it? It was *you, your* people, who searched my home and shop after Johnny died. You took his computer, the papers from his briefcase. You needed to know what my husband knew."

Simon walked to the table and poured two stiff whiskeys. "Don't you know the story of the scorpion, Maggie? He rescues a tiny animal from a raging river, then stings it to death when they reach the shore." He swallowed the alcohol, watching her face. "It's my nature, Maggie. Don't ask me to apologize for it."

"The scorpion just uses his nature as a damned excuse. People I care about almost died, Simon. I need some answers. Did Dane get away?"

He looked at her sharply, nodded. "You haven't seen Beckett?"

"Not—since the beach. He put me in the ambulance and left." She touched his arm. "He went after Dane, didn't he?"

"Mike could have stopped Dane on the beach. But you were hurt. He had to make a choice. Couldn't change *his* nature, either. I didn't count on that. Let it be, Doc."

He looked at his watch. "They're holding my plane for DC. I've got ten minutes. Ask your questions."

She took a deep swallow of fiery whiskey, ignoring the pain in her arm. "Where are TJ and Zach?"

"Medivaced by 'copter to the trauma unit here in Aix. The kid's okay," he added, seeing her face, "thanks to you. He's going to be fine. The kid's a trooper. Scared, groggy, some hypothermia. But talking, Maggie. A few words, anyway. The docs are making him take it real slow. But he sure found a way to ask for you." He looked at her. "I told TJ that I was Sofia's friend—and he told me what he remembers about his mother's death."

A silver knife flashed in the darkness of her mind. Maggie shuddered. "Dane killed Sofia," she told him, "and threatened her child so he would remain silent." Her eyes filled with tears. "What a horrible burden for a little boy."

"Here, dammit, you're freezing. Come over by the fire." Simon took her arm and caught her sudden wince. "You ought to be in that hospital yourself, Doc."

She pulled away from him. "Why aren't you telling me about Zach?"

"He was hurt, Maggie. Trying to stop Orsini."

"No!" she cried. "He told me they were very close. Victor wouldn't have hurt Zach."

"Details are sketchy. But there was a fight on the yacht. Zach was shot."

Just like Michael. She felt the ice close around her heart. "Is he alive, Simon?"

"Yeah. It's bad, Maggie. But Zach made it through the surgery. He's alive. Orsini could have killed him. But he didn't."

"Zach insisted that Victor was like a father. You haven't found Orsini?"

"Probably hiding in those islands where he spent the last year on his yacht. Porquerolles, Port-Cros, who knows? There are hundreds of Mediterranean islands, thousands of hidden inlets." He stopped, looking at her ashen face. "But you know that already."

"Victor was in the Porquerolles? Oh God. It's where Johnny died."

"Your husband must have tracked Orsini to those islands. We'll find Orsini, Doc. Got to. Because there was a king's fortune of stolen art and music on that yacht, all gone when we got there. And that art was just the tip of the iceberg. God knows where the rest of his collection is hidden."

She gazed at him in confusion. "Art? All this, because of missing *art*?"

Simon shrugged. "And music. Orsini was selling pieces to private collectors, to finance acts of terror against us. The only things left behind on that yacht were a smashed violin, a small forgotten painting, and..."

"Zach."

"Yeah. Victor just left Law there, bleeding all over the floor of the salon."

She remained stonily quiet.

"Zach Law will be okay, Maggie."

Sugarman poured another whiskey for himself. He downed the burning liquid in one long swallow. "Gotta blow. Dane isn't finished with us yet. We think he's headed for New York, but we don't know what he's planning."

"Simon. Something Dane said to me...on the beach. But I can't remember." She felt the shudder of her body. "It just won't come."

"Think hard. You've got to remember, Maggie, it's important." He leaned closer to her, handed her a small printed card. "*Really* important. As soon as you know, call me here."

Simon stopped at her door. "You deserve to know—I found the journal Sofia hid. Priceless, she gave us everything. Orsini's investors, clients, bank accounts, hired guns. Dynamite stuff."

So much hurt, all because of the names in a small notebook. "Where was it, Simon?"

"Right in front of our noses. Sofia's boy had it all along. The journal had been rolled like a cee-gar and tucked into TJ's stuffed bear." He hesitated at the door. "Did Fee ever send you anything? A music manuscript, maybe? Maybe she talked about it?"

"She wrote that she'd taken a valuable manuscript from Victor, but I never saw it."

"Then it's still out there, somewhere." He gave her a brief salute and closed the door behind him.

Maggie stood alone in the silent room staring into the fire, hugging the thick robe to her shivering body and trying to shut out the images of wild seas and a silver knife and Dane's grotesque smiling face, so close to hers.

*You're only alive because I let you live, my Juliet.*

* * *

In the small safe house in the hills north of Marseilles, the man known as Dane stared at his image in the cracked mirror over the sink.

The long fair hair, the mustache and diamond earring were gone. The dark-browed face that looked back at him wore thick tinted glasses and the tri-cornered European priest's cap called a biretta. The purple bruise on the side of his face was completely hidden by the theatre make-up and the thick, curling gray hair.

Almost time for your next performance, he told himself, adjusting the collar of the long black cassock once more. Pain shot through his burned hand. He cursed and reached for the new black leather gloves. Hunching his shoulders, he watched his reflection in the mirror. Perfect. He nodded and turned his attention to the passports and tickets scattered on the table.

Most of the documents, including a first-class Olympic Airways ticket from New York to Athens, were issued to an unpronounceable Greek name. The remaining papers, issued to one Monsignor Hervé Chalfont, included a passport with his current likeness and a Lufthansa ticket from Frankfurt to the United States.

They would be watching the Nice airport. But his jet for Germany left from a private airfield near Arles in less than two hours. Money talked. From there, an eight-hour flight to the US. With luck he would be in the safe house by the time the sun rose over the east coast. Twenty-four hours after that a rich—a *very* rich—businessman would be on his way to Greece. Not even Victor knew about the house on Mykonos. He would disappear completely.

Just one last job.

One final role to play.

# CHAPTER EIGHTY-SIX

"*Bonsoir,* Madame O'Shea." The night manager at the inn smiled at Maggie as she entered the small lobby. "I hope your friends at the hospital are doing well?"

"The little boy is going to be fine, *Monsieur, merci bien.*"

Maggie pulled the heavy, borrowed jacket more closely around her shoulders. She'd driven herself to the hospital and found TJ curled in a corner bed, wrapped in blankets, a muscular policewoman reading by his bedside.

"Hey, TJ," she said with a gentle shake of his shoulder. "You saved my life."

"Mag...gee." The raw, hesitant voice was the most miraculous music she'd ever heard.

He had thrown his arms around her neck. "I didn't want that man to hurt you, Maggie," he whispered against her neck, "not like...my mama. I saw the knife!"

"I know, honey. You were very brave. But you should be resting your voice." She grinned at him. "You sound just like a frog."

They'd laughed and she'd held him while he bombarded her with his rasping questions and fears until the small voice was no more than a whisper and, exhausted, he finally slept. She stayed with him for a long time, watching him sleep.

Then she'd gone to Zach's room.

In the small quiet lobby of her hotel, Maggie closed her eyes, but still she saw the image of Zach's face on the white pillow. The tubes, the bandages, the machines that registered every breath and heartbeat with a whirring, frightening sound.

*Fight, Zach*, she'd told him, fight for Brian and TJ. Fight for your life. She'd touched his scarred face. "You really are a beautiful man," she'd whispered.

"*Madame?*" The concerned voice of the hotel manager broke into her thoughts. "We will miss you and *Mon Colonel, Madame.* Your room will be called 'The Music Room' from now on. We have decided to leave the piano there." She tried to smile at him, but knew that he saw the sadness that touched her face. "*Mon Colonel* looked very tired, also," he ventured.

"He's back? Thank God." She turned toward the lift.

"Back, *oui, Madame.* But heading to the airport," said the manager with dismay. "He settled his bill and had me call for a taxi."

But she was gone, running up the narrow stairs.

* * *

He stood by the fire, feet apart, left hand in the pocket of his tweed jacket, right hand swirling one final glass of whiskey as he stared into the flames. Shiloh lay curled on the hearth rug, watching him, the flames turning his fur to gold.

*Just five more minutes*, Beckett bargained.

Time to go home, old man, he thought. Taxi's waiting. Dane's gone to ground. Victor as well, along with a vast fortune in art. Only the devil knows where he's hidden those pieces. Sugar is somewhere over the Atlantic by now. And Maggie, well, her room is empty. She's with Zach, of course.

He looked down at the Golden. "By tomorrow she'll be gone, too, back to Zach Law and her family and a life of music that doesn't include us."

Shiloh's eyes flickered in the light, seeming to glow with sadness.

This mission was over. It was time for him to walk away. *Time to let her go.* What the devil was he waiting for, anyway?

Momentary insanity, under control now. Pick up the duffel bag. Slip the leash on Shiloh. Forget shining green eyes and lips that tasted like the sea.

*Go.* But still he gazed into the fire. And all he could see was the image of a woman standing on a dark beach, lit by flashing blue lights, holding on for dear life to a small boy and a three-legged dog.

He heard the sound of the door opening behind him, breathed the soft scent of roses in the air. His heart was beating like the whump of a 'copter blade but he was afraid to turn around and so he continued to stare into the fire.

"Mrs. O'Shea," he said softly, smiling, watching the leaping flames.

There's still a chance, he told himself. I can still leave.

"Colonel," she said.

The husky voice drew him, no hope for it, and he turned, eyes questioning, seeking hers. Everything around him seemed to blur, and all he could see was Maggie, standing in the firelight. She'd pulled her hair up and tucked it inside the knitted hat.

Her gaze swept over his duffel bag, waiting by the door. "Could you just leave me then, without saying goodbye?"

"I've never done a harder thing."

"I thought we..."

"Yes," he said simply. "We did."

"Then don't go, Michael."

"I couldn't stop Dane or Orsini. They're still out there, you're still in danger. You shouldn't be here."

"You saved my life. You protected my son's life. Where else would I be?"

He looked over at the Golden. "See, when she says things like that..."

His sleek head resting on his paw, Shiloh gazed back at him with an expression of amusement.

Maggie smiled at the dog. "This is where he tells me to go home. Again."

Beckett gazed down at her. "The soldier wants you to go, ma'am. But the man wants you to stay."

The room behind her was very dark. The firelight caught the planes of her face, her eyes blazing. Very slowly, as if drawn by the heat, she walked toward him, past the cleared desk, past the untouched bed, past the packed and waiting duffel bag. Then she was in front of him, looking up with those smoldering eyes.

"It's not finished between us."

He looked down at this woman who stood before him, who changed his life early one morning in an ancient French cemetery under a lavender sky.

*If I don't touch her*, he bargained, *I'll still be able to leave.*

Like a man caught in a dream, his hand came up. He pushed the cap back from her head so that it fell to the floor, her hair tumbling like dark water over her shoulders.

"Don't go," she said again. "I couldn't bear it."

His eyes held hers. "If I stay, Maggie, there'll be no turning back for me."

"I don't want you to turn back. I don't want to be anywhere else right now. Only with you."

He smiled crookedly at her. "But?"

"But—" She looked down at her wedding ring, twisted it on her finger.

"I know you're not ready," he said.

"Every step I take toward the future is taking a step away from my husband. It feels like I'm betraying him."

"You loved each other when he died, I get that. It doesn't just go away. But your husband would want you to be happy."

"I'm scared," she whispered. "Scared of what I felt for you the night you gave me the piano. What I felt when you kissed me on the beach."

"You think that I'm not afraid?" he said. "Afraid because you're the only woman I've ever known who would run into eight lanes of traffic to save a three-legged dog, the only woman who would jump overboard into a raging black sea to rescue a little boy." He shook his head, still astonished by her bravery.

"I couldn't stop my husband's death, Michael. But I could damned sure do something for the dog and that child."

"A woman like you doesn't belong with a man like me."

"I have news for you, Colonel, you're the last person I want in *my* life as well! You'll make me fall for you, and then...then you'll die, just like Johnny died!"

"I'm not going to leave you."

He stepped closer, cupped her face in both hands and tilted her head back. "It's barely a week since I laid eyes on you. But the first time I saw you in the cemetery, I knew."

"That I was trouble?"

"That I'd met my downfall."

"I'm not the same woman you met in that cemetery. I'm—tougher. Stronger."

"Couldn't you just have gone for—oh, I don't know—maybe less impulsive, unpredictable and confusing?" He looked over at the Golden. "Every conversation with her is like trying to teach a kangaroo to limbo."

Shiloh gazed back at them as if in deep contemplation. Maggie laughed. "For so many months," she said, shaking her head, "my life hasn't seemed to fit me. But now, with you, I'm starting to feel as if I know who I am again."

"I didn't want to fall for you," said Beckett. "Tried so damned hard *not* to. But it just *is*."

They were close enough to feel each other's breath.

"I was drowning, Colonel. And then you were there..."

He placed his hands on her shoulders. "You are the most intensely beautiful, infuriating, brilliant woman I have ever known," he said. "You take away the shadows."

* * *

The small clock on the mantel began to chime the midnight hour. She looked up at him—this formidable army colonel who wanted only to roam the blue hills of Virginia with a dog named Shiloh, a man who had frightened her and given her a piano and protected the life of her son. A man who looked at her with such fierce yearning that at last she felt the pain locked for so long inside her tremble and shatter into a thousand pieces.

"I want to be alive again," she whispered. "But we can't... I'm not ready to..."

His silver brows spiked with amusement. "To make love? I have no doubt, Maggie, that making love to you will be as astonishing as a sunrise. But my plane leaves at dawn. And I'm not a hit-and-run kind of guy, right, Shiloh?"

The Golden barked once.

"This is about much more than the physical," he said. "Not that I haven't been thinking about it." He gave her his crooked grin. "This is about emotional intimacy, and you know it. It's about two lost people finding each other." He reached out slowly, caught the collar of her coat, pulled her closer. "But I could stay here with you. For a while."

"You're talking too much." Her hands moved over his face and rested on the bandages over his eye. "Your stitches..."

"The devil with the stitches."

Without taking her eyes from him, she dropped her coat to the floor.

Her t-shirt said *Handel with Care.*

They didn't speak.

He gathered her in his arms and drew her down on the rug in front of the fire.

She touched his mouth with her fingers.

His grasp tightened around her waist and pulled her body closer.

He lifted her hair and brushed his lips across the hollow of her neck. Slipped her sweater off her shoulder, touched his lips to her skin.

"You have a tattoo," he murmured.

"It's a treble clef."

He shook his head at her.

The Golden moved closer, settling against her hip.

Beckett stoked up the fire.

They shared bread and cheese in the streaming shadows.

He wrapped her in a soft blanket.

They drank sweet red wine.

"Better than a cold beer on a hot night," he murmured.

She laughed.

He found Chopin on the small radio.

"Being with you is like music," she whispered.

He lifted her hand to his lips, kissed the inside of her wrist.

She touched her forehead to his.

He wrapped his arms around her and told her, "Being with you is like being home, in my mountains. An endless big sky in your eyes. A light in the window..."

She twined her fingers in the silver chain around his neck while she listened.

Then, "Just keep saying my name, Colonel," she said. "I want to hear it over and over."

"Maggie. Maggie." His lips found hers. "Maggie."

# CHAPTER EIGHTY-SEVEN

AIX-EN-PROVENCE. PAST MIDNIGHT, JULY 12

Victor Orsini stood at a tall, open, casement window, staring out into the darkness.

*Where is my son tonight? Is Thomas still alive?*

He had to find out.

His fingers closed into tight fists. *I did not love you enough,* he told his son.

But it was too late for anguish. He'd been lost for too long. His chance was gone. He would make the O'Shea woman pay for what she'd done to him—if she was still alive.

* * *

The bedroom was swathed in shadows. They sat together on the floor in front of the fire, Maggie's head against Beckett's shoulder. The Golden's head was in her lap.

The air was quiet, flickering. A log dislodged, falling to the hearth in a loud shower of sparks. Both Beckett and the Golden jolted against her.

"Michael," she said, reaching to stroke and reassure the dog. "Do you trust me?"

A beat of silence. Then, "Yes." She could hear the shimmer of surprise in his voice.

She took his hand. "Can you tell me what happened to you? To both of you..."

He gazed into the flames, still and silent. Gripping her hand tightly, he closed his eyes and began to speak.

"The Middle East. A hell of a place. Neon skylines on the edge of desert. Conflict not only in the war zones, but cultural. A museum with modern art, a woman who walks miles to get there because she's not allowed to drive.

"And then—the moonscape of Afghanistan. Nothing prepares you for it. It was my third tour in Helmand Province. A quiet morning. I was in the village on recon with my team. There was this kid, Farzad. Eleven, twelve. Friendly kid, always hanging around. There was just something about him, you know? He had a little sister, and a thin, wild Golden that followed him everywhere. Only mutts in the village, but the Golden had belonged to some US contractor." He shrugged. "The local kids loved soccer, it was the only escape for some of them. So that morning I'd brought a bright red soccer ball with me."

\* \* \*

This morning the square is busy, hot and dusty, surrounded by white cubes of houses with dark, open windows.

He tosses the soccer ball across the square. A bright red sphere against the high sky. The little girl, her brother Farzad, and the Golden all run after it. The children are shouting, laughing. Smiling.

He smiles, too, watching them.

The red ball spins through the air.

Again. Again.

The boy runs up to him, grabs his hand, squeezes. "You will take us home with you one day?" the child asks, eyes huge in the thin face. "We will play soccer every day together?"

He smiles down at Farzad. And wonders, not for the first time, if there is any way he can take this smart gentle boy and his little sister home with him.

He lifts the ball once more, sends it sailing high across the dusty square. He hears Farzad's sister squeal with delight just as he sees the glint of the sun on metal in one of the windows overlooking the square.

All sound stops.

The sudden scream of automatic gunfire split the air.

A shout, *Allahu Akbar!*

A flash of brilliant light.

"Incoming!" he shouts, throwing himself toward the boy. But the boy runs from him.

More explosions, blooming in the sky. *He is on the ground. The earth beneath him is stained red. Sharp and pulsing. He's been hit.*

He raises his head, sees the boy racing across the square toward his sister. The gold dog chases him, barking frantically.

*Christ, the kids. No, Farzad! Don't—*

*Allahu Akbar!*

The dog launches into the air, his front paws hitting the boy, pushing him down. Covering him.

Bright flashes, a terrible scream. The whining spit of bullets, the smell of burning flesh. The roar of thunder, a searing blast of heat.

Dust exploding around him, shattered glass, blood everywhere.

An animal's high howl of fear and pain. Then silence.

He staggers to his feet, struggles across the square.

Past the soccer ball, glistening in a pool of blood.

He sees Farzad's sister, crumpled and still. Gone.

The dog is covered in blood, lying on top of the boy. They are not moving.

*No! Farzad...*

Somehow he gathers the boy and the dog against him, lifts them both against his chest, and begins to stagger across the shimmering square toward safety.

The sounds of automatic gunfire echo around him.

* * *

Maggie reached up to wipe the tears from his face. "Farzad didn't make it," she said.

"No. He died cradled in my arms. I never got to bring him home. If only I hadn't..." He swiped angrily at the tears. "I went into the darkness for the all right reasons," he said, "but I didn't know it would shatter my soul. Now, somehow, I have to learn to live with it."

She put her arms around him and held on tight.

# CHAPTER EIGHTY-EIGHT

*The sailboat slid sickeningly across the roaring water toward the rocks. Chimes rang wildly in the darkness, while in the distance a phone rang and rang...*

"Oh, God!" Maggie jolted up, looking wildly around the fire-lit room. Then she saw Michael.

Beckett looked down at her. "I trusted you tonight. It's your turn. Tell me about the nightmares."

Her eyes widened with sudden understanding. "It was *you* that first night in Aix, in my bedroom. You came to me, when I was dreaming. You tasted of brandy. You said, 'I've got you.'"

"Yes."

"I dream," she said, "that I'm playing the piano—the Grieg Concerto—late at night on a faraway beach. There's a terrible storm. A telephone is ringing loudly, insistently. And all around me, the echo of chimes. Then Johnny's sailboat appears, flying across the sea. Suddenly it explodes, and I'm in the water, search-ing for him...drowning with him." She buried her face in her hands. "I thought I faced the nightmares this afternoon. In the sea. But—"

"But there's more to the dream than the water."

"Yes. I'll never know what happened to Johnny that day."

"You deserve to know the truth," said Beckett. There was an odd expression in his eyes.

"Sugar doesn't think that your husband's death was an acci-dent. He believes that your husband was murdered."

Her entire body began to tremble. Blood hammered in her ears, blinding lights burst behind her eyes. Her fingers tightened on his arm. "But I was told it was an accident! I never questioned it. I just accepted..."

Beckett put his arms around her and held her, as if he could keep her from shattering. "Months before Sofia died, your husband was working on a story about the financing of terrorists. When he went off in search of your godson, all the dots began to connect and he realized who Victor Orsini was. He was ready to expose Orsini," Beckett said. "He was endangering Orsini's operation."

Her eyes reflected her horror. "Please, no..."

"There's no way to prove it, Maggie. Two people who'd gotten close to Orsini in the past disappeared. There are too many subtle ways to disguise a killing. Hit and run, mugging, heart attack. A boating accident..."

That's why Johnny has been coming to me in my dreams all these months. For the truth. For justice.

*Victor Orsini had my husband killed.*

"I think some part of me always knew," she whispered.

The mantel clock struck two a.m.

"I need to help you find him, Michael. Victor Orsini is the man responsible for my husband's death. The closer I can get to him, the more I can hurt him."

"And the more he could hurt *you*. Leave this to me. And Sugar. We have the resources to—"

"He killed my husband, Michael!"

"We don't know for sure. So we find him, get a confession, bring him to trial—"

"Confession..." A chill raced through her.

"What is it, Maggie?"

"That's it. You said 'confession.' I've remembered what Dane said to me on the beach."

Immediately Beckett's head came up, listening and alert. "Tell me. It could be important."

"He had me pinned beneath him, I couldn't move. He called me his Juliet. Then he—" she shuddered—"he tore my jeans and murmured something religious. It didn't make sense. He talked about... 'priestly vestments,' and 'dancing at a wedding.' He was going to rape me, Michael, and he behaved as if it were some sort of ceremony."

"Goddamned bastard," he said, holding her against his chest. He stiffened. "Christ, that's it! He's going to be disguised as a priest."

Beckett jumped up, clicked the locks on his briefcase, and ran his eyes down a list of scheduled events. "That must be the target! I have to get a military flight to DC." He reached for his phone.

"Can't Simon do it?"

"He's already on a flight to New York." He bent to touch her cheek. "Dane and I have a score to settle." Then he stopped. "I don't want to leave you to deal with your husband's death alone."

"It's the only way I *can* deal with it." She looked steadily into his eyes. "You've got to go. Dane must be stopped. And for me, after all these months, the knowing is better than the not knowing. Just come back to me."

He dropped to one knee, tilted her head back, and kissed her. "I'll come back to you. That's a promise."

Beckett shouldered his duffel bag and looked down at her. He reached for his computer case, called to the Golden, and moved toward the door.

"Making love to you, Magdalena O'Shea," he said, "is as inevitable as sundown." And then, "*Count on it.*"

Then he and his dog were gone, back into the shadows.

* * *

Maggie stared at the closed door. You've given me so much, Michael. And now, one more gift. Now I have a way to say goodbye to Johnny.

You have a job to do. *But so do I.*

"I made a vow to you, Johnny O'Shea," she said out loud in the flickering darkness. "I damn well intend to keep my promise."

It was time to confront the man who ordered the death of her husband.

# CHAPTER EIGHTY-NINE

10:45 a.m.

Dane stood in a narrow, dark bedroom, fingering the hand-crafted plastic weapon that would be taped to his leg. "The Secret Service are the best at what they do," he murmured. "But—"

But he was better. He had all the right credentials, the disguise. The plan. The key was to act as if he belonged. And he did that perfectly. There would be no reason to suspect him.

He looked into the mirror over the bureau, took in the curling gray hair, the darkened eyes beneath the glasses, the stooped shoulders, the puffed cheeks above the tight collar. "Even if the agents have photographs," he said aloud to the image, "no one here could recognize you."

He turned away from the mirror, smoothing the heavy black costume with a steady hand.

He was ready. One more glance in the mirror, a minor adjustment, a final check of his weapon, and then he moved toward the door.

"I have done a thousand dreadful things," he quoted, "As willingly as one would kill a fly."

* * *

11:02 a.m.

The bomb dogs had come and gone. All clear.

*So far.*

In the glittering glass-enclosed Boat House Restaurant in

New York City's Central Park, Sugarman gazed out over the sea of faces that gathered for the First Lady's birthday celebration luncheon. He could see her, just past the flowers, smiling at the German Chancellor and her husband.

The small phone on his hip buzzed to life. The Jesuit priest had just entered the restaurant.

Sugarman moved through the crowd.

\* \* \*

11:58 a.m.

Three hundred miles to the south, deep within the campus of Georgetown University in Washington, DC, there was an air of expectancy in the small Dahlgren Chapel.

Masses of white roses had transformed the simple chapel into a snowy garden. In the flickering candlelight, an array of prominent faces waited, watching each other while the organist filled the arched nave with the beauty of Pachelbel's Canon in D. The scent of roses was heavy in the air.

Several members of the Cabinet and Congress were already seated on the red, cushioned chairs. The British Ambassador whispered with newspaper scions, celebrities, and captains of industry. The newest Supreme Court Justice, a friend of the bride's mother, took her place in a front pew with family and close friends. In the rear of the chapel, paparazzi pressed against velvet ropes while cameras flashed.

Just to the right of the altar, beneath stained glass windows glowing with high noon sunlight, a row of Jesuits and nuns sat with heads bowed in devotion.

At both entrances to the little church, watchful men in dark suits waited, eyes constantly moving over the candlelit faces.

A smiling young man in a tuxedo escorted the Admiral's wife and family to their seats in the front row. Twenty young men and women in blue robes rose, sheet music open in their hands. A Jesuit in snowy vestments walked out onto the altar. The tall and slightly bemused young groom took his place and looked expectantly down the white-carpeted aisle.

The organist struck the first stirring chords of Mendelssohn's triumphant Wedding March. The guests stood. Beyond the altar, a stooped old nun in a black habit dropped her missal and stooped to retrieve it. As she bent forward, her long black veil swung forward to hide her face.

*　*　*

12:33 p.m.

In New York City, just moments before the President was about to toast the First Lady and their distinguished luncheon guests, Sugarman moved to the front table and leaned down until his mouth was against the Jesuit's ear. "I'm your nightmare, pal. Better finish your prayers, because those folks coming toward us across the room? They're all pals of mine, from the FBI."

The old priest looked at him with shocked eyes.

*　*　*

1:07 p.m.

In the Georgetown University chapel, the Admiral kissed his granddaughter's cheek before she turned toward her groom. The long white satin skirt brushed his wheelchair as his radiant grandchild passed by.

Colonel Michael Beckett entered the chapel and moved down the side aisle.

"Almighty and Eternal Father," intoned the celebrant, "we ask your blessing on this man and this woman..."

Beckett stopped beneath an archway and stared at the clergy seated beyond the altar. One of the Jesuits leaned forward. Just behind him, an elderly nun knelt down, bowing her veiled head in silent prayer. The bride bent toward her groom.

"...today we have come together in God's house to celebrate the union..."

Beckett moved forward, stopping behind a white pillar.

Very carefully, he scanned the faces of the black-clad priests and nuns who sat in the rows so close to the Admiral and his wedding guests. Where are you, Dane? asked Beckett, staring at each face. Too old, too young, wrong sex. Too dark, too heavy, too short. In the flickering light of the tall tapers, the faces of the priests swam before his eyes.

"...to love and honor, in sickness and in health..."

*He has changed his appearance*, Beckett reminded himself.

A gray-haired priest raised his head slowly.

A tall, stooped nun grasped the wooden crucifix on her breast with a gloved hand.

Beckett stopped, alerted by the unexpected movement. There was something wrong. Damn, what was he missing?

*The glove...*

"...so long as you both shall live..."

The old priest closed his missal.

The nun's hand moved beneath a fold of her black habit. The dark veil fell forward to shield her face. *Why a glove?*

The bride and groom knelt down.

The priest's hand moved upward.

"Pronounce you man and wife..."

The choir stood and began to sing a triumphant *Hallelujah*.

The Admiral took his wife's hand and looked toward the bride.

The tall nun turned slightly. Beckett's eyes were on her hands. The gloves.

The dark veil shifted, fell back. A pale face, narrow lips moving in prayer.

The profile! thought Beckett, staring at Dane's hawk-like nose. The gloved hand...to hide an injury? To hide a man's hands?

*He was dressed as a nun.*

The bride smiled at her husband.

Beckett shouted a warning.

The nun spun around, stood quickly and took aim.

Beckett launched his body across the aisle.

The Admiral turned in shock.

In the front row, several women screamed.

Beckett's fist smashed into the nun's arm just as a shot was fired.

Unaware of the unfolding tragedy, the organist high in the loft reached his crescendo. As twenty choral voices soared into the high spaces, the blast of Dane's weapon echoed outward, shattering the small chapel with reverberating sound.

In the front pew, the Admiral fell back as a bright red rose bloomed like a grotesque flower on the side of his face and spilled down onto the starched formal shirt.

\* \* \*

Several hundred miles to the north, at a secure and very private airfield in Queens, Sugarman watched the President and First Lady of the United States shake hands with the German Chancellor and the embattled President of France. Listened as the somber president said, "The Middle East is our next focus. We will go forward together."

Sugarman shook his head. *Sometimes, a priest is just a priest.*

He stood on the shadowed tarmac and watched until all three Lear jets disappeared into the shining sunlit sky.

# CHAPTER NINETY

It was almost sunset in Provence when Maggie stood at the tall, carved gates of Saint Paul de Mausole monastery in the town of Saint-Rémy-de-Provence.

She looked cautiously through the heavy grillwork into a small shaded garden. All quiet. She'd been told that the beautiful old building where Van Gogh had lived was now actually part monastery and part convalescent home.

And a place to hide. A place for a monster to go to ground.

She pulled her sweater more tightly around her shoulders. She had gone to the hospital that morning, as soon as Michael left for the airport. She had kissed a sleeping TJ, then gone to Zach's room. There, deep in the pocket of Zach's jacket, she'd found the pearl-handled revolver he'd taken from Celeste LaMartine's hands at the Cézanne museum in Aix. Then she had curled into a chair and kept vigil over her son's father until, just after three p.m., Zach had opened his eyes.

She told him that TJ was fine. She told him that his son, Brian, was safe. She asked him where Victor would go to hide, and he whispered the answer. She kissed his forehead and went to find his doctor.

*He's going to live, Madame.*

Then she was gone, driving east in the small rental car as fast as she dared.

Now, standing outside the monastery's thick stone walls, her hands were shaking. She touched the hard cold metal of Celeste's revolver in the pocket of her jeans. Could you kill him if you have to, she asked herself once more. *Could you?*

A deep and terrible fear washed over her. If you let this go, she told herself, you won't be able to live with yourself. She slipped her hand into her pocket, her fingers closing around the smooth handle of the pistol.

*Who have I become?*

The setting sun slanted over the high tiled roof and touched her face. *The bright day is done*, she thought, *and we are for the dark.*

Just do it. Zach had told her that there was a hidden walled garden, beyond the fountain, where the monks went to pray at sunset.

She pushed open the heavy wooden gate.

\* \* \*

"It's over, Admiral."

Sugarman stood in a small curtained room in Georgetown University Hospital's ER. Monitors beeped softly behind him.

The older man in the hospital bed shook his pale, bandaged head. "You're wrong, Sugar. We don't have Orsini. We don't have Dane, thanks to Beckett's bumbling. We don't have jack shit."

"You have your life, Admiral. And so does your granddaughter, her groom, and all your wedding guests, thanks to *Colonel* Mike Beckett." Sugarman shook his head. "Dane's a goddamn Houdini. He counted on the crowd's panic, set off the smoke bombs, used the choir for cover. Beckett had to choose between the bride—your *granddaughter*—and the terrorist. What would you have done?"

"A true soldier would have sacrificed the bride," said the Admiral without a moment's hesitation. Then his breath rasped out. "But I'm grateful he didn't. So Dane got away once again."

"Disappeared into the university's underground tunnels. But we'll find him."

"I wouldn't hoist my sails just yet. Now, if there's nothing else, help me into my wheelchair. We've got work to do."

"Just one tiny problem, Admiral. It's not 'we' any longer."

Sugarman dropped a sheaf of papers onto the lap of the CIA Deputy Director.

"What's this?"

"A few photocopies. Read 'em and weep, as they say."

The watery blue eyes scanned the first lines, then flew to Sugarman's face.

"From Orsini's files?" The scraping voice was as dry as tinder ready to burst into fire. "But—you told me you found nothing."

"I lied."

"Damn you, Sugar. Why?"

"Three little words, Admiral. '*Skull and Bones*.'"

"Don't go there, Sugar."

"You were—still are—a member of Yale's oldest secret society, right? So is Orsini. Yeah, you'd already graduated. But you knew each other, didn't you. Fellow Bonesmen and all that. He called you for help, didn't he, way back when he discovered his father's war crimes. *You* helped him hide those paintings. And then you blackmailed him. Demanded he join the CIA, use his father's fortune to do your bidding—"

The old man threw the papers to the blanket. "The thing about a secret society, Sugar, is...it's *secret*."

"You had an account with Orsini, Admiral. You became one of his clients, using CIA money you transferred to a private Cayman bank account. It's right there in black and white, pal. All the names and account numbers. Under your watch, the CIA has been transferring major funds into Orsini's empire for years. Money that's been used to finance acts of terrorism against our allies. And *against the United States*, you sick bastard."

"You won't find my name anywhere in Orsini's journal."

"You're too smart for that, aren't you, Admiral? Sure you are. So you used a Cut-Out."

"I beg your pardon?"

"A pardon is probably not in your cards. You couldn't afford to use your own name, so you had someone else front for you. Someone else, who invested CIA money with Orsini for you."

Sugarman leaned closer to the Admiral. "Vanessa Durand," he said.

"Vanessa Durand is an art gallery owner in Paris and Rome, nothing more."

"Admit it, Admiral. Durand really worked for you." Sugarman stared at him and waited.

"Dammit, Sugar, you don't know everything. It all came from our eighties CIA op, under Casey. *Veil*. Good God, man, we had Prince Bandar in our pockets, funding covert operations for ten mil. We funded anti-Quaddafi efforts in Chad, we prevented the communists from coming to power in Italy..."

"And Orsini?"

"For years he took care of things for us, financing terror groups through his network. In the Gulf, Eastern Europe, Africa. Central America. Assassinations, coups, troublesome leaders. Disrupting anti-US elections. All paid for with *our* money...until Ravello."

\* \* \*

The narrow blue door set in the monastery wall swung open. Victor Orsini walked out into the first evening shadows of the hidden garden.

Maggie stood as still as one of the stone statues, behind a bright burst of bougainvillea. She studied the cruel, bull-like features, the barrel chest, the dark robes. The setting sun was behind him, casting a blue shadow across his eyes. He held an enormous white Persian cat against his chest.

She slid her hand into her pocket, felt the security of the small pistol, and stepped out from behind the wall of pink flowers.

At the sound of her footstep on the stony path, he turned and shaded his eyes against the bright falling sun. "Who's there?"

"Magdalena O'Shea."

Orsini's nod was fatalistic. "I've been expecting you."

She walked toward him, and then stopped. They stood staring at each other, five feet apart.

"Have you come here to kill me, Magdalena?"

"I've come to look into your damned eyes," she told him quietly.

"To hear you say the words. To find justice for my husband." She took a shuddering breath. "I've come to stop you."

"Your husband couldn't stop me. No one can. Not Sugarman, not Gideon. Certainly not you."

"I *will* stop you," she said. "You ordered the murder of my husband, you filthy monster. You're responsible for the death of my best friend. You tried to kill my son." The words scraped from her mouth. "I loved them. Why? Why did Fee and Johnny have to die?"

Coal-black eyes stared into hers. He stroked the cat with thick, sun-browned fingers. A heavy gold ring flashed in the light.

And in her memory—a ring, flashing blue.

"You dare to stand here, Magdalena, so righteous. So innocent. But *you* told Sofia to leave me, didn't you? To take my boy—my son—and run. Sofia left me because of you. And then *you* tried to take my son away from me!"

Maggie felt the rage crawl up her throat. She backed away from him as the horror threatened to choke her. "You're twisting the truth," she whispered. "You don't even know how awful you are. Fee left you to protect Tommy."

"The truth?" He lifted his face toward the orange sun. "The truth is that I wanted Fee found, Magdalena. I wanted my wife and my son to come home. I did not want her to die."

"Liar. She loved you once, Victor. What happened to you?"

He turned to study the rosebushes that spilled across the path. "I confused love with possession. And I never told her the truth about my family," he murmured, reaching out to touch a rose that shimmered with fire in the dying light. "Even so, Sofia called me her 'Bright Angel.' Because somehow she knew that, like Lucifer, I'd fallen to earth with my wings on fire."

Maggie's eyes were locked on his thick fingers, caressing the rose petals. "You gave Fee your mother's sapphire ring," she said.

A flash of blue. Where had she seen it? On Fee's finger? No. *Dane's* hand. It was Dane who murdered Fee and took her ring...

Orsini turned back to her. "I loved her, in my way."

"Given the choice," she said, "men like you will always choose power over love."

He shrugged. "I thought Sofia could save me. But no one could."

"Save you from what?"

"The sins of the father. They said my father was a random mugging victim, but the truth is, he took his own life. At the end of the day, he could not live with his guilt." He looked down at the cat held against his chest, and spoke as if to himself. "I thought for years that I could make amends."

"Then why did my husband have to die? You had no reason to hurt him."

"I had the best reason of all. His death would hurt *you*." He shrugged. "But that is not what happened. Your husband suspected that my father collaborated with the Nazis, stole priceless art and music during the war. And that I used those stolen treasures to finance my operations. Of course, I wanted him stopped. Johnny O'Shea was getting too close to finding me. I could not allow him to expose the truth about my past."

"You bastard."

"But I did not order his death."

Maggie inhaled, stunned by his words. *He's lying*. And yet...

Orsini smiled. "The sea, and the storm, took care of that. Or so I was told..." He shook his head at the strange vagaries of fate. "Your husband was doing you a favor, searching for your godson. But what he found was leading him directly to me. To my secrets."

"I don't give a damn about your filthy secrets."

"Perhaps you should."

"What does that mean?"

Orsini stroked the Persian cat held against his chest. "At the end, Sofia discovered my secrets," he said. "You were her dearest friend, she sent you letters all the time. Did she tell you what she found? Did she send you the manuscript of sheet music that she stole from me? Or tell you where she'd hidden it?"

"She wrote that she took a rare violin concerto that belonged to you."

"*Stole* from me. The most amazing musical discovery in the last two hundred years. It will turn the music world upside down."

Her eyes were locked on his. "A Holy Grail of music..."

He smiled coldly at her. "I *wanted* you to come to France," he admitted. "I thought that you would know where the score was. Or lead me to it."

She shook her head. "I know Fee took the concerto from you before Zach had a chance to authenticate it. But no, I have no idea where it is. It may stay lost forever."

"I *must* have it. It was to be the find of the century, the signature piece for my sister. And the road to my own redemption. To return something beautiful that was lost. To replace ugliness with *glory*..."

"Your sister was Bianca Farnese."

His head came up sharply.

"I know what happened in Ravello, Victor. Your sister was a brilliant violinist. She didn't deserve to die."

He shook his bull's head slowly. "No. But I will have my revenge. On all of you." He gazed blindly toward the sky. "Do you know the best way to hurt someone, Magdalena?"

She stared at him, sickened.

"Take away the person they love the most. You have taken away everything else that mattered to me. My art. Gideon. My wife. *My son.*" Black eyes burned into hers. "I know about your colonel, Magdalena. Imagine how he would suffer if he loses you. How your *son* would suffer."

"Murderer," she whispered. "I hope you rot in hell."

"I do not deny that I am ruthless. But I am not amoral. I am a once-moral man, at war."

She saw the glint of black metal appear over the cat's fur, pointing at her heart.

She held out her hands.

Suddenly, tumbling into the air, the monastery chimes rang out from the chapel bell tower.

# CHAPTER NINETY-ONE

"Ravello."

In the flickering light of the ER, the Admiral looked down at his veined hands. "It all went wrong when Orsini's sister was killed in that damned CIA operation in Italy. Bianca Farnese wasn't supposed to die at that concert in Ravello, Sugar. The front-running Italian candidate for Prime Minister wanted to meet her, wanted to hear her perform. He was a charismatic Communist. And we wanted to shut him down. So we used her performance to get him to Ravello. The Communist and the US Ambassador to Italy, together in the front row. It was perfect. A win-win for us."

"Until the bomb went off at the wrong time," said Sugarman, suddenly understanding.

The Admiral nodded. "The Tartini was supposed to be the signal. Somehow we blew it and in a split second we took away the one person in all the world that Orsini cared about. And then all of a sudden he was coming after *us*, Sugar. With our own damned money." The silver head shook wearily. "He blamed us, of course. Began to sell his art to private collectors, amassed a fortune to finance his own acts of terror. Against *us*. The ultimate act of revenge. I couldn't do anything without incriminating the agency. Or myself."

"Because Orsini blamed you. He would never have done business with you, would he, Admiral? He wanted to take you down."

The old man turned away to stare out the window.

"Right. But you needed *him*, didn't you, to do your dirty work for you." Sugarman snapped his fingers. "Enter Vanessa Durand. You had her in your pocket."

The Admiral's eyebrows were coal slashes on the pale forehead. "I was close, Sugar. The wind was at my back, I was almost past the three-mile limit. If it hadn't been for..."

Sugarman smiled. "Yeah. Beckett. And a valiant concert pianist."

"Listen to me, Sugar. I still have access to millions of dollars in secret Cayman accounts. There's still time for damage control."

"That ship has sailed, Admiral. I put the proof in The Man's hand myself, just hours ago."

The fire went out of the bright blue eyes, extinguished like a flame in a sudden wind. "*You* threw me overboard, Sugar?" The parchment skin was bone-white on the shocked face. "Good God, man, why?"

"Because of Sofia Orsini. Sofia needed help when she ran from Orsini. She'd become friendly with Vanessa Durand, Victor's art dealer. Fee turned to her friend, a woman she trusted." Sugarman's dark eyes flashed with pain. "But Vanessa told you that, didn't she?"

"No."

"Yes. Vanessa worked for you, she told you about Fee, and you got word to Orsini." Rage burned in his voice. "*You* told Orsini where Sofia was hiding. You're the monster responsible for her death."

"I couldn't let that journal fall into anyone else's hands."

Sugarman was moving toward the door. He stopped, stiffened. "Johnny O'Shea..." he said. "You thought Johnny O'Shea was going to find the truth. Not about Orsini. About *you*. You arranged for Vanessa, your *agent*, to send him to that art curator in Hyères. Arranged for the curator to tell Johnny that Orsini was hiding on a yacht in the Porquerolles. Arranged for a bomb on a sleek white sailboat."

"You're navigating through murky moral waters, Sugar.

That art dealer in Hyères is long gone. You can't prove any of it." The Admiral turned away to stare out over the black treetops. "And by the way, Sugar. That phone call you insist Orsini made to his *Skull and Bones* friend at Yale, asking for help? He made *two* phone calls that night. To two of us, not just one. There's someone else out there who knows the truth about Orsini, Sugar. Someone else knows about the money, the art. It's not over."

"Then I'll just have to keep looking for that other person, won't I, Admiral?"

Through the open window, Sugarman could smell the magnolia blossoms and hear the soft fluttering as a fresh wind rocked the narrow branches.

"When the bough breaks..." said Sugarman. Then he closed the door softly behind him.

\* \* \*

The chimes of Saint Paul de Mausole's monastery bells echoed over the shifting shadows in the hidden garden, calling the monks to Evensong.

*Chimes.* Maggie raised her head, listening. And froze.

In that instant, the answers tore into her, like a knife stabbing through fog. Finally, the last pieces of her nightmare's puzzle fell into place. She closed her eyes, forcing herself to see the stormy, windswept beach of her dream. She was sitting at the grand piano, her scarf like a banner in the wind, and she raised her head to listen. And heard...what?

A telephone, ringing loudly, endlessly, in the darkness. And—chimes! The echo of church chimes. A monastery? No. A convent.

The final message from her husband, written in his calendar. *Begin at the beginning, CFSMC.* She thought of the last letter from Sofia, then the phone call from an unidentified woman. Sofia had sought refuge in the Convent of the Fog. *CF?* Suddenly she saw it all, like finding the last pages of a long lost concerto.

She had to get to the island, to the convent. Had to leave *now*, before Orsini realized...

She spun away from the man with the gun.

"Not so fast, Magdalena."

Orsini's hand moved and the white cat growled in his arms. She heard the faint click of a hammer being cocked on his gun.

"You have taken my son from me," said Orsini. "Where is Tommy, damn you? What have you done with my son?"

"Your son is safe."

"Return him to me."

"It's too late, Victor. Gideon will testify against you. So will Celeste LaMartine."

"Gideon is alive?" For just an instant, the dark eyes gleamed at her with a strange light. Then the eyes hooded and the barrel shoulders shrugged. "It no longer matters. And Celeste would never turn against me."

"You've destroyed her life with Gideon, you shot the man she loves." cried Maggie. "She must hate you now. Almost as much as I do."

The barrel of Orsini's gun moved back and forth. "Let us finish this little drama, then."

Maggie stood straight and still in the hot, pulsing light. She stared at the man who was responsible for the deaths of her husband and her best friend. Wasn't he? Oh God.

Very slowly Maggie drew the revolver from the pocket of her jeans until it was aimed at Victor Orsini's chest. "I will not let my life be shattered again," she told him.

His thick fingers gripped the huge cat firmly against his heart. "You won't shoot," he said to her.

The small pistol was shaking in her hand. High on the silver monastery wall a blue shutter shifted, swung slowly open. Somewhere behind her she could hear the low drone of bees in the poppies and the late-day song of the cicadas. She felt the hot white light of the spinning sun wash across her face.

*The bright day is done...*

She stared into the terrible black hole of Orsini's gun. She couldn't breathe.

Shoot him, her mind screamed. Just aim past the cat and shoot!

Orsini stepped closer, looking into her eyes. "If you kill me," he whispered. "you will never know the truth about Sofia. Or what really happened to your husband the night he died." He smiled. "Don't you want to know the truth?"

"More than anything," she whispered.

Orsini moved, flinging the cat toward the bushes. A flare of sunlight on gun metal.

A shot, shattering the stillness.

A frozen moment of silence.

Maggie closed her eyes and pulled the trigger.

A second later, three more gunshots, crashing like cymbals through the dying light while the chimes rang and rang above her head.

# CHAPTER NINETY-TWO

The old iron gate was locked.

Maggie pressed the bell a second time, peering through the black bars into the sixth-century Benedictine convent. Couvent de la Brume. The Convent of the Fog, abbreviated, in her husband's calendar, as "CF."

*Go back to the beginning*, he'd written.

On the far side of the ancient cloister, a blue door set deep within the stone wall opened. Maggie caught her breath. A nun, almost wider than she was tall, stepped into the mist-wreathed garden.

Maggie still could not wrap her mind around everything that had happened in the last twenty-four hours. The French Sûreté detectives had released her in Saint-Rémy at dawn, after two phone calls from Simon Sugarman and a third call from a man they referred to only as "Sir." It had not been her bullet—found embedded in the monastery's stone wall—that killed Orsini. He had been shot twice by Celeste LaMartine, from behind a blue-shuttered window high on the monastery wall. One of the bullets had found his heart.

Once released, Maggie had gone immediately to the airport. Now, hours later, she stood at the high iron bars, the fingers of fog cool against her cheek, waiting for the nun to unlock the gate. In the distance, she could hear the muffled thunder of waves pounding against the rocks.

So much of her time with Orsini was still a blur. But she

could remember the flash as his arm moved. He had fired first, his shot wide. Deliberately? She would never know. And then, terrified, she had looked into the menacing black barrel of his gun, closed her eyes and pulled the trigger of the small pistol. She still had no idea if she'd fired in self-defense or because she wanted justice for her husband and her best friend. Oh, yes, she had aimed at his heart and fired.

Hadn't she? Or had she aimed at the stone wall behind him?

She closed her eyes and heard Orsini's shot, felt the release of her own bullet, and then heard two more shots, apparently fired by Celeste. But she had heard *five* gunshots, hadn't she? Who had fired the final bullet?

The nun approached her, holding a huge iron key, her eyes questioning. "Welcome, Madame O'Shea. I trust there is a good reason why you have insisted that I break our vow of silence?"

"The most important reason of all, Sister. I must speak with Soeur Marie Clair."

The rest of her husband's note, scribbled in his calendar... CFSMC. *Convent of the Fog, Soeur Marie Clair.* The sister who, according to Fee's last letter, had hidden Fee and Tommy for days in the convent. The same woman who had called Maggie late one night, to tell her that Fee was dead.

The loud ringing of the telephone. And then, when Maggie had answered, she'd heard the convent's chimes in the background, drowning out the woman's voice.

*The ringing phone, the chimes of her nightmare.*

The nun hesitated, then unlocked the huge gate, swung it open, gestured for her to enter. "Soeur Marie Clair is no longer with us."

Maggie stepped inside the gate and gazed down at the nun. "Where can I reach her?"

The nun shook her head. "She died last October of pneumonia."

Maggie reached out, grasped the nun's arm. "Just—tell me, please. Is Marie Clair the same sister who found the body of my friend, Sofia Orsini, in the chapel on the cliffs last fall?"

The nun stiffened, then sank down next to her on the hard bench. "Who are you?"

"Magdalena O'Shea. Sofia Orsini's best friend. Her son's godmother."

Maggie watched the nun's skin pale beneath the white wimple.

"Magdalena," repeated the nun.

"Yes."

The nun touched Maggie's arm, leaned closer. "Soeur Marie Clair was an excellent nurse," she began. "She befriended your friend, Sofia, and her little boy from the moment they showed up at the convent gate. She is the one who found Madame Orsini on the floor of the cliff chapel."

Maggie felt the grief rise in her throat. "Oh, dear God."

"There had been a struggle, but there was no sign of the child. Madame had been bleeding for hours, her knife wounds terrible. We could not find her pulse..."

Maggie turned to her, holding her breath. "But?"

"Come with me," said the nun.

* * *

Maggie followed the nun through the cloister and into the small, high-roofed convent chapel. In the late-day gloom, she saw the simple stone altar, the worn wall tapestries, an ancient organ set against the far wall. Off to the side, a small, glassed cabinet glimmered with the flicker of candlelight. Inside, an open manuscript.

Maggie stopped, drawn inexplicably toward the case. Somehow she knew it was important.

She moved closer and caught her breath, staring in shock at the torn, stained pages before her. Her hands moved involuntarily, aching to touch the paper, the notations. The cascade of black notes.

"It can't be..."

The manuscript, opened like a book in the glass case, looked to be some eighty pages thick. The paper appeared to be very old, faded, marked with penciled scribbles, violent jabs, erasures worn into holes. Musical notes spilled across the two pages she could see, furious and impatient, marked by splatters of black ink, drops of sealing wax.

Swoops, gouging, splashes, smudges, dark smeared blotches.

But still the musical notes shone through. Electric, desperate. Savage.

And she knew she was looking at the electricity of genius.

Across the bottom of the right page, a scrawled name. An autograph. She bent closer, holding her breath.

"Jesus God," she breathed. "*Beethoven!*"

It appeared to be a concerto for violin, one she had never heard before. One the world had never heard? He'd only written one violin concerto. And now...*another*?

It had to be the manuscript Fee had stolen from Victor. Hidden in plain sight in a tiny fog-bound chapel...

Again her fingers brushed the glass with reverence. *Beethoven.* The real thing, she thought, gazing at the blotched, ancient pages. The Holy Grail of music.

"Mrs. O'Shea? Are you coming?"

The nun's voice broke into her thoughts. She forced herself to look up, smile.

"Yes, Soeur, I'm coming."

And she followed the white-wimpled nun out into the fog-lit garden.

* * *

The nun stopped at a small gate, gesturing Maggie forward. "Soeur Marie Clair found your friend just moments before death. She was able to stop the bleeding. Your friend did not die that morning, Madame O'Shea." The nun shook her head. "But, we knew she was in terrible danger. We did not know whom to trust. God forgive us, we thought her boy was dead. We wanted only to protect her from more pain. She has only spoken two words since that terrible day. Thomas. And Magdalena."

Shading her eyes, Maggie moved into the garden.

The convent garden, wreathed in a silvery fog, sloped down toward the sea. Bright flowers and twisted trees spilled along the paths like ghosts in the shimmering light. She could hear the waves thundering in the distance.

There, by the rocks—a bench, a woman. Very still. Facing out to the sea.

Barely able to breathe, Maggie walked toward her across the damp, misted grass.

She stopped just behind the woman. Looking down at a mass of black hair, shot now with strands of silver, she laid a gentle hand on the thin, bony shoulder.

The woman startled, then turned.

Deep blue eyes gazed without recognition into Maggie's.

*Fee's eyes.*

"Fee," whispered Maggie. "It's me. Maggie. Oh, God, Fee. You're *alive*!"

She dropped to the bench, encircling Sofia Orsini in the safety of her arms. "It's going to be okay," she said against her friend's cheek. "Your son is alive. Tommy is waiting for you."

Sofia Orsini pulled away to gaze at Maggie. Her eyes widened. Just for a moment, a flicker of light behind the vacant sea-blue.

"Magdalena..."

# CODA
(in music, a passage formally ending a composition)

*Is this chair empty? Is the king dead?*
—Shakespeare, *Richard III*

## TWO MONTHS LATER

### GREECE

The last lights glimmered and dimmed around the harbor of Mykonos as dawn touched the wine-dark edge of the Aegean Sea with a faint pink glow.

Soon, in the relentless sun of midday, the cubed homes scattered on the hills of this Cycladic island would shine with a blinding white radiance against the brilliant blue of sky and sea. But now the hillside was cloaked in shadows that spilled across the houses and olive trees and the terrace high above the sea. There, a man stood alone in the dark like a sleepless Odysseus, thinking about a woman with night-black hair.

Soon, the sun would edge over the horizon and the sea would flash with azure light. It would touch the harbor cafés with gold and climb the hillside, lighting each home with white flame. Soon it would wash across the terrace and touch the man, turning his pale wheat hair to fire and burning like twin torches in the glittering mirrored eyes.

### BOSTON

She had never seen her beloved Symphony Hall spark with so much electricity.

Maggie O'Shea, resplendent in a strapless tube of midnight blue, leaned forward to look down from her center box. In the theatre below her, the expectant faces glowed like stars in the glittering light from the chandelier.

A waving hand in the center aisle caught her eye. Simon Sugarman, standing next to the newly appointed deputy director of the CIA, smiled and gave her the thumbs-up sign.

She hadn't seen him since Aix, the night before that terrible moment in the monastery garden when gunshots had shattered the morning stillness and Victor Orsini had fallen at her feet.

Maggie returned Sugarman's wave with a shake of her head. When his team had searched Victor's yacht, they'd discovered one small Cézanne left behind—a portrait since proven to have been stolen from a Jewish banker in 1943. So now Sugar was back in Washington, searching for art missing since World War II and "doing what he had to do." But still he called her, late at night when dark memories wouldn't let him sleep. "The art's still missing, the bad guys are still out there," he would say. "Just be careful. It's not over."

She remembered so clearly that day three months earlier, when he'd shown up on the doorstep of her music shop to talk about the death of Sofia Orsini. It had begun with one woman's courage, one woman's profound love for her child. Sugar had asked her to find Fee's son. To make it right. *For Sofia*, thought Maggie, nodding at Sugarman.

She closed her eyes for a moment, thinking of Fee. The nuns, afraid for Sofia's life, had hidden her, cared for her, planted flowers on the grave that held the body of Soeur Marie Clair and pretended that Fee was dead. Fee was living, now, in a small medical facility in Aix. Getting stronger day by day. Able, at last, to recognize her son. Able to hold him.

*Healing*. For both of them. Mother and son.

Maggie smiled, picturing the moment when she had reunited mother and son for the first time. Tommy, racing down the long white hall of the clinic, arms stretched in front of his pumping body, calling out for his mother. The look on Fee's face as she enveloped her son in her arms.

No, this was not a night for sadness. Maggie turned her gaze to her new grandson, sleeping so peacefully in his mother's arms just a few seats away, and then her eyes were drawn back to the stage, where the empty chairs and music stands waited for the members of the Boston Symphony Orchestra. Where a black Steinway Concert Grand Piano stood center stage, alone in the spotlight.

"Is it time yet?"

The flutelike voice broke into her thoughts. She smiled at the little boy sitting on her right.

"Almost, TJ. Did I tell you how handsome you look in your new suit?"

"Zach helped me pick it out," whispered the child. Maggie nodded, pleased that TJ had begun to use Zach's given name. The formal guardianship was now legal, until Sofia was well enough to be with her son once more.

"TJ has good taste, doesn't he?" said Zach, who sat to the boy's right. He ruffled the child's newly-trimmed hair. Just beyond Zach, Cameron Law sat watching his son and the little boy with a wistful, yearning expression in his faded eyes. Father and son had spoken twice and formed a tenuous truce. Just keep trying, she told the old man silently.

In a few days, Zach would return to Aix with TJ, to work on the authentication of the Beethoven manuscript—the Violin Concerto in E minor, stolen in Florence during World War II from a Jewish collector of music. A violin concerto never played in a concert hall, never heard by an audience. Hidden for decades—and now, perhaps the greatest classical music find of the century.

Zach leaned forward, scattering her thoughts. He nodded toward the stage and looked into Maggie's eyes. "Nervous?"

Her bare shoulders shrugged as she held out her shaking fingers. "Not a tremor," she lied. "What about you, Mr. Composer?"

He held out his left hand. "Like a rock."

"Will you two stop," whispered Luze Jacobs. "I'm a nervous

wreck." She and her husband sat behind Zach and TJ. The velvet chair behind Maggie was still empty.

"Relax, Luze. The worst that can happen is that he blanks on the opening passage."

Theatre lights flashed as members of the orchestra moved onto the stage and found their places. The first violinist stroked his bow, sounding the long A note to tune the instruments. As the audience stirred at the familiar sound, Maggie glanced once more over her shoulder at the empty chair and sighed.

She hadn't seen Michael since the morning he'd left her in Provence. There'd been a postcard from Geneva and brief scattered phone calls, the last one waking her at midnight from Afghanistan. Then a bright orange t-shirt mailed from Istanbul that proclaimed *Musicians Duet Better*.

She blushed in the darkness and raised cool fingers to her cheeks. She wasn't even certain that tonight's invitation had reached him.

The theatre darkened. It was that magical moment just before the conductor strode onto the stage, when all things were possible. In the sudden quiet, Maggie closed her eyes, intensely aware of the empty seat behind her. Just one year ago, her heart told her, you would have been waiting for Johnny.

*Just because I can't see you anymore*, her heart whispered, *doesn't mean you're not here.* And then, *I kept my promise, Johnny.*

It was time. She looked down at her wedding ring for a long moment, then gently slid it off her finger and slipped it into the hidden pocket of her gown. Whether or not Michael Beckett came tonight, she was ready to move on with her life.

At that moment her son appeared on the stage.

Tall, slim, with dark curling hair, Brian emerged from the wings of the concert hall and approached the piano with rapid steps, back straight, arms swinging slightly at his sides. Exactly like his father had, so many years before. Maggie's heart skipped in her chest as applause filled the great hall with sound.

A classical musician by education, he'd been practicing his father's concerto since they'd met. She watched her son now as he stood in front of the piano in his tuxedo, so proud and handsome and fine. He looked up toward their box, dark eyes searching for his wife, Laura, and the tiny baby boy wrapped in her arms. Then his eyes moved to his mother—and his father. Maggie saw him give a slight nod of recognition, then a quick, self-conscious bow. That chore over, he turned and sat down at the piano. She watched him lift his hands above the keys and pause for a moment, as if listening.

As Brian's fingers came down on the keys, Zach's hand reached for hers in the darkness. She squeezed his fingers in silent recognition of the overwhelming love and pride they shared for their extraordinary son. And their astonishing new grandson.

*The healing power of music,* she thought. *And the healing power of love.*

Then she sat back and listened to the opening bars of the American premiere of the Piano Concerto No. 1 in D minor— *The Lost Concerto* explained the program notes—composed by Zachary Law.

*Zach's concerto, lost to her for almost thirty years, given life tonight in their son's hands.*

Then the pure notes were falling around her like stars and the roof fell away and she felt herself lifted on the wings of the music, high into the night sky.

A sound in the darkness behind her and the sudden sweet scent of lilacs as a strong hand closed over her naked shoulder. A spray of blossoms spilled onto her lap in a pool of white snow.

"I've come to take you home to my Blue Mountains, ma'am," murmured a soft Virginian voice in her ear.

The music swelled around her. "I'm ready, Michael."

When she leaned back, his arms came around her. "I've got you," he murmured.

Now, once more, she could hear the music.

The powerful notes of Zach's concerto flew toward them like bright sparks in the pulsing darkness.

Full of pain. And passion.

And promise.

# AUTHOR'S NOTE

Thank you for joining me in Maggie's world.

More than anything, I wanted to tell a good story, create characters with depth, and paint pictures with words. And, whenever possible, make the reader *feel*.

*The Lost Concerto* was written over several years. Like my first novel, *Firebird*, much of the plot comes from the *New York Times*, the *Washington Post*, *Time Magazine*, and *NBC Nightly News*. References to the CIA's "Veil" operation are based on Bob Woodward's fascinating book on secret American foreign policy in the 1980s—*Veil: The Secret Wars of the CIA, 1981–1987*.

As for the settings and locations, there are some places that just speak to you.

Many years ago I exited the underground Paris Metro by elevator and found myself surrounded by the shrill cries of thousands of birds. The moment I entered the high, shadowed aisles of the Bird Market (Marché aux Oiseaux), I knew that one day it had to be a scene in a novel. The Bird Market still opens in Louis Lepine Square on Sunday mornings.

Likewise, I spent a morning wandering the twisting paths of Cimetière du Père Lachaise with my children, and knew I would one day send my characters up those same paths.

Also in Paris, Sacré Coeur, Musée d'Orsay, Notre Dame, Sainte Chapelle's stained glass windows, the house boats along the Seine, Jardin du Luxembourg's puppets and carousel, the gorgeous old Opera House, and the Café de la Paix.

The tiny Italian town of Ravello, perched high above the

Amalfi Coast and host to an annual summer music festival, is another place of inspiration. We arrived just after the final performance, but I will never forget standing on the Villa Rufolo's outdoor orchestra ledge, surrounded by empty chairs and music stands, overlooking the distant Mediterranean. Victor Orsini's sister, and their story, came alive for me at that moment.

In Provence, Aix-en-Provence. The Archbishop's Palace, Cézanne's studio, and Deux Garçons are real and wonderful places, as is the unforgettable Abbaye de Sénanque to the north. Every July, the Festival d'Art Lyrique et de Musique is held in Aix-en-Provence, although traditionally it is a showcase for Opera.

Both Relais Odette in Paris and Maggie's inn in Aix-en-Provence exist only in my imagination but were inspired by two beautiful French inns that I visited several years ago. The vineyard of Le Refuge also exists only in my head.

The missing musical score discovered in the last chapters of *The Lost Concerto* is based on a true experience at a cathedral in Toledo, Spain, where, in a small, narrow chapel at the end of a dark corridor, we found a nun—almost wider than she was tall—guarding priceless original works of art by El Greco, Dalí, Picasso, and Murillo. All hidden in plain sight.

Over the centuries, thousands of musical scores and valuable instruments have been documented as stolen, destroyed accidentally or purposely, or simply disappeared. A composition by a young Mozart was found in a notebook in an Austrian attic in 2012; a lost trumpet concerto by Mozart is still missing. A Vivaldi Flute Concerto, lost for 300 years, was found in Scotland. A lost Piano Concerto by Beethoven was found in the British Museum. A Bach wedding cantata was found in Japan, while a Benjamin Britten orchestration for Les Sylphides appears to have been discovered not long ago in a New Jersey warehouse. Pieces that are still missing by composers include Haydn, Sibelius, Brahms, and Liszt, while the Art Loss Register lists eighteen missing Stradivarius violins.

You may be interested to know that, like *Firebird,* a good percentage of the net proceeds from *The Lost Concerto* will go to my SunDial Foundation, Inc., which, since 1998, has benefited our most vulnerable women, children, and families. SunDial supports inner city food banks, education, health, shelter, child protection, the arts and economic development, with an emphasis on programs that promote dignity, independence, and safety, and combat poverty, hunger, sickness, and homelessness. (sundialfoundation.org)

As mentioned in my dedication, my son, Sean, was the inspiration for Maggie's vocation and her beloved classical music pieces. I am not a musician, and any mistakes regarding music are all mine. For those of you who love classical music, I have listed several of "Maggie's" favorites below.

Bach – Cello Suite No. 1 (Yo Yo Ma)
Beethoven – Piano Concerto No. 1 in C major
Beethoven – Piano Concerto No. 5 in E-flat (The Emperor)
Beethoven – Concerto in D major for violin
Beethoven – 5th Symphony
Chopin – Piano Concerto in E minor
Chopin – Ballade No. 4 in F minor
Grieg – Piano Concerto in A minor
Haydn – Symphony No. 45 – "The Farewell"
Liszt – Hungarian Rhapsody No. 2, C-sharp minor
Mozart – Piano Concerto No. 19 in F major
Mozart – Piano Concerto No. 21 in C (associated with Elvira Madigan)
Paganini – Caprice No. 24 in A minor
Rachmaninoff – Piano Concerto No. 2 in C minor
Tartini – Violin Sonata in G minor (the Devil's Trill)
Tchaikovsky – Piano Concerto No. 1 in B-flat minor
Tchaikovsky – Concerto in D major for violin
Vivaldi – The Four Seasons

CPSIA information can be obtained at www.ICGtesting.com
Printed in the USA
LVOW11s2200141016

508351LV00013B/8/P